Works by the same Author.

Chronicles of the Schonberg-Cotta Family.

The Early Dawn.

Diary of Kitty Trevylyan.

Winifred Bertram.

Each of the above 4 vols., in the same Series, and uniform in size and binding with this.

Mary, the Handmaid of the Lord.
One Vol., 16mo.

The Song without Words.
Dedicated to Children. Square 16mo.

Published by M. W. DODD,
By arrangement with the Author.

THE

Draytons and the Davenants

A STORY OF

THE CIVIL WARS.

By the Author of

"CHRONICLES OF THE SCHONBERG-COTTA FAMILY,"
ETC., ETC.

New York:
M. W. DODD, 506 BROADWAY.
1866.

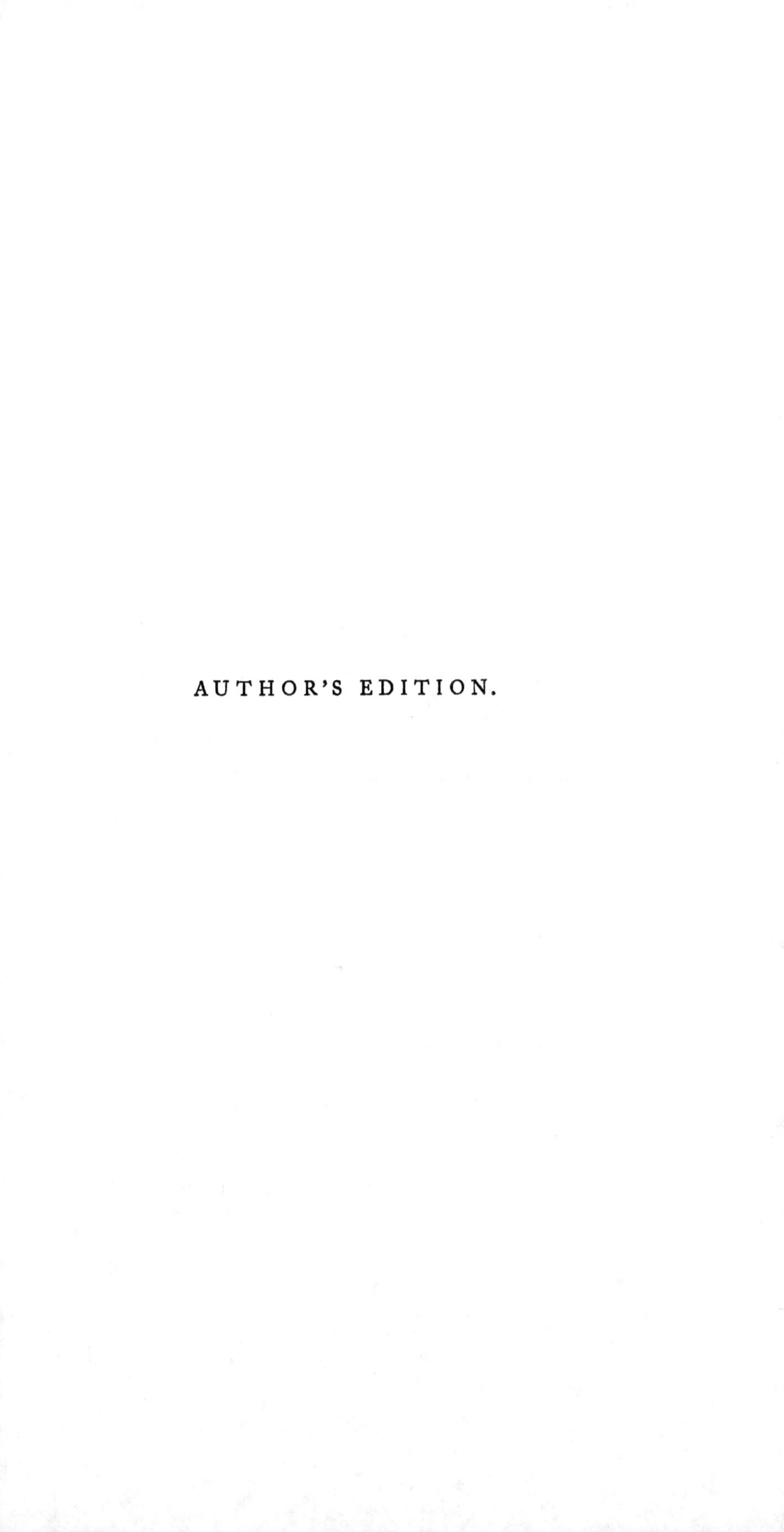

AUTHOR'S EDITION.

CARD FROM THE AUTHOR.

"The Author of the 'Schonberg-Cotta Family wishes it to be generally known among the readers of her books in America, that the American Editions issued by Mr. M. W. Dodd, of New York, alone have the Author's sanction."

NOTICE.

This Volume will be followed next year by a supplementary Volume covering the period of the Commonwealth and the Restoration, and embracing incidents connected with the Early History of this country.

THE

Draytons and the Davenants

INTRODUCTORY.

YESTERDAY at noon, when the house and all the land were still, and the men, with the lads and lasses, were away at the harvesting, and I sat alone, with barred doors, for fear of the Indians (who have of late shown themselves unfriendly), I chanced to look up from my spinning-wheel through the open window, across the creek on which our house stands. And something, I scarce know what, carried me back through the years and across the seas to the old house on the borders of the Fen Country, in the days of my childhood. It may have been the quiet rustling of the sleepy air in the long grasses by the water-side that wafted my spirit back to where the English winds sigh and sough among the reeds on the borders of the fens; it may have been the shining of the smooth water, furrowed by the track of the water-fowl, that set my memory down beside the broad Mere, whose gleam we could see from my chamber window. It may have been the smell of this year's hay, which came in in sweet, soft gusts through the lattice, that floated me up to the top of the tiny haystack, made of the waste grass in the orchard at old Netherby Manor, at the foot of which Roger, my brother, used to stand while I turned up the hay, assisted by our Cousin Placidia (when she was condescending), and by our Aunt Gretel, my mother's sister, whenever we had need of her. Most probably it was the hay. For, as the excellent Mr. Bunyan has illustriously set forth in his work on the Holy War, the soul hath five gates through which she holdeth parlance with the outer world. And correspondent with these outer gates from the sensible world in space, meseemeth, are as many inner gates into the inner, invisible world of thought and time; which inner gates open simultaneously with the outer, by the same spring. But of all the mystic springs which unlock the wondrous inward world, none act with such swift, secret magic as those of the Gate of Odors. There stealeth in unobserved some delicate perfume of familiar field flower or garden herb, and straightway, or ere she is aware, the soul is afar off in the world of the past, gathering posies among the fields of childhood, or culling herbs in the old corner of the old garden, to be laid, by hands long since cold, in familiar chambers long since tenanted by other owners.

Wherefore, I deem, it was the new, sweet smell

of our New England hay which more than anything carried me back to the old house in Old England, and the days so long gone by.

With my heart in far-off days, I continued my spinning, as women are wont, the hand moving the more swiftly for the speed wherewith the thoughts travel, until my thoughts and my work came to a pause together by the flax on my distaff being exhausted. I went to an upper chamber for a fresh stock, and while there my eye lighted on an old chest, in the depths whereof lay many little volumes of an old journal written by my hand through a series of buried years.

An irresistible attraction drew me to them; and as I knelt before the old chest, and turned over these yellow leaves, in some cases eaten with worms, and read the writing—the earlier portions of it in large, laborious, childish characters, as if each letter were a solemn symbol of weighty import—the later scrawled hastily in the snatched intervals of a busy and tangled life—I seemed to be looking through a series of stained windows into the halls of an ancient palace. On the windows were the familiar portraits of a little eager girl, and a young maiden familiar to me, yet strange. But the paintings were also window-panes; and, after the first glance, the painted panes seemed to vanish, and I saw only the palace chambers on which they looked. Not empty chambers, or shadowy, or silent, but solid, and fresh, and vivid, and full of the stir of much life; so that, when I laid down those old pages, and looked out through the declining light over these new shores, across this new sea, towards the far-off England which still lives beyond, it seemed for a moment as if the sun setting behind the wide western woods, the strip of golden corn-fields, the reapers returning slowly over the hill, the Indian burial-mounds beside the creek, the trim new house, my old quiet self, were the shadows, and that Old World, in which my spirit had been sojourning, still the living and the real.

Neighbor Hartop's cheery voice roused me out of my dream, and I hurried down to open the door, and to set out the harvest supper.

But as I look at the old crumpled papers again to-day, the past lives again once more before me, and I will not let it die.

There is an hour in the day when the sun has set, and all the dazzle of day is gone, and the dusk of night has not set in, when I think the world looks larger and clearer than at any other time. The sky seems higher and more heavenly than at other hours; and yet the earth, tinted here and there on its high places with heavenly color, seems more to belong to heaven. The little landscape within our horizon becomes more manifestly a portion of a wider world. And is there not such an hour in life? Before it passes let me use the light, and fix in my mind the scenes which will so soon vanish into dreams and silence.

The first entry in those old journals of mine is:

"*The twenty-eighth day of March, in the year of our Lord sixteen hundred and thirty-seven.*—On this day, twelve years since, King Charles was proclaimed King at Whitehall Gate, and in Cheapside; the while the rain fell in heavy showers. My father heard the herald; and my Aunt Dorothy well remembers the rain, because it spoiled a slashed satin doublet of my father's (the last he ever bought, having since then been habited more soberly); also because many of the people said the weather was of evil promise for the new reign. But father saith that is a superstitious notion, unworthy of Christian people.

"Also my father was present at the king's coronation, on the 5th of February in the following year. Our French Queen would not enter the Abbey on account of her Popish faith. When the king was presented bareheaded to the people, all were silent, none crying God save the King, until the Earl of Arundel bade them; which my father saith was a worse omen than if the clouds poured down rivers."

These in large characters, each letter formed with conscientious pains.

The second entry is diverse from the first. It runs thus:

"*April the tenth.*—The brindled cow hath died, leaving an orphan calf. Aunt Gretel saith I may bring up the calf for my own, with the help of Tib the dairy-woman."

The diversity between these entries recalls many things to me. On the day before the first entry, father brought to Roger my brother, my Cousin Placidia, and me, three small books stitched neatly together, and told us these were for us to use to note down any remarkable events therein. "For," said he, "we live in strange and notable times, and you children may see things before you are grown, yea, and perchance do or suffer such things as history is made of."

The stipulation was, that we were each to write independently, and not to borrow from the other; which was a hard covenant for me, who seldom then meditated or did anything without the co-operation or sanction of Roger.

After much solitary pondering, therefore, I arrived at the conclusion that history especially concerns kings and queens, and lesser people only as connected with them. That is, when there are kings and queens. In the old Greek history I remembered there were heroes who were not kings, but I supposed they did instead. But the English history was all made up of what happened to the kings. One was shot while hunting; another was murdered at Berkeley Castle; the little princes were smothered in the Tower. King Edward III. gained a great victory at Creçy in France; King Henry V. gained another at Agincourt. Of course other people were concerned in these things. Sir Walter Tyrrel shot the arrow by accident that killed King William, and some wicked people must have murdered King Edward and the little princes on purpose. And, of course, there were armies who helped King Edward and King Henry to gain their victories; but none of these people would have been in history, I thought, except as connected with the kings. At the same time I thought it was of no use to relate things which no one belonging to me had had anything to do with, because any one else could have done that without my taking the trouble to write a note-book at all. Therefore it seemed to me that my father, and even my father's slashed satin doublet, fairly became historical by having been present at the King's proclamation, and Aunt Dorothy by having commented thereon.

The second entry was caused by an entirely different theory of history, having its origin in a talk with Roger. Roger said that we never can tell what things are historical until afterwards, and that therefore the only way was to note down what honestly interests us. If these things prove afterwards to be things which interest the world, our story of them becomes part of the world's story, and, as such, history to the people who care for us. But to note down feeble echoes of far-off great events, in which we think we ought to be interested, is no human speech at all, Roger thought, but mere monkey's imitative chattering. Every one, Roger thinks, sees everything just a little differently from any one else, and therefore if every one would describe truly the little bit they do see, in that way, by degrees, we might have a perfect picture. But to copy what others have seen is simply to depart with every fresh copy a little further from the original. If, for instance, said he, the nurse of Julius Cæsar had told us nursery stories of what Julius Cæsar did when he was a little boy, it would have been history; but the opinions of Julius Cæsar's nurse on the politics of the Roman republic would probably not have been history at all, but idle tattle.

With respect to kings and queens being the only true subjects for history, also, Roger was very scornful. He had lately been paying a visit to Mr. John Hampden, Mr. Oliver Cromwell, and others of my father's friends, and he had returned full of indignation against the tyranny of the court and the prelates. The nation, he said wise men thought, was not made for the king, but the king for the nation. And, to say nothing of the Greek history, the Bible history was certainly not filled up with kings and queens, but with shepherds, herdsmen, preachers, and soldiers; or if with kings, with kings who had been shepherds and soldiers, and who were saints and heroes as well as kings.

All which reasoning decided me to make my next entry concerning the calf of the brindled cow, which at that time was the subject in the world which honestly interested me the most. If my father, or Roger, or Cousin Placidia, or Aunt Gretel, ever became historical personages (and, as Roger said, who could tell?), then anecdotes concerning the calf of the cow which my father owned and Aunt Gretel cherished, and which Cousin Placidia thought it childish to care so much about, might become, in a secondary sense, historical also. At all events, I resolved I would not be like Julius Cæsar's nurse, babbling of politics.

The next entry was:

"*August* 4, 1637.—Dr. Antony has spent the evening with us, and is to remain some days, at father's entreaty, to recruit his strength; Aunt Dorothy having knowledge of medicinal herbs, and Aunt Gretel of savory dishes, which may be of use to him. He hath narrowly escaped the jail-sickness, having of late visited many afflicted good people in the prisons through the country, as is his custom. 'Sick and in prison,' Dr. Antony saith, 'and ye visited me,' is plain enough to read by the dimmest light, whatever else is hard to understand. He told us of two strange things which happened lately. At least they seem very strange to me.

"In the Palace Yard at Westminster, on the 30th of last June (while Roger and I were making hay in the pleasant sunshine of the orchard), Dr. Antony saw three gentlemen stand in the pillory. The pillory is a wooden frame set up on a platform, where wicked people are fastened helplessly like savage dogs, with their heads and hands coming through holes, to make them look ridiculous, that people may mock and jeer at them. But father and Dr. Anthony did not think these gentlemen wicked, only at worst a little hasty in speech. And the people did not think them ridiculous; they did not mock and jeer at them, but kept very still, or wept. Their names were Mr. Prynne, a gentleman at the bar, Dr. John Bastwick, a physician; and Mr. Burton, a clergyman of a parish in London. There they stood many hours while the hangman came to each of them in turn and sawed off their ears with a rough knife, and then burnt in two cruel letters on their cheeks, S. L., for seditious libeler. Dr. Anthony did not say the three gentlemen made one cry or complaint, but bore themselves like brave men. But the bravest of all, I think, was Mrs. Bastwick, the doctor's wife. She stayed on the scaffold, and bore to see all her husband's pain without a word or moan, lest she should make him flinch, and then received his ears in her lap, and kissed his poor wounded face before all the people. Sweet, brave heart! I would fain have her home amongst us here, and kiss her faithful hands like a queen's, and lay my head on her brave heart, as if it were my mother's! The sufferers made no moan; but the people broke their pitiful silence once with an angry shout, and many times with low, hushed groans, as if the pain and shame were

2*

theirs (Dr. Anthony said), and they would remember it. And Mr. Prynne, when the irons were burning his face, said to the executioner, 'Cut me, tear me, I fear not thee; I fear the fire of hell.' Mr. Burton spoke to the people of God and his truth, and how it was worth while to suffer rather than give up that. And at last he nearly fainted, but when he was borne away into a house near, he said, with good cheer, 'It is too hot to last.' (He meant the persecution.) But the three gentlemen are now shut up in three prisons—in Launceston, Lancaster, and Caernarvon. And father and Dr. Antony say it is Archbishop Laud who ordered it all to be done. But could not the king have stopped it if he liked?

"But will Roger and I ever turn over the hay again in the pleasant June sunshine, without thinking how it burned down on those poor, maimed and wounded gentlemen? And one day I do hope I may see brave Mistress Bastwick and tell her how I love and honor her, and how the thought of her will help me to be brave and patient more than a hundred sermons.

"Dr. Antony's other story was of one Jenny or Janet Geddes, not a gentlewoman, for she kept an apple stall in Edinburgh streets, and, moreover, does not appear to have used good language at all. The Scotch, it seems, do not like bishops, and, indeed, will not have bishops. But Archbishop Laud and the king will make them. On Sunday, the 23d of last July, a month since, one of Archbishop Laud's bishops began the collect for the day in St. Giles's Cathedral, Edinburgh. Jenny Geddes had brought her folding stool (on which she sat by her apple stall, I suppose) into the church, and when the bishop came out in his robes (which Archbishop Laud likes of many colors, while the Scotch, it seems, will have nothing but black), she took up her stool and flung it at the bishop's head, calling the service, the mass and the bishop a thief, and wishing him very ill wishes in a curious Scottish dialect, which, I suppose, I do not quite understand; for it sounded like swearing, and if Jenny Geddes was a good woman (although not a gentlewoman) she would scarcely, I should think, swear, at least not in church. Whether the bishop was hurt or not, no one seems to know or care. I suppose the stool did not reach his head. But it stopped the service. For all the people rose in great fury, not against Jenny Geddes, but against the bishop, and the archbishop, and the prayer-book, and against all bishops and all prayers in books, not in Edinburgh only, but throughout the land. Which shows, father said, that a great deal of angry talk had been going on beforehand in the streets around Jenny Geddes' apple stall. There must always be some angry person, father said, to throw the folding stool, but no one heeds the angry person unless there is something to be angry about."

A very long entry, which lost me many hours and many pages.

And about the passages in my own history which it led to, not a word. Indeed, throughout these journals I notice that it is more what they recall than what they say which brings back the past to me. I wonder if it is not thus with most diaries. For to keep to Roger's rule of writing the things which really interest us at the time seems to me scarcely possible; because at the time we scarcely know what things are most deeply interesting us, and if we do, they are the very things we cannot write about. Underneath the things we see and think and speak about are the great, dim, silent places out of which we ourselves are growing into being, and where God is at work. The things we are beginning to see we can *not* see, the things we are feeling without knowing what we feel, the dim, struggling thoughts we cannot utter or even think. Without form and void is the state of a world being created. When the world is created, the creation is a history, and can be written. While it is being created, it is chaos, and from without can only be described as without form and void—from within, in the chaos, not at all. The Creator only understands chaos, and knows the chaos before the new creation from the mere waste and ruin of the old.

To understand the past is only partly possible for the wisest men.

To understand the present is only possible to God.

Because to understand the present would be to foresee the future. To see through the chaos would be to foresee the new creation.

Wherefore it seems to me all diaries are of value not as records, but as suggestions. And all self-examination resolves itself at last into prayer, saying, "What I see not, teach Thou me."

"Search me and try me, and see Thou, and lead Thou me."

The passages in my history that this story of Dr. Antony led to, arise before me as clearly as if they happened yesterday, although in the Journal not a hint of them is given.

The Sunday after Dr. Antony had told us those terrible things about the sufferings in the pillory, Roger and I had gone to our usual Sunday afternoon perch in an apple-tree in the corner of the orchard furthest from the house. We had taken with us for our contemplation a very terrible delineation, which was the nearest approach to a picture Aunt Dorothy would let us have on the Sabbath-day. This she permitted us, partly, I believe, because it was not the likeness of anything in heaven or earth (nor, I hope, under the earth), and partly on account of the very awful thoughts it was calculated to inspire.

It was a huge branching thing like our old family tree. But at the root of the tree, where would be the name of Adam or Noah, or Æneas of Troy, or Cassibelaun, or whoever else was recognized as the head of the family, stood the sacred name of the Holy Trinity. From this trunk forked off two leading branches, one representing the wicked and the other the just, with the words written along them to show that the very same mercies and means of grace which produce repentance and faith and love in the hearts of the just, produce bitterness and false security and hatred of God in the hearts of the wicked. Further and further the branches diverged until one ended in an angel with wings, and the other in a mouth of a horrible hobgoblin with a whale's mouth, a dragon's claws, and a lion's teeth, and both were united by the lines,—

"Whether to heaven or hell you bend,
God will have glory in the end."*

* A similar tree is to be seen in the beginning of Bunyan's Pilgrim's Progress, in the edition of 1698.

Most terrible was this delineation to me, sitting that sunny autumn day in the apple-tree, especially because if you were once on the wrong branch, it was not at all pointed out how you were ever to get on the right. All seemed as irrevocable and inevitable as that point in our own pedigree where Edwy, the eldest son, became a Benedictine monk and vanished into a thin flourish, and Walter, the second son, married Adalgiva, heiress of Netherby Manor, and branched off into us. And it looked so terribly (with unutterable terror I felt it) as if it mattered as little to the Holy Trinity what became of any one of us, as to Cassibelaun or Noah what became of his descendants, Edwy or Walter.

So it happened that Roger and I sat very awe-stricken and still in our perch in the apple-tree, while the wind fluttered the green leaves around us, and the sunbeams ripened the rosy apples for their work, and then danced in and out on the grass below for their play. And I remember as if it were yesterday how the thought shuddered through my heart, that the same sun which was shining on Roger and me, on that last 30th of June, making hay in the orchard, was at that very same moment scorching those poor wounded gentlemen in the pillory in the Palace Yard, and not losing a whit of its glory to us by all the anguish it was inflicting, like a blazing furnace, on them. And if this fearful tree were true, did it not seem as if it were the same with God?

I sat some time silent under the weight of this

dread. It made me shiver with cold in the sunshine, and at length I could keep it in no longer, and said to Roger, in a whisper, for I was half afraid to hear my words,—

"Oh, Roger, why did not God kill the devil?"

At that moment something shook the tree, and I clung to Roger in terror. I could not see what from among the thick leaves where we were sitting. I trembled at the echo of my voice. The dark thoughts within seemed to have brought night with its nameless terrors into the heart of day. But Roger leant down from the branch, and said,—

"Cousin Placidia! For shame! You shook the tree on purpose. I heard the apples fall on the ground, and you are picking them up. That is cheating."

For the fallen fruit was the right of us, children.

Said Placidia in a smooth, unmoved voice,—

"I came against the stem of the tree by accident, and perhaps I did shake it a little more than I need, when I heard what Olive said. They were very wicked words, and I shall tell Aunt Dorothy."

"You may tell any one you like," said Roger indignantly. "Olive did not mean to say anything wrong. You are cruel enough to sit in the Star-chamber, Placidia."

"She is exactly like our gray cat," he continued to me, as she glided away, "with her soft, noiseless ways, and her stealthy, steady following of her own interests. When the fowl-house was burnt down last year, and the turkeys were screaming, and the hens cackling, and every one flying hither and thither trying to save somebody or something, I saw the gray cat quietly licking her lips in a corner over a poor singed chicken. I believe she thought the whole thing had been set on foot to roast her supper. And Placidia would have done precisely the same. If London were on fire, and she in it, I believe she would contrive to get her supper roasted on the cinders. And the provoking thing is, she thinks no one sees."

Roger was not often vehement in speech, but Placidia was our standing grievance, his and mine. There were certain little unfairnesses, not quite cheating, certain little meannesses, not quite dishonesties, and certain little prevarications, not quite lies, which always excited his greatest wrath, especially when, as often happened, I was the loser or the sufferer by them.

"Do you think she will tell Aunt Dorothy?" I said, for that very morning Placidia and I had had a quarrel, she having pinched my arm where it could not be seen, and I having to my shame bitten her finger where it could be seen.

"I don't know, and I don't care," said Roger loftily. "What is the good of minding? I suppose we must all go through a certain quantity of punishment, Olive, and it is to be hoped it will do us good for the future, if we did not deserve it by the past. At least Aunt Dorothy says so. Go on with what you were saying."

So I recurred to my question.

"Oh, Roger, I wish I knew why God did not destroy the devil in the beginning, or at least not let him come into the garden. Because, then, nothing would have gone wrong, would it? Eve would not have eaten the fruit. Mr. Prynne and Dr. Bastwick would not have been set in the pillory. And I should not, most likely, have quarrelled with Placidia, because, I suppose, Placidia would not have been provoking."

"I wish I knew why my Father lets Cousin Placidia live with us, and always be making us do wrong," said Roger.

"She is an orphan, and some one must take care of her, you know," I said. "Besides, surely, Father has reasons, only we don't always know."

"And I suppose God has reasons," said Roger reverently, "only we don't always know."

"But the devil is all bad," said I, "and will never be better; and Cousin Placidia may. It could not be for the devil's own sake God did not kill him, for he only gets worse; and I do not see how it could be for ours."

"The devil was not always the devil, Olive," said Roger, after thinking a little while. "He was an angel at first."

"Then, O Roger," said I eagerly, for the perplexity lay heavy on my heart, "why did not God stop the devil from ever being the devil? That would have been better than anything."

Roger made no reply.

"It cannot be because God could not," I pursued, "because Aunt Dorothy says He can do everything. And it cannot be because He would not, because Aunt Gretel says He hates to see any one do wrong or be unhappy. But there must be some reason; and if we only knew it, I think everything else would become quite plain."

"I do not see the reason, Olive," said Roger, after a long pause. "I cannot see it in the least. I remember hearing two or three people discuss it once with Father and Aunt Dorothy; and I think they all thought they explained it. But no one thought any one else did. And they used exceedingly long and learned words, longer and more learned the further they went on. But they could not agree at all, and at last they became angry, so that I never heard the end. But in two or three years, you know, I am going to Oxford, and then I will try and find out the reason. And when I have found it out, Olive, I will be sure to tell you."

"But that is not at all the most perplexing thing to me, Olive," he began, after a little silence; "because, after all, if we or the angels were to be *persons* and not *things*, I don't see how it could be helped that we might do wrong if we liked. The great puzzle to me is, why we do anything, or if we can help doing anything we do; that is, if we are really persons at all, and not a kind of puppets."

"Of course we are not puppets, Roger," said I. "Of course we can help doing things if we like. I do not think that is any puzzle at all. I could have helped biting Placidia's finger if I had liked—that is, if I had tried. And that is what makes it wrong."

"But you did not like it," said Roger, "and so you did not help it. And what was to make you like to help it, if you did not?"

"If I had been good, I should not have liked to hurt Placidia, however provoking she was," I said.

"And what is to be good?" said he.

"To like to do right," I said. "I think that is to be good."

"But what is to make you like to do right?"

"Being good, to be sure," said I, feeling myself helplessly drawn into the whirlpool.

"That is going round and round, and coming to nothing," said Roger. "But leaving alone about right and wrong, what is to make you do anything?"

"Because I choose," said I, "or some one else chooses."

"But what makes you choose?" said he. "What made you choose, for instance, to come here this afternoon?"

"Because you wished it, and because it was a fine afternoon; and we always do when it is," said I.

"Then you chose it because of something in you which makes you like to please me, and because the sun was shining. Neither of which you could help; therefore you did not really choose at all."

"I *did* choose, Roger," said I. "I might have

felt cross, and chosen to disappoint you, if I had liked."

"But you are not cross; you are good-tempered, on the whole, so you could not help liking to please me."

"But I am cross sometimes with Placidia," I said.

"That is because, as Aunt Gretel says, your temper is like what our mother's was, quick but sweet," said he; "and that is a deeper puzzle still, because it goes further back than you and your character, to our mother's character, that is to say; and if to hers, no one can say how much further, probably as far as Eve."

"But sometimes," said I, "for instance, when you talk like this, my temper is tempted to be cross even with you, Roger. But I choose to keep my temper, and it must be I myself that choose, and not my temper or my mother's."

"That is because of the two motives, the one which inclines you to keep your temper is stronger than the one which inclines you to lose it," said he. "But there is always something before your choice to make you choose, so that really you *must* choose what you do, and therefore you do not really choose at all."

"But I do choose, Roger," said I. "I choose this instant to jump down from this tree—so—and go home."

"That proves nothing," said he, following me down from the tree with provoking coolness; "you chose to jump down, because there is a wilful feeling in you which made you choose it, and that is part of your character, and probably can be traced back to Eve, and proves exactly what I say."

"I am not free to do right or wrong, or anything, Roger!" I said. "Then I might as well be a horse, or a tree, or a stone."

"I suppose you might, if you were," said Roger drily.

"Is there no way out of the puzzle, Roger?" I said.

"I do not see any," he said; "at least not by thinking. But there seems to me no end to the puzzles, if one begins to think."

He did not seem to mind it at all, but rather to enjoy it, as if it were a mere tossing of mental balls and catching them.

But I, on the other hand, was in great bewilderment and heaviness, for I felt like being a ball myself, tossed helplessly round and round, without seeing any beginning or end to it, and it made me very unhappy.

We came back to the house at supper-time with a vague sense of some judgment hanging over our heads. Aunt Dorothy met us in the porch with a switch in her hand.

"Naughty children," said she, "Placidia says she heard you using profane language in the apple-tree, taking God's holy name in vain."

"I was not speaking so much of God, Aunt Dorothy," said I in confusion, "as of the devil."

"Worse again," said Aunt Dorothy, "that is swearing downright. It is as bad as the cavaliers at the Court. Hold out your hand, Roger; and, Olive, go to bed without supper."

Roger scorned any self-defence. He held out his hand, and received three sharp switches without flinching. Only at the end he said,—

"Now I shall tell my father how Placidia stole the apples and get justice done to Olive."

"You will tell your father nothing, sir," said Aunt Dorothy. "I have sent Placidia to bed three hours ago for tale-bearing, and given her the chapter in the Proverbs to learn. And you will sit down and learn the same, and both of you say it to me to-morrow morning before breakfast."

This was what Aunt Dorothy considered even-handed justice. Time, she said, was too precious to spend in searching out the rights of children's quarrels, and human nature being depraved as it is, all accusations had probably some ground of truth, and all accusers some wrong motive. And in all quarrels there is always, said she, fault on both sides. She therefore punished accused and accuser alike, without further investigation. I have observed something of the same plan pursued since by some persons who aspire to the character of impartial historians. But it never struck me as quite fair in the historians or in Aunt Dorothy. However, I must say, in Aunt Dorothy's case, this mode of administering justice had a tendency to check accusations. It must have been an unusually strong desire of vengeance, or sense of wrong, which induced us to draw up an indictment which was sure to be visited with equal severity on plaintiff and defendant. And although our sense of justice was not satisfied, and Roger and I in consequence formed ourselves into a permanent Committee of Grievances, the peace of the household was perhaps on the whole promoted by the system. The embittering effects were, moreover, softened in our case by the presence of other counteracting elements.

I had not been long in bed according to the decrees of Justice in the person of Aunt Dorothy, when Mercy, in the person of Aunt Gretel, came to bind up my wounds.

"Olive, my little one," said she, sitting down on the side of my bed, "what hast thou been saying? Thou wouldst not surely say anything ungrateful against the dear Lord and Saviour?"

Whereupon I buried my face in the bed-clothes, and sobbed so that the bed shook under me.

She took my hand, and bending over me, said tenderly,—

"Poor little one! Thou must not break thy heart. The good Lord will forgive, Olive, will forgive all. Tell me what it is, darling, and don't be afraid."

Still I sobbed on, when she said,—

"If thou canst not tell me, tell the dear Saviour. He is gentler than poor Aunt Gretel, and knows thee better. Only do not be afraid of Him, nothing grieves Him like that, sweet heart; anything but that."

Then I grew a little calmer, and moaned out,—

"Indeed, Aunt Gretel, I did not mean anything wicked. But it is so hard to understand.

There are so many things I cannot make out. And oh, if I should be on the wrong side of the tree after all! If I should be on the wrong side of the tree!"

And at the thought my sobs burst forth afresh.

Aunt Gretel was sorely perplexed. She said—

"What tree, little one? Where is thy poor brain wandering?"

"The tree with God at the beginning," said I, "and with heaven at one end and hell at the other, and no way to cross over if once you get wrong, and God never seeming to mind."

"A very wicked tree," said Aunt Gretel. "I never heard of it. The only tree in the Bible is the Tree of Life. And of that the blessed Lord will give freely to every one who comes—the fruit for life and the leaves for healing. Never mind the other, sweet heart."

"If there were only a way across!" said I, "and if I could be sure God did care!"

"There is a way across, my lamb," said she. "Only it is not a way. It is but a step. It is a look. It is a touch. For the way across is the blessed Saviour Himself. And He is always nearer than I am now, if you could only see."

"And God does care," said I, "whether we are lost or saved?"

"Care! little Olive," said she. "Hast thou forgotten the manger and the cross? That comes of trying to see back to the beginning. *He* was in the beginning, sweet heart, but not thou or I! He *is* the beginning every day and for ever to us.

Look to Him. His face is shining on you now, watching you tenderly as if it were your mother's, my poor motherless lamb. Whatever else is dark, that is plain. And you never meant to grieve or question Him! You did not mean to say the darkness was in Him, Olive! You never meant that. Put the darkness anywhere but there, sweet heart —anywhere but there. There is darkness enough, in good sooth. But in Him is no darkness at all." And then she murmured, half to herself, "It is very strange, Dr. Luther made it all so plain, more than a hundred years ago. And it seems as if it all had to be done over again."

"Didst thou say thy prayers, my lamb?" she added.

I had. But it was sweet to kneel down with Aunt Gretel again, with her arms and her warm dress folded around me, and say the words after her, the Our Father, and the prayer for father and Roger and all.

But when I came to ask a blessing on Cousin Placidia, my lips seemed unable to frame the words.

"Thou didst not pray for thy cousin, Olive," said Aunt Gretel.

"She is so very difficult to love, Aunt Gretel," said I; "she often makes me do wrong. And I bit her finger this morning."

Aunt Gretel shook her head.

"Poor little one," said she, "ah, yes! It is always hardest to forgive those we have hurt."

"But she pinched my arm where no one could see," said I.

"It will not help thee to think of that, poor lamb," said Aunt Gretel, "what thou hast to do is to forgive. Think of what will help thee to do that."

"I can't think of anything that helps me," said I.

"Dost thou wish anything bad to happen to thy cousin?" said Aunt Gretel, after a pause. "If thou couldst bring trouble on her by praying for it, wouldst thou do it?"

"No, not from God," said I. "Of course I could not ask anything bad from God."

"Then wouldst thou ask thy father to send her away, poor neglected orphan child that she was?"

"No, no, Aunt Gretel," I said, "not that. But I should like to see her punished by Aunt Dorothy."

"How much?" said Aunt Gretel.

"I am not sure. Only as much as she quite deserves."

"That would be a good deal for us all," said she; "perhaps even for thee a little more than going to bed one night without supper."

"Then until she was good," said I.

"Thou wishest thy cousin to be good, then?" said Aunt Gretel. "Then thou canst at least pray for that."

"It would make the house like the Garden of Eden, I think," I said, "before the tempter came, if Placidia were only not so provoking."

"Would it?" said she, gravely. "Art thou then always so good? Then, perhaps, thou canst ask that thy cousin's trespasses may be forgiven, even if *thou* canst not forgive her, and hast *none of thine own* to be forgiven!"

"O, Aunt Gretel," said I, suddenly perceiving her meaning, "I see it all now! It is the bit of ice in my own heart that made everything dark and cold to me. It is the bit of ice in my own heart!"

She smiled and folded me to her heart.

And then she prayed once more for Placidia the orphan, and for me, and Roger, that God in His great pity would bless us and forgive us, and make us good and loving, and like Himself and His dear Son who suffered for us and bore our sins."

And after that I did not so much care even whether Roger brought the answer he promised from Oxford or not.

And it flashed on me for an instant, as if the answer to Roger's other puzzle might come somehow from the same point; as if it answered everything to the heart to think that light and not darkness, love and not necessity, are at the innermost heart of all. For love is at once perfect freedom and inevitable necessity.

But before I fell asleep, while Aunt Gretel was still sitting on the bedside with her knitting, I heard her say to herself—

"Not so very strange—not so strange after all, although Dr. Luther did make it all clear as sunshine more than a hundred years ago. It is that bit of ice in the heart, that bit of ice that is always freezing afresh in the heart."

But Aunt Dorothy, on a night's consideration, thought the affair of the apple-tree too important to be passed over, as most of our childish quarrels were, without troubling my father about them.

Accordingly the next morning we were summoned into my father's private room, where he received his rents as a landlord, and sentenced offenders as a magistrate, and kept his law-books, and many other great hereditary folios on divinity, philosophy, and things in general. A very solemn proceeding for me that morning, my conscience oppressed with a sense of having done some wrong intentionally, and I knew not how much more without intending it.

Gradually, Roger and I standing on the other side of the table, with the law-books and the mathematical instruments my father was so fond of between us, he drew from us what had been the subject of our conversation.

Then, to my surprise, as we stood awaiting our sentence, he called me gently to him, and, seating me on his knee, pointed out a paper spread on a huge folio volume, which lay open before him. It was a diagram of the sun and the planets, with the four moons of Jupiter, the earth and the moon, complicated by circles and lines mysteriously intersecting each other.

"Olive," said he, "be so good as to explain that to me. It is made by a gentleman who learned about it from the great astronomer Galileo, and is meant to explain how the earth and the sun are kept in their places." I looked at the complication of figures and lines and magical-looking signs, and then in his face to see what he could mean.

"You do not understand it?" he said, as if he were surprised.

"Father," said I, "a little child like me!"

"And yet this is only a drawing of a little corner of the world, Olive—the sun and the earth and a few of the planets in the nook of the world in which we live. The whole universe is a good deal harder to understand than this."

"Father," said I, ashamed and blushing, "indeed I never thought I could understand these things—at least not yet; I only thought you might, or some wise people somewhere."

"Olive," said he, in a low voice, tenderly and reverently, stroking my head while he spoke, "before the great mysteries you and Roger have fallen on, I can only wonder, and wait, and say like you, '*Father, a little child like me!*' And I do not think the great Galileo himself could do much more."

But to Roger he said, rising and laying his hand on his shoulder—

"Exercise your wits as much as you can, my boy; but there are two kinds of roads I advise you for the most part to eschew. One kind are the roads that lead to the edge of the great darkness which skirts our little patch of light on every side. The other are the roads that go in a circle, leading you round and round with much toil to the point from which you started. I do not say, never travel on these—you cannot always help it. But for the most part exercise yourself on the roads which lead somewhere. The exercise is as good, and the result better." And he was about to send us away.

But Aunt Dorothy was not at all satisfied. "That Signor Galileo was a very dangerous person," she said. "He said the sun went round, and the earth stood still, which was contrary at once to common sense, the five senses, and Scripture; and if chits like Roger and me were allowed to enter on such false philosophy at our age, where should we have wandered at hers?"

"Not much further, Sister Dorothy," said my Father, "if they reached the age of Methuselah. Not much further into the question, and not much nearer the answer."

"I see no difficulty in the question at all," said Aunt Dorothy. "The Almighty does everything because it is His will to do it. And we can do nothing except He wills us to do it. Which answers Olive and Roger at once. All doubts are sins, and ought to be crushed at the beginning."

"How would you do this, Sister Dorothy?" asked my Father; "a good many persons have tried it before and failed."

"How! The simplest thing in the world," said Aunt Dorothy. "In the first place, set people to work, so that they have no time for such foolish questions, and genealogies, and contentions."

"A wholesome plan, which seems to be very generally pursued with regard to the whole human race," said Father. "It is mercifully provided that those who have leisure for such questions are few. But what else would you do?"

"For the children there is the switch," said Aunt

Dorothy. "They would be thankful enough for it when they grew wiser."

"So think the Pope and Archbishop Laud," replied my Father; "and so they set up the Inquisition and the Star Chamber."

"I have no fault to find with the Inquisition and the Star Chamber," said Aunt Dorothy, "if they would only punish the right people."

"But sometimes we learn we have been mistaken ourselves," said Father. "How can we be sure we are absolutely right about everything?"

"*I am*," said Aunt Dorothy, emphatically. "Thank Heaven I have not a doubt about anything. Heresy is worse than treason, for it is treason against God; and worse than murder, for it is the murder of immortal souls. The fault of the Pope and Archbishop Laud is that they are heretics themselves, and punish the wrong people."

This was a point often reached in discussions between my Father and Aunt Dorothy, but this time it was happily closed by the clatter of a horse's hoofs on the pavement of the court before the house.

My father's face brightened, and he rose hastily, exclaiming, "A welcome guest, Sister Dorothy—the Lord of the Fens—set the table in the wainscoted parlour."

He left the room, and we children watched a tall, stalwart gentleman, well known to us, with a healthy, sunburnt face, alight from his horse.

"The Lord of the Fens, indeed!" said Aunt Dorothy in a disappointed tone, as she looked out of the window. "Why, it is only Mr. Oliver Cromwell of Ely, with his coat as slovenly as usual, and his hat without a hat-band. I am as much against gewgaws as any one. If I had my way, not a slashed doublet, or ribboned hose, or feather, or lace, should be seen in the kingdom. But there is reason in all things. Gentlemen should look like gentlemen, and a hat without a hat-band is going too far, in all conscience. The wainscoted parlour, in good sooth! Why, his boots are covered with mud, and I dare warrant it, he will never think of rubbing them on the straw in the hall. And they will get talking, no one knows how long, about that everlasting draining of the Fens. I can't think why they won't let the Fens alone. They did very well for our fathers as they were, and they were better men than we see now-a-days; and if the Almighty made the Fens wet, I suppose he meant them to be wet; and people had better take care how they run against His designs. And they say the king is against it, or against somebody concerned in it, so that there is no knowing what it may lead to. All Scotland in a tumult, and the godly languishing in prison, and our parson putting on some new furbelow and setting up some new fandango every Sabbath; and a godly gentleman like Mr. Oliver Cromwell (for he is that, I don't deny) to have nothing better to do than to try and squeeze a few acres more of dry land out of the Fens!"

But Roger whispered to me,—

"Mr. Hampden says Mr. Cromwell would be the

greatest man in England if things should come to the worst, and there should be any disturbance with the king."

At that moment my father called Roger, and to his delight he was allowed to accompany him and our guest over the farm.

And the next entry in my Journal is this,—

"Mr. Oliver Cromwell of Ely was at our house yesterday. Roger walked over the farm with him and my father. Their discourse was concerning twenty shillings which the king wants to oblige Mr. Hampden of Great Hampden to lend him, which Mr. Hampden will not, not because he cannot afford it, but because the king would then be able to make every one lend him money whether they like it or not, or whether they are able or not. They call it the ship-money. Concerning this and also concerning some good men, ministers or lecturers, whom Mr. Cromwell wishes to set to preach the Gospel to the people in places where no one else preaches, so that they can understand, but whom Archbishop Laud has silenced with fines and many threats, Aunt Dorothy thinks it a pity godly men like Mr. Hampden and Mr. Cromwell should concern themselves about such poor worldly things as shillings and pence. Regarding the lecturers, she says that they have more reason. Only, she says, it is a wonder to her they will begin with such small insignificant things. Let them set to work, root and branch (says she), against Popery under false names and in high places, and these lesser matters will take care of themselves. But father says, 'poor worldly things' are just the things by which we are tried and proved whether we will be faithful to the high unworldly calling or not. And 'small insignificant things' are the beginnings of everything that lives and endures, from a British oak to the kingdom of heaven."

CHAPTER II.

May Day, 1638.

"HIS morning, before break of day, I went to bathe my face in the May dew by the Lady Well. There I met Lettice Davenant with her maidens. She was dressed in a kirtle of grass-green silk, with a blue taffetas petticoat, and her eyes were like wet violets, and her brown hair like wavy tangles of soft glossy unspun silk, specked and woven with gold, and she looked like a sweet May flower, just lifting itself out of its green sheath into the sunshine, and all the colours changing and weaving into each other, as they do in the flowers. And she laid her soft, little hand in mine, and said her mother loved mine, and she wished I would love her, and be her friend. And she kissed me with her dear, sweet, little mouth, like a rosebud—like a child's. And I held her close in my arms, with her silky hair falling on my shoulder. She is just so much shorter than I am. And her heart beat on mine. And I will love her all my life. No wonder Roger thinks her fair.

"I will love her all my life, whatever Aunt Dorothy says.

"Firstly, because I cannot help it. And secondly, because I am sure it is right—right—right to love; always right to love—to love as much, as dearly, as long, as deep as we can. Always right to love, never right to despise, or keep aloof, or turn aside. Sometimes right to hate, at least I think so; sometimes right to be angry, I am sure of that; but never right to despise, and always—always right to love.

"For Roger and I have looked well all through the Gospels to see. And the Pharisee despised, the Priest and the Levite passed by, and the disciples said once or twice, send her away. But the Lord drew near, called them to Him, touched, took in His arms, loved, always loved. Loved when they were wandering—loved when they would not come; loved even when they 'went away.'

"And Aunt Gretel thinks the same. Only I sometimes wish we had lived in the times she speaks of, told of in certain Family Chronicles of hers, a century old. For then it was the people with the wrong religion who despised others, and were harsh and severe. And they went into convents, which must have been a great relief to the rest of the family. And now it seems to be the people with the right religion who do like the Pharisees. And they stay at home, which is more difficult to understand, and more unpleasant to bear."

A very vehement utterance, crossed through with repentant lines in after times, but still quite legible, and of interest to me for the vanished outer world of life, and the tumultuous inward world of revolt it recalls.

For that May morning, on my way home through the wood, I met the village lads and lasses bringing home the May; and when I reached the house, it was late; the serving men and maidens had finished their meal at the long table in the hall, and Aunt Dorothy sat at one end of the table, which crossed it at the top, and span; and Cousin Placidia sat silent at the other end and span, the whirr of their spinning-wheels distinctly reproaching me in a steady hum of displeasure, until I was constrained to reply to it and to Aunt Dorothy's silence.

"Aunt Dorothy, prithee, forgive me. I only went to bathe my face in the May dew by the Lady Well. And there I met Lettice Davenant."

"I never reproached thee, child," said Aunt Dorothy. "There is too much license in this house for that. But this, I will say, the excuse is worse than the fault. How often have I told thee not to stain thy lips with the idolatrous title of that well? And as to bathing thy face in the May dew, Olive, it is Popery—sheer Popery."

"Not Popery, sister Dorothy," said my Father, looking up from his sheet of news just brought from London. "Not Popery; Paganism. The custom dates back to the ancient Romans, probably to the festival of the goddess Maia, mother of Mercury, but here antiquarians are divided."

"And well they may be," said Aunt Dorothy, "what but sects and divisions can be expected from such tampering with vanities and idolatries? For my part, it matters little to me whether the custom dates to the modern or the ancient Romans, or to the Hittites, the Perizzites, the Amorites, and the Jebusites. Whoever painted the idol, I have little doubt who made it. And of the two I like the unchristened idols best."

"Not quite, sister Dorothy, not always," remonstrated my Father, "it is certainly a great mistake to worship the Virgin Mary. But the Moloch to whom they burned little children was worse, much worse."

"If he was, the less we hear about him the better, Brother," said Aunt Dorothy. "But as to the burning I see little difference. You can see the black sites of Queen Mary's fires still. And Lettice Davenant has been up at the court of the new Queen Marie (as they call her);—an unlucky name for England. And little good she or hers are like to do to our Olive."

On which I turned wholly into a boiling caldron of indignation; and to what it might have led I know not, had not Aunt Gretel at that moment intervened, ruddy from the kitchen fire, and with the glow of a pleasant purpose in her kindly blue eyes.

"They are like to have the blithest May to-day they have seen for many a year," said she. "Our Margery, the daughter of Tib the dairywoman, is to be queen. And a better maiden or a sweeter face there is not in all the country side. And Dickon, the gardener's son at the Hall, is her sweetheart, and the Lady Lucy Davenant has let them deck the bower with posies from her own garden, and they are coming from the Hall, the Lady Lucy and Sir Walter, and Mistress Lettice and her five brothers, to see the jollity."

"Tell Tib's goodman to broach a barrel of the best ale, sister Gretel," said my Father, "and we will go and see."

This was said in the tone Aunt Dorothy never answered, and she made no remonstrance except through the whirr of her spinning-wheel, which always seemed to Roger and me to be a kind of "*famulus*," or a second-self to Aunt Dorothy (of course of a white not a black kind), saying the thing she meant but would not say, and in a thousand ways spinning out and completing, not her thread only, but her life and thought.

My Father soon rose and went to the farm. Aunt Dorothy span silent at one end of the table, and Cousin Placidia at the other; while I sat too indignant to eat anything, and Aunt Gretel moved about in a helpless, conciliatory state between.

"The Bible does speak of being merry, sister Dorothy," said she at length, metaphorically putting her foot into Aunt Dorothy's spiritual spinning, as she was wont to do.

"No doubt it does," said Aunt Dorothy. "'Is any merry among you, let him sing psalms.'"

"I am sure I wish they would," said Aunt Gretel, "there is nothing I enjoy so much. And," pursued she, waxing bold, "after all, sister Dorothy, the whole world does seem to sing and dance in the green May; the little birds hop and sing, (sing love-songs too, sister Dorothy), and the leaves dance and rustle, and the flowers don all the colours of the rainbow."

"As to the flowers," said Aunt Dorothy, "they did not choose their own raiment, so no blame to them, poor perishing things. I hold they were clothed in their scarlet and purple, like fools in motley, for the very purpose of shaming us into being sober and grave in our attire. The birds, indeed, may hop and sing if they like it. Not that I think they have much cause, poor inconsiderate creatures, what with the birds'-nesting, and the poaching, and Mr. Cromwell draining the fens. But they have no foresight, and they have not immortal souls, and if they're to be in a pie to-morrow they don't know it; and they are no worse for it the day after."

"But," said Aunt Gretel, "we have immortal souls, and I think that ought to make us sing a thousand-fold better than the birds."

"We have not only souls, we have sins," said Aunt Dorothy; "and there is enough in sin, I hold, to stop the sweetest music in the world when the burden is felt."

"But we have the Gospel and the Saviour," said Aunt Gretel, "glad tidings of great joy to all people."

"Tell them, then, to the people," said Aunt Dorothy; "get a godly minister to go and preach them to the poor sinners in the village, and that will be better than setting up May-poles and broaching beer barrels."

"I do tell them whenever I can, sister Dorothy," said Aunt Gretel meekly, "as well as I can. But the best of us cannot always be listening to sermons."

"We might listen much longer than we do if we tried," said Aunt Dorothy, branching off from the subject. "In Scotland, I am told, the Sabbath services last twelve hours."

Aunt Gretel sighed; whether in compassion for

the Scottish congregations, or in lamentation over her own shortcomings, she did not explain.

"But," she resumed, "it does seem that if the good God meant that there should have been no merry-making in the world he would have arranged that people should have come into the world full-grown."

"Probably it would have been better if it could have been so managed," said Aunt Dorothy; "but I suppose it could not. However that may be, the best we can do now is to make people grow up as soon as they can, and not keep them babies with May games, and junketings, and possetings."

"But," said Aunt Gretel timidly, "after all, sister Dorothy, the Bible does not give us any strict rules by which we can judge other people in such things."

"I confess," replied Aunt Dorothy, "that if there could be a thing to be wished for in the Bible (with reverence I say it), it is just that there *were* a few plain rules. St. Paul came very near it when he was speaking of the weak brethren at the idol-feasts; but I confess I do think it would have been a help if he had gone a little further while he was about it. Then, people would not have been able to pretend they did not know what he meant. I do think it would have been a comfort if there could have been a book of Leviticus in the New Testament."

"But your Mr. John Milton," said Aunt Gretel, "in his new masque of Comus, which your brother thinks beautiful, introduces music and dancing."

"Mr. Milton is a godly man," said Aunt Dorothy, "but, poor gentleman, he is a poet; and poets cannot always be expected to keep straight, like reasonable people."

"But Dr. Martin Luther himself dearly loved music," said Aunt Gretel, driven to her final court of appeal, "and even sanctioned dancing, in a Christian-like way, without rioting and drunkenness."

"Dr. Luther might," rejoined Aunt Dorothy. "Dr. Luther believed in consubstantiation, and rejected the Epistle of St. James. And, besides, by this time he has been in heaven, it is to be hoped, for nearly a hundred years, and there can be no doubt he knows better."

Aunt Gretel was roused.

"Sister Dorothy," she said, "Dr. Luther does not need to be defended by me. But I sometimes think if he came to England in these days he would think some of you had gone some way towards painting again that terrible picture of God, which made the little ones fly from Him instead of taking refuge with Him, and which it took him so much toil to destroy."

And she fled to the kitchen, rosier than she came, but with tears instead of smiles in her eyes.

"If people could enjoy themselves harmlessly, without rioting and drunkenness," said Aunt Dorothy, half yielding, "there might be less to be said against it."

"What is rioting, Aunt Dorothy?" asked Placidia from her spinning-wheel.

"Idling and romping, and doing what had better not be done nor talked about."

"Because, Aunt Dorothy," said Placidia solemnly, "I saw Dickon trying to kiss our Tib's daughter, Margery, behind the door; and she would not let him. But she laughed and did not seem angry. Is that rioting?"

"Dickon may kiss Margery as often as he likes without hurting you or any one, Placidia," said Aunt Dorothy, incautiously. "Margery is a good honest girl, and can take care of herself. And you have no right to watch what any one does behind doors. You, at least, shall not go to the May-pole to-day, but shall stay with me and learn the thirteenth of First Corinthians."

"I do not wish to go to any rioting or May games," said Placidia. "I like my spinning and my book. I never did care for dancing and playing and fooling, Aunt Dorothy, I am thankful to say."

"Don't be a Pharisee, Placidia," said Aunt Dorothy, turning hotly on her unwelcome ally. "Better play and dance like a flipperty-gibbet, than watch what other people do behind doors, and tell tales."

And I left them to settle the controversy, while I went to join Aunt Gretel, who was in my Father's chamber preparing for me such sober decorations in honor of the festivities as our Puritan wardrobes admitted of. It was a great day for me; chiefly for the expectation of meeting the Lady Lucy and the sweet maiden Lettice.

I was starting full of glee when the sight of Aunt

Dorothy, spinning silently in the hall as we passed the door, with Placidia beside her, threw a little shadow over my contentment. Aunt Dorothy so completely represented to me the majesty of law, and at the bottom of our hearts both Roger and I so trusted and honored her, that in spite even of my Father's sanction, something of misgiving troubled me at the sight of her grave face. With a sudden impulse I ran back, and, standing before her, said—

"Aunt Dorothy, you are not angry. I shall not dance, only look, and soon be at home again, and all will go on the same as ever."

She shook her head, but more sorrowfully than angrily.

"Eve only looked," said she, "but nothing went on the same evermore."

At that moment my father came back to seek me, and, catching Aunt Dorothy's last words, he said kindly but gravely, "Do not let us trouble the child's conscience with our scruples. It is a serious danger to force our scruples on others. When experience of their own peculiar weaknesses and besetments has led them to scruple at things for themselves, it is another matter. But to add to God's laws is almost as tremendous a mistake as to subtract from them. Our additions, moreover, are sure to end in subtractions in some other direction. Indifferent things done with a guilty conscience lead to guilty things done with an indifferent conscience. In inventing imaginary sins you create real sinners."

"Well, brother, it is as you please," said Aunt Dorothy, "but I should have thought our new parson reading from that blasphemous 'Book of Sports' from the pulpit, commending the people to dance around the May-poles on the Sabbath afternoons, was enough to turn any serious person against them."

"Nay; that is exactly one of the strongest reasons why I go to-day," said my father. "I go to show that it is not the May-poles we scruple at, but the cruel robbing of the poor by the desecration of the day given them by God for higher things."

And he led me away. But my free, innocent gladsomeness was gone.

Conscience had come in with her questionings, and her discernings and her dividings. I was not sure whether God was pleased with me or with any of us. Even when I looked at the garlanded May-pole, I thought of the old tree in Eden with its pleasant fruit, which I had embroidered with a serpent coiled round it, darting out his forked tongue at Eve. I wondered whether if my eyes were opened I should see him there, writhing among the hawthorn garlands, or hissing envenomed words into the ear of our Tib's Margery as she sat in her royal bower of green boughs crowned with flowers, or gliding in and out among the dancers, as hand in hand they moved singing around the May-pole, wreathing and unwreathing the long garland which united them, and making low reverences, as they passed, to their blushing Queen. I wondered whether the whole thing had some mysterious connection with idolatry, and heaven itself were after all watching us with grieved displeasure, like Aunt

Dorothy, and secretly preparing fiery serpents, or a rain of fire and brimstone, or a thunder storm, or whatever came instead of fiery serpents and fire and brimstone in these days when there were no more miracles.

These thoughts, however, all vanished when the family appeared from the Hall. The Lady Lucy was borne by two men in a sedan-chair which she had brought from London, a thing I had never seen before. It so happened that I had never seen the Lady Lucy until that day. The family had been much about the court, and on the few occasions on which they had spent any time at the Hall, the Lady Lucy's health had been too feeble to admit of her attending at the parish church with the rest of the family. From the moment, therefore, that Sir Walter handed her out of the chair and seated her on cushions prepared for her, I could not take my eyes from her, not even to look at Lettice. So queenly she appeared to me, such a perfection of grace and dignity and beauty. Her complexion was fair like Lettice's, but very delicate and pale, like a shell; and her hair, still brown and abundant, was arranged in countless small ringlets around her face. On her neck and her forehead there was a brilliant sparkle and a glitter, which must, of course, have been from jewels; and her dress had a sheen and a gloss, and a delicate changing of gorgeous colours on it which must have been that of velvet and brocade and rare laces. But in my eyes she sat wrapped in a kind of halo of unearthly glory. I no more thought of resolving it into the texture of any earthly looms than if she had been a lily or a star. All around her seemed to belong to her, like the moonbeams to the moon or the leaves to a flower. Not her dress only, but the green leaves which bent lovingly down to her, and the flowery turf which seemed to kiss her feet. If I thought of any comparison, it was Aunt Gretel's fairy-tale of the princess with the three magic robes, enclosed in the magic nut-shells, like the sun, like the moon, and like the stars.

Even Sir Walter, burly, and sturdy, and noisy, and substantial as he was, seemed to me to acquire a kind of reflected glory by her speaking to him. And her seven sons girdled her like the planets around the sun, or like the seven electors Aunt Gretel told us about around the emperor. But when at last her eyes rested on me, and she whispered something to Sir Walter, and he came across and doffed his plumed hat to my father, and then led me across to her, and she looked long in my face, and then up in my father's, and said, "The likeness is perfect," and then kissed me, and made me sit down on the cushion beside her with her hand in mine, I thought her voice like an angel's, and her touch seemed to me to have something hallowing in it which made me feel safe like a little bird under its mother's wing. The silent smile of her soft eyes under her smooth, broad, unfurrowed brow, as she turned every now and then and looked at me, fell on my heart like a kiss. And I thought no more of Eve and the serpent, or Aunt Dorothy, or anything, until she rose to go. And then she kissed me again. But I scarcely seemed to care that she should kiss me. Her presence was an embrace; her smile was a kiss; every tone of her voice was a caress. A tender motherliness seemed to fold me all round as I sat by her. As she left me she said softly,—

"Little Olive, you must come and see me. Your mother and I loved each other." Then holding out her hand to my father, she added,—

"Politics and land-boundaries, Mr. Drayton, must not keep us any longer apart."

He bowed, and they conversed some time longer; but the only thing I heard was that he promised I should go and see her at the Hall.

I think every one felt something of the soft charm there was in her. For, quiet and retiring as she was, when she left, a light and gladness seemed to go with her. Before long the dancing and singing stopped, the tables were set on the green, and the feasting began, and we left and went home.

"Oh, Roger," said I, when we were alone that evening, "there can be no one like her in the world."

"Of course not," said Roger decisively. "Did I not always say so?"

"But you never saw her before."

"Never saw her, Olive? How can I help seeing her every Sunday? She sits at the end of the pew just opposite mine."

"She never came to church, Roger."

"Never came to church? Who do you mean?"

"Mean? The Lady Lucy, to be sure."

"Oh," said Roger, "I thought, of course, you were speaking of Mistress Lettice."

But when we came back to Netherby, full as my heart was of my new love, there was something in Aunt Dorothy's manner that quite froze any utterance of it, and brought me back to Eve and the apple. Yet she spoke kindly,—

"Thou lookest serious, Olive," said she. "Perhaps thou didst not find it such a paradise after all. Poor child, the world's a shallow cup, and the sooner we drain it the better. I think better of thee than that thou wilt long be content with such May games and vanities. Come to thy supper."

But my honesty compelled me to speak. I did not wish Aunt Dorothy to think better of me than I deserved.

"It *was* rather like paradise, Aunt Dorothy," I said.

"Paradise around a May-pole," said she compassionately. "Poor babe, poor babe!"

"It was not the May-pole," said I, my face burning at having to bring out my hidden treasure of new love; "not the May-pole, but Lady Lucy."

"Lady Lucy took a fancy to the child, Sister Dorothy," said my father, "and asked her to the Hall." And lowering his voice he added, "She thought her like Magdalene."

I had scarcely ever heard him utter my mother's Christian name before, and now it seemed to fall from his lips like a blessing.

Aunt Dorothy's brow darkened.

"Thou wilt never let the child go, brother?"

He did not at once reply.

"Into the very jaws of Babylon, brother? The Lady Lucy is one of the favourites, they say, of the Popish Queen."

"Very probably," said my father dryly, "I do not see how the Queen or any one else could help honouring or favouring the Lady Lucy."

My heart bounded in acquiescence.

"They say she has a chapel at the Hall fitted up on the very pattern of Archbishop Laud, and priests in coats of no one knows how many colours, and painted glass, and incense. Thou wilt never let the poor unsuspecting lamb go into the very lair of the Beast?"

"There are jewels in many a dust-heap, Sister Dorothy, and the Lady Lucy is one," said my father a little impatiently, for Aunt Dorothy had the faculty of arousing the latent wilfulness of the meekest of men. "Let us say no more about it. I have made up my mind."

Had he known how deep was the spell on me, he might have thought otherwise. For, ungrateful that I was, having lost my heart to this fair strange lady, I sat chafing at Aunt Dorothy's injustice, in a wide-spread inward revolt, which bid fair to extend itself to everything Aunt Dorothy believed or required. All her life-long care and affection, and patient (or impatient) toiling and planning for me and mine, blotted out by what I deemed her blind injustice to this object of my worship, who had but kissed me twice, and smiled on me, and said half-a-dozen soft words, and had won all my childish heart!

And yet, looking back from these sober hours, I still feel it was not altogether an infatuation. Such true and tender motherliness as dwelt in Lady Lucy is the greatest power it seems to me that can invest a woman.

All mothers certainly do not possess it. On some, on the contrary, the motherly love which passionately enfolds those within is too like a bristling fortification of jealousy and exclusiveness to those without. Or rather (that I dishonour not the most sacred thing in our nature), I should say, the mother's love which is from above is lowered and narrowed into a passion by the selfishness which is not from above. And some unmarried women possess it, some little maidens even who from infancy draw the little ones to them by a soft irresistible attraction, and seem to fold them under soft dove-like plumage. Without something of it women are not women, but only weaker, and shriller, and smaller men. But where, as in Lady Lucy, the whole being is steeped in it, it seems to me the sweetest, strongest, most irresistible power on earth, to control, and bless, and purify, and raise, and the truest incarnation (I cannot say anything so cold as image), the truest embodying and ensouling of what is divine.

But that night it so chanced that I, who had fallen asleep lapped in sweet memories of Lady Lucy and in the protection of Aunt Gretel's presence, was awakened by the long roll of a thunder-peal which seemed as if it never would end.

For some time I tried to hide myself from the flash and the terrific sound under the bed-clothes. But it would not do. At length I sprang speechless from my little bed to Aunt Gretel's. She took me in close to her. And there, with my head on her shoulder, speech came back to me, and I said, in a frightened whisper (for it seemed to me like speaking in church),—

"Aunt Gretel, will the last trumpet be like that?"

"I do not know, Olive," said she quietly. "More awful, I think, yet plainer, for we shall all understand it, even those in the graves; and it will call us home."

"O Aunt Gretel," I said at last, "can it have anything to do with the May-pole?"

"What, sweet heart! the thunder?"

"It is God's voice, is it not? Does not the Bible say so? And it does sound like an angry voice," I whispered, for the windows were rattling and the house was quivering with the repeated peals, as if in the grasp of a terrible giant.

"There is much indeed to make the good God angry, my lamb, much more than May-poles."

"Yes," said I, "there were the three gentlemen in the pillory! That must have been worse certainly. But do you think God can be angry with me, Aunt Gretel?"

"For what, sweet heart?"

"For loving Lady Lucy," said I; "she is so very sweet."

"God is never angry with any one for loving," said Aunt Gretel, "only for not loving. But there is a better voice of God than the thunder, Olive," added she. "A voice that does not roar but speaks, sweet heart. Hast thou never heard that?"

I was silent, for I half guessed what she meant.

"'*It is I, be not afraid,*'" she said, in a low, clear tone, contrasting with my awe-stricken whisper. "Whenever you do not understand the voice that thunders, sweet heart, go back to the voice that speaks, and that will tell thee what the voice that thunders means."

"Aunt Gretel," said I, after a little silence, "it seemed to me as if Lady Lucy were like some words of our Saviour's. As if everything in her were saying in a soft dove's voice, 'Suffer the little children to come unto Me.' Was it wrong to think so? It seemed as if I were sitting beside my Mother, and then I thought of those very words. Was it wrong?"

"Not wrong, my poor motherless lamb," said she, "no, surely not wrong. Remember, Olive, from Paradise downwards the worst heresy has been slander of the love of God; distrust of His love, and disbelief of the awful warnings His love gives against sin. Whenever we feel anything very tender in any human love, we should feel as if the blessed God were stretching out His arms to us through it, and saying, 'That is a little like the way I love thee. But only a little, only a little.' "

And the thunder rolled on, and the lightning that night cleft the great elm by the gate, so that in the morning it stood a scorched and blackened trunk.

And Aunt Dorothy said what an awful warning it was. But to me, if it was an "awful warning," it stood also like a parable of mercy. I could not exactly have explained why; but I thought I could read the meaning of the Voice that thundered by the Voice that spoke.

I thought how He had been scathed and bruised for us.

And I pleaded hard with my father that the old scathed tree might not be felled. For to me its great bare blackened branches seemed to shelter the house like that accursed tree which had spread its bare arms one Good Friday night outside Jerusalem, and had pleaded not for vengeance, but for pity and for pardon.

I think the resentment of injustice is one of the first-born and strongest passions in an ingenuous heart. And to this, I believe, is often due the falling off of children from the party of their parents. They hear hard things said of opponents; on closer acquaintance they find these to be exaggerations, or, at least, suppressions; the general gloom of a picture being even more produced by effacing lights than by deepening shadows. The discovery throws a doubt over the whole range of inherited beliefs, and it is well if in the heat of youth the revulsion is not far greater than the wrong; if in their indignation at discovering that the heretic is not an embodied heresy, but merely a human creature believing something wrong, they do not glorify him into a martyr and a model.

For Roger and me it was the greatest blessing that our father was just and candid to the extent of seeing (often to his own great distress and perplexity) even more clearly the defects of his own party which he might correct, than of the other side, which he could not; and that Aunt Gretel was apt to see all opinions and characters melted into a haze of indiscriminate sunshine by the light of her own loving heart.

Our indignation, therefore, during the period of our lives which followed on this May-day was almost entirely directed against Aunt Dorothy.

My idol remained for some time precisely at the due idolatrous distance, enshrined in general behind a screen of sweet mystery, with occasional flashes of beatific vision; the intervals filled up with rumours of the music, and breaths of the incense of the inner sanctuary, enhanced by what I deemed the unjust murmurs of the profane outside.

My father fulfilled his promise of taking me to the Hall. On our way to Lady Lucy's drawing-chamber I caught a glimpse through a half-open door into her private chapel, which left on my memory a haze and a fragrance of coloured light falling on the marble pavements through windows like rubies and sapphires, of golden chalices and candelabras, of aromatic perfumes, with a rise and fall of sweet chords of sacred music, all blended together into a kind of sacred spell, like the church bells on Sunday across the Mere. The Lady Lucy herself was embroidering a silken church vestment with gold and crimson; skeins of glossy silk of brilliant colours lay around her, which thenceforth invested the descriptions of the broidered work of the tabernacle for me with a new interest. She received my father with a courtly grace, and me with her own motherly sweetness. She made me sit on a tabouret at her feet, while she conversed with my father, and gave me a French ivory puzzle to unravel. But I could do nothing but drink in the soft modulations of her voice without heeding what she said, except that the discourse seemed embroidered with the names of the King and the Queen, and the Princes and Princesses, which seemed as fit for her lips as her rich dress was for her person. She seemed to speak with a gentle raillery, reminding him of old times, and asking why he deserted the court. But his words and tones were very grave. Then, as he spoke of leaving, she unlocked a little sandal-wood cabinet, and took out a locket containing a curl of fair hair, and she said softly, "This was Magdalene's!" and held it beside mine. And then, as she carefully laid it aside again, the conversation for a few moments rose to higher things, and a Name higher than those of kings and queens was in it. And she said reverently, "In whatever else we suffer, that good part, I trust, may be mine and yours! as we know so well it was hers." And my father seemed moved, took leave, and said nothing more until we had passed through the outer gate, when in the avenue Lettice met us, cantering on a white palfrey, in a riding coat laced with red, blue and yellow; and springing off, left her horse to go whither it would, as she ran to welcome me, saying a thousand pretty, kindly things, while I, in a shy ecstasy, could only stand and hold her hand, and feel as if I had been transported, entirely unprepared, straight into the middle of a fairy tale.

After that for some weeks there was a stream of courtly company at the Hall, and Roger and I only saw Lettice and occasionally the Lady Lucy at church, or met them now and then in our rides and rambles by the Mere or through the woods. But whenever we did meet there was always the same eager cordial greeting from Lettice, and the same affectionate manner in her mother. And from time to time we heard, through Tib's sweetheart Dickon, of the gracious little kindnesses of both mother and daughter, of their thoughtful care for tenant and servant, of the honour in which they were held by prince and peasant. And so on me and on Roger the spell worked on.

The Draytons were of as old standing in the parish as the Davenants. Indeed, if tradition and our family tree spoke true, many a broad acre around Netherby had been in the possession of our ancestors, maternal or paternal, when the forefathers of the Davenants had been holding insignificant fiefs under Norman dukes, or cruising on very doubtful errands about the northern seas. Our pedigree dated back to Saxon times; the porch of the oldest transept of the church had, to Aunt Dorothy's mingled pride and horror, an inscription on it requesting prayers for the soul of one of our progenitors; and the oldest tomb in the church was ours. But while our family had remained stationary in place as well as in rank, the Davenants had climbed far above us. Our old Manor House had received no additions since the reign of Elizabeth, when the third gable had been built with the large embayed window, and the three terraces sloping to the fish-pond and the orchards, while on the other side of the court extended, as of old, the cattle-sheds and stables. Meantime, the old Hall of the Davenants had been degraded into farm-buildings, whilst a new mansion, with sumptuous banqueting halls and dainty ladies' withdrawing-chamber like a palace, had gradually sprung up around the remains of the suppressed Priory, which had been granted to the family; the ancient Priory Church serving as Lady Lucy's private chapel, the monks' refectory as the family dining-hall, whilst all signs of farm life had vanished out of sight, and scent, and hearing.

During the same period, the new transept of our parish church, which had been the Davenants' family chapel, had become enriched with stately monuments, where the effigies of knight and dame rested under decorated canopies. The titles and armorial bearings of many a noble family were mingled with theirs on monumental brass and stained window; whilst the plain massive architecture of our hereditary portion of the church was not more contrasted with the rich and delicate carving of theirs than were we and our servingmen and maidens, in our plain, sad-colored stuffs, unplumed, unadorned hats, caps or coifs, and white linen kerchiefs, with the brocades, satins, and velvets, ostrich feathers and jewels, ribboned hosen and buckled shoes of the Hall.

The contrast had gone deeper than mere externals, as external contrasts mostly do, in this symbolical world. In the Civil Wars, when no political principle was involved, it had chanced that the Draytons and the Davenants had seldom been on the same side. But at and after the Reformation the difference manifested itself plainly and steadily.

The Davenants had recognized Henry VIII.'s supremacy to the extent of receiving from him a grant of the lands belonging to the neighbouring abbey. But it had probably cost them little change of belief to return zealously to the old religion, under the rule of Queen Mary; whereas the Draytons, adhering with Saxon immobility to the Papal authority when Henry VIII. discarded it, had slowly come round to the conviction of the truth of the reformed religion by the time it became dangerous; and we hold it one of our chief family distinctions that we have a name closely connected with us enrolled among the noble army in "Fox's Book of Martyrs." Indeed, throughout their history, our family had an unprosperous propensity to the dangerous side. The religious convictions, so painfully adopted and so dearly proved, throughout the reign of Elizabeth given our ancestors, a leaning to the Puritan side; deep religious conviction binding them from generation to generation to the noblest spirits of their times, whilst a certain almost perverse honesty and inflexibility of temper naturally drove them to resist any kind of pressure from without, and a taste for what is solid and simple rather than for what is elegant and gorgeous, whether in life or in ritual, inclined them to the simplest forms of ecclesiastical ceremonial.

It was this strong hereditary Protestantism which had led my Father to join the religious wars in Germany. He held King Gustavus Adolphus, the Swede, to be the noblest man and the greatest general of ancient or modern times. And he held that the fearful conflict by which that great king turned the tide against the Popish arms was little less than a conflict between truth and falsehood, barbarism and civilization, light and darkness. It was enough to make any one believe in the necessity of hell, he said, to have seen, as he had, the city of Magdeburg, ten days after Tilly's soldiers had sacked it, when scarce three thousand corpse-like survivors crept around the blackened ruins where lay buried the mangled remains of their fourteen thousand happier dead. To see that, said my Father, would make any one understand what is meant by the *wrath* of the *Lamb*; and that there are things which can make a gospel of vengeance as precious to just men as a gospel of mercy. And some foretaste of that merciful vengeance, he said, had been given already. For after Magdeburg it was said Tilly never won a battle. My Father fought with the Swedish army till the death of the king, on the sixth of November, 1632; and that day of his victory and death at Lützen, was always kept in our household as a day of family mourning.

Had Elizabeth been on the throne, my Father used to say, and Cecil at the helm of state, it would not have been the little northern kingdom of Sweden which should have stemmed the torrent of Popish and Imperial tyranny, while England stood by wringing helpless womanish hands, beholding her brethren in the faith tortured and slaughtered, her own king's daughter exiled and dethroned, and, at the same time, her brave soldiers and sailors trifled to inglorious death by thousands at the bidding of a musked and curled court favourite at Rhé and Rochelle.

It was in Germany that my Father met my mother. She was a Saxon from Luther's own town, Wittemberg. Her name was Reichenbach, and her family retained affectionate personal memories of the great Reformer, as well as an enthusiastic devotion to his doctrines. She and Aunt Gretel (Magdalene and Margarethe) were orphan daughters of an officer in the Protestant armies. And I often count it among my mercies that our family history linked us with more forms of our religion than one, and extended our horizon beyond the sects and parties of England.

Our mother died two years after my father's return to England, leaving him us two children, and the memory of a love as devoted, and a piety as simple, as ever were.

It was during these years she made the acquaintance with Lady Lucy. They had been very closely attached, although political differences, and the long absences of the Davenants at Court, had prevented much intercourse between the families since her death.

Roger recollected her face and voice and her foreign accent, and one or two things she said to him. I remember nothing of her but a kind of brooding warmth and care, tender caressing tones, and being watched by eyes with a look in them unlike any other, and then a day of weeping and silence and black dresses and sad faces, and a wandering about with a sense of something lost. Lost for ever out of my life. As much as by any possibility could be, Aunt Gretel made up the tenderness, and Aunt Dorothy the discipline; and my father did all he could to supply her place by a fatherly care softened into an uncommon passion by his sorrow, and deepened into the most sacred principle by his desire to remedy our loss. Yet, in looking back, I feel more and more we did indeed inevitably lose much. All these balancing and compensating cares and affections and restraints from every side yet missed something of the tender constraints and the heart-quickening warmth they would have had all living, blended, and consecrated in the one mother's heart. Yet to Roger, perhaps, the loss was at various points in his life even greater than to me.

If she had lived, perchance the lessons we had to learn after that May Day would have been learned with less of blundering and heat. Yet how can I tell? It seems to me the true painter keeps his pictures in harmony not by mixing the colours on the palette, but by blending them on the canvass, not by painting in leaden monotonous grays, but by interweaving and contrasting countless tints of pure and varied colour. And in nature, in history, in life, it seems to me the Creator does the same.

Yes, God forbid that in lamenting what we lost I should blaspheme the highest love—the love which, as Aunt Gretel says, takes every image of human affection, and fills and overfills it, and casts it away as too shallow; in its unutterable intensity putting as it were a tender paradox of slander on even a mother's love for her babes, and saying, "They may forget, yet will not I."

For that love, we believe, gave and took away, and has led us through fasting and feasting, dangers and droughts, Marahs and Elims, chastenings and cherishings, ever since.

Chapter III.

T length the time arrived when my dark ages of mystery and adoration were to to close. The pestilence so constantly hovering over the wretched wastes of devastated Germany had been brought to Netherby by a cousin of my mother's, who had come on a visit to us. He fell sick the day after his arrival, and died on the third day. That evening Tib, the dairywoman, sickened, and before the next morning, Margery, her daughter. A panic seized the household. My father accepted Lady Lucy's gen erous offer, to take charge of Roger and me, we happening to have been from the first secluded from all contact with the sick. Aunt Dorothy made a faint remonstrance. There were, said she, contagions worse than any plague. If her brother would answer for it, to his conscience, it was well. She, at least, would wash her hands of the whole thing. But my father had no scruples. "He only hoped," he said, "that Lady Lucy might touch us with the infection of her gracious kindliness; Olive would

be only with her, and as to Roger and the rest of the household, if he was ever to be a true Protestant, the time must come when he must learn, if necessary, to protest."

So much to Aunt Dorothy. To Roger himself, he said, in a low voice, as we were riding off, with his hand on the horse's mane,—

"Remember, my lad, there is no true manliness without godliness."

Aunt Gretel watched and waved her hand to us from the infected chamber window where she sat nursing Margery; and when I opened my bundle of clothes that evening, I found in the corner a little book containing my mother's favorite psalms copied in English for us, the 46th (Dr. Luther's own psalm), the 23d, and the 139th.

Thus armed, Roger and I sallied forth into our enchanted castle.

To be disenchanted. Not to be repelled, but certainly to be disenchanted. Not by any subtle spell of counter-magic, or rude shock of bitter discovery, but by the slow changing of the world of misty twilight splendours, of dreams and visions, guesses and rumours, into a world of daylight, of sight and touch.

My first disenchantment was the Lady Lucy's artificial curls. She allowed me to remain with her while her gentlewoman disrobed her that evening. I shall never forget the dismay with which I beheld one dainty ringlet after another, of the kind called "heart-breakers," disentangled from among her hair—itself still brown and abundant—and laid on the dressing-table. The perfumes, essences, powders, ointments, salves, balsams, crystal phials, and porcelain cups, among which these "heart-breakers" were laid, (mysterious and strange as they were to me who knew of no cosmetics but cold water and fresh air,) seemed to me only so many appropriate decorations of the shrine of my idol. But the hair was false, and perplexed me sorely, Puritan child that I was, brought up with no habits of subtle discernment between a deception and a lie.

The next morning brought me yet greater perplexity. I slept in a light closet in a turret off the Lady Lucy's chamber. The Lady Lucy's own gentlewoman came in to dress me, but before she appeared I was already arrayed, and was kneeling at the window-seat of my little arched window, reading my mother's psalms.

I thought she came to call me to prayers, with which we always began the day at home; my father reading a psalm at daybreak and offering a short solemn prayer in the Hall, where all the men and maidens were gathered, after which we sat down at one table to breakfast as the family had done since the days of Queen Elizabeth. But when I asked her if she came for this, she smiled, and said it was not a saint's day, so that it was not likely the whole household would assemble, though no doubt my Lady and Mistress Lettice would attend service with the chaplain in the chapel. But she said I might attend Lady Lucy in her chamber before she rose. I gladly accepted, and Lady Lucy invited me to partake of a new kind of confection called chocolate, brought from the Indies by the Spaniards, which finding I could not fancy, she sent for a cup of new milk and a manchet of fine milk-bread on which I breakfasted. Then she began her dressing; and then ensued my second stage of disenchantment. Out of the many crystal and porcelain vases on the table, her gentlewoman took powders and paints, and to my unutterable amazement actually began to tint with rose-colour Lady Lucy's cheeks, and to lay a delicate ivory-white on her brow. She made no mystery of it; but I suppose she saw the horror in my eyes, for she laughed and said,—

"You are watching me little Olive, with great eyes, as if I were Red Riding Hood's wolf-grandmother. What is the matter?"

I could not answer, but I felt myself flush crimson, and I remember that the only word that seemed as if it could come to my lips, was "Jezebel." I quite hated myself for the thought; the Lady Lucy was so tender and good! Yet all the day, through the service in the chapel, and my plays with Lettice, and my quiet sitting on my favorite footstool at Lady Lucy's feet, those terrible words haunted me like a bad dream: "and she painted her face and tired her head and looked out at a window." A thousand times I drove them away. I repeated to myself how she loved my mother, how my father honored her, how gracious and tender she was to me and to all. Still the words came back, with the visions of the false curls, and the paint, and the powder. And I could have cried with vexation that I had ever seen these. For I felt sure Lady Lucy was inwardly as sweet and true as I had believed, and that these were only little court customs quite foreign to her nature, to which she as a great lady had to submit, but which no more made her heart bad than the washed hands and platters made the Pharisees good. Yet the perfect image was broken, and do what I would I could not restore it.

My third disenchantment was more serious.

At the ringing of the great tower bell for dinner, summoning the household and inviting all within hearing to share the hospitality of the Hall, a cavalcade swept up the avenue, consisting of the family of a neighbouring country gentleman. Lady Lucy who was seated at her embroidery frame in the drawing-chamber, was evidently not pleased at this announcement. "They always stay till dark," she said, "and question me till I am wearied to death, about what the queen wears, what the princesses eat, or how the king talks, as if their majesties were some strange foreign beasts, and I some Moorish showman hired to exhibit them. Lettice, my sweet, take them into the garden after dinner, or I shall not recover it."

Yet when the ladies entered she received them with a manner as gracious as if they had been anxiously expected friends. I reasoned with myself that this graciousness was an inalienable quality of hers, as little voluntary or conscious as the soft tones of her voice; or that probably she repented of having spoken hastily of her visitors and compensated for it by being more than ordinarily kind. But when it proved that they had to leave early, and she lamented over the shortness of the visit, and yet immediately after their departure threw herself languidly on a couch, and sighed, "What a deliverance!" I involuntarily shrank from her to the farthest corner of the room, and watching the departing strangers, wished myself departing with them.

I stood there long, until she came gently to me and laid her hand kindly on my head. I looked up at her, and longed to look straight into her heart.

"Tears on the long lashes!" said she, caressingly. "What is the matter, little one?"

My eyelids sank and the tears fell.

"What ails thee, little silent woman?" said she, stooping to me.

I threw my arms around her and sobbed, "You are *really* glad to have me, Lady Lucy; are you not? You would not like me to go?"

She seemed at first perplexed.

"You take things too much to heart, Olive, like your poor mother," she said at last, very gently. "Those ladies are nothing to me; and your mother was dear to me, Olive, and so are you."

But in the evening when I was in bed she came herself into my little chamber, and sat by my bedside, like Aunt Gretel, and played with my long hair in her sweet way; and then before she left, said tenderly,—

"My poor little Olive, you must not doubt your mother's old friend. I am not all, or half I would be, but I could not bear to be distrusted by you. But you have lived too much shut up in a world of your own. You wear your heart too near the surface. You bring heart and conscience into things which only need courtesy and tactics. You waste your gold where beads and copper are as valuable. I must be courteous to my enemies, little one, and gracious to people who weary me to death; but to you I give a bit of my heart, and that is quite a different thing."

And she left me reassured of her affection, but not a little perplexed by this double code of morals. That one region of life should be governed by the rules of right and wrong, and another by those of politeness, was altogether a strange thing to me.

Meantime Lettice and I were rapidly advancing from the outer court of courtesies into the inner one of childish friendship, spiced with occasional sharp debates, and very undisguised honesties towards each other; as Lettice and her brothers initiated me and Roger into the various plays and games in which they were so much superior to us, and we became eager on both sides for victory. A very new world this play-world was to us, who had known scarcely any toys but such as we made for ourselves, and no amusements but such as we had planned for ourselves.

Very charming it was to us at first, the billiard-table, the tennis-court, or pall-mall; and great delight Roger took in learning to vault and throw the dart on horseback, to wheel and curvet, or pick up a lady's glove at full speed, and in the various courtly exercises and feats, Spanish, French, or Arabian, which the young Davenants had learned from their riding-master. Naturally agile, he had been trained to thorough command of his horse, by following my Father through flood and fen, while his eye had learned quickness and accuracy from hunting the wild fowl, and tracking hares and foxes through the wild country around us, and these accomplishments came easily enough to him. Yet with all these ingenious arrangements for passing the time, it seemed to hang more heavily on hand at the Hall than at Netherby; it came, indeed, to Roger and me as something completely new that any arrangements should be needed to make the time pass quickly. What with spinning, and sewing, and my helping my Aunts, and his learning Greek, and Latin, and Italian of my Father, and helping him about the farm, our holiday hours had always seemed too brief for half the things we had to do in them. Every morning found an eager welcome from us, and every evening a reluctant farewell; and it was not until we spent those days at the Hall that the question, "What are we to do next?" ever occurred to us, not in hesitation which to select of the countless things we had to do in our precious spare hours, but as an appeal for some new excitement.

Moreover, while in outward accomplishments and graces we felt our inferiority, in many things we could not but feel that our education had been far more extensive than that of the Davenants.

Allusions to Greek and Roman history, and to new discoveries in art and science, and even to stories of modern European wars, which were as natural to us as household words, were plainly an unknown tongue to them. Even on the lute and the harpsichord, Lettice's instructions had fallen short of those my father had procured for me, although her sweet clear voice, and her graceful way of doing everything, made all she did seem done better than any one else could have done it.

The brothers, for the most part, laughed off their deficiencies, and often made them seem for the moment a kind of gentlemanlike distinction, bantering Roger as if learning were but a little better kind of servile labour, beneath the attention of any but those who had to earn their bread. All that kind of thing, they said, was going out of the mode. The late King James had tired the court out with overmuch pedantry and learning; the present king indeed was a grave and accomplished gentleman, but merrier days were coming in with the French queen's court and the young princes, when the "gay science" would be the only one much worth cultivating by men of condition. Meantime the elder brothers paid me many choice and graceful compliments on my hands and my hair, my eyes and my eye-lashes, my learning and my accomplishments, jesting now and then in a courtly way on my sober attire; and, child that I was, sent me looking with much interest and wonder at myself in the long glass in Lady Lucy's drawing-chamber, to see if what they said was true. I remember, one afternoon, after a long survey of myself, I concluded that much of it was, and thanked God that evening for having made me pleasant to look at. A few years later, the danger would have been different.

But Lettice was of a different nature from all her brothers except one. Generously alive to whatever was to be loved or admired in others, and ready to depreciate herself, she wanted Roger and me to teach her all we knew. She made him hunt out the books which would instruct her in Sir Walter's neglected library. She sat patiently three sunny mornings trying to learn from Roger the Italian grammar, which she had pleaded hard he should teach her, she made him read the poetry to her, and said it was sweeter than her mother's lute. But on the fourth morning her patience was exhausted;—she declared it was a wicked prodigality to waste the sunny hours in-doors, and danced us away to the woods; and all Roger's remonstrances could not bring her back to such unwonted work. Indeed the more he remonstrated, the more idle and indifferent she chose to be, insisting instead on showing him some new French dance or singing him some snatch of French song she had learned from the Queen's ladies, until he gave up in despair; when she declared that but for his want of patience she had been fairly on the way to become a feminine Solomon.

It was Monday when our visit commenced, so that we were no longer strangers in the house by the following Sunday. But we were not prepared for the contrast between the Sundays at Davenant

Hall with those at Netherby. At our own home, grave as the day was, there was always a quiet festival air about it. The hall was fresh swept, and strewn with clean sand. My Father and my Aunts, the maids and men, had on their holiday dresses. That morning at prayers we always had a psalm, and the mere thrill of my voice against my Father's rich deep tones was a pleasure to me. Then after breakfast Roger and I had a walk in the fields with him, and he made us hear, and see a hundred things in the ways of birds and beasts and insects that we should never have known without him. One day it was the little brown and white harvest-mouse, which, by cautiously approaching it, we saw climbing by the help of its tail and claws to its little round nest woven of grass suspended from a corn-stalk. Another day it was a squirrel, with its summer house hung to the branch of a tree with its nursery of little squirrels; and its warm winter house, lined with hay, in the fork of an old trunk; or a colony of ants roofing their dwellings in the wood with dry leaves and twigs. Or he would turn it into a parable and show us how every creature has its enemies, and must live on the defensive or not live at all. Or he would watch with us the butterfly struggling from the chrysalis, or the dragon-fly soaring from its first life in the reedy creeks of the Mere to the new life of freedom in the sunshine. Or he would point out to us how the field-spider had anticipated military science; how she threw up her bulwarks and strengthened every weak point by her fairy buttresses, and kept up the communication between the citadel and the remotest outwork. Or he would teach us to distinguish the various songs of the birds, the throstles, the chaffinches, the blackbirds, or the nightingales. God, he said, had filled the woods with throngs of sacred carollers, and melodious troubadours, and merry minstrels; some with one sweet monotonous cadence, one bell-like note, one happy little "peep" or chirp, and no more, and others overflowing with a passion of intricate and endlessly varied song; and it was a churlish return for such a concert not to give heed enough to learn one song from another. Or, together, we would watch the rooks in the great elm grove behind the house, how strict their laws of property were, the old birds claiming the same nest every year, and the young ones having to construct new ones. Or he would tell us of the different forms of government among the various creatures; how the bees had an hereditary monarchy, yet owned no aristocracy but that of labour, killing their drones before winter, that if any would not work neither should he eat; and how the rooks held parliaments. Everywhere he made us see, wonderfully blended and balanced, fixed order, with free spontaneous action; freaks of sportive merriment, free as the wildest play of childhood, with a fixedness of law more exact than the nicest calculations of the mathematicians; "service which is perfect freedom;" delicate beauty with homely utility; lavish abundance with provident care. And everywhere he made us feel that the spring of all this order, the source of all this fullness, the smile through all this humour and play of nature, the soul of all this law, was none other than God. So that often after these morning walks with him we fell into an awed silence, feeling the warm daylight solemn as a starry midnight, with the Great Presence; and entered the church-porch almost with the feeling that we were rather stepping out of the Temple than into it; that, sacred as was the place of worship and of the dead, it was not more sacred or awful than the world of life we left to enter it.

The other golden hour of our golden day (for Sunday was ever that to us), was when in the evening he read the Bible with Roger and me in his own room. I cannot remember much that he used to say about it. I only remember how he made us reverence and love it; its fragments of biography which make you know the people better than volumes of narrative; its characters that are never mere incarnations of principles, but men and women; its letters that are never mere sermons concentrated on an individual; its sermons that are never mere dissertations peculiarly applicable to no one time or place, but *speeches* intensely directed to the needs of one audience, and the circumstances of one place, and *therefore* containing guiding wisdom for all; its prayers that are never sermons from a pulpit, but brief cries of entreaty from the dust or flaming torrents of adoration piercing beyond the stars, or quiet asking of little children for daily bread; its confessions that are as great drops of blood wrung slowly from the agony of the heart; its hymns that dart upward singing and soaring in a wild passion of praise and joy.

I can recall little of what my father said to us in those evening hours, but I remember that they left on our minds the same kind of joyous sense of having found something inexhaustible which came from our morning walks. They made us feel that in coming to the Bible, as to nature, we come not to a cistern or a stream or a ponded store, though it might be abundant enough for a nation; but to a Fountain, which, though it might seem at times but a gentle bubbling up of waters just enough for the thirsty lips which pressed it, was, nevertheless, living, inexhaustible, eternal, because it welled up from the fullness of God.

The usual name for the Sabbath in our home was the Lord's Day, because of our Lord's Resurrection. On other days my Father read to us, and made us read and love other books—books of history and science as well as of religion, Shakespeare, Spenser, the early poems of Mr. John Milton, and, when we could understand them, the Italian poet Dante, or Davila, and other great Italians who spoke nobly of order and liberty.

But on this day of God he never read but from these two divine books, Nature and the Holy Scriptures.

In church we had not always any sermon at all. Preaching had not been much encouraged since the days of Queen Elizabeth. Occasionally one of the lecturers, or gospel preachers, whom Mr. Cromwell and other good men were so anxious to supply at their own cost, used, in our earlier days, to enter our pulpit and arouse us children with bursts of earnest warning or entreaty (our parish minister then being a meek and conformable person). But Archbishop Laud soon put a stop to this, and sent us a clergyman of his own type, who fretted Aunt Dorothy by changing the places and colours of things, moving the communion-table from the middle of the church, where it had stood since the Reformation, to the East End, wearing white where we were used to black, and coats of many colours where we were used to white, and in general moving about the church in what appeared to us Puritan children, uninstructed in symbolism, a restless and unaccountable manner; standing when we had been wont to sit, kneeling when we had been wont to stand, making little unexpected bows in one direction and little inexplicable turns in another, in a way which provided matter of lively speculation to Roger and me during the week, since we never knew what new movement might be executed on the following Sunday. But to Aunt Dorothy these innovations were profanities, which would have been utterly intolerable had she not consoled herself by regarding them as signs of the end of all things. For what to Mr. Nicholls, the parson, was the "beauty of holiness," and to our father "personal peculiarities of Mr. Nicholls," and to Aunt Gretel but one more of our "incomprehensible English customs," were to Aunt Dorothy the infernal insignia of the "Mother of abominations."

She therefore remained resolutely and rigidly sitting and standing as she had been wont, a target for fiery darts from Mr. Nicholls' eyes, and a sore perplexity to Aunt Gretel, who, never having mastered our Anglican rubric, had hitherto had no ceremonial rule, but to do what those around her did, and was thus thrown into inextricable difficulties between the silent reproaches of Aunt Dorothy's compressed lips if she did one thing, and the suspicious glances of the Parson's eyes if she did another.

On our return Aunt Dorothy frequently made us repeat the sixteenth and seventeenth chapters of the Revelation. We understood that she regarded both these chapters as in some way directed against Mr. Nicholls. In what way—we discussed it often—Roger and I at that time could never make out. The great wicked city, with ships, and merchants, and traders, and pipers, and harpers, seemed to us more like London town, with the Court of the King. than like the parish church at Netherby. But however that may be, I am always thankful for having learned it. Many and many a time, when in after life the world has tempted me with its splendours, or straitened me with its cares, and I have been assailed with the Psalmist's old temptation at seeing the wicked in great prosperity, the grand wail over the doomed city has pealed like a triumphal march through my soul, and the whole gaudy pomp and glory of the world has lain beneath me in the power of that solemn dirge, like the tinsel decorations of a theatre in the sunbeams, whilst above me has arisen, snow-white and majestic, the vision of the Bride in her fine linen "clean and white,"—of the City coming down from heaven "having the glory of God."

Aunt Gretel, on the other hand, would frequently quiet her ruffled spirits after her perplexities, by making Roger and me read to her the fourteenth chapter of the Romans, ending with, "We then that are strong ought to bear with the infirmities of the weak. Let every one of us please his neighbour for his good to edification. For even Christ pleased not Himself."—A rubric which secretly seemed to us to have two edges, one for Aunt Dorothy and one for Mr. Nicholls, but of which Aunt Gretel contrived to turn both on herself.

"You see, my dears," she would say, "that is a rule of which I am naturally very fond. Because, of course, I am one of the weak. And it certainly would be a relief to me if those who are strong would have a little more patience with me. But then it is a comfort to think that He who is stronger than all does bear with me. For He knows I do not wish to please myself, and would be thankful indeed if I could tell how to please my neighbours." Which seemed to us like the weak bearing the infirmities of the strong.

After this learning and repeating our chapters from the Bible, while my Father and my Aunts were going about the cottages and villages near us on various errands of mercy, Roger and I had a free hour or two, during which we commonly resorted in summer to our perch on the apple-tree, and in winter to the chamber over the porch where the dried herbs were kept, where we held our weekly convocation as to all matters that came under our cognizance, domestic, personal, ecclesiastical, or political. Placidia was not excluded, but being four years older, she preferred "her book" and the society of our Aunts. Then came the sacred hour with our Father in his own chamber. Afterwards in winter, we often gathered round the fire in the great hall, we in the chimney-nook, and the men and maidens in an outer circle, while my Father told stories of the sufferings of holy men and women for conscience' sake, or while Dr. Antony (when he was visiting us) narrated to us his interviews with those who were languishing for truth or for liberty in various prisons throughout the realm.

And so the night came, always, it seemed to us, sooner than on any other day. Although never until our visit at Davenant Hall did I understand the unspeakable blessing of that weekly closing of the doors on Time, and opening all the windows of the soul towards Eternity; the unspeakable lowering and narrowing of the whole being which follows on its neglect and loss. To us the Lord's Day was a day of Paradise; but I believe the barest Sabbath which was ever fenced round with prohibitions by the most rigid Puritanism, looking rather to the fence than the enclosure, rather to what is shut out than to what is cultivated within, is a boon and a blessing compared with the life without pauses, without any consecrated house for the soul built out of Time, without silences wherein to listen to the Voice that is heard best in silence.

It was a point of honor and a badge of loyalty with many of the Cavaliers to protest against the Puritan observance of the Sabbath. The Lady Lucy, indeed, welcomed the sacred day, as she did everything else that was sacred and heavenly. She sang to her lute a lovely song in praise of the day from the new "Divine Poems" of Mr. George Herbert, and told me how he had sung it to his lute on his death-bed only a few years before, in 1632.

"On Sunday heaven's gates stand ope,"

she sang; and I am sure they stood ever open to her.

But the rest of the family, whilst reverencing her devout and charitable life, seemed to have no more thought of following it than if she had been a nun in a convent. Indeed, in a sense, she did dwell apart, cloistered in a hallowed atmosphere of her own.

Her husband and her sons requested her prayers when they went on any expedition of danger, as their ancestors must have sought for the intercessions of priest or canonized saint. The heavier oaths, except under strong provocation, were dropped (by instinct rather than by intention) in her presence; and mild adjurations, as by heathen gods or goddesses, or by a lover's troth, or by a cavalier's honor, substituted for them. They would listen fondly as she sang "divine poems" to her lute, and declare she had the sweetest warbling voice and the prettiest hands in His Majesty's three kingdoms. But it never seemed to occur to them that her piety was any condemnation, or any rule to them. Indeed, she had so many minute laws and ceremonies that, easily as they suited her, it would have been difficult to fit them into any but a lady's life of leisure. She had special prayers and hymns for nine o'clock, mid day, three o'clock, six o'clock. And once awakening in the night I heard sounds like those of her lute stealing from the window of the little oratory next her chamber. She had what seemed to me countless distinctions of days and seasons, marked by the things she ate or did not eat, which she observed as strictly as Aunt Dorothy her prohibitions as to not wearing things. Only in one thing Lady Lucy was happier than Aunt Dorothy; for whilst Aunt Dorothy fondly wished for a book of Leviticus in the New Testament, and could not find it, Lady Lucy had her book of Leviticus,—not indeed exactly in the New Testament, but solemnly sanctioned by the authority of Archbishop Laud.

A complex framework to adapt to the endless varieties and inexorable necessities of any man's life, rich or poor, in court, or camp, or city; or indeed of any woman's, unless provided with waiting gentlewomen.

In fact, the Lady Lucy herself sometimes spoke with wistful looks and sighs of Mr. Farrar's Sacred College at Little Gidden (not far from us), between Huntingdon and Cambridge, where the voice of prayer never ceased day nor night, and the psalter was chanted through in a rotatory manner by successive worshippers once in every four-and-twenty hours.

Sir Walter and her sons never attempted to imitate her. She floated in their imagination, in a land of clouds, between earth and heaven. Her religion had a dainty sweetness and solemn grace about it most becoming, they considered, to a noble lady; but for men, except for a few clergymen, as inapplicable as Archbishop Laud's priestly vestments for the street or the battle-field.

In our Puritan homes there was altogether another stamp of religion. Whatever it might lack in grace and taste, it was a religion for men as much as for women, a religion for the camp as much as the oratory. Rough it might be often, and stern. It was never feeble. It had no two standards of holiness for clergy and laity, men and women. All men and women, we were taught, were called to love God with the whole heart; to serve him at all times. If we obeyed we were still (in our sinfulness) ever doing less than duty. If we disobeyed, we were in revolt against the King of heaven. There were no neutrals in that war, no reserves in that obedience.

And unhappily the Lady Lucy's family, in surrendering any hope of reaching her eminence of piety, surrendered more. For, it is not elevating, it is lowering, to have constantly before us an image of holiness which we admire but do not imitate.

In the morning the household met in the Family Chapel (the Parish Church being for the present avoided until danger of the infectious sickness was over). In the afternoon, Sir Walter and his sons loyally played at tennis and bowls with the young men of the household. And in the evening there was a dance in the hall, in which all joined.

The merriment was loud, and reached Lettice and me where we sat with the Lady Lucy and her lute.

Yet now and then one of the boys would come in and complain of the tedium of the day. It was such an interruption, they said, to the employments of the week, and just at the best season in the year for hunting, and with their father's hounds in perfect condition and training. Tennis they said, was all very well for boys, and Morris-dancing for girls, but there was no real sport in such things after all, except to fill up an idle hour or two. The next day there was to be a rare bear-baiting at Huntingdon, and the day after a cock-fight in the next village. And at the beginning of the following week Sir Walter had promised to give them a bull to be baited. And the Book of Sports, in their opinion, let the Puritans say what they like, was too rigid by half in prohibiting such true old English sports on Sundays.

The Lady Lucy said a few pitiful tender words on behalf of Sir Walter's bull, which they listened to without the slightest disrespect, or the slightest change of mind—kissing her hand and laughingly vowing she was too tender and sweet for this world at all, and that if she had had the making of it she would certainly have left bears and bulls altogether out of the creation.

It was without doubt a long and dreary Sunday

to Roger and me. It would naturally have been long and melancholy anywhere without our Father.

I missed the busy work of the week, which made it not only a sacred day but a holiday. I missed Aunt Dorothy's laws which made our liberty precious.

But to Roger the day had had other trials.

In the evening he and I had a few minutes alone together in the window of the drawing-chamber.

"Oh, Roger," said I, "I am afraid it cannot be right; but I am so glad Sunday is over."

"So am I—rather," he said.

"Has it seemed long to you? I thought I heard your voice in the tennis-court all the afternoon."

"You did not hear mine," he said.

"You did not think it right?" I asked, "I wondered how they could."

"I am not sure about its being right or wrong for other people," said Roger. "But I was sure it was wrong for me. My Father would not have liked it, and, therefore, I could not think of doing it; especially when he was away."

"Were they angry?" I asked.

"Not exactly," he said. "They only laughed."

"*Only* laughed!" said I. "I think that is worse to bear than anything."

"So do I," he said.

"But you did not hesitate?"

"Not after they laughed, certainly," said he. "That set my blood up, naturally; for it was not so much at me as at my Father and all of us. They said I was too much of a man for such a crew."

"They laughed at Father!" said I, in horror.

"Not by name," said he, "but at all he thinks right—at the Puritans, or Precisians, as they call us."

"What did you do, Roger?" I said.

"Walked away into the wood," he replied.

"Why did you not come to us?" I asked.

"Because they told me to go to you," he said, flushing.

"That was a pity; we were singing sweet hymns."

"I heard you," he said. "But I do not think it was a pity I did not come.

"What did you find in the wood, then?" said I.

"I do not know that I found anything," he said.

"What did you do then, Roger?"

"I went to the Lady Well, and lay down among the long grass by the stream which flows from it towards the Mere, and separates my Father's land from Sir Walter's, at the place where you can see Davenant Hall on one side and Netherby among its woods on the other. And I thought."

"What did you think of?" said I.

"I thought I had rather live as a hired servant at my Father's than as master here," said he.

"Was that all?" said I.

"I thought of our talk in the apple-tree about our being puppets, or free."

I was silent.

"And Olive," he continued, "I seemed like some one waking up, and it flashed on me that God has no puppets. The devil has puppets. But God has free, living creatures, freely serving him. And I thought how glorious it would be to be a free servant and a son of his. And then I thought of the words, 'Thou hast redeemed us to God by thy blood;' not from God, Olive, but to God, to be his free servants for ever."

"That was a great deal to think, Roger," said I. "I think you did find something in the wood."

"I found I *wanted* something, Olive," he said very gravely; "and I thought of something Mr. Cromwell once said when people were talking about sects and parties,—'To be a seeker is to be of the best sect next to being a finder.' He meant to be seeking happiness, or wealth, or peace, or anything in the world, Olive, but to be seeking God."

We were looking out across the woods to the Mere, which we could also see from Netherby. The water was crimson in the sunset, and beyond it the flats stretched on and on, dark and shadowy except where the rows of willows and alders in the distance, and some cattle on an enbankment, stood out distinct and black, like an ink etching, against the golden sky.

And something in Roger's words made the sky look higher and the world wider to me than ever before.

The next week, Lady Lucy's eldest son, Harry, came from London to the Hall with an acquaintance of his, Sir Launcelot Trevor.

I thought Harry Davenant the most polished gentleman I had ever seen. He was the first person who ever called me Mistress Olive, and treated me with a gentle deference as if I had been a woman. I admired his manners exceedingly. His voice, though deep and strong, had something of the soft cadence of Lady Lucy's. He always saw what every one wanted before they knew it themselves. He always seemed to listen to what you said as if he had something to learn from every one. His whole soul always appeared to be in what he was saying or what you were saying, and yet there seemed to be another kind of porter-soul outside, quite independent of this inner soul, always on the watch to render any little courtesy to all around. I supposed these courtly attentions had become an instinct to him, so that he could attend to them and to other things at the same time, as easily as we can talk while we are eating or walking.

He was his mother's greatest friend. Sir Walter never was this. He was always almost lover-like in his deference and attention to her, stormy and soldier-like as his usual manner was. But into her thoughts he did not seem to care to enter, any more than into her oratory. They had some portion of their worlds in common, but the largest portion, by far, apart. And the younger boys were like him, more or less. But whatever Lady Lucy might have missed in him was well made up to her in her eldest son.

He was a cavalier to her heart,—grave, religious, cultivated,—a soldier from duty, but finding his delight in poetry and music, and all beautiful things made by God or by man. It was a great interest to me to sit at Lady Lucy's feet and listen to their discourse about music and painting,—about the great Flemish painter Rubens, who had painted the ceiling of the king's banqueting-house at Whitehall, the grand building which Mr. Inigo Jones had just erected; and about the additions the king had lately made to his superb collection of pictures. He and Lady Lucy spoke of the purchase of the cartoons of Raffaelle and of other pictures by this great master, and by Titian, Correggio, and Giulio Romano, or by Cornelius Jansen and other Flemish painters, with as much triumph as if each picture had been a province won for the crown. He spoke also with the greatest enthusiasm of the painter Vandyke, who was painting the portraits of the Royal Family, and the great gentlemen and ladies of the Court. He had brought a portrait of himself by Vandyke as a present to his mother, (only, he said, as a bribe for her own by the same hand); and it seemed to me that Mr. Vandyke must be as fine a gentleman as Harry Davenant himself, or he never could have painted so perfectly and nobly the noble features, the grave almost sad look of the eyes, the long chestnut-coloured love-locks, the courtly air, and the dress so easy and yet so rich.

All this was very new discourse to me; paintings, especially religious paintings such as the Holy Families and Crucifixions by the foreign masters which Harry Davenant described, never having been much encouraged among us.

When he spoke of music and poetry I was more at home, and when he alluded with admiration to the Masque of Comus by Mr. John Milton, I felt myself flush as at the praise of a friend.

For the names revered at Davenant Hall and at Netherby were usually altogether different. For instance, of Archbishop Laud and Mr. Wentworth (afterwards Lord Strafford), whom Lady Lucy and her son seemed to regard as the two pillars of church and state, I had only heard as the persecutors of Mr. Prynne, and the subvertors of the liberties of the nation.

But indeed the nation itself seemed to be little in Harry Davenant's esteem, except as a Royal Estate with very troublesome tenants who had to be kept down; and liberty, which in our home was a kind of sacred word, fell from his lips as if it had been a mere pretext for every kind of disorder.

With all his refinement, however, it did seem strange to me that Harry Davenant should enter with apparent zest into the bull-baiting, bear-baiting, and cock-fighting which were the festivities of the next week. But he said these were fine old English amusements, and it was right to show the people that the polish of the court did not make the courtiers dainty or womanish, or prevent their entering into these manly sports.

Sir Launcelot Trevor was a man of a different stamp. He had bold handsome features, black hair, black eyes, and low forehead, a face with those sharp contrasts of colour some people think handsome. But there was something in him from which, even as a child, I shrank, although he paid the most finished compliments to the Lady Lucy, Lettice, and me, and to everything we did or said. His compliments always seemed to me like insults. When Harry Davenant spoke of Beauty in women, or pictures, or nature, he made you feel it something akin to God and truth, to reverence and give thanks for.

When Sir Launcelot spoke of Beauty, he made you feel it a thing akin to the dust, to be fingered and smelt and tasted, and then to fade and perish.

Harry Davenant's was a polish bringing out the grain, as in fine old oak. Sir Launcelot's was like a glittering crust of ice over a stagnant pond, with occasionally a flaw giving you a glimpse into the black depths beneath.

But I suppose it was the way in which he behaved to Roger that more than anything opened my eyes to what he was. So that, behind all his bland smiles on us, I always seemed to see the curl of the mocking smile with which he so often addressed Roger. From the first they seemed to recognize each other as antagonists.

Two days after his coming Sir Walter's bull was to be baited in a field near the village. Lettice and I were standing in the hall porch, debating whether we ought at once to report to Lady Lucy a dangerous adventure from which we had just escaped, or whether it would alarm her too much, when we heard voices approaching in eager and rather angry conversation. First Sir Walter's rather scornful,—

"Let the boy alone. If his father chose to bring him up as a monk or a mercer it is no concern of yours or mine."

Then Sir Launcelot's smooth tones.

"Far from it. Is there not indeed something quite amiable in such compassion as Mr. Roger displays for your bull? In a woman it would be irresistible. Should we not almost regret that the hardening years are too likely to destroy that delightful tenderness?"

Then Roger's voice, monotonous and low, as always when he was much moved.

"I see nothing more manly, Sir Launcelot, in tormenting a bull than a cockchafer, when neither of them can escape. My Father says it is not so much because it is savage, as because it is mean, that he will have nothing to do with cock-fighting or bear and bull baiting."

Then a chorus of indignant disclaimers of the comparison from the boys.

"If you are too tender to stand a bull-baiting, how would you like a battle?"

But the next moment little Lettice, sweet, generous Lettice (herself Roger's prime tormentor when he was left to her), confronting the whole company—the five brothers and Sir Launcelot—and seizing her father's hand in both hers, exclaimed,—

"For shame on you all, Robert and George, and Roland, and Dick, and Walter" (Harry was not there, and she scornfully omitted Sir Launcelot); "you are all baiting Roger. And that is worse than baiting a dozen bulls. Don't let them, Father. He has done a braver thing this very day for us than baiting a hundred bulls. This very morning he faced that very bull in the priory meadow; not an hour ago. We were crossing it, Olive and I, and the bull ran at us, and Roger saw him and leapt over the hedge and fronted him, holding up my scarlet kerchief, which I had dropped, and then moved slowly backward, never turning till we were safe over the paling beyond the bull's reach."

Sir Walter's eyes kindled as he turned and held out his hand to Roger.

"Why did you not tell me of this, my boy?" he said.

"I did not think it had anything to do with it," said Roger quietly. "I did not know any one thought I was a coward."

Sir Launcelot took off his plumed hat and bowed low to Lettice.

"Heaven send me such a fair defender, Mistress Lettice, when I am assailed."

She looked up in his face with her large deep eyes, and said indignantly,—

"I am not Roger's defender. He was mine."

He laughed, but not pleasantly.

"Few would take much heed of such a danger for such a reward," he said.

After this he professed to treat Roger with the profoundest deference.

"A hero and a saint, a Don Quixote and one of the godly, all in one," he said, "and such a paragon at sixteen! What might not England expect from such a son?"

He was, moreover, continually referring questions of conscience to Roger; asking him whether it was consistent with Christian compassion to play at tennis; he had heard of a tennis-ball once hitting a man in the eye, and who could say but that it might happen again? or whether he seriously thought it charitable to ride horses with sharp bits, since it was almost certain they did not like it! or whether certain equestrian feats were not positively profane, since they were brought to Europe by the Moors; or whether indeed there was not a text forbidding the riding of horses altogether.

He did not venture on these taunts when Harry Davenant was present. But he generally contrived to make them with such a quaint and good-humoured air that the boys joined in the laugh, and Roger, having neither so nimble nor so practised a wit, could only flush with indignation, and then with vexation at himself that he could not control the quick rush of blood which always betrayed that he felt the sting.

Sir Launcelot had many of the qualities which command the regard of boys—an indifference to expenditure sustained by the Fortunatus purse of an unbounded capacity for getting into debt, which passed for generosity ("if the worst comes to the worst," said he; I can but make interest with the king, for a monopoly"); a wit never too heavily weighted to wheel sharp round on an assailant; skill and quickness in all the accomplishments of a cavalier, from commanding a squadron of horse to tuning a lady's lute; a dashing courage which shrank from no bodily danger; (*brave* I could not call him, for to be brave is a quality of the spirit, and spirit it was very difficult to conceive Sir Launcelot had, except such as there is in a mettlesome horse); a kindly instinct which would make him take care of his horses or dogs, or fling a piece of money to a crying child; or in the wars share his rations with a hungry soldier (plundering the next Puritan cottage to repay himself). For cruel he was not, at least not for cruelty's sake; if his pleasures, whether at the bull-baiting or bear-baiting, or of other baser kinds proved cruelty to others, that was not his intention, it was only an attendant accident, not, ("of course,") to be avoided, since life was short and enjoyment must be had, follow what might.

But of all that went on in the tennis-court and the riding-ground I knew little, except such glimpses as I have given, until long afterwards, when Lettice, who heard it from her brothers told me; Roger scorning to breathe a word of complaint on the subject, either while at the Hall or after our return.

But oh! the joy when one morning my Father came up to the Hall with two led horses following him, the speechless joy with which, rushing down from Lady Lucy's drawing chamber, I met him at the great door and threw myself into his arms as he dismounted.

"Why, Olive," he said, "you are like a small whirlwind."

Yet I shed many tears when the moment came to go. Lady Lucy, if no more a serene goddess, and embodiment of perfect womanhood to me, was in some sense more by being less. I loved her as a dear, loving, mother-like woman. Her tender words that night by my bedside—"Olive, I am not all or half I would be. But I could not bear to be distrusted by you." And all her frank, gracious, considerate self-forgetful ways had made my heart cling with a true, reverent tenderness to her, far deeper rooted than my old idolatry. And Lettice, generous, eager, willful as the wind, truthful as the light, now imperious as an empress, now self-distrustful and confiding as a little child, her sweet changing beauty seemed to me only the necessary raiment of the ever-changing, varying, yet constant heart, that glowed in the brilliant flush of her cheek, and beamed or flashed through her eye.

Lettice and I were friends by right of our differences and our sympathies, by right of a common antagonism to Sir Launcelot Trevor, and our common conviction of our each having in Roger and in Harry Davenant the best brothers in the world. Lettice and Harry royalist, and Roger and I patriots to the core; they devoted to the King and the Queen Marie, and we to England and her liberties; they persuaded that Archbishop Laud was a new apostle, we that he was a new Diocletian.

I shall never forget the joy of waking early the next morning in my old chamber, and looking up and seeing the sheen of the morning in the Mere, and watching Aunt Gretel asleep in the bed close to mine, and hearing the first solitary crow of the king of the cocks, and then the clacking of his family as they woke up one by one; the bleating of the sheep in the orchard meadow, and the lowing of cows in the sheds—the lowing of White-face, and Beauty my own orphaned calf, and Meadow-sweet;

and then the cheery voice of Tib, the dairy-woman, recovered from the sickness, remostrating with them on their impatience; and the calls of Bob, Tib's husband, to his oxen, as he yoked them and drove his team a-field; and mingled with all, the deep soldierly bay of old Lion, the watch-mastiff, and the sharp business-like bark of the sheep-dogs driving the flocks to fresh pastures. It was such a delight to be among all the living creatures again. It felt like coming out of an enchanted castle, drowsy with perfumes and languid strains of music, into the fresh open air of God's own work-a-day world—a world of daylight, and truth, and judgment, and righteousness, and duty.

I was dressed before Aunt Gretel was fairly awake, and down among the animals, eager to learn from Tib the latest news of all my friends in field and poultry-yard.

But Roger was out before me. And before breakfast we had visited nearly all our familiar haunts—the heronry by the Mere, the creek where the water-fowl loved to build among the rushes, the swan's nest on the reedy island, the shaded fish-ponds in the orchard, the little brook below where he and I had made the weir, the bit of waste low-ground which the brook used to flood, which with Bob's help we had dyked and embanked into corn-ground for Roger's pigeons.

My very spinning task with Aunt Dorothy was a luxury. I could scarcely help singing with a loud voice as I span; my heart was singing and dancing every moment of the day. The lessons for my Father were a keen delight, like a race on the dykes in a fresh wind; the Latin grammar was like poetry to me. It was such a liberation to have come into a busy, every-day, working world again; —a world of law, and therefore of liberty, where every one had his task, and every task its time, and the play-hours were as busy as the working-hours to heads and hands vigorous with the rebound of real necessary labour.

All the world became thus again our play-ground, and all the creatures our play-mates, by the mere fact that when not at play we, too, were fellow-workers with them—working as hard in our way as ant or bee, or happy building bird, or cleansing winds, or even the glorious ministering sunbeams themselves, whose work was all joyous play, and whose play was all world-helpful work.

An then it was inspiring to hear once more the great old honoured names of our childhood—Sir John Eliot (honoured in his dishonoured grave), and Hampden, and Pym, and Sir Bevill Grenvil (loyal then to his country and his King, and afterwards, as he believed, to his King for his country's sake), and Mr. Cromwell, who whether in Parliament, in the Fens, or on the "Soke of Somersham," understood liberty to be, liberty to restrain the strong from oppressing the weak—liberty to speak the truth loud enough for all the world to hear.

I thought I began to understand what was meant by, "Thou hast set my feet in a large room." For it seemed like coming forth from the ante-room of a court presence-chamber, with low-toned voices, perfumed atmosphere, constrained, soft movements, into our own dear, free Old England, where we might run, and sing, and freely use every free faculty to the utmost, beneath the glorious open heavens, which are the Presence-chamber of the Great King.

CHAPTER IV.

HE very afternoon of Roger's and my return from Davenant Hall Dr. Antony came on one of his ever-welcome visits. He had, by dint of much trouble and perseverance, obtained access to Mr. Prynne, in his solitary cell at Caernarvon, and to Mr. Bastwick and Mr. Burton, in theirs, in Launceston and Lancaster Castles; and afterwards to the prisons to which they were removed, in Guernsey, Jersey, and the Scilly Islands, and also to old Mr. Alexander Leighton, in his prison, after his most cruel mutilations.

Often in the summer Dr. Antony left his patients for a season, to visit such throughout the land as were in bonds for conscience' sake, bearing them the tidings, so precious to the solitary captive, that in the rush of life outside they were not forgotten; taking them food or physic, and such poor bodily comforts as were permitted by the hard rules of their imprisonment, and bringing back messages to their friends and kinsfolk. This last year Dr. Antony himself (as we heard from others) had been somewhat impoverished by a fine of £250 sterling, to which he had been sentenced by the Star-Chamber on account of these visits of compassion; although there was no law against them.

This time he brought us grievous tidings from many quarters; and very grave was the discourse between him and my Father.

Everywhere disgrace and disaster to our country; the French Huguenots cursing our Court for encouraging them to insurrection, and then sending ships against them to Rochelle (though, thank Heaven! scarcely one of our brave sailors would bear arms against their Protestant brethren—officers and men deserting in a body when they discovered against whom they had been treacherously sold to fight); our own fisheries on the east coast sold to the Hollanders, and the capture of one of our Indiamen by Dutch ships; the Barbary corsairs landing on the coast near Plymouth, and kidnapping our countrymen and countrywomen from their village homes, to sell them as slaves to the Moors in Africa; the King of Spain, the very pillar of Popery and persecution, the sworn foe of our religion and our race from the days of the Armada, permitted to recruit for his armies in Ireland; the Government, with Wentworth (traitor to liberty) and Archbishop Laud at the head of it, weak as scorched tow to chastise our enemies abroad, yet armed with scorpions against every defender of our ancient rights at home. The decision but lately given by the judges against the brave and good Mr. Hampden as to ship money, placing our fortunes at the mercy of the Court, who chiefly valued them as means wherewith to destroy our liberties; Justice Berkeley declaring from the judgment-seat that Lex was not Rex, but that Rex was Lex; thirty-one monopolies sold, thus making nearly every article of consumption at once dear and bad. The sweeping, steady pressure of Lord Strafford's (Mr. Wentworth) "Thorough" wrought into a vexation for every housewife in the kingdom, by the king's petty monopolies. The heavy links of Wentworth's imperious despotism, filed and twisted by Archbishop Laud's petty tyrannies into needles wherewith to torture tender consciences, and wiry ligatures wherewith to tie and bind every limb. "Regulations as to the colours and cutting of vestments, worthy (Aunt Dorothy said) of a court tailor, enforced by cruelties minute and persevering enough for a malignant witch." Dark stories, too, of private wrong, wrought by Wentworth in Ireland, worthy of the basest days of the Roman emperors; tales of royal forests arbitrarily extended from six miles to sixty, to the ruin of hundreds of gentlemen and peasants; disgraceful news of faith broken with Dutch and French refugees welcome to the heart of England since the days of Elizabeth, made secure with rights confirmed to them by James and by King Charles himself, now forbidden by Archbishop Laud to worship God in the way for which their fathers had suffered banishment and loss of all things,—driven to seek another home in Holland, and in their second exile ruining the flourishing town of Ipswich, where they had lived, and carrying over the cloth-trade which was the support of our eastern counties to our rivals the Dutch.

"You have a copy of Fox's Book of Martyrs?" Dr. Antony asked of my Father, after he had been speaking of these lamentable things.

"What good Protestant English household is without one?" exclaimed Aunt Dorothy; "least of all such as this, whose forefathers are enrolled in its lists."

"Take good care of it, then," Dr. Antony replied, "for the Primate hath forbidden another copy to be printed, under the penalties the Star-Chamber will not fail to enforce."

"The times are dark," he continued, "dark and silent. I stood this spring by the grave of Sir John Eliot, in the Church of the Tower; as brave, and loyal, and devout a gentleman as this nation ever knew, killed by inches in prison for calmly pleading the ancient rights of England in his place in Parliament, and then his body refused to his family for honourable burial among his kindred in his parish church in Cornwall, and cast like a felon's into a dishonoured grave in the precincts of the prison where he died. And I thought how it might have thrown a deeper shadow over his deathbed if he could have foreseen how, during these six years, the tyranny would be tightened, and the voice of the nation never once be heard in her lawful Parliaments."

"The voice of the nation is audible enough to those who have ears to hear," said my Father.

"Yea, verily" said Dr. Antony, "if you had journeyed through the country as I have, you would say so. When will kings learn that moans and subdued groans between set teeth are more dangerous from human lips than any torrents of passionate speech?"

"And," added my Father, "that there is a silence even more significant and perilous than these!"

"But there are two points of hope," said Dr. Antony. "One is the Puritan colony in New England, where our brethren have exchanged the vain struggle with human blindness and tyranny for the triumphant struggle with nature in her primeval forests and untrodden wilds. Four thousand good English men and women, and seventy-seven clergymen, have taken refuge there during these last twenty years. Not poor men only, for they have taken many thousand pounds of English money, or money's worth, with them, forsaking country and comfortable homes for the dear liberty to obey God rather than man. And these plantations, after the severest struggles and privations, are beginning to grow.

"What they hope and mean to be is shown by this, that two years since, while food was still hard to win from the wilderness, and roads and bridges had yet to be made, the plantation of Massachussetts voted £400 for the founding of a college. Such an act might seem more like the foresight of the fathers of a nation than the care of a little exiled band struggling for existence with the Indians, the wilderness, and a hostile Court at home.

"The other point of hope is the Greyfriars' Church in Edinburgh, where, on the 1st of last March, after long prayers and preachings, the great congregation rose, gathered from all corners of the kingdom,—nobles, gentlemen, burgesses, ministers, lifted their hands solemnly to heaven, and swore to the Covenant." Then Dr. Antony took a manuscript paper from the breast of his coat, and read: "'We abjure,' they swore, 'the Roman Antichrist,—all his tyrannous law made upon indifferent things against our Christian liberty; his erroneous doctrine against the written Word, the perfection of the law, the office of Christ, and His blessed Evangel; his cruel judgments against infants departing this life without the sacraments; his blasphemous priesthood; his canonization of men; his dedicating of kirks, altars, days, vows to creatures; his purgatory, prayers for the dead, praying or speaking in a strange language; his desperate and uncertain repentance; his general and doubtsome faith; his holy water, baptizing of bells, conjuring of spirits, crossing, saving, anointing, conjuring, hallowing of God's good creatures.' 'We, noblemen, barons, gentlemen, burgesses, ministers, and commons, considering the danger of the true Reformed religion, of the king's honour, and of the public peace of the kingdom by the manifold innovations and evils generally contained and particularly mentioned in our late supplications, complaints, and protestations, do hereby profess, and before God, his angels, and the world, solemnly declare that with our whole hearts we agree and resolve all the days of our life constantly to adhere unto and defend the foresaid true religion, and forbearing the practice of all novations already introduced in the matter of the worship of God, or approbations of the corruptions of the public government of the Kirk, till they be tried or allowed in free Assemblies and in Parliaments, to labour by all means lawful to recover the purity and liberty of the Gospel.' 'Neither do we fear the aspersions of rebellion, combination, or what else our adversaries, from their craft and malice, could put upon us, seeing what we do is well warranted, and ariseth from an unfeigned desire to mantain the true worship of God, the majesty of our king, and the peace of the kingdom, for the common happiness of ourselves and posterity. And because we cannot look for a blessing of God on our proceedings except with our subscription we gave such a life and conversation as becometh Christians who have renewed their covenant with God, we therefore promise to endeavour to be good examples to others of all godliness, soberness, and righteousness, and of every duty we owe to God and man. And we call the living God, the Searcher of hearts, to witness, as we shall answer to Jesus in that great day, under pain of God's everlasting wrath and of infamy; most humbly beseeching the Lord to strengthen us with his Holy Spirit for this end.' And this," added Dr. Antony, "has been sworn to not in the Greyfriars' Church alone; but by crowds, signed with their blood on parchment spread on the stones of the churchyards in Edinburgh and Glasgow; yea, in church after church, in city, village, and on hill-side, from John o'Groats' House to the Borders, from Mull to Fife, with tears, and shouts, and fervent prayers."

"And this means?' said my Father.

"It means that the Scottish nation will rather die than submit to Archbishop Laud's ceremonies and canons; but that they mean neither to die nor to submit; that every covenanted congregation will be a recruiting ground, if necessary, for a covenated army; that the oath sworn in the Kirk they are prepared to fulfil on the battle-field."

"And a goodly army they might soon discipline," said my Father, "with the military officers they have trained under the great Gustavus."

"It means," added Dr. Antony, lowering his voice, "that they are ready to kindle a fire for religion and liberty in Scotland which will not stop at the Borders, and will find fuel enough in every county in England."

"The Court had better, for its own peace, have heeded Jenny Geddes' folding-stool," said my Father.

"For his own peace," rejoined Aunt Dorothy, "but scarcely for ours."

From that time (1638), through more than a quarter of a century, public and private life were so intertwined that no faithful history can divide them. In quieter times, while the great historical paintings are being wrought in parliament-houses and palaces, countless small family-pictures are being woven entirely independent of these in countless homes. But in times of revolution, national history and private story are interwoven into one great tapestry, from which the humblest figure cannot be detached without unravelling the whole web.

Such times are hard, but they are ennobling. Or at least they are enlarging. Faults, and ordinary virtues become crimes, or heroical virtues, by mere force of temperature and space. Principles are tested; pretences are dissolved by the fact of being pretences. Such times are ennobling, but they are also necessarily tragical. All noble lives—all lives worth living—are expanded from the small circles of everyday domestic circumstances into portions of the grand orbits of the worlds. Yet, doubtless, thereby in themselves such lives must often become fragments instead of wholes, must seem in themselves unfinished, must be in themselves inexplicable.

But, indeed, are not the histories of nations, and revolutions themselves, even the grandest, but fragments of those greater orbits of which we scarcely, even in centuries, can trace the movement? Is it any wonder then that national histories as well as personal should often seem tragical? As now, alas, to us! poor tempest-tossed fragments of the ship's company which we deemed should have brought home the argosies for ages to come, driven to these untrodden far-off shores; whilst to England, instead of the golden fleece of peace and liberty, our enterprise may seem but to have brought a tyranny more cruel and a court more corrupt. Yet may there be something in the future which, to those who look back, will explain all!

For England; and perhaps even for these wild shores which we fondly call New England!

Can it be possible that we *have* won the Golden Fleece, and have brought it *hither?*

There is something, moreover, in having lived in times of storm. The temperature is raised at such times; all life is keener, colour more vivid, and growth more rapid.

A nation in revolution is, in more ways than one, like a ship in a storm. The dividing barrriers of selfishness are dissolved for a time into a common passion of patriotic hope, purpose, and endeavour. We feel our common humanity in our common throbs of hope and fear, in our common efforts for deliverance. And we are (or ought to be) nobler, and more large of heart for ever afterwards. And I think the greater part are. Perhaps, in some measure, all; unless, indeed, it be the ship's cats, who, no doubt, privately pursue the ship's mice with undeviating purpose through the raging of winds and waves, and look on the strife of the elements as a providential arrangement to enable them to fulfil their mousing destinies with less interruption.

And what such times of revolution do for a nation, ought not Christianity, the great perpetual revolution, to do for us always?

The great hindrance seems to me to be, that it is so much easier to be partizans than patriots, whether in the Church or State.

If men would do for the country what they do for the party, what a country we should have!

If Christians would do for the Church what they do for their sect, what a world we should have!

For a quarter of a century, from the signing of the Covenant in the High Kirk of Edinburgh, the long struggle went on. Nor has it ceased yet, though the combatants have changed, and the battle-field.

The Scottish covenanted congregations grew quickly indeed into a covenanted army, and advanced to the border. The King, by Archbishop Laud's counsel, disbelieving in the Covenant, proclaimed that if within six weeks the Scotch did not renounce it, he would come and chastise them (in a fatherly way) with an army. The King and Archbishop Laud regarded the Covenant as a freak of rebellious misguided children. The Scotch regarded it as the portion of the eternal law of God which they then had to keep; and would keep, or die.

A difference not to be settled by royal proclamation.

The Scotch had the advantage of *being* their own army, ready to fight for their Divine law; while the king had to pay his army with the coin of the realm, and never could inspire them to the end with the conviction that they were fighting for anything but coin of the realm.

The coin of the realm, moreover, lay in the keeping of those dragons called Parliaments, which his majesty had termed "vipers" at their last meeting, and in a letter to Strafford, had compared to "cats," tameable when young, "cursed" if allowed to grow old, and which he had therefore banished underground for eleven years into shadow and silence.

When, therefore, the king and the Covenanted army met on the borders, it was found that the Scotch, commanded, as my Father said, by old Gustavus Adolphus's officers; every regiment as in that old Swedish army, also a congregation, meeting morning and evening round its banner of "Christ's crown and covenant," for prayer was a rock against which the English army might vainly break; but from which, as the event proved, it preferred to ebb silently away, the pay for which only it professed to fight, being, moreover, exhausted.

The king took refuge in a treaty, promising to leave Kirk affairs in the hands of the Kirk, and to call a free assembly. Poor gentleman, his promises were still believed to have some small amount of truth in them, and a pacification was effected.

Then came the moment of hope for those who had been watching those movements with the intensest interest in England.

Of the two evils, a remonstrating Parliament in London and a fighting Kirk in Scotland, the former now appeared to the king the least. In the keeping of the Parliament, dragon-monster as it seemed to him, lay the gold. And once more, after a silence of eleven years, on the 15th of April, 1640, the Parliament was summoned; a weapon welded by the wrongs and the patience of eleven years into a temper the king had done well to heed.

Pym and Hampden were the chief spokesmen, and Mr. Cromwell sat for Huntingdon.

At the last Parliament they, and brave men like them, had wept bitter tears at the king's arbitrary measures, and at his false dealing.

At this Parliament there were no tears shed. There were no disrespectful or hasty words spoken.

It was as if in spirit they met around the grave of the martyred Sir John Eliot, and would do or say nothing to dishonour the grave to which since last they met he had been brought for liberty.

But no portion of the hoarded treasure could the king force or cajole from their grasp. The court insisted on supplies. The Parliament insisted on grievances.

And on May the 5th, the king dissolved the Parliament.

My Father wept with emotion when he heard it. "They would have saved him!" he said. "They would have saved the country and the king!"

Said Aunt Dorothy grimly, "The king prefers armies to parliaments; and no doubt he will have his choice."

A second royal army was raised by enforcing ship-money, seizing the pepper of the Indian merchants, and compelling loans, filling the towns and cities with angry men who dared not resist, and the prisons with brave men who dared. And to rouse the country further, the queen appealed publicly for aid to the Roman Catholics, whilst Archbishop Laud demanded contributions of the clergy. Earl Strafford, recalled from Ireland, was appointed commander-in-chief. The court endeavoured also to enkindle the fury of the old Border war-memories; but the Borderers were brethren in the faith, and, refusing to hate each other, combined in hating the bishops.

The second army melted like the first, after some little heartless fighting in a cause they hated; having distinguished itself mainly by shouting its sympathy with the Puritan preachers in the various towns through which it passed; by insisting on testing whether its commanders were Papists before it would follow them to the field; and by draining the king's treasury, so that he could proceed no further without once more looking to the dreaded guardians of the gold.

"They meet in a different temper from the last," my Father said, as we walked home from the village, where we had eagerly hastened to meet the flying Post, who galloped from one patriot's house to another with printed sheets and letters containing the account of the king's opening speech on the 3d of November; "as different as the sweet May days of promise during which the Little Parliament debated, from the gray fogs which creep along the Fens before our eyes to-day. Summer, and hope, and restitution brightened before that April Parliament. Over this lower winter, storms, and retribution; slow clearing of the stubble-fields of centuries, stern ploughing of the soil for better harvests, not to be reaped, perchance, by the hands that sow."

For the six months between had been ill-filled by the court party.

I remember now how one day during those months my Father's hands trembled and his voice grew low as a whisper as he read to us a letter telling how a poor reckless young drummer lad, who, when on leave from the army in the north, had joined a wild mob of London apprentices in an attack on Lambeth Palace, had been racked and tortured in the Tower to make him confess his accomplices; and torture failing to make him base, poor boy, how he had been hanged and quartered the day after.

"They dared not torture Felton a few years since for the murder of Buckingham," my Father said, "and now they twist this boy's offence into treason, because, forsooth, a drum chanced to be sounded by the mob, that the poor misguided lad may suffer the traitor's doom, and the honour of his Holiness, their Pontifex Maximus, their Archangel, as they call him, be avenged."

(These were the things that silenced the pleadings of pity in good and merciful men when, in after years, the Archbishop was brought to the scaffold.

Now that the crime and its avenging all are past, and victim, slayer, avenger, all have met before the great Bar, it is hard to recall the passion of indignation these deeds awakened in the gentlest hearts when they were being done with little chance of ever being avenged. But is not the most inflexible judgment the offspring of outraged mercy?)

All through that summer the king, the archbishop, and Strafford went on accumulating wrongs on the nation, too surely to recoil on themselves.

There may have been many tyrannies more terrible. Never could there have been one more irritating, more ingenious in sowing discontents in every corner of the land.

The archbishop in convocation made a new canon,

requiring every clergyman and every graduate of the universities to take an oath that all things necessary to salvation were contained in the doctrine and discipline of the Church of England, as distinguished from Presbyterianism and Papistry.

I remember that canon especially, because it brought Roger home from Oxford, where he had been studying during the past two years, and was about to take his degree, and led to results, sad indeed for us, though not exactly among the miseries to be set down to the archbishop. Roger would not swear, he said, against the religion of half the kingdom, at least without understanding it better.

From Northamptonshire, Kent, Devonshire,—old conservative Kent and the loyal West,—came up indignant petitions against this canon. London was exasperated by the committal of four aldermen who refused to set before the king the names of those persons within their wards who were able to lend his majesty money; every borough in the kingdom was aroused by the *presence* of its members ignominiously dismissed from the dissolved Parliament; nine boroughs were still more deeply moved by the *absence* of their members, imprisoned the day after the dissolution in the Tower. Every day brought reports of some fresh victim fined in the Star-Chamber on account of the odious ship-money. Especial complaints came from the North, which Strafford was grinding with the steady pressure of his presence in the council at York.

And meantime the friendly Scots were practically

inculcating Presbyterianism and the advantages of armed resistance in the four counties beyond the Tees, where they had been left in possession until they received the price wherewith the king had paid them for rebellion.

There was much stir and movement in the land all through those months. Netherby lay close to the high road, and we had many visitors. Mr. Cromwell once, on his way to Cambridge, brief in speeech and to the point, hearty in look, and word, and gesture, and also at times in laughter. Mr. Hampden, dignified and courtly as any nobleman of the king's court. Mr. Pym, with firm, close-set lips and grave eyes. He came more than once on horseback, and put up for the night, on one of the many rides he took at that time around the country to stir up the patriots to act together. My father also was often absent at meetings of the country party at Broughton Hall, near Oxford, where Roger, being at the university, sometimes met him.

So the summer passed on, its perishable things fading, and its enduring things ripening into autumn. Crop after crop of royal promises budded and bloomed and bore no fruit, until the people grew sorrowfully to understand that royal words, like flowers cultivated into barrenness in royal gardens, were never purposed to bear fruit, but only to attract with empty show of blossom. The nobles petitioned for a Parliament; ten thousand citizens of London, in spite of threats, petitioned for parliament; and at last once more the king summoned it.

A month afterwards, early in December, my Father called the household around the great hall fire to hear a letter from Dr. Antony:

"*To my very loving friend,*
"*Roger Drayton, Esq.,*
"*November 28th.*
"*Present these.*

"HONOURED SIR,—Let us rejoice and praise God together. My occupation is gone. The prisons bid fair to be cleared of all save their rightful tenants. Parish after parish will welcome back faithful ministers, undone and imprisoned by Star-Chamber and High Commission. Heaven send the prison persecutions have made their voices strong and gentle, and not bitter and shrill; for I have found the devil not locked out by prison-bolts. And too surely also he will find his way into triumphal processions such as we have had in London to-day, on behalf of Mistress Olive's old friends, Mr. Prynne, Mr. Bastwick, and Mr. Burton. But let me set my narrative in order.

"A fortnight before the Parliament was opened two thousand rioters had torn down the benches in St. Paul's, where the cruel High Commission were sitting, shouting that they would have no bishop, no High Commission. Now these disorders cease. Once more the gag is off the lips of every borough and county in Old England; and the bitter helpless moans and wild inarticulate cries which have vainly filled the land these eleven years give place to calm and temperate speech. Petitions and remonstrances pour in from north, south, east and west; some brought by troops of horsemen. The calmest voices are heard more clearly.

"'He is a great stranger in Israel,' said Lord Falkland, 'who knoweth not that this kingdom hath long laboured under great oppression both in religion and liberty. Under pretence of uniformity they have brought in superstition and scandal; under the titles of reverence and decency they have defiled our Church by adorning our churches. They have made the conforming to ceremonies more important than the conforming to Chistianity.'

"Said Sir Edward Deering, in attacking the High Commission Court,—

"'A Pope at Rome will do me less hurt than a patriarch at Lambeth.'

"Said Sir Benjamin Rudyard,—

"'We have seen ministers, their wives, and families, undone against law, against conscience, about not dancing on Sundays. They have brought it so to pass, that under the name of Puritans all our religion is branded. Whosoever squares his actions by any rule divine or human, he is a Puritan; whosoever would be governed by the king's laws, he is a Puritan; he that will not do whatsoever other men will have him do, he is a Puritan.'

"The Commons had not sate four days when, on the 7th of November, by warrant of the house, they sent for Mr. Pryne, Mr. Bastwick, and Mr. Burton, from their prisons beyond the seas, to certify by whose authority they had been mutilated, branded, and imprisoned.

"And now after three weeks these three gentlemen, freed from their sea-washed dungeons in Jersey, Guernsey, and the Scilly Islands, have this day arrived in the city. All the way from the coast they have been eargerly welcomed, escorted by troops of friends with songs and garlands, from town to town.

"Five thonsand citizens of condition rode forth on horseback to meet them, among them many a citizen's wife, and all with bay and rosemary in their hats and caps, to do honour to those their enemies had vainly sought to shame. I trow brave Mrs. Bastwick, who stood tearless by her husband at the pillory, and who hath not been suffered to see him in his prison since, thought it no shame to unman him by shedding tears of joy to-day. Old gray-haired Mr. Leighton, moreover, bent with imprisonment and torture, and young John Lilburn, for whom Mr. Cromwell so fervently pleaded, were there to share the triumph, all marked with honourable scars from the Star-Chamber. This outside the city. And within, at Westminister, another victory —not a triumph but a victory—not festive, but solemn and tragical, as victories on battle-fields are wont to be.

"This day at the bar of the House of Peers, about three of the clock in the afternoon, Mr. Pym, in the name of all the Commons of England, impeached Thomas, Earl of Strafford, of high treason. And this night Lord Strafford lodges in the Tower.

"He is too stately a cedar that there should not be something great in his fall.

"Scorning the Commons' message, with a proud-glooming countenance the earl made towards his place at the head of the board. But at once many bade him void the house. Sullenly he had to move to the door till he was called. There he, at whose door so many vainly waited, had to wait till he was summoned. Loftily he stood to hear the sentence of the House. He was commanded to kneel, and on his knees he was committed prisoner to the Keeper of the Black Rod. He would have spoken, but he who had silenced England for eleven years was sternly silenced now, and had to go without a word. In the outer room they demanded his sword. The earl cried to his serving-man with a loud voice to take my Lord-Lieutenant's sword. A crowd thronged the doors of the House as he stepped out to his coach. No fellow capped to him before whom yesterday not a noble in England would have stood uncovered with impunity. One cried to another, 'What is the matter?' 'A small matter, I warrant you,' quoth the earl. Coming to where he had left his coach he found it not, and had to walk back again through the gazing, gaping crowd. He was not suffered to enter his own coach, but was carried away a prisoner in that of the Keeper of the Black Rod.

"And this night he lodges—scarce, I trow, rests or sleeps—in the Tower. Will the memory of his old companion in the days before he turned traitor to England and liberty, our noble murdered patriot Eliot, haunt his memory there? From his *ghost* the earl is safe enough. Such ghosts are in other keeping and other company. And for the earl's *memory*, darker recollections than that of Eliot with all his wrongs may well haunt it, if report speaks truth; recollections which the Old Tower itself, with all its chambers of death, can scarce outgloom.

"But Lord Strafford is not a man to dream while there is work to be done, or to look back when life may hang on his wisdom in looking forward.

"The first stroke is struck, but the cedar is not felled yet. Nor can any surmise what it may bring down with it if it falls.

"Your faithful servant and loving friend.

"LEONARD ANTONY.

"Roger will like to hear that his friend Mr. Cromwell presented the petition for poor John Lilburn, (some time writer for Mr. Prynne) that was scourged from Westminster to the Fleet prison. And also that he hath warmly espoused the cause of certain poor countrymen whom he knows near St. Ives, robbed of their ancient pasture-rights on a common tyrannously enclosed by one of the queen's servants.

"Mr. Cromwell seemed to take these poor men's wrongs sorely to heart, and spoke with a flushed face and much vehement eloquence concerning them, in a voice which certain courtiers thought loud and untunable, clad in a coat and band they thought unhandsome and made by an 'ill country-tailor,' and in a hat without a hatband. But the Parliament hearkened to him with much regard, and gave great heed to what he counselled."

Roger's eye kindled.

"Mr. Cromwell will never forget the old friends for the new," said my Father, "nor pass by little duties in rushing to great ends."

Then our household broke into twos and threes debating the news.

Aunt Dorothy shook her head. "I do mourn over it," said she. "Mr. Cromwell might do great things. And here are the Church and State all on fire, and the Almighty sending His lightnings on the cedars of Lebanon and the oaks of Bashan, while Mr. Cromwell keeps harping on these petty worldly things; on the wrongs of an insignificant servant of Mr. Prynne's, which no doubt would get set right of themselves when once the great battle is fought; and on whether some poor clodpoles near St. Ives get a few acres more or less to feed their sheep on. And, meanwhile, the sheep of the Lord's pasture wandering on the mountains without pasture or shepherd! I do think it a pity, too, that Mr. Cromwell does not change his tailor; we ought to provide things honest in the sight of all men. Not but that I will say," she concluded, "Mrs. Cromwell and the maidens might take some of these matters on herself."

I remember that night asking Aunt Gretel if she thought it would be wrong to put Earl Strafford's name into my prayers. He was not exactly an enemy of *mine*, or there would be a *command* to do so; and he certainly was not a friend, nor, now, any longer "one in authority." But it went to my heart to think how in a moment all his glory seemed turned to dishonor, the crowd gaping on him, and no man capping to him.

"What wouldst thou pray for, Olive?" said Aunt Gretel. "Certainly not that he may have power again, and set up the Star-Chamber, and send the three gentlemen to the pillory once more."

"Would he do that if he got out of the Tower?" said I.

"The wise and good men think so, or they would not have him sent there," said she.

"But might he not be better always afterwards?" I asked.

"The people cannot trust that he would," she said. "Even if he promised ever so much and intended it, they could not at once trust him."

"Is it too late then for him to be forgiven?" I said.

"Too late, it seems, for men to forgive him," said she, very gravely.

"But never too late for God?" I said.

"No, never too late for God," said she, slowly. "Because God knows when we really intend to give up sinning, even when we can do nothing to show it to men. So it is never too late for Him to take His prodigals home to his bosom."

"Then I can ask for that," said I. And I did.

But that night there sank down on my heart for the first time (the first time of so many in the solemn years that followed) the terrible words, "*Too late*;" the terrible sense that an hour may come when, if repentance towards God is still possible, reparation to man and mercy from man is possible no longer.

This fervour of patriotic life which animated us all at Netherby made us rather hard, I am afraid, on Cousin Placidia.

Throughout the year, after our sojourn at Davenant Hall, she had tried Roger and me (and I believe also secretly Aunt Dorothy) very seriously by becoming in her way exceedingly religious. One winter morning when Roger and I were busy with my father about our Italian lessons at one end of the hall, the following discussion took place between Placidia and Aunt Dorothy over their spinning near the hearth. Placidia had seen, she informed Aunt Dorothy, the vanity of all things under the sun, the folly of pride, and the wickedness of all worldly pomp, and she wished decidedly to take her place "on the Lord's side," to work out betimes her own salvation, and to secure for herself an abundant entrance into the kingdom. Aunt Dorothy spoke of the heart being deceitful, and hoped Placidia would make sure of her foundation. Placidia rejoined with some slight resentment as to any doubts of her orthodoxy, that she humbly trusted she knew as well as any one, that *every one's* heart was indeed deceitful above all things and desperately wicked, that is, every ungodly person's; indeed one only needed to look around in any direction to see it. Aunt Dorothy replied that, for her part, she found *her own* heart still very ingenious in deceiving her, and in need of a great deal of daily watching.

Placidia admitted the necessity. Indeed, she said, that on a review of her life she felt that, although she had been mercifully preserved from many infirmities which beset other people, (her temper being naturally even, and her tastes sober,) still no doubt she shared in the universal depravity. But she had, like Jacob at Bethel, she said, made a solemn covenant with God, promising to give Him henceforth His due portion of her affections and substance; she had signed and sealed it on her knees, and she believed she was accepted, that she was on the Lord's side, and that, as with Jacob, He would henceforth be on hers.

Aunt Dorothy's spinning-wheel flew with ominous rapidity, but some moments passed before she replied. Then she said,—

"My dear, I trust that you know the difference between a *covenant* and a *bargain.* The patriarch Jacob, on the whole, no doubt meant well, but I never much liked his 'ifs' and 'thens' with the Almighty. The best kind of covenants, I think, are those which begin on the other side. As when the Lord said to Abraham, 'Fear not, Abraham, I am thy shield and thy exceeding great reward.' Or, 'I am the Almighty God, walk before me and be thou perfect.' Then follow the promises, lavish as His riches, which fill heaven and earth; free as the air He gives us to breathe. When God gives there is no limit, no reserve, no condition. But, on the other hand, neither is there reserve, or condition, or limit when He demands. It is not so much for so much, but *all* surrendered in absolute trust. It is,

'Be thou perfect;' it is, 'Leave thy country, and thy kindred, and thy father's house;' it is, 'Give me thy son, thine only son Isaac, whom thou lovest.' Is this what you mean by a covenant with God? Think well, for He 'is not mocked.' His hand is larger than ours, as the sea is larger than a drinking-cup; but He will not accept our hands half full."

Said Placidia,—

"Aunt Dorothy, I have no intention whatever of being half for the world and half for God. I have no opinion at all of the religion which can dance round May-poles on the week-day, and attend the worship of God on Sundays; or fast and pray on Fridays, wear mourning in Lent, and be decked out in curls, and laces, and jewels, on feast-days. I have made up my mind never to wear a feather, or a trinket, or a bit of lace to my band, or a laced stomacher, nor to use crisping-tongs, nor to indulge in any kind of 'dissoluteness in hair,' nor ever to sport any gayer colour in mantle or wimple than gray, or at the most 'liver colour.' I have not the least intention, Aunt Dorothy, of trying to serve two masters. I know in that way we gain nothing. But I do believe that those that honour Him He will honour, and that godliness hath promise of the life that now is as well as of that which is to come."

"The Lord's honours are not often like King Ahasuerus's," said Aunt Dorothy, gravely; "the crowns of those He delighted to honour have sometimes been of fire, and their royal apparel of sackcloth. There is such a thing," she continued, her wheel whirling like a whirlwind, "as serving *only one* master, yet that not the right one, though taking His name. And we are near the brink of that precipice whenever we seek any reward from the Master beyond His 'Well done.' '*I* am thy shield,'" she concluded, "'*I*, the *Lord Himself*;' not what He promises or what He gives, though it were to be the half of His kingdom."

By this time my Father's attention had been aroused to the discussion, and rising from the table and approaching the spinners, he said,—

"What you say, sister Dorothy, reminds me of some words I heard lately in a letter of Mr. Cromwell's. 'Truly no creature hath more cause,' he wrote, 'to put himself forth in the cause of his God than I. I have had plentiful wages beforehand, and I am sure I shall never earn the least mite.'"

"Yea, verily," said Aunt Dorothy, "Mr. Cromwell may waste too much thought on draining and dyking; but he is a godly gentleman, and he understands the Covenant."

Cousin Placidia, however, pursued her course, and continued a living rebuke to Roger and me if we indulged in too noisy merriment, and to any of the maids who were tempted into a gayer kirtle or ribbon than ordinary. On Sunday she was never known to smile, nor on any other day to laugh, except in a mild moderate manner, as a polite concession to any one who expected it in response to a facetious remark.

Her conversation meantime became remarkably

scriptural. She did not allow herself an indulgence which she did not justify by a text; if her dresses wore longer than usual, so as to spare her purse, she looked on it as a proof that she had been marvellously helped with wisdom in the choice. If she escaped the various accidents which not unfrequently brought me into disgrace, and my clothes to premature ruin, she regarded it as an interference of Providence, like to that which watched over the Israelites in the wilderness.

Indeed, it seemed to Roger and me that Placidia's primary meaning of being "on the Lord's side" was, that in a general way the Almighty should do what she liked; and that in particular the weather should be arranged with considerate reference as to whether she had on her new taffetas or her old woolsey. Great therefore was our relief, although great also our astonishment, when Aunt Dorothy announced to us one day that Cousin Placidia was about to be married to Mr. Nicholls, the vicar of Netherby.

"Are you not surprised?" I ventured to ask of my Father. "Cousin Placidia is such a Precisian, as they call it, and Mr. Nicholls thinks so much of Archbishop Laud."

"Not much surprised, Olive," he said. "I think Placidia's religion and Mr. Nicholls' are a little alike. Both have a great deal to do with the colour and shape of clothes, and with the places and times at which things are done, and the way in which they are said. And both are prudent persons, desirous of taking a respectable place in the world in a religious way. I should think they would agree very well."

But Aunt Dorothy was at once indignant and consoled.

"I never quite trusted Placidia's professions," said she; "but this, I confess, goes beyond my fears. A person who never passes what he calls the altar without making obeisances such as the old heathens made to the sun and the moon, and who, not six months ago, defiled the house of God with Popish incense!"

But Cousin Placidia had explanations which were quite satisfactory to herself.

"She had had so many providential intimations," she said (one of the habits of Placidia that always most exasperated Roger was her way of always doing what she wished, because, she said, some one else wished it; and since she had become religious, she usually threw the responsibility on the Highest Quarter)—"intimations so plain, that she could not disregard them without disobedience. Mr. Nicholls' coming to Netherby at all was the consequence of a series of most remarkable circumstances, entirely beyond his own control. The way in which the prejudice against each other, with which they began, had by degrees changed into esteem, and then into something more, was also very remarkable. And what was most remarkable of all was, that on the very morning of the day when he proposed to her, she had—quite by chance, as it might seem, but that there was no such thing as chance—opened the Bible on the passage, 'Get thee out from thy country, and from thy kindred, and from thy father's house, into a land that I will shew thee: and I will bless thee.' "

"But, my dear," remarked Aunt Gretel, to whom, Aunt Dorothy being unapproachable, Placidia had made this explanation—"my dear, you are *not* going to leave your country, are you? and you *do* know the land to which you are going."

"Of course," said Placidia, "there are always differences. But the application was certainly very remarkable. Mr. Nicholls quite agreed with me, when I told him of it."

"No doubt, my dear, no doubt," said Aunt Gretel, retreating. "But there does seem a little difference in your opinions."

"Uncle Drayton says we should look on the things in which we agree, more than on those in which we differ," said Placidia. "Besides, if Aunt Dorothy would only see it, I really trust I have been already useful to Mr. Nicholls. He said, only yesterday, he thought there was a good deal to be said in favour of some late ordinances of the Parliament against too close approach to Papistical ceremonies. Mr. Nicholls had never any propension towards the Pope; and he thinks now that, it may be, his canonical obedience to Archbishop Laud led him to some unwise compliances. But the powers that be, he says, must always have their due honour. The great point is, to ascertain which powers be, and which only seem to be. And now that the Parliament has impeached Archbishop Laud, and sent him to the Tower, this is really an exceedingly difficult question for a conscientious clergyman, who is also a good subject, to determine."

Aunt Gretel did not pursue the subject, she being always in fear of losing her way, and straying into wildernesses, when English politics or rubrics came into question.

And in due time Placidia became Mistress Nicholls, and removed to the parsonage, with a generous dowry from my Father, and everything that by the most liberal interpretation could in any way be construed into belonging to her, down to a pair of perfumed Cordova gloves which had been given her by some gay kinswoman, and, having been thrown aside in a closet as useless vanities, cost Aunt Dorothy a long and indignant search. Everything might be of use, said Placidia, in their humble housekeeping. And she had always remembered a saying she had once heard Aunt Gretel quote from Dr. Luther,—"that what the husband makes by earning, the wife multiplies by sparing."

"An invaluable maxim," she remarked, "for people in narrow circumstances, who had married from pure godly affection, without passion or ambition, despising all worldly considerations, like herself and Mr. Nicholls."

It was a strange Christmas to many in England, that first in the stormy life of the Long Parliament. Earl Strafford had been in the Tower since the 28th of November. A week before Christmas day Archbishop Laud had been impeached and committed to custody. There was no thought of the Parliament dispersing. Mr. Pym and others of the patriot members were occupied with preparing for Lord Strafford's trial, which did not begin until the 22nd of the following March.

On the other hand, faithful voices, long silent in prisons, were heard again in many pulpits throughout the land.

Judge Berkeley, who had given the unjust decision in favour of ship-money, was seized on the bench in his ermine, and taken to prison like a common felon.

The great thunder-cloud of Star-chamber and High Commission Court had dispersed. The Puritans and Patriots breathed once more, and the great voice of the nation, speaking at Westminster the words which were deeds, while it quieted the cries and groans of the oppressed country, set men's tongues free for earnest and determined speech by every hall hearth, and every blacksmith's forge, and ale-house, and village-green, and place of public or social talk throughout the country.

The blacksmith's forge in Netherby village was indeed a place well known to Roger and me. Job Forster, the smith, a brave, simple-hearted giant from Cornwall (given to despising our inland peasants, who had never seen the sea, and suspected of being the mainstay of a little band of sectaries in the neighborhood), having always been Roger's chief friend; while Rachel, his gentle, sickly, saintly little wife (whom he cherished with a kind of timorous tenderness, like something almost too small and delicate for him to meddle with), had always given me the child's place in her motherly heart, which no child had been given to their house to fill. Whenever we were missed in childhood, it was commonly to Job Forster's forge we were sought and found. And by this means we learned a great deal of politics from Job's point of view, as well as many marvellous stories of God's providençe by sea and land, which seemed to us to show that God was as near to those who trust Him now, as to the Israelites of old, which, also, Job and Rachel most surely believed.

But, meantime, while the clouds over England seemed scattering, a heavy cloud gathered over us at Netherby.

The Davenant family had come to the Hall for the Christmas festivities. We met often during the time they were there, more than ever before. The ties of friendship and of neighbourhood seemed to prevail over the party strife which had so long kept us apart.

Hope there was also that those party conflicts at last might cease with the disgrace of the hated Lord-Lieutenant.

His sudden abandonment of the patriot side, his rapid rise, and his lofty, imperious temper, had not failed to make enemies even among those of his own party. Sir Walter Davenant said he had no liking for turn-coats. They always over-acted their new part, and commonly did more to injure the party they joined than the party they betrayed. The haughty earl once out of the way, the king would listen to truer men and better servants.

The Lady Lucy held in detestation the earl's private character. The king, she said, was a high-minded gentleman, an affectionate husband and father, his presence and life had done much to reform the court; the earl was a man of commanding ability, but his hands were not pure enough to defend so lofty a cause. Better men, she thought, if in themselves weaker, would yet form stronger stays for the throne of the anointed of God. If Lord Strafford were displaced, she thought, the best men of all parties would unite; would understand each other, would understand their king, and all might yet go well. My Father, though less sanguine, was not without hope, although on rather different grounds. While Lady Lucy believed that Lord Strafford's violence and evil life were a weakness to the cause she deemed in itself sacred, my Father thought that Lord Strafford's power of character and mind were a fatal strength to the cause he deemed in itself evil. The earl once gone, he believed the king would never find such another prop for his arbitrary measures, the lesser tyrant would fall like an arch with the key-stone out, and the king would yield, perforce, to the just demands of the nation.

However, for the time, Lord Strafford's imprisonment formed a bond of sympathy between the two families, to Roger's and my great content. Much friendly rivalry there was in the Christmas adornment of the two transepts with wreaths of ivy and holly, ending in a free confession of defeat on our part, as our somewhat clumsy bunches of evergreen stood out in contrast with the graceful wreaths and festoons with which Lettice had made the memory of the Davenants green.

For a moment she enjoyed her triumph, and then begging permission to make a little change in our arrangements, with that quick perception of hers, and those fairy fingers which never could touch anything without weaving something of their own grace into it, in an hour or two she had made the massive columns and heavy arches of our ancestral chapel light and graceful as the most decorated monument of the Davenants, with traceries of glossy leaves and berries.

Lettice's birthday was on Twelfth Night. She was fifteen, nearly two years younger than I was, and three than Roger.

There was great merry-making at the Hall that day. In the morning distributings of garments to all the maidens in the parish of Lettice's age, by her own hands. She had some kindly or merry word for every one, and throughout the day was the soul of all the festivities. There was such a fullness of life and enjoyment in her; such a power of going out of herself altogether into the pleasures or wants of others. She seemed to me the centre of all, just as the sun is, by sending her sunbeams everywhere. While every one else was full of the thought of her, she was full only of shining into every neglected corner and shy blossom, making every one feel glad and cared for, down to Gammer Grindle's idiot boy.

It was a wonderful joy for me to be Lettice's

friend. I had almost as much delight in her as Sir Walter, who watched her with such pride, or Lady Lucy, whose eyes so oft moistened as they rested on her. She would have it that Roger and I must be at her right hand in everything.

In the afternoon Harry Davenant came with Sir Launcelot Trevor. Harry looked rather grave, I thought, but he was naturally that; and Lettice's gaiety soon infected him so that he became foremost in the games, which lasted until the sun went down, and the servants and villagers dispersed to kindle up the twelve bonfires. But Sir Launcelot looked sorely out of temper. His heavy brows quite lowered over his keen, dark eyes, so that they flashed out beneath like the stormy light under a thunder cloud. He scarcely bent to my Father or to any of us; and although he was lavish as ever of compliments to Lady Lucy and Lettice, his brow scarcely relaxed to correspond with the lip-smiles with which he accompanied them.

When the sun was fairly set, the twelve fires were kindled, this time on the field in front of the Hall, in honour of Lettice, instead of as usual on the village green.

We waited to see them burn up, and then we left. Roger stayed behind us. There was to be songs and dances round the fires, and then feasting in the Hall late into the night. But Roger only intended to remain a little while to see the merriment begin.

I remember looking back for a last glimpse of the fires as they leapt and sank, one moment lighting up every battlement, of the turrets, and all the carving of the windows with lurid light, and flashing back from the glass like carbuncles; the next substituting for the reality their own fantastic light and goblin shadows, so that not a corner or gable of the old building looked like itself. And I remember afterwards that close by one of the fires were standing Roger and Lettice, and Sir Launcelot, near each other; Roger piling wood on the fire at Lettice's direction, and Sir Launcelot standing a little apart with folded arms watching them. His face looked red and angry. I thought it was perhaps because of the angry glare of the flames. Yet something made me long to turn back and bring Roger away with us. It was impossible. But involuntarily I looked back once more: the flames leapt up at the moment, and then I saw Sir Launcelot and Roger as clearly as in daylight, apparently in eager debate.

I lingered to watch them, but just then the fitful flames fell, I could see no more, and I had to hasten on to follow my Father and Aunt Gretel home.

Before we reached home the clouds, which had been threatening all day, began to fall in showers of hail. We had not been in an hour when, as we were sitting over the hall fire, talking cheerily over the doings of the day, Roger suddenly entered, his face ashen-white, his eyes like burning coals, and, in a low voice, called my Father out to speak to him outside. For a few minutes, which seemed to me hours, we sat in suspense, Aunt Gretel's knitting falling on her lap, in entire disregard of consequence to the stitches—Aunt Dorothy's spinning-wheel whirling as if driven by the Furies. Then my Father returned alone, as pale as Roger.

He seated himself again, with his arms on his knees and his hands over his face—an attitude I had never seen him in before. It made him look like an old man; and I remember noticing for the first that his hair was growing gray.

No one asked any questions.

At length, in a calm, low voice, my Father said,—

"Roger and Sir Launcelot Trevor have quarrelled. Roger struck Sir Launcelot, and he fell against one of the great logs of the bonfires. He is wounded severely, and Roger is going to ride to Cambridge for a physician."

"In such a night!" said Aunt Gretel; "not a star; and the hail has been driving against the panes this half hour!"

"It is the best thing Roger can do," said my Father, quietly.

The next minute we heard the ring of a horse's hoofs on the pavement of the court, and then the sound of a long gallop dying slowly away on the road amidst the howling of the wind and the clattering of the hail.

But no one spoke until the household were gathered for family prayer.

There was no variation in the chapter read or in the usual words of prayer; only a tremulous depth in my Father's voice as he asked for blessings on the son and daughter of the house.

And afterwards, as I wished him good-night, he leant his hand on my head, and said—

"Watch and pray, Olive—watch and pray, my child, lest ye enter into temptation."

Then I knelt down, and hid my face on his knee, and said—

"O Father, Roger must have been sorely provoked—I am sure he was. I am sure it was not Roger's fault—I am sure; so sure! Sir Launcelot is so wicked, and I will never forgive him."

"Roger said it *was* his fault, my poor little Olive," replied my Father, very tenderly, "and that he will never forgive *himself*. And whatever Sir Launcelot said or did, you *must* forgive him, and pray that God may forgive him; for he is very seriously hurt, and may die."

"Roger would be sure to say that," I said. "He is always ready to blame himself and excuse every one else. But, O Father, God will not let Sir Launcelot die! What can we do?"

"Pray! Olive," he said in a trembling voice—"pray!" and he went to his own room.

But all night long, whenever I woke from fitful snatches of sleep, and went to the window to look if the storm had passed, and if Roger were coming, I saw the light burning in my Father's window.

The last time Aunt Gretel crept up softly behind me, and throwing her large wimple over me, drew me gently away.

"I have kept such a poor watch for Roger!" I said; "and see! my Father's lamp is burning still. He has been watching all night."

"There is Another watching, Olive," she said, softly, night and day. The Intercessor slumbers not, nor sleeps. It is never dark now in the Holiest Place, for he is ever there; and never silent, for He is ever interceding."

Chapter V.

HEN I awoke again, the cheerful stir of life had begun within and without the house—the ducks splashing in the pond in the front court; the unsuccessful swine and poultry grunting and cackling out their bill of grievances against their stronger-snouted or quicker-witted rivals; Tib's cheery voice instructing her cows and calves; and at intervals the pleasant regular beat of the flail in the barn, where they were thrashing the corn,—striking steady time to all the busy irregular sounds of animal life, and bringing them into a kind of unity.

All these homely, quiet sounds seemed stranger to me than the howling of the winds, and fitful clattering of the hail, through the night. They made me feel impatient with the animals, and with Tib, and with the inflexible every-day course of things. Was not Roger—our own Roger—in agony worse than mortal sickness, in suspense whether or not his hand had dealt a death-blow. Were not we in dreadful suspense whether his whole life might not be overshadowed from this moment as with a curse?

And yet the calves must be fed, and the swine snuff at their troughs and grudge if they be not satisfied, and the ducks splash and preen themselves as if nothing was the matter.

There are many seasons in life when the quiet flow of the stream of every-day life, as it prattles past our door among the familiar grasses and pebbles, falls on the heart with a sense of inflexibility more terrible than the storm which ploughs the waves of the Atlantic into mountains, and snaps the masts of great ships like withered corn stalks.

But that morning was the first on which I learned it.

The storm had quite passed. The dawn was still struggling with the cold winter moonlight. Far off the gray morning shone with a steely gleam on the creek of the Mere, were I used to sit quite still for hours while Roger angled, holding his fish-basket, amply rewarded at last by his dictum that there was one little woman in the world who knew when to hold her tongue, and by the reflecting glory of his triumph when he brought the basket of fish to Tib for my father's supper. Only last autumn, and now it seemed as if it had happened in another life.

Close to us in the high-road the moonlight still glimmered on the pools.

Aunt Gretel was dressed and gone. My last sleep had been sound. I reproached myself for my hard-heartedness in sleeping at all.

It was still dusk enough to show the faint red

light in my Father's chamber. Was he still watching?

My question was answered by the sound of the psalm coming up from the hall, where the household were gathered for family prayer. This reminded me that it was the Sabbath-day, the only day on which we used to sing a psalm at morning prayers. I knelt at the window while they sang. I heard my father's voice leading the psalm, and Aunt Dorothy's deep second, and Aunt Gretel's tremulous treble; but not Roger's. I felt so strange to be listening, instead of joining in the song. Such a thing had never happened to me before. Aunt Gretel must have thought it good for me to sleep on, and have crept down stairs like a ghost. But the feeling of being *outside* was terrible to me that morning. It brought back my old terror about being "on the wrong side of the tree." But not so much for myself. For Roger! for Roger! What if he should be feeling left outside like this!—outside the prayers, outside the hymns, outside the holy family gatherings, outside the light and the welcome! That morning I felt something of what must be meant by the *outer* darkness. The darkness outside! Even the "darkness" did not seem to me so terrible as the being *outside!* For it showed there was a within—a home; light within, music within, the Father's welcome within and we outside! Could it be that Roger was feeling this now?

All this rushed through my heart as I knelt to the music of the family psalm.

Then, dressing hastily, I went down.

"Roger has been here, Olive," said my Father, answering my looks. "He brought the chirurgeon to the Hall, and came home an hour since, and then went back again to watch."

"Then Sir Launcelot is not out of danger," I said.

"No," he replied; "but there is hope."

There was no morning walk for us that day. My Father went to his chamber, my aunts to theirs, and I to the chamber where the dried herbs lay, partly because it was Roger's and my Sunday parliament-house, and partly because from it I could see the towers of Davenant Hall.

In our Puritan household we were brought up with great faith in the virtues of solitude. A very solemn part of our ritual was, "Thou, when thou prayest, enter into thy closet, and shut thy door, and pray to thy Father which is in secret." "The one minute and unmistakable rubric," my Father called it, "in the New Testament." For he used to say, "not only is the solitary place the place for the Redeemer's agonies and the apostle's bitter weeping; it is the place of the largest assemblies. For therein passing the barriers of the congregation, we enter into the assembly and Church of the first-born, and into the temple not made with hands, eternal in the heavens. Any religion," said he, "whose secret springs do not exceed its surface waters, will evaporate in the burden and heat of the day."

We went to church as usual, and slowly and silently we were coming away, avoiding as much as possible the usual greetings with neighbours, and

I feeling especially anxious to escape Placidia's sympathy.

But that was impossible. However, as she joined us she looked really anxious; too anxious even to find an appropriate text. She took my hand kindly, and said—

"We must hope for the best, Olive."

And there was something in the "we," and the briefness of her words, which brought tears into my eyes, and made me think I might still have been keeping a hard place in my heart which would have to be melted.

But we had only just left the church-yard, and gone a few steps beyond the gate on the field-path to Netherby (I walking behind the rest), when a soft hand was laid on my shoulder, and my face was drawn down to Lettice Davenant's kisses, as in a low voice she said—

"Oh, Olive, I am sure Sir Launcelot will get well. My Mother has been saying prayers all night. And Roger is so good. Indeed, it was not nearly half Roger's fault. Sir Launcelot did say terribly provoking things about the Precisians, and hypocrisy, and your Father."

"*What* did he say, Lettice?" I asked, passionately.

"My Mother says we ought to forget bitter words," she said; "and I think we ought—at all events, until he gets better."

"Oh, Lettice," I implored, "tell me, only me! That I may know, if he should *not* get better. Roger told my Father it was all his fault; but I know—I always knew—it was not. I shall know this if you will not tell me another word, and perhaps think even worse things than were said."

"It was not so much the words—they were ordinary enough—it was the tone," said she. "And, besides, it is so difficult to repeat any conversation truly; and it was all in such a moment, I can scarcely tell. It began about Lord Strafford, and about Mr. Hampden and Mr. Pym being canting hypocrites, and Mr. Cromwell being a beggarly brewer; and then Sir Launcelot muttered something in a whining tone about wondering that Roger's Father permitted him to indulge in such ungodly amusements as bonfires; and Roger said it was not fair to attack when he knew there could be no retort (meaning because I was there); and Sir Launcelot said he believed the Precisians never thought it fair to be attacked except behind some good city walls. And then followed a fire of words about cowardice, and hypocrisy, and treason; and then something about your father having taken care to leave the German wars in good time for his own safety. Then I saw Roger's hand up, thrusting Sir Launcelot away, rather than striking him, I thought. But the next instant Sir Launcelot lay on the ground, with his head against a jagged log, the other end of which was in the bonfire, and Roger was pulling him back, and Sir Launcelot swearing something about a "Puritan dog" and being "murdered." And then I saw the blood flowing from a wound in his head. I gave Roger my veil to staunch it with. But it would not stop. Sir Launcelot fainted; and Roger told me to run to my Mother. In five minutes all the people were on the spot, and Roger was on horseback riding of for the physician. There! I have told you all I know" she said, "whether I ought or not. But don't tell Roger. For I tried to comfort him by saying how he had been provoked. But it did not comfort him in the least. He looked quite fierce at me—at me!" said little Lettice, the tears overflowing, "when he was always so kind! And he said there was no excuse for murder. He was wild with trouble," she continued, sobbing, "not a bit like himself, Olive; and since that I cannot tell what to say to him. Your ways and ours are not exactly the same, you know. So I have been with my Mother in her oratory. It is so hard to understand anybody. But I hope God understands us all. I do hope He does. My Mother could not find one of the church prayers that quite fitted. But she joined two or three together, in the Collects, and the Visitation of the Sick, and the Litany, which seemed to say all she wanted wonderfully. I never knew how much they meant before. And it does seem as if God must hear; and Roger always so good. He may say what he likes, always so good, to me and to every one!"

Lettice's tears opened the sluices of mine, and were a great comfort; and it was a comfort, too, to think of those dear kind voices joining in Lady Lucy's oratory.

When we reached home, the great table was spread in the hall, and the serving-men and maidens were standing round it.

My Father moved to the head and asked the blessing on the meal, then he said,—

"Friends, the hand of God is heavy on me to-day, and you will not look that I should eat bread while a life is in peril through deed of one who is to me as my own soul. I might brave it out, and put on a cheerful countenance. But I would have you know I am humbled. The blows of an enemy we may face as men. Beneath the rod of the Lord we must bow like smitten children. And I would have you know I do. Yet I cannot refrain from telling you also that it was for bitter words against good men that the blow was struck. So much I must say for the boy, though God forbid I should hide the sin."

He left the hall, and every eye was moist as it followed him.

The general judgment was anything but harsh against Roger, as was easy to see from the few low broken words which interrupted the silence of that sorrowful meal, and from the response of Tib, to whom I secretly ventured to tell how sorely Roger had been provoked.

"No need to tell me, Mistress Olive!" said she. "That Sir Launcelot is enough to rouse a saint, his groom told my Margery's Dickon. And they may say what they like, but I wouldn't give a farthing for any saint that can't be roused."

It was not the public verdict Roger had to fear. Aunt Dorothy took my Father's place at the head of the table, her face white and rigid, carving the meat, but eating not a morsel, nor uttering a word. Aunt Gretel moved about on one pretence and another, holding half-whispered discourse with the elder servants of the house, from the broken snatches of which I gathered that she fell into great historical difficulties in her double anxiety to say nothing harsh of the wounded gentleman, and at the same time to prove that Roger had meant no harm. And I, meantime, could scarce have sat through that terrible meal at all, but for Roger's stag-hound Lion, who nestled in close to me, pressing his great head under my hand, and calling my attention by a soft moan, and from time to time secretly relieving me of the food I could not touch, bolting it in a surreptitious manner, regardless of consequences, which said as plainly as possible, "Thou and I understand each other. Our hearts are in the same place. I eat, not because I care a straw about it, but to please thee and help *him*." Only once, when my tears fell fast on his nose, as I stooped over him to hide them, his feelings betrayed him, and his great paws appeared for a moment on the clean Sabbath cloth, as with an inquiring whine he started up and tried to lick my face, which I supposed was his way of figuratively wiping away my tears. But at the gentlest touch on his paws he subsided, casting one anxious glance at Aunt Dorothy, who, however, neither saw him nor the brown foot-prints on the tablecloth. Always afterwards he maintained his gentlemanlike reserve, limiting all further expression of his feelings to spasmodic movements of his tail, and to his great soft wistful eyes, which he never took off from me. For dogs always know when anything is the matter. Their misfortune is they can never make out what it is. Roger's ancient foe, the old gray cat, meantime made secretly off with a piece of meat which Lion had dropped. And I caught sight of her slowly luxuriating over it in a corner, entirely regardless of the family circumstances.

Every most trivial incident in that day glows as vividly and distinctly in my memory, in the fire of the passion that burned through it all, as every detail of the carving of Davenant Hall in the flames of the twelve bonfires.

The meal passed in a silence so deep that every whisper of Aunt Gretel's and every moan of Lion's were clearly heard. But afterwards the men slunk hastily away to the farm-yard and stables, and Tib with bones and fragments to her hens and pigs, and the maidens began to clear away the wooden trenchers and our pewter dishes, the clatter and rattle sounding singularly noisy without the cheerful talk which generally accompanied it.

Aunt Dorothy, Aunt Gretel, and I, went, at his summons, into my Father's justice-room. "Where two or three are gathered together," said he; and without further preamble we all knelt down while he prayed, in a few words and quiet (to the ear). For he seemed to feel the great, loving, omnipotent Presence; not far off, where cries only could reach, but near, close, overshadowing, indwelling, too near almost for speech. And we felt the same.

When he ceased, it was some minutes before we

rose. And the silence fell on me like an answer, like an "Amen," like one of those "Verilys" which shine through so many of the Gospel words, and illumine them so that they may read in the dark; in the dark when we most need them.

Before we left, I told him of Lady Lucy and Lettice praying the Collects for Roger in her oratory.

My Father turned away with trembling lips to the window. Aunt Gretel sobbed. Aunt Dorothy said, with a faint voice,—

"God forgive me if I said anything of Lady Lucy I should not have said."

We had not left the room when Lettice's white palfry flashed past the door, and in another moment she had met us in the porch.

"Sir Launcelot will live!" she said. "The physician says there is every hope; and he sleeps. If he wakes better, all will be right; and Roger waits to see, because he still fears. But I am sure all will be well. And I could not bear you should wait; so my mother let me come."

In his thankfulness my Father forgot the stately courtesy with which he usually treated Lettice, and stooping down, took her in his arms, as if she had been me, and kissed and blessed her, and called her "God's sweet messenger and dove of hope!" and prayed she might be so all her life. And Aunt Gretel disappeared to tell every one. But Aunt Dorothy stood still where she was, and covered her face with her hands and wept unrestrainedly in a way most uncommon with her.

Lettice, with her own sweet instinct when to come and when to go, was on the steps by the door in a moment (anticipating her groom's ready hand), on her white pony, waving her hand to us as we watched her in the porch, and away out of sight, escaping our thanks, and leaving us to our hope.

Slowly the dispersed household, who had all been invisily bound to the centre they nevertheless would not approach, gathered in the hall from stall, and shed, and field.

And then my Father said,—

"Friends, God has given us hope. Therefore let us pray." And for a few minutes we all knelt together while he prayed, in brief trustful words, ending with the Lord's Prayer, in which all the voices joined, at least all that could, for there were many tears.

Then my Father read Luther's Psalm, "God is our refuge and strength, a very present help in time of trouble."

And we felt it was true. And so the service ended. And once more the household scattered. For Roger had yet to return, and we all felt a family-gathering would be a welcome he could ill bear. So Aunt Dorothy went to her chamber, and Aunt Gretel to her German hymn-book by the fireside, and I to my place at her feet, and then to watch from the porch. For my Father went out to meet Roger.

And of that meeting neither of them ever spoke.

They came back together, my Father's hand on

Roger's shoulder, half as on a child's for tenderness, half as an old man's on a son's for support.

"Sir Launcelot is out of danger!" said my Father, when he came into the hall.

Roger kissed me and Aunt Gretel as he passed, and took my hand and tried to say something; but said nothing, only let me sob a minute on his shoulder, and then went up to his chamber.

We were used rather to repress than to give utterance to feeling in our Puritan households. And Lion was the only person who made much show of what he felt, twisting and whining and fondling round Roger in a way very unsuited to his giant bulk. We heard him pacing after Roger to the foot of the great staircase. Upstairs no dog under Aunt Dorothy's rule would venture, under the strongest excitement; so after lying expectant at its foot for some time, Lion returned to express his satisfaction in a more composed manner to me.

At family-prayer that night, my Father made one brief allusion of fervent thankfulness to the mercy of the day. More neither he nor Roger could have borne.

And so that Sabbath of unrest ended. To us, but not to Roger; although I only learned this long afterwards. For no lamp marked the watch of agony he kept that night. And on his haggard countenance, when he came down the next morning, no one dared question nor comment.

For while others rejoiced in the deliverance, he writhed in agony under the burden and in the coils of his sin. The accident of the log being at hand, that might have made it murder, and the other accident, that the wound had not been an inch nearer the temple or a barley-corn deeper, made absolutely no difference in the burden that weighed on him. If Sir Launcelot had died, the punishment would have been heavier; but not the remorse. And although his living was the deepest cause of thankfulness, yet it was no lightening of the sin. For it was the *fountain* of the sin within that was Roger's misery; the fountain deep in the heart.

Now he began to feel the meaning of the words, "Out of the heart." Now the old difficulties he and I had discussed in the apple-tree and in the herb-chamber rushed back on him. Now he began to feel that it was no mere entertaining question in metaphysical dynamics whether he was a free agent or not, but a question of moral and eternal life or death.

Could he have resisted the temptation to strike Sir Launcelot? Or could he not? His hand had stirred to deal that blow, at the bidding of the bitter anger in his heart, as instinctively and almost as unconsciously as the indignant blood had rushed to the cheek. What had stirred the sudden movement of anger in his heart? Far bitterer words from the lips of a stranger had not moved him as those mocking tones of Sir Launcelot's. The strength of that fatal impulse was but the accumulated force of the irritation of countless petty provocations, not retaliated outwardly, but suffered to ferment in the heart. Nor was that last sin altogether rooted in sin. Roger's search into his own heart was made with too intense a desire of being true to himself and to God for him to fall into that blind passion of self-accusing. It had been more than half-rooted in justice, just anger against injustice, generous indignation against ungenerous slander, truth revolting against falsehood. And so gradual (and in part so just) had been the growth of deep-rooted detestation of Sir Launcelot's character, that the last act—which might have been crime in the eyes of man, which was crime in the eyes of God, whose judgment is not measured by consequences—had become almost as irresistible and instinctive as the movement of the eyelid to sweep a grain of dust from the eye.

When, then, could he have begun to resist? *When* would it have been possible to stem the little stream which had swollen into a torrent that had all but swept his life into ruin? *Where* was the point where sin and virtue, hatred which leads to murder, and justice which is the foundation of all virtue, began to intertwine until they were ravelled inextricably beyond his power to sever or distinguish? Had there ever been such a point? Must not all, he being as he was by nature, and things being as they were, and Sir Launcelot being as he was, have necessarily gone on as it had, and led to the result it led to?

But here came in the low inextinguishable voice of conscience.

"This anguish is no fruit of inevitable necessity. It was sin—it was sin. I have sinned." And then—

"I have sinned, because there is sin *in me.* Sin in me; no mere detached faults, no isolated wrong acts, but a fountain of evil within me, from which every evil thing proceeds. Out of the heart—out of the heart; not from without, not something merely *in* me. It is *I myself* that am sinful, that have sinned. This one evil thing, which, unlike all other seemingly evil things, storms or frosts, or corruption and death itself, never produces good fruit, but only evil fruit, is springing in an inexhaustible flow from the depths of my innocent being."

"Free?" I am *not* free! I am in bondage. I am a slave. I am tied and bound. Yet this bondage is no excuse; it is the very essence of my sin. I cannot explain it; but I feel it. I feel it in this anguish which I cannot escape any more than we can escape from anguish in the bones by writhing. For this is not the anguish of blows or of wounds, but of disease within, growing from my inmost heart, preying on my inmost life. O God, I have sinned, I am a sinful man. In me is no help. Is there none in the universe, none in Thee?"

Then from the depth of the anguish came the relief. The thought flashed through him—

"Unless one worse than the worst conception man ever formed of the devil is the Maker of man and the Omnipotent Ruler of the world, it is impossible that we should be so powerless in ourselves to overcome sin, and so agonized in remorse for it, and yet that there should be no deliverance."

That thought made a lull in his anguish for a

time, a silence; that thought, and the mere exhaustion of the conflict. For his thoughts had whirled him round until thought, with the mere rapidity of motion, became imperceptible. In the centre of the whirlwind there was stillness, and therein he lay prostrate, dumb, and exhausted.

But not alone.

On his mind, wearied out with vain thinking, on his heart, numb with suffering, fell in the pause of the storm old sweet, familiar words, still small voices, soft echoes of sacred hymns learned in childhood; those old familiar, simple words, wherewith the Spirit, moving like a dove on the face of the waters, knows how to win entrance into souls tempest-tossed, when new words, though wise and deep as an archangel's, would only sweep past its closed doors undistinguished from the wail of the winds, or the raging of the seas on which it tosses.

Old familiar words,—

"Go in peace, thy sins are forgiven thee."

Words of healing to so many!

Forgiveness; not as a far-off result of a life of expiation, but free, complete, present. Peace; not after years of doubtful conflict, but now, to strengthen for the conflict. Yet these were not the words he most wanted then. It was not so much that guilt pressed on him as a burden, as that sin bound him like a chain. Not peace he most wanted, but power; freedom to fight, power to overcome. It seemed to him as if what he longed for was not so much "Go in peace," as "Come! and I will chasten thee, smite thee low, humble thee in the dust; but make thee whole."

Not soft words of comfort, but strong words of hope and promise, were what he needed, and they did not seem to come.

He crept out of the house before dawn to obtain tidings at the Hall of Sir Launcelot, and to quiet the restlessness of his heart by outward movement.

On his way he passed the forge where Job Forster, the blacksmith, lived alone with his wife at the edge of the village opposite to ours, on the way to the Hall.

There was a light in Job's window; a strange sight in his orderly and childless home. The red glare it cast across the road was struggling with the growing dawn. As Roger approached, it was put out; and just when he reached the door it was opened, and Job's tall figure issued forth.

Job strode forward and grasped Roger's hand.

"Thee had best not be roaming about the country by theeself in the dark like a ghost," said he. "It's wisht!"

"Is anything the matter?" asked Roger, diverting the conversation from himself.

"There's nought the matter with us," said Job.

"There was a light in your window, so I thought Rachel might be ill," said Roger.

"There's nought ailing with us," repeated Job; and after some hesitation he added, "We were but thinking of thee."

"You used not to need a lamp to think by," said Roger, touched more than he liked to show.

"No, nor to pray by," said Job. "But we wanted a promise, she and I." (Job seldom called his wife anything but *she.*) "We wanted a promise, Master, for thee. For she thought the devil would be sure to be busy with thee just now, and so did I."

"Did you find one?" asked Roger.

"They are as plenty as the stars," said Job, "but we couldn't light on the one that would fit. And it's bad work hammering them promises to fit if they don't go right at first."

"As many as the stars, and not one that fits me!" said Roger, unintentionally betraying the struggles of the night. "Peace, and pardon, and everything every one wants, but not what I want. You found none, Job! Then, of course, there was nothing more to be done. You and Rachel wouldn't give in easily."

"Well, Master Roger," said Job, "we didn't. But we came to a stand, and for a while gave up looking altogether. And I sat down on one edge of the bed and she on the other, and we said nothing. But she wept nigh as bitter as Esau, for she ever had a tender heart for thee, having none of her own, and thee no mother. When all at once she flashed up through her tears, and said, 'Why, Job, we've gone a-hunting for a promise, and we've got them all to our hand. All in Him! Yea and amen, in Him! We've forgotten the blessed Lord!' Then it struck me all of a heap what fools we were; and

I could have laughed for gladness, but that she might have thought I'd gone mazed. So I only said, 'Why, child, here we've been chattering like cranes, as if we'd been all in the twilight, like poor old Hezekiah. We've been hunting for the promises, and we've got the Gift! We've been groping for words, and we've got the Word.' So we knelt down again, and begged hard of the Lord to mind how He was tempted and forsaken, and to mind thee, Master Roger, and help thee any way He could. And we rose up wonderful lightened, she and I. And then the promises came falling about us as thick as hail; and uppermost of them all, 'If the Son shall make you free, you shall be free indeed;' 'Reconciled to God by His death; saved by His life;' and, 'I am come that they might have *life.*'"

"Job," said Roger, "I think that will do; I think that will fit me."

"Maybe, Master Roger," said Job. "They're mighty words. But, please God, thee and she and I never forget what we learnt to-night. Words are not so strong always the thousandth time as the first. But His voice goes deeper every time we hearken to it. And every sore needs a fresh salve. But His touch is a salve for all sores. Never you be such a fool as we were, Master Roger. Never you go creeping back into the dark hunting for a promise and forget that they are all, yea and amen, in the Lord. No more if's or maybe's, or peradventure's, but yea and amen in Him for us all for ever."

Roger grasped Job's hand in silence, and went on to hear tidings of Sir Launcelot.

The night had been quiet; the fever had subsided, and the danger was over. And Roger came back to his chamber at Netherby to give thanks to God. For danger averted from others, for a curse averted from himself, but above all, for the glorious promise of freedom now and for ever—freedom to overcome sin, freedom to serve God. Freedom in the liberating Saviour, life in the Life, sonship in the Son, now and for ever.

The various streams of the various lives which had been flooded into one by the common anxiety about Roger and Sir Launcelot soon shrank back into their various separate channels.

Ah! if we could all keep at the point, "*I will arise*," or better still, at the place where the Father meets us, how good, and lowly, and tender-hearted we should be! No, "*thou never gavest me a kid;*" no, "*this thy son, which hath devoured thy substance!*" Strange that the memory of such moments (and what Christian life can be without such?) should not keep the heart ever broken and open. The best way towards this, no doubt, is to have such an arising and such an embracing every day we live. I am sure we need it. However, we did not exactly do this at that time at Netherby.

Aunt Dorothy, on thinking matters over with her "sober judgment," thought it a duty to warn us against the "spirit of bondage," which, with all her sweetness, had restrained poor Lady Lucy's prayers to the limits of the Prayer-book. Cousin Placidia, the immediate anxiety having subsided, could not but feel that Roger's vehemence had added another step to the distance which already separated them. Once on that Pharisaic height, to which, alas! we so easily rise without any trouble of climbing, being puffed up thither by windy substances within and without, other people's falls necessarily increase our comparative elevation above them; and whether this is caused by their descent or by our ascent is difficult to determine; just as in the case of one boat passing another, it is difficult by the mere sense of sight to ascertain which is moving. Not that Placidia asserted this conscious superiority by reproaches. Did she need to descend to speech? Was not her life a reproach? That placid life, unbroken by any movement deeper than the soft ripples of an approving conscience; or a calm disapproval of any one attempting an encroachment on her rights,—which of course she never permitted. Had she not heard of Archbishop Laud's cruelties to the three gentlemen in the pillory with no further emotion than a gentle regret that the three gentlemen could not have held their tongues? Had she not, on the other hand, heard the tidings of Lord Strafford's arrest, and the destruction of the Star-Chamber Court, with no more vehement feeling than a remark on the vanity of human greatness, and a gentle hope that it might lead to the abolition of the very inconvenient monopolies on pepper and soap?

Had she not always warned Roger and me against

severity on Sir Launcelot? Had she not even gone the length of pronouncing him a very fine gentleman? And what could be more striking than the subsequent justification of her warnings by the revengeful act to which Roger had been betrayed?

Under all these circumstances, Placidia's forbearance must have seemed to herself remarkable. She uttered no rebuke, she pointed no moral, by reminding us of her prophetical sayings. She merely towered above us on her serene heights, a little higher, a little more severe—a very little—than before. And she called me "Olive, my dear," and Roger "poor Roger." But that was partly, no doubt, on account of her being married.

Roger bore her superiority most meekly. Indeed, I believe he felt it as much as she did. For Roger *did* remain at that point of penitence and pardon where the heart keeps sweet, and lowly, and tender. Which, most certainly, I very often did not. For Placidia's condescension, especially to Roger, chafed me often past endurance.

Only once I remember his being roused.

She had been saying (I forget in what connection) that she hoped Roger would not be *too* much cast down. "It was never too late to turn over a new leaf; and then there was the consoling example of the Apostle Peter. There was reason to believe that the Apostle Peter was a wiser and better man all his life from his terrible fall. And we know that 'all things work for good,'" said she, "'to them that are called.'"

Then Roger, sitting at the other end of the hall

cleaning his gun, as we believed out of hearing, suddenly rose, and coming to where we were sitting, stood before Placidia with compressed lips and arms folded tightly on his breast,—

"Cousin Placidia," he said, "never, never say that again. St. Peter was not wiser and better, or even humbler for denying Christ. No doubt he was wiser, and better, and tenderer for *that look*, for ever and ever; and better for the bitter weeping; but not for the denial, not for the sin."

Said my Father, who came in behind Roger as he spoke, laying his hand on Roger's shoulder,—

"True, Roger, true; but though sin can never work for good, the memory of sin may; and at any point in the lowest depths where we turn our back on the husks and our face to the Father's house, God will meet us, and from that moment make the consequences, bitter as they may be, begin to work for good to us."

"To *us!* Father, to us," said Roger, "but to others—how to others? To those our misdoing may have misled or confirmed in evil? We may stop a rock hurled down a precipice. But who can stop all it has set in motion, or undo the ruin it has wrought in its way?"

"*Nothing* works for good," said my Father mournfully, "to those whose faces are turned from God. But He can help us, and will, if we set our whole hearts to it, to counter-work the evil we have wrought. Counter-work, I say, not undo; for to undo a deed done is impossible even to Omnipotence. And that makes sin the one terrible and unalterably evil and sorrowful thing in the world, and the only one."

The words fell heavily on my heart. Was this the gospel? I thought. Evil never, never to be undone, sin never to be the same as if it had not been? Placidia said no more until Roger and my Father went out on the farm together, and we were left alone with Aunt Gretel, and then she observed in her deliberate way, with a slow shake of her head,—

"I hope Cousin Roger is not still in the dark. I trust he understands the gospel—"

"What do you mean by the gospel, Placidia?" said I, half roused on Roger's account and half troubled on my own.

Placidia, always ready (at that time) with a theological definition, neatly folded and packed, entered into a disquisition of some length as to what she understood by "the gospel." In a deliberate and business-like manner she undertook to explain the purposes of the Almighty from the beginning, as if she had, in some inexplicable way, been in the confidence of Heaven before the beginning, and comprehended not only all the purposes of the Eternal, but the reasons on which these purposes were founded. The effect produced on my mind was as if the whole life-giving stream of redeeming love flowing from the glorious unity of the living God, the Father, the Son, and the Holy Spirit, had been frozen into a rigid contract between certain high sovereign powers for the purchase of a certain inheritance for their own use, in which the utmost care was taken on all sides that the quantity paid and the quantity received should be precisely equivalent. It was as if the whole living, breathing world, with its infinite blue heavens, its abounding rivers, its waving corn-fields, its heaving seas, and all that is therein, had been shrivelled into a map of estates, in which nothing was of importance but the dividing lines. These "dividing lines" of her system might, for aught I knew, be correct enough, might be those of the Bible itself; but the awful Omnipresence, the real holy indignation against wrong, the love, the life, the yearning, pitying, repenting, immutably just, yet tenderly forgiving heart which beats in every page of the Bible, had vanished altogether. All the while she spoke, as it were in spite of myself, the words kept running through my head, "They that make them are like unto them."

At the close she said, turning to Aunt Gretel,—

"I think I have stated the gospel clearly. I only hope Cousin Roger understands it."

"I am sure I do not know, my dear," said Aunt Gretel (for Aunt Gretel, being always afraid of in some way compromising Dr. Luther by any confusion in her theological statements, seldom ventured out of the text of Scripture). "I am sure, my dear, I do not know. I am no theologian. And it is a blessing that the Holy Scriptures provide what Dr. Luther calls a gospel in miniature for those who are no theologians: 'God so loved the world that He gave His only begotten Son, that whosoever believeth in Him should not perish, but have everlasting life.' That is my gospel, my dear. It is shorter, you see, than yours, and I think rather better news; especially for the wandering sheep and prodigal sons, and all the people outside, and for those who, like me, trust they have come back, but still feel, as I do, very apt to go wrong again."

"Mr. Nicholls always says I have rather a remarkably clear head for theology," said Placidia. "But gifts differ, and we have none of us anything to be proud of."

"No doubt, my dear," said Aunt Gretel. "At least I am sure I have not. But I cannot say I think the punishment, or at least the sad consequences of sin are all exactly taken away for us, at least in this life. For instance, there is Gammer Grindle's grandchild, poor Cicely, as pretty a girl as ever danced around the May-pole, that people say Sir Launcelot Trevor tempted away to London, and left to no one knows what misery there. (If it was not Sir Launcelot, may I be forgiven for joining in an unjust accusation; but he was seen speaking to her the evening before she left.) Now if Sir Launcelot were to repent, as I pray he may, that would not bring back the lost innocence to little Cicely; nor do I see how the thought of her could ever bring anything but a bitter agony of remorse to him."

("Ah," interposed Aunt Dorothy, who had joined us, "*I did* speak my mind, I am thankful to say, about those May-poles.")

"What *is* forgiveness, then?" resumed Placidia. "And what is the good of being religious, if we are to be punished just the same as if we were not forgiven?"

"The blessing of forgiveness," said Aunt Dorothy, "is *being forgiven;* and the good of being godly is, I should think, *being* godly."

"Forgiveness, my dear," added Aunt Gretel, "What is forgiveness? It is welcome back to the Father's heart. It is the curse borne for us and taken from us out of everything, out of death itself. It is God with us against all our sins, God for us against all our real foes. It is the broken link re-knit between us and God. It is the link broken between us and sin. What would you have better? What could you have more? Once on the Father's heart, can we not well leave it to Him to decide what pain we can be spared, and what we can *not* be spared, without so much the more *sin*, which is so infinitely worse than any pain."

"My theology," Aunt Dorothy continued, "is the doctrine Nathan taught when he said to David, 'The Lord hath put away thy sin, but the child shall die,'—and to the Apostle Paul when he wrote, 'God is not mocked; whatsoever a man soweth that shall he also reap:' the theology our fathers taught us; no gospel of *tolerating* sin, but of *forgiving* and *destroying* it. 'Christ has redeemed us from the curse of the law, being made a curse for us.' He has brought us under the rod of the covenant, having Himself 'learned obedience through the things which He suffered.' There is as much mercy and as much justice in one as in the other. I hope, my dear," she concluded, "you and Mr. Nicholls do indeed understand the gospel. But, I confess, people who get into the Covenant so very easily do puzzle me. They say the anguish all but cost Dr. Luther his life, and Mr. Cromwell his reason."

Placidia, from her double height of spiritual serenity and semi-clerical dignity, looked mildly down on Aunt Dorothy's suggestions.

"Aunt Dorothy," said she, "I have often thought, you scarcely comprehend Mr. Nicholls and me. But it is written, 'Woe unto you when all men speak well of you.' And as to Cousin Roger's Gospel, I should call it simply the Law."

Soon after Placidia rose to leave. But as she was putting on her mufflers, she remarked, as if the thought had just occurred to her,—

"Aunt Dorothy, those three beautiful cows Uncle Drayton gave me, I am a little anxious about them: the glebe farm is on high ground, and the grass is not so rich as they have been used to, and I was saying to Mr. Nicholls yesterday morning that I was sure Uncle Drayton would be quite distressed if he saw how much less yellow and rich the butter was than it used to be. And Mr. Nicholls said he quite felt with me. And Uncle Drayton is always so kind. So I said I thought I had better be quite frank with Uncle Drayton. You know I always am frank, and speak out what I think. It is no merit in me. It is my nature, and I cannot help it. And Mr. Nicholls said he thought I had. And yesterday evening it happened that we were passing the meadow by the Mere, and there were no cattle on it. And I said to Mr. Nicholls at once, what a pity that beautiful grass should run to seed, and our butter be such a poor colour. And Mr. Nicholls saw it at once. And he advised me—or I suggested and he approved of it, I cannot be certain which (and I am always so anxious to report everything exactly as it happened)—at once to go to Uncle Drayton and ask him if he would allow our three cows just to stand for a little while in that meadow, while there are no other cattle to put in it, just to prevent the pasture running to waste, which I know would be quite a trouble to Uncle Drayton if he thought of it, only no one can be in every place at once, and no doubt he had forgotten it."

"*Very few* people's eyes can be in every place at once, certainly, Placidia," said Aunt Dorothy, with point. "But it so happens that your uncle had not forgotten that meadow. And this morning Bob drove all our cows there."

"Oh," said Placidia, "that is quite enough. I only felt naturally anxious that nothing should be wasted, especially when we happened to be wanting it. But, of course, a poor parson's wife cannot expect such butter as you have at Netherby; only I always remember the 'twelve baskets,' and how important it is 'nothing should be lost,' and the virtuous woman at the end of the Proverbs. I shall always have reason to be grateful to you, Aunt Dorothy, for making me learn so much Scripture."

"Thank you, my dear," said Aunt Dorothy, "you always had an excellent memory. But it is very important with the Holy Scriptures, at least the English version, not to read them from right to left."

So Cousin Placidia departed, leaving Aunt Dorothy with a comfortable sense of having defeated a plot.

But half an hour afterwards my Father came in.

"Poor Placidia," said he, "I met her on her way home, and I really was quite touched by her gratitude for those few cows I gave her, and also by the feeling she expressed about Roger. It seems the glebe pasture does not agree with the beasts as well as ours, and she had been rather troubled about the butter, but had not liked to speak of it, especially when we were in such anxiety about Roger. It really shows more delicacy of feeling than I thought Placidia possessed, poor child. And it shows how careful we ought to be not to form uncharitable judgments. So I ordered Bob to put those three cows with ours in the Mere meadow for a little while."

"Did Placidia mention the Mere meadow?" said Aunt Dorothy.

"Well, I cannot be sure, but I think she did; and I think it was a very sensible suggestion."

"What did Bob say?" said Aunt Dorothy, grimly.

"Bob spoke rather sharply," said my Father; "he is apt to be very free-spoken at times; he said he had like to look well to our pastures if we were to give change of air to all Mistress Nicholl's cattle. It was not likely, Bob thought, they would be in any hurry to change back again."

"Well, there *are* men," murmured Aunt Dorothy, "who are as harmless as doves, and there *are* women who are as wise as serpents. And the less the two meet the better. I don't care a rush who feeds

Placidia's cows; but it is almost more than I can bear that she thinks no one sees through her schemes."

But Placidia had triumphed. And the parsonage cows never needed any further change of residence.

It irks me somewhat to intertwine these rough dark threads with the story of those so dear to me, but the whole would drop into unmeaningness without them. Placidia and Mr. Nicholls made many a calumny of the enemy's comprehensible to me. For in later days it became the fashion to assert that characters of that stamp formed the staple of our Commonwealth men and women. Characters of this stamp win Naseby and Worcester! save the persecuted Vaudois! make England the reverence of the world! conceive the "Pilgrim's Progress," the "Areopagitica," and the "Living Temple!" sacrifice two thound livings for conscience sake!

No! Pharisees, doubtless, there were among us, as, alas, doubtless there is the root of Pharisaism within us. But they were of the make of Saul the disciple of Gamaliel, not of those who tithed the "mint, anise, and cummin."

At first it seemed to me that Placidia's "Gospel" was more likely to be fulfilled in Roger's case than his own forebodings.

Good seemed to come out of that hasty act of his rather than evil. The feeling he, usually so self-repressing, had shown about Sir Launcelot, revealed him in a new light to Lady Lucy.

"I thought him rather stony, I must confess," she said; "but now I see it was only a little of your Puritan ice, if I may say so without offence; and that there is an ocean of feeling below. My dear, now all has ended well, he really must not take it so much to heart. He has grown too grave. We cannot have precisely the same standard for young men, with all their temptations and strong passions, as for sweet innocent girls sheltered tenderly in homes, with our softer natures. I should always wish to be severe to myself. But young men; ah, my child, the king is a good man, but if you had seen a little even of our Court, you would think Roger an angel."

Compared with Sir Launcelot, I most sincerely believed he was. But this double standard was unknown in our Puritan home. One law of righteousness, and purity, and goodness we knew, and only one, for man and woman. And in this I learned to think Aunt Dorothy's grimmest sternness more pitiful than Lady Lucy's pity. I do not wish to set down what seemed to me Lady Lucy's mistakes to any sect or any doctrine. In theory all Christian sects are agreed as to the moral standard. But I believe in my heart it was the high moral standard set up, in those days, chiefly (never only) in our Puritan homes, which will be the salvation of England, if ever that pest-house, called the Court, is to be cleansed, and if England ever is to be saved.

Lady Lucy's religion was one of tender, devotional emotions, minute ceremonial, and gorgeous ritual. When braced up by Christian principle, it was beautiful and attractive. The Puritan religion was one of principle and doctrine. When inspired by Divine love, it was gloriously deep and strong.

Meantime, with Sir Walter and his boys, Roger had manifestly risen many degrees by his "spirited conduct." Sir Launcelot's jests, they admitted, could bite, and it was just as well he should have a lesson, though rather a severe one.

Sir Launcelot himself, moreover, took a far different demeanour towards Roger. "Saints with that amount of fire in their temper," he observed, "might be dangerous, but were certainly not despicable!"

And as to Lettice, whose moral code was chivalrous rather than Scriptural, and to whom generosity was a far more admirable virtue than justice, and honour a more glorious thing than duty, she said candidly she was delighted Roger had lost his temper for once, just to show every one how much heart and spirit he had.

"You and I knew what he was, Olive," said she; "but I wanted the rest to feel it too."

And yet there was something lost. Slowly I grew to see and feel it.

Firstly, in the relative position of Roger and Sir Launcelot. Deeds of violence inevitably place the one who does them morally below the one who suffers. There had been a real honour to Roger in Sir Launcelot's previous mockery; there was a real dishonour in the assumption he now made that Roger stood on his own level. Moreover, Roger's own generous self-reproach deprived him of the power of retort.

And secondly (but chiefly), in Lettice's altered feeling about Sir Launcelot. Roger never spoke of him; but now that he had recovered, I felt that I could not forget how, by Lettice's own account, he had provoked the blow; nor could I see that the fact of his having received a blow which he had provoked in any way made his character different from what it had been. Many debates we had on the subject, for we met often during those weeks—those weeks of winter and early spring, when the whole nation was in suspense about Lord Strafford's trial, watching during the ploughing and sowing of the year the solemn reaping of the harvest he had sown. One of these debates in particular I remember, because of the way in which it closed.

It was on Thursday, the 13th of May (1641). We had met in the wood by the Lady Well. There seemed a marvellous melody that day in the music of the little spring, as it bubbled up into its stone trough, and echoed back from the stone roof of the little sacred cell the monks had lovingly made for it seven hundred years ago. The inscription could still be read on the front:—

> " Ut jucundas cervus undas
> Æstuans desiderat,
> Sic ad rivum Dei vivum
> Mens fidelis properat."

Lettice and I knelt and listened to it.

"It is as if all the bells in fary-land were ringing," said she at length, softly; "only hear how the soft peals rise and fall, and go and come, and how one sound drops into another, and blends with it, and flows away and comes back, and meets the next, until there is no following them."

"Then," said I, "there must have been choirs and church-bells in fairy-land, for there is surely something sad and sacred in the sound. It sounds to me like those bells the legends tell us of, buried beneath the sea, tolling up to us from far beneath the dark waters of the past."

Then Lettice fastened back her long hair, and stooped down and drank of the crystal water, bathing her face as she drank.

"Those Israelitish soldiers understood how to enjoy water," said she, rising from her draught. "That is delicious."

For we were tired and thirsty with gathering lapfuls of the blue-bells, of which the woods were full.

As she stood, her moist parted lips, the rich glow on her cheeks, her eyes dancing with life, her arms full of flowers, she said,—

"It never seems enough to look at the beautiful world, Olive. I seem to want another sense for it. I want to drink of it like this spring; to take it to my heart, as I do these flowers. And I suppose that is why I delight to gather them, just as when I was a little child. Do you understand?"

I did; but I thought of the inscription on the Lady Well.

"I suppose we do want to get nearer, Lettice," I

said; "we want to drink of the Fountain. We want to rest on the Heart."

"Do you think that is what this strange unsatisfied longing means," said she, "which all great joys and all very beautiful things give me?"

For a few moments she was silent. Then she said,—

"What life there is everywhere! Everything seems filled too full of joy, and brimming over—the birds into songs, the fields into flowers, and the trees into leaves, the oldest and gayest of them. And I feel just like them all, Olive. On such a morning one must love every one and everything, altogether regardless of their being lovable, just for the sake of loving. Olive," she added, with one of her sudden turns of thought, "to-day you must forgive Sir Launcelot from the very bottom of your heart, once for all."

"Oh, Lettice," said I, "I do forgive him. I really think I did, long since; at least for everything but his forgiving Roger in that gracious way, as if Roger had nothing to forgive him. I have forgiven him, but I cannot think him good."

"Ungenerous!" said she, half in jest and half in earnest; "you ought to think every one good on such a morning as this. Besides, Sir Launcelot always speaks so kindly and generously of you: he says you are goodness itself."

"I cannot think what is not true, just because the sun shines and the birds sing," said I, "and I certainly cannot think any one good because they call me good, or goodness itself. How *can* I, Lettice?

How *can* I believe a thing because I wish to believe it?"

"Truth, truth!" said she, a little petulantly, "truth and duty, and right and wrong, I wish those cold words were not so often on your lips. There are others so much warmer and more beautiful—nobleness and generosity, and loyalty and devotion, those are the things I love. Yours is a world of daylight, Olive. I like sunshine, glowing morning and evening like rubies and opals, veiling the distance at noon with its own glorious haze. I hate always to see everything exactly as it is, even beautiful things; and ugly things I never will see, if I can help it."

"I love to see everything exactly as it is," said I; "I want, and I pray, to see everything as it is. And in the end I am sure that is the way to see the real beauty of everything in the world. For God has made it, and not the devil. And therefore we need never be afraid to look into things. And I shall always think truth and duty the most beautiful words in the world."

"Very pretty!" said she perversely; "and under all those beautiful words you bury the fact that you will never forgive poor Sir Launcelot."

"I have long forgiven him," said I; "but I cannot think him good, if I tried for ever, until he is. I cannot help thinking of poor little Cicely, Gammer Grindle's grandchild, wandering lost in London."

"Hush, Olive, hush," said she passionately, "that is ungenerous and unkind. I will not listen to village gossip. My Mother says we must not be harsh in judging those whose temptations we cannot estimate. But she means to do all she can in London to help poor Cicely."

"Oh, Lettice," said I, "it is not a question of *more* or *less* pity, but of *who* needs our pity most."

"You are all alike," she rejoined; "yet I love you all, and I love you, Olive, dearly. Without your Puritan training, Olive, you and Roger would have been the best people and the pleasantest in the world; but as my Mother says, all these severe doctrines of law, and justice, and truth, do make people harsh in judging others, and bitter in resenting wrong."

I could say no more. She had taken refuge under the shadow of Roger's hasty act, and the argument was closed.

When we reached Davenant Hall an unusual crowd was gathered at the front door—a silent eager throng—around a horseman whose horse was covered with foam, from the speed with which he had come. It was Harry Davenant. And the tidings he brought were that on yesterday morning Lord Strafford had been beheaded on Tower Hill, a hundred thousand people gathered there to see; but through all the silent multitude neither sighs of sympathy nor sounds of triumph.

The servants silently dispersed. Harry's horse was led to the stables, and we went in with Lady Lucy, Sir Walter, and Sir Launcelot, into the hall.

"That is what they were doing in London while we were gathering blue-bells!" said Lettice. And she threw her flowers on the stone floor. "I will never gather any more."

She buried her face in her hands and burst into tears—"Cruel, cruel," she said, "of the king, of the queen, to let him die."

"It was the Parliament which hunted him to death," said Harry, bitterly. "And the king did try to save him."

"The Parliament is wicked, and hated him, and I don't care what they did," said Lettice, looking up with a flushed face; "but the king, oh, Mother, you said the king would never let Lord Strafford die. What is the use of being a king if kings can only *try* to do things like other people. I thought kings could *do* the things they thought right. He was faithful to the king, was he not, Mother?"

"A devoted servant to the king Lord Strafford surely was," said Lady Lucy, "whether a good counsellor or no. I did not think the king would have given him up. Did no one plead for him?" she asked.

"He pleaded with a wonderful eloquence for himself," said Harry Davenant, "that might well-nigh have turned the heads of his bitterest enemies, and did win the hearts of every one who heard him."

"But the king did try to save him?" said Lady Lucy, clinging to this.

"The king called his privy council together," said Harry Davenant, "last Sunday, when the bill of attainder had passed through the Lords and Commons, and said he had doubts and scruples about assenting to it, and asked their advice. Dr. Juxon, Bishop of London, counselled him never to consent to the shedding of what he believed innocent blood. But the rest of the council advised him to yield.—And the king yielded."

"Some people," he continued, "think the king was justified by a letter the earl wrote him on the Tuesday before, wherein he offered his life in this world to the king with all the cheerfulness; nay, even counselled the sacrifice to reconcile him to his people, saying, 'To a willing man there is no injury done.'"

"Oh, Harry," said Lettice, "the king could give him up *after that?*"

"It is said the earl scarcely believed it when he heard it, and that he laid his hand on his heart and exclaimed, 'Put not your trust in princes.'"

"And well he might!" exclaimed Lettice, her tears dried by the fire of her indignation.

"Hush, child, hush," said Lady Lucy.

"The king made another effort to save him," Harry continued; "he wrote to the Lords recommending imprisonment instead of death; and at the end of the letter he added a postscript: 'If he must die, it were charity to relieve him till Saturday.'"

'A miserable, cold request!" exclaimed Lettice, vehemently; "more cruel than the sentence."

"I would have expected this from his father," murmured Sir Walter, "but not from the king." Then turning from a painful subject, he added, "The earl died bravely, no doubt."

"As he passed the windows of the chamber where Archbishop Laud was, he bowed to receive his blessing, and he said, 'Farewell, my lord, God protect your innocence.' He marched to the Tower Hill more with the bearing of a general leading his army, than a sentenced man moving to the scaffold. At the Tower Gate the lieutenant desired him to take coach, fearing the violence of the people, but the earl refused: 'I dare look death in the face,' said he, 'and I hope the people do. Have you a care I do not escape, and I care not how I die, whether by the hand of the executioner or by the madness of the people. If that give them better content, it is all one to me.' And so, after protesting his innocence, saying he forgave all the world, and sending a few affectionate words to his wife and four children, he laid his head on the block. There was no base triumphing in the crowd, I will say that for them; they behaved like Englishmen. The earl fell in silence. But in the evening the brutish populace cried out in exultation, 'His head is off! his head is off!' and the city was blazing with bonfires. The people feel they have gained the first step in a victory. The Court thinks it has made the furthermost step in concession, and that thenceforward all must be peace. Would to heaven the king and the Court might be right; but it is hard to say."

It was dusk before all this converse was ended and I left the Hall. Harry Davenant persisted in guarding me across the fields to Netherby, until we came to the high road close to the house. There he took leave.

"My Father would like to see you," I said.

"Mr. Drayton would be courteous to his mortal enemy," said he.

"We are not enemies," I said, a little pained.

"Heaven forbid," he replied; "but I had better not come, not to-day. The fall of the earl scarcely means the same thing in your home as in ours."

"There will be no mean triumphing over Lord Strafford's death at Netherby," I said, with some indignation.

"There will be no low, or ungenerous, or mean thing said by one of the Draytons!" he said, warmly. "But I had better not see Mr. Drayton this evening."

And waving his plumed hat, he vaulted over the stile; and I felt he was right. Looking back at the turn leading to the house, I saw he was watching me from the field. But as I turned the corner and came in sight of the gables of the Manor, a foreboding came on me, as of siftings and severings to come—of a few pebbles, or a few rushes, gently giving the slightest turn to the course of the two little trickling springs, and their waters flowing, ever after, by different banks, and falling at last into the oceans which wash the shores of opposite worlds. But not Lettice, never Lettice; the whole world, I thought, should be no barrier to sever us from Lettice! Nor should all the political or ecclesiastical differences in the world ever check or chill the current of our love and reverence to all the true, and brave, and just, and good, and godly. For politics, even ecclesiastical politics, are of time; but truth, and courage, and justice, and goodness, and godliness, are of God, and are eternal.

CHAPTER VI.

HE six months of the year 1641, from early May till November, shine back on me beyond the stormy years which part them from us, like a meadow bright with dew and sunshine on the edge of a dark and heaving sea. Beyond those months, in the further distance, stretches the dim Eden of childhood, with its legends and its mysteries, and its gates of Paradise scarcely closed. Bordering them, on the further side, glooms the broad shadow of Roger's temptation and bitter repentance. On the hither side heaves the great intervening sea of civil war. But through all, that little sunny space beams out, peaceful, as if no stormy waves beat against it; distinct, as if no long space of life parted it from us.

Did I say childhood was the Eden? Then youth is the "garden planted eastward in Eden," the Paradise which "the Lord God plants" in the outset of the dullest or stormiest life, where the river which compasseth the land flows over golden sands, "and the gold of that land is good." Not childhood, surely, but early youth, "the youth of youth," is the golden age of life. Childhood is the twilight. Youth is the beautiful dawn. Childhood is the dream and the struggling out of it; youth is the conscious, joyful waking. If childhood has its fairy robes spun out of every gossamer, its fairy treasures in every leaf; it has also its eerie terrors woven of the twilight shadows, its overwhelming torrents of sorrow having their fountains in an April shower, as it steps uncertainly through the unknown world. And neither its joys, nor its sorrows, nor its terrors, nor its treasures, can it utter.

Childhood is the dim Colchis where the Golden Fleece lies hidden; youth is the Jason that brings thence the "Argosy." Childhood is the sweet shadowy Hesperides, lying dreamily in the tropic sunshine, where the golden fruit ripens silently among the dark and glossy leaves. Youth is the Hero who penetrates the garden and makes it alive with human music, and wins the fruit and bears it forth into the free wide world. If childhood is the golden age, youth is the heroic age, when the heart beats high with the first consciousness of power, and the first stir of half-conscious hopes; when the earth lies before us as a field of glorious adventure, and the heaven spreads above as a space for boundless flight; before we have learned how mixed earth's armies are, how slow the conquests of truth; how seldom we can fight any battle here without wounding some we would fain succour; or win any victory in which some things precious as those borne aloft before us in triumph, are not trailed in the dust behind us, dishonoured and lost.

Not that the most vivid and golden hopes of youth are delusions. God forbid that I should blaspheme His writing on the heart by thinking so for an instant! It is but that the Omniscient, who knows the glorious End that is to be, sets us in youth on the mountain-tops to breathe the pure air of heaven, foreshortening the intervening distance from these heights of hope and by its sunny haze, as eternity foreshortens it to Him; that, forgetting the things that are behind, and overspanning the things that are between, every brave and trusting heart may go down into the battle-field strong in the promise of the End, of the Triumph of Truth that shall yet surely be, and of the Kingdom of Righteousness that shall one day surely come.

Such, at least, was youth to us; to Lettice Davenant, and Roger, and me. And, looking back, this sunny time of youth seems all gathered up into those six months before the beginning of the Civil War.

For we were continually meeting through that summer; and the land was quiet. At least so it seemed to us at Netherby.

The king had granted Triennial Parliaments; had granted that this Parliament should never be dissolved like its predecessors by his arbitrary will, but only with its own consent; had seemed, indeed, ready to grant anything. Strafford, the strong prop of his despotism, had fallen; Archbishop Laud, his instigator to all the petty irritations of tyranny, which had well-nigh driven the nation mad, lay helpless in the Tower; the unjust judges, who had decreed the evil decrees about ship-money, had fled, disgraced, beyond the seas. What then might not be hoped, if not from the king's active good-will, at least from his passive consent? There had, indeed, been an attempt to bring Pym and Hampden into the royal councils, and if this had not quite succeeded, at least the patriot St. John was solicitor-general.

During much of the summer, after assenting to everything the Parliament proposed, the king sojourned in Scotland. It was true that the reports that reached us thence were not altogether satisfactory. There were rumours of army-plots encouraged in the highest quarters; rumours of some dark plot called "The Incident," intending treachery against Argyle and others; of His Majesty going with five hundred armed men to the Scottish Parliament, to the great offence of all Edinburgh; rumours that the English Parliament, hearing of "The Incident," had demanded a guard against similar outrages, if any "flagitious persons" should attempt them.

But for the most part, hope predominated over fear with us at Netherby. One thing was certain; a Parliament alive to every rumour stood on guard for the nation at St. Stephen's, vowed together by a solemn "Protestation" to do or suffer ought rather than yield our ancient rights and liberties, and until the note of warning came thence, the nation might peacefully pursue its daily work; not asleep, indeed, and with arms not out of reach, but for the present called not to contend, but to work and wait.

There was just enough of stir in the air, and of storm in the sky, to quicken every movement without impeding it; to take all languor out of leisure, to make moments of intercourse more precious, and friendships ripen more quickly.

We were still one nation, we owned one law, one throne, one national council. We were still one national Church, gathering weekly in one house of prayer; kneeling, at least at Easter, although with some scruples, around one Holy Table; together confessing ourselves to have "gone astray like lost sheep;" together giving thanks for our "creation and redemption;" kneeling reverently, and with one voice saying, "Our Father which art in heaven;" together standing as confessors of one Catholic faith, and with one voice repeating the ancient creeds; together praying (in the words ordered in King James' reign) for our sovereign lord King Charles, and (in the form his own reign first appointed) for the High Court of Parliament, under him assembled.

There were indeed words and postures and vestments which were not to the liking of all, which to some were signs of irritating defeat and to others of petty triumph; but in general—especially since the Book of Sports had been silenced, and Archbishop Laud had been kept quiet (and Mr. Nicholls had forsaken his more novel practices)—there was a strong tide of truth and devotion in the ancient services, which swept all true and devout hearts along with it.

And besides, there was, at this period, with some of the Puritans, a hope of peacefully affecting some slight further reformation, so that even Aunt Dorothy was less controversial than usual; contenting herself with an occasional warning against going down to Egypt for horses, or against Achans in the camp, and an occasional hope that, while his words were smoother than butter, the enemy had not war in his heart. But she did not distinctly explain whether by these Achans and Egyptian cavalry she meant Mr. Nicholls, Placidia, Lady Lucy, Lettice or the king; or, on the other hand, the little band of Separatists or Brownists whom we met from time to time coming from their worship in a cottage on the outskirts of the village, against whom she considered my Father not a little remiss in his magisterial duty. These apparently inoffensive people were suspected of Anabaptist tendencies. Aunt Gretel even associated them in her own mind with some very dangerous characters of the same name at Münster. It was, indeed, the utmost stretch of her toleration, to connive at our Bob and Tib's occasional attendance at their assemblies; but the consideration of Tib's discreet years, and Bob's discreet character, and Aunt Dorothy's somewhat indiscreet zeal, had hitherto induced her to do so, her conscience being further fortified by my Father's solemn promise to bring these sectaries to justice if ever they showed the slightest tendency towards polygamy or homicide. They consisted chiefly of small freeholders and independent hand-workers, the tailor, the village carpenter, and at the head, Job Forster, the blacksmith; Tib and Bob were, I think, the only household servants among them. They were few, poor, and quiet, doing nothing at their meetings, it seemed, but read the Bible, listen to one reading or explaining it, and praying: some among them having scruples as to whether it might not be a carnal indulgence to sing hymns. Occasionally they were strengthened by the visit of a preacher of their way of thinking from Suffolk, where the sect was more numerous. They were good to each other; not hurtful to any one else. They would certainly, every one of them, have died or gone into destitute exile for the minutest scruple of their belief or disbelief, being satisfied that every thread of the broidered work of their tabernacle was as divinely ordered as the tables of the law written with the finger of God. But as yet there was nothing to show what their enthusiasm would do when it was enkindled to action, instead of smouldering in passive endurance; nothing to show what germs of vigorous life lay dormant in that little company, each holding his commission, as he believed, direct from God. Yet from these, and such as these, at the touch of Oliver Cromwell, sprang into life that crop of Ironsides terrible as Samsons, chaste as Sir Galahad, unyielding as Elijah before the threats of Jezebel, unsparing as Elijah with the prophets of Jezebel on Carmel, which overthrew power after power in the state; made England the greatest power in the world;

and if the only human hand that could command it had been immortal, might have ruled England and the world to this day.

So many hidden germs of life lie around us undeveloped everywhere. In the primeval forests of this, our New England, when one race of trees is felled, a succession of another kind springs up self-sown in their stead. If the first had *not* been felled what would have become of the seeds of the second? Would they have perished, or waited dormant through the ages, till their hour should come?

But I am creeping back to Roger's ancient puzzle of Necessity, wherewith he bewildered me of old as we sat in the apple-tree at Netherby.

And after all, however these things be, it is only the king's ministers that are changed in the universal government of the nations. The King never dies.

Meantime these sectaries were the only outward schism in the unity of the Church and Nation, as represented at Netherby. Korahs, Dathans, and Abirams, Aunt Dorothy called them, or (when she was most displeased) "Anabaptists," and would (theoretically) have liked them to be made examples of in some striking and uncomfortable way; harmless enthusiasts my Father called them, and let them alone; well-meaning persons with dangerous tendencies, Aunt Gretel considered them, and made them possets and broth when they were ill. In Lady Lucy's eyes they were misguided schismatics; in Sir Walter's, self-conceited fools; in Harry Davenant's, vulgar fanatics. Of all our circle, I think, none cared to find out what they really meant and wanted, except Roger, who, especially after his great trouble, had always the most earnest desire not to misjudge any one; or, indeed, to *judge* any one as from a judgment-seat above them. And Roger said they believed they had found God, and were living in His Presence, as truly as Moses, or Elijah, or any to whom He appeared of old, which made everything else seem to them infinitely small in comparison; that they wanted, above all things, to do what God commanded, whenever they knew what it was, which made every homeliest duty on the way towards that end seem to them part of the "service of the sanctuary," any mountain of difficulty but as the small dust of the balance; every obstacle as the chaff before the whirlwind. Convictions which gave an invincible power of endurance, and could give a tremendous force of achievement, as events proved.

To this better estimate of them, Roger was, no doubt, partly led by his friendship for Job Forster. Job, indeed, through the whole of these six months, so calm and full of hope to us at Netherby, continued to forebode storms. "The weather was brewed," he said, "on the hills and by the sea; and folks who were bred on the flats, out of sight of sea and hills, and who only knew one-half of the world, could not reasonably be expected to understand the signs of the sky. The Lord, in his belief, had plenty of work to do on his anvil yet, before the swords were beaten into ploughshares and the spears into pruning-hooks. It was more likely the ploughshares would have to be beaten into swords, and pruning-hooks into spears."

And the village coulters, spades, and mattocks, received from Job's hammer treatment all the more vigorous on account of the warlike figures they supplied.

Moreover, Rachel, his wife, looking out from her chamber-window one stormy night across the Fens, had seen wonders in the heavens, black-plumed clouds, marshalled like armies, rolling far away to the east, till the rising sun smote them to a blood-red; while high above, from behind these, one white-winged arm, as of an archangel swept across the sky untouched by the red glow of battle, raised majestically, as if to warn or to smite.

"There is something terrible going on somewhere," she had said, "or else something terrible to come."

And Job, to whom Rachel's words had always a tender sacredness in them, woven of the old reverence of our northern race for the prophet-woman; of sacred memories of the inspired songs of Deborah and Hannah, interpreted by his belief that the people of the Bible were not exceptional but typical; and of his own strong love for her—believed Rachel's visions with entire unconsciousness how much they were reflections of his own convictions. "How," he would say, "could a feeble creature like her, nurtured and cherished like a babe, and busy all her life in naught but enduring sicknesses or doing kindnesses, know aught of wars and battle-fields, unless it was of the Lord?" So Job foreboded, and we hoped, and the summer months passed on.

Scarcely a day passed on which we and the Davenants did not meet, especially Roger, and Lettice, and I; for Roger had taken his degree, and having overworked at it, was constrained to be idle for a while; and the boy Davenants were most of the time in London. At church, at the Hall, at the Manor, riding, coursing, hay-making, nutting, boating on the Mere; on rainy days, hunting out wonderful old illuminated manuscripts in Sir Walter's library, or by the organ in my Father's, singing glees and madrigals; making essays at Italian poetry, generally resulting in translations, metrical or otherwise, by Roger, for Lettice's benefit. Lettice reigning in all things, by a thousand indisputable royal rights; as pupil; as sovereign lady; as the youngest; as the most adventurous; as the most timid; by right of her need of care, and her clinging to protection; by right of minority, she being one, and we two; by right of her true constancy and her little seeming ficklenesses; by right of her brilliant, ever-changing beauty, and all her nameless, sweet, tyrannical, winning, willful ways; by right of all her generous self-forgetfulness, and delight to give pleasure; and firstly and lastly, by right of the subtle power which, through all these charms, stole into Roger's heart, and took possession of it, unchallenged and unresisted, then and for ever.

We spoke little of politics. Lettice never had any, except loyalty to the king; and at this time her loyalty was sorely tried by reason of her perplexity and distress at what seemed to her the ungenerous desertion of Strafford in his need.

There were no forbidden topics between us. There was one, indeed, which by tacit mutual consent we always avoided, and that was all that concerned Sir Launcelot Trevor. Lettice, always scenting from afar the least symptom of what could pain, never approached what had been the cause of so much anguish to Roger; and me she never freed from the suspicion of a certain sisterly injustice in my sentiments towards my brother's enemy. But a very insignificant and unnecessary chamber indeed was this to be locked out of the palace of delights through which we three roamed at will together. Nor can I remember one pang of vexation at my own falling from the first place to the second in Roger's thoughts. If I had not loved Lettice on my own account as I did, there was nothing in Roger's love for her that could have sown one miserable seed of jealousy in my heart. If he loved her most, he was more to me than ever before. The reflection of his tender reverence for her fell like a glory on all women for her sake. He was more to all for being most to her. Mean calculations of more or less, better or best, could not enter into comparison in affections stamped with such a sweet diversity. All true love expands, not narrows; strengthens, not weakens; anoints the eyes with eye-salve, not blinds; opens the heart, and opens the world, and transfigures the universe into an enchanted palace and treasure-house of joys, simply by giving the key to unlock its chambers, and the vision to see its treasures.

This was the innermost heart of the joy of those our halcyon days, that Roger and Lettice and I were together. We three made for ourselves our new Atlantis. We should have made it equally in the dingiest street of London city. Only, there the joy within us would have had to transform our world into a paradise. At Netherby, riding over the fields with the fresh air in our faces, or roaming the musical woods, or skimming the Mere while Roger rowed, and dipping our hands in the cool waters, or talking endlessly on the fragrant garden terraces of the Manor and the Hall, it had not to transform, only to translate.

Outside this inner world of our own lay a bright and friendly world all around us. First, our Father, sweet Lady Lucy, and Aunt Gretel—scarcely indeed outside, except by the fact of their not quite understanding what we had within, regarding us, as they fondly did, as dear happy children not yet out of our paradise of childhood; next Aunt Dorothy, Job Forster, and Rachel, guarding us as fondly, though anxiously, as on the unconscious eve of encounter with our dragons and leviathans; and beyond, the village, of which we were the children; the country, which was our mother; the world, of which we were the heirs. For to us in those days there were no harassing Philistines, no crushing Babylon; no Egyptians behind, nor Red Sea before. The world was to be conquered, but not as a prostrate foe, rather as a willing tributary to Truth and

Right. The kings of Tarshish and of the isles were to bring presents; Sheba and Seba were to offer gifts. The wilderness and the solitary place were to be glad for us, and the desert was to rejoice and blossom as the rose.

Meanwhile Lady Lucy came back to her old place in my heart. Her sweet motherliness seemed to brood like the wings of a dove over our whole happy world.

Harry Davenant came more than once to the Hall, and stayed a few days, to Lady Lucy's perfect content, and entered into our pursuits as keenly as any of us. Only with him there was always an undertone of sadness, a despondency about the country and the world, a bitterness about the times, a slight cynicism about men and women, inevitable, perhaps, to a noble spirit like his, which (as it seems to me) has lost its way, and strayed into the backward current, contrary to all the generous forward movements of the age; but strongly contrasted with the steadfast, hopeful temper no danger could daunt and no defeat could damp, which characterized the nobler spirits on the patriot side. The noble Sir Bevil Grenvill had bitter thoughts of his contemporaries; the generous Lord Falkland craved for peace and welcomed death. Eliot, Pym, Hampden, Cromwell, Milton, looked for liberty; believed in the triumph of truth; thought England worth fighting for, living for, if needful, dying for; they braved death indeed like heroes, they met it like Christians, but they did not long for it like men sick and hopeless of the world. If God had willed it so, they had rather have lived on, because of the great hopes that inspired them, because they believed that not fate nor the devil were at the heart of the world, or at the head of the nations; but God.

Yet about such men as Harry Davenant there was an inexpressible fascination. There is something that irresistibly touches the heart in heroism which, like Hector's of Troy, is nourished, not by hope, but by duty; which sacrifices self in a cause which it believes no courage and no sacrifice can make victorious, and bates no jot of heart when all hope has fled.

And to me he was always so gentle a friend. We had so many things in common; our love for his Mother, his reverence for my Father's goodness, justice, and wisdom; his generous appreciation of Roger; a certain protecting, shielding tenderness we both had for Lettice, who was, indeed, a creature so tender, and dependent, and willful, so likely to rush into trouble, so sure to feel it, that no womanly heart could help feeling motherlike toward her.

Yet there always seemed a kind of half-acknowledged barrier between us, even from the first, more distinctly acknowledged afterwards, which gave a strange mixture of frankness and reserve, of nearness and separation, to our intercourse; wherein, perhaps, lay something of its charm.

And across this world of ours flashed from time to time during those months lofty visions of nobleness and wisdom from other spheres; especially during the last six weeks when the Parliament was in recess, and many a worthy head found a night's shelter in the guest-chamber at Netherby.

Mr. Hampden was in Scotland as Parliamentary Commissioner, keeping watch over the king; Mr. Pym, at his lodgings in Gray's Inn Lane, keeping guard for the nation. But Mr. Cromwell went home in the recess to his family at Ely, and spent some hours with us on his way back to London. He was forty-two years old then, my Father said, and his hair was not without some tinge of gray; tall, all but six feet in stature, and firmly knit. Many things seemed to lie hidden in the depths of his grave eyes; a subdued fire of temper flashing forth at times sufficiently to show that at the heart of this gravity lay not ice but fire; a hearty humour, as of a soul at liberty, grasping its purpose firmly enough to be able to give it play—keen to descry likenesses in things unlike, inner differences in things similar, absurdities in things decorous, and the meaning of men and things in general through all seemings. Yet withal, capacities and traces of heart-deep sorrow, as of one who had looked into the depths on many sides and found them unfathomable. Moreover, above all, his were eyes which *saw;* not merely windows through which you looked into the soul. Aunt Gretel said there was a look in him which made her think of a portrait of Dr. Luther which she had seen in her youth. He loved music, too, which was another resemblance to Dr. Luther. He was always kind to us children, and now he spoke fondly of his two "little wenches" at home—Bridget (afterwards Mistress Ireton), a little beyond my age, and Elizabeth (Mistress Claypole), then about eleven, his dearly-loved daughter; and the two blithe little ones, Mary and Frances, about five and three. Methought his eyes rested with a sorrowful yearning on Roger; and my Father told us, after he left, he had only two years before, in May, buried his eldest son Robert, about nineteen, which was Roger's age. This son was buried far from home, at Felsted Church in Essex; a youth whose promise had been so great that the parson of the parish where he died had inserted a record of him in the parish register, which reads like a fond epitaph amidst the dry unbroken list of names and dates. Mr. Cromwell spoke also with much reverence of his aged mother, who dwelt in his house at Ely.

Mr. Cromwell was full of a firm confidence in the future of the church and the country; but, like Job Forster, he seemed to think there was much to be done and gone through before the end was gained. On his way through the village he had held some converse with Job Forster while having his horse shod; and he said something of such men as Job being the men for a Parliament army, if ever such an army should be needed.

Whilst Job, on his part, as he told us afterwards, was deeply moved by his interview with Mr. Cromwell. "He was a man," said Job, "who had been in the depths, and had brought thence the sacred fire, which made two or three of his words worth a hundred spoken by common men."

Then towards the close of that happy time there was one evening in Octobėr which lingers on my memory as its golden sunset lingered on the many-coloured autumn woods.

We were standing on the terrace at Netherby, overlooking the orchard, Roger, Lettice, and I, in the fading light; Lettice twining some water-lilies Roger had just gathered from the pond. Through the embayed window of the wainscoted parlour, which stood open, poured forth the music of my Father's organ, in chords rich and changing as the colours of the sunset on wood, and meadow, and Mere.

Mr. John Milton was the musician, and as the intertwined harmonies flowed from his hands

> "In linked sweetness long drawn out,
> His melting voice through mazes running,
> Untwisted all the chains that tie
> The hidden soul of harmony."

As we listened, enrapt by the power of the music, which seemed

> "Dead things with imbreathèd sense, able to pierce,
> And to our high-raised phantasy present
> That undisturbed song of pure concent
> Aye sung before the sapphire-coloured throne
> To Him that sits thereon."—

the lilies dropped from Lettice's fingers, and she

sat like the statue of a listening nymph; the knitting fell from Aunt Gretel's lap, and the tears came into her eyes, and, thinking of my mother, she murmured "Magdalene!" Roger and I were leaning on the window-sill, and all of us were so unconscious of anything present, that Lady Lucy had advanced from the other end of the terrace near enough to touch me on the arm without my hearing a footstep.

By her side stood a courtly-looking young clergyman, with dark hair flowing from under his velvet cap, and dark, meditative eyes, yet with much light of smiles hidden in them, like dew in violets. Him she introduced as "Dr. Taylor, one of His Majesty's chaplains." He was not yet eight-and-twenty years of age, but was in mourning for his first wife, but lately dead.

Mr. Milton joined us soon with my Father. He was a few years older than Dr. Taylor, but in appearance much more youthful; with his brown un-Puritan love-locks, his short stature, his face determined, almost to severity, yet delicate as a beautiful woman's.

And then between these two, while we listened, ensued an hour's converse, like the antiphons of some heavenly choir.

Names of ancient heroes and philosophers—Egyptian, Assyrian, Greek, Latin—dropped from their lips like household words. Until at last they rose into a chorus in praise of liberty, of conscience, and of thought; Dr. Taylor, I thought, basing his argument more on the dimness of human vision, and

Mr. Milton on the inherent and victorious might of truth. Dr. Taylor pleading for a charitable tolerance for error, Mr. Milton for a generous freedom for truth; the which converse I often recalled when, in after years, we read the Liberty of Prophesying by the one, and the Liberty of Printing by the other.

As they spoke, the glory faded from the sky and the golden autumnal woods, and when they ceased, and we stepped from the terrace into the gloom of the dark wainscoted parlour, it seemed to me as if we had stepped out of a fragrant and melodious elysium into a farm-yard, so homely and unmeaning, like the cacklings or lowings of animals, did all common discourse seem afterwards.

The next day, when Mr. Milton had left us, and we were speaking together of this discourse, Aunt Gretel said it was like beautiful music, only, being mostly in a kind of Latin, was, of course, beyond her comprehension. Aunt Dorothy only consoled herself for what she regarded as the dangerous licence of their conclusions, by the thought that their path to them was too fantastic and fine for any common mortals to tread. And my Father said afterwards that it seemed to him as if Dr. Taylor's learning and fancy hung around his reason like the jewelled state-trappings of a royal palfrey; you wondered how his wit could move so nimbly under such a weight of ornament; whilst Mr. Milton's learning and imagination were like wings to the strong Pegasus of his wisdom, only helping him to soar. When Dr. Taylor spoke of the learned stories of the ancients, they seemed like a treasury wherewith to adorn his fancies or to wing his airy shafts. But to Mr. Milton they seemed an armory common to him and to the wise men of whom he spoke, and to which he had as free access as they; to draw thence weapons for his warfare and theirs, and to add thereto for the generations to come.

Yet brilliant and glowing as their speech was, Roger would have it that Mr. Cromwell's brief and rugged words had in them more of the red heat that fuses the weapons wherewith the great battles of life are fought. For we spoke often of that evening, Roger, and Lettice, and I, in the few short days that remained of our golden age of peace.

Scarcely a fortnight after that evening at Netherby, tidings of the Irish massacre thrilled through all the land with one shudder of horror and helpless indignation for the past; awakening one bitter cry for rescue and vengeance in the future.

On the 20th of October the Parliament had met again.

It was a gray and comfortless evening early in November when a Post spurred into the village of Netherby, and stopped at Job Forster's forge to have some slight repair made in the gear of his horse.

Rachel was there immediately with a jug of ale for the weary rider and water for his horse. The horseman took both in silence.

"Thou art scant of greetings to-day, good-master," said Job, as he busied himself about the broken bit, without looking in the rider's face.

But Rachel, who had caught in an instant the weight of heavy tidings on the stranger's face, laid her hand with a silencing gesture on her husband's arm.

Then Job looked up, and meeting the horseman's eye, dropped the bit, and said abruptly,—

"What tidings, master? We are not of those who look for smooth things."

"Rough enough," was the reply. "A hundred thousand Protestants,* men, women, and children, surprised, and robbed, and massacred in Ireland, scarce more than a sennight agone. At morning, met with good-days and friendly looks by the Papists around them; before evening, driven from their burning homes, naked and destitute, into the roads and wildernesses. Thousands murdered amidst their ruined homes; happy those who were only murdered, or murdered quickly; no mercy on age or sex, no memory of kindness; treachery and torture; women and little children turning into fiends of cruelty. Dublin itself only saved by one who gave warning the evening before. But the worst was for the women, and the little helpless tortured babes."

"Softly, softly, master," said Job; for Rachel had fallen on his shoulder fainting. "She can bear to

* This was the number commonly believed among us at the time. Since I have heard it disputed. But that the slaughter and the atrocities were terrible, there can be no doubt.

hear any dreadful thing, or to see any dreadful sight, if she can be of any help; but this is too much for her."

Gently he bore her in and laid her on the bed, and hesitated an instant what to do, not liking to leave her.

"She always seems to know whether it's me or any one else, even when she's clean gone like this," he said; "but yet I dare not hinder the Post."

"Leave her to me, Job," I said; "she'll not feel strange with me."

And after a moment's further pause, lifting her into an easier position, he went out.

Sprinkling water on her face and chafing her hands, breathing on her lips and temples, as I had seen Aunt Gretel do in such a case, I had the comfort of soon seeing Rachel languidly open her eyes. For a moment there was a bewildered, inquiring look in them, but quickly it gave place to a mournful collectedness.

"I knew it—I knew it, Mistress Olive!" she said, "I knew something must come. But I thought the judgment would fall on the Lord's enemies; and Job and I have been pleading with Him for mercy, even on them. I never thought the sword would fall on the sheep of His pasture. Least of all on the lambs," she added; "on the innocent lambs. But maybe, after all, that *was* His mercy. They are but gone home by a cruel path, poor innocents—only gone home." Then a burst of tears came to her relief; a neighbour came in to help; and I left to go home without further delay.

The few minutes which I had spent at Rachel Forster's bedside had sufficed to gather all the village around the forge; women with babies in their arms and little ones clinging to their skirts; men on their way home from the day's labour with spades and mattocks on their shoulders; the tailor needle in hand; the miller white from the mill; women with hands full of dough from the kneading-trough; none waiting to lay aside an implement, none left hehind but the bedridden, yet none asking a question, or uttering an exclamation, as they passed around the messenger, drinking in the horrible details of the slaughter. Only, in the pauses, a long-drawn breath, or now and then a suppressed sob from the women.

Job meanwhile continued, as was his wont, working his feelings into the task he had in hand, so that long before the villagers were weary of listening while the Post told the cruel particulars, heightening the excitement and deepening the silence, the bit was mended, every weak point of hoof or harness had undergrone Job's skillful inspection, and offering the messenger another draught at the beer-can, he said to him in his abrupt way,—

"Whither next, master? We may not delay such tidings."

"I have letters for Squire Drayton of Netherby Manor," was the reply.

"Trust them to me," said Roger.

"The best hands you can trust them to," said Job.

In consideration of the urgent need of haste, the

Post gave us a letter in Dr. Antony's writing to Roger, and in another minute was out of sight beyond the turn of the village street.

A little murmur arose among the village-gossips. "No need for breaking a Post short like that, goodman Forster," said the miller's wife; "sure he knows his own business best."

"What did we need to hear *more*, goodwife?" was Job's reply. "All England has to hear it yet! Thousand of prayers have to be stirred up throughout the land before night. And haven't we heard enough to make this night a night of watching? Hearkening to fearful tales helps little; and talking less. For this kind goeth not out but with prayer and fasting."

And Job turned away into his cottage. But as Roger and I hastened up the street, the village had already broken into little eager groups, and the words, "the Irish Popish Army," and "the Popish Queen," came with bitter emphasis from many voices.

Deep was the excitement at home when we brought the terrible tidings. Dr. Antony's letter too dreadfully confirmed them, telling how the House of Commons received the news, brought in by one O'Conolly, in an awe-stricken silence; how nearly all Ulster, the head-quarters of the Protestants, was still in the hands of the insurgents; the towns and villages in flames.

"Tilly and Magdeburg!" were the first words that broke from my Father's lips. "The same strife, the same weapons, the same fiendish cruelty, in the name of the All Pitiful. If such another conflict is indeed to come, God send England weapons as good wherewith to wage it; soldiers that can pray; and, if such can be twice in one generation, another Gustavus!"

Fervently he pleaded that night together with the gathered household for the robbed and bereaved sufferers in Ireland. Far into the night Roger saw the lamp burning in his window. No doubt he had sought Job Forster's Refuge.

But the next morning, when we came in to breakfast, he had taken down the old sword he had worn through the German wars; and was trying its edge.

"The good God keep us from war, Brother!" said Aunt Gretel, trembling at the thoughts that old weapon recalled, "I was thinking we might search out our stores for woolseys and linseys. They will be sure to be sending such to the poor sufferers, and they will be building orphan houses."

"Citadels have to be built and kept first!" said my Father. "There are times when war is as much a work of mercy as clothing the naked and feeding the hungry."

"But war with *whom*, Brother?" said Aunt Dorothy, pointedly. "It is little use lopping the branches and sparing the tree. What has become of the Irish Popish army the king was so loth to dismiss? Of what avail is it to smite a few poor blind fanatics, when the Popish queen and her Jesuits rule in the Palace? It wearies me to the heart to hear of honest men like Mr. Hampden, Mr. Pym, and all of them, impeaching Lord Strafford and imprisoning Archbishop Laud, who, I believe (poor deluded man), thought himself doing God's service; and yet kissing the hand that appointed Laud and Strafford, and would sign death-warrants for every patriot and Puritan in the kingdom to-night, if it were safe."

"Mr. Hampden, Mr. Pym, and Mr. Cromwell are doing their best to make it *not* safe, Sister Dorothy," was my Father's reply. "And meantime there is more strength in silence than in invective."

"A Parliament of women," said Aunt Dorothy, "would have gone to the point months since, and let the king understand what they meant."

"Probably," said my Father, "but the great thing is to *gain* the point."

Unusually early in the day for her, Lady Lucy appeared at the Manor, with Harry and Lettice walking beside her horse.

She looked very pale as my Father led her into the wainscoted parlour.

"Mr. Drayton," she said, "who ever could have dreamed of such tidings! The only ray of comfort is that they may help to unite our distracted country. There can be but one mind throughout the land about such deeds as these. The king went at once to the Scottish Parliament with the news, to seek their counsel and aid. Now at least the king, parliament, and nation, will be one in their indignation."

"It would be well if the king had dismissed before this the Irish Catholic army which Lord

Strafford raised for him," said my Father. "It is well known that its officers have been in communication with the assassins."

"The king did send orders to disband it long since," she said.

"Yes, *public* orders," my Father replied; "but there are rumours of secret instructions having accompanied, not precisely to the same effect."

"Rumours!" she said eagerly; "Mr. Drayton, mere rumours! You are too just and generous to listen to a vulgar report, with the king's word against it."

"Madam," he replied, very gravely, "it would have been the salvation of the country long since if the king's word had been a sufficient reply to attacks on his policy. There is nothing so revolutionary as falsehood in high places."

"You call the king a revolutionist?" she said.

"I call untruth the great revolutionist," he replied. "Without truth and trust all communities must ultimately fall to pieces, with more or less noise, according as they are assailed by a strong hand from without, or simply crumble from within. The ruin is certain."

"But all good men must be agreed in detesting these barbarous deeds," she said. "Even the Earl of Castlehaven, a Catholic, has said that all the water in the sea would not wash off from the Irish the stain of their treacherous murders in a time of settled peace."

"No doubt there are Catholics, madam, who speak the truth and hate injustice," said my Father.

"You are unjust, you are cruel to His Majesty," she said, with tears in her eyes, "if you could be unjust or cruel to any one."

"Lady Lucy," he replied, "this is a time for all men who fear God and love England to be united. Would Lord Strafford (could he come back among us) contradict the words wrung from him when the king signed his death-warrant? Would he say, 'Put your trust in princes?'"

Harry Davenant passionately interposed.

"It is too bad to drive the king to actions he detests, and then to reproach him for them. He would have saved Lord Strafford, as all men know, if he could. It is the distrust of the country that has compelled the king to have recourse to subtleties no gentleman would choose."

"Harry Davenant," said my Father, "I am confident no measure of unjust distrust would drive you to the policy of making promises you never meant to keep."

"My life is simple, sir," was the mournful reply, "and it is my own. If I choose any evil to myself, rather than go from my word, or imply the thing I do not mean, I am at liberty to do so. But the king's life is manifold. He stands before the Highest with the nation gathered up into his single person. He stands above the nation as the anointed representative of the King of kings. God himself is only indirectly King of nations by being King of kings. He stands between the past and the future with a sacred trust of prerogative and right to guard and transmit. It is not for us to apply the standards of our private morality to him."

"Apply the standards of Divine morality to all!" said my Father. "Truth is the pillar of heaven as well as of earth. There is no bond of society like a trusted word."

"At least, sir," rejoined Harry Davenant, gently but loftily, "it is not for me who eat the king's bread to say or hear ought disloyal to him. Nor will I." And he rose to leave.

My Father held out his hand to grasp his.

"One word more," he said, "disloyalty is a terrible word, and we may hear more of it in these coming years. Let me say to you, once for all, the question is not of loyalty or disloyalty, but to whom our loyalty is due. I believe it is to England and her laws; to the king if he is faithful to these."

"What tribunal can judge the king?" Harry Davenant replied.

"More than one," said my Father, solemnly. "The English laws he has sworn to maintain; the eternal Lawgiver from whom you say he holds his crown, whose laws of truth and equity are no secret, and are as binding on the peasant as the prince."

Lady Lucy's manner had a peculiar tenderness in it to me as she wished me good-bye.

"Very difficult times, Olive!" she said, kissing me; "but we will remember women have one work at all times; to make peace and pour balm into wounds."

And Lettice whispered to me and Roger,—

"Don't believe those wicked things about the king, or I shall not be able to come to Netherby."

Roger looked sorely perplexed.

"But how can we help believing them," he said, "if we find them true?"

"I can always help believing things I don't like," she said. "Wishing is half way to believing." And she slipped away, leaving a very heavy shadow on Roger's face as he turned back to the house.

"Not quite so clear, Olive," said Aunt Dorothy, when I repeated to her Lady Lucy's words as a proof of her good will. "There are times when Deborah is as necessary as Barak, and more so. And then there was Judith, a valiant and godly woman, although she is in the Apocrypha. And there are times when the knife is kinder than all the balm in Gilead."

"Knives are never safe, however," added my Father, "except in hands that use them for the same purpose as the balms."

The intercourse of the two families did not cease after that little debate. It rather became more frequent. The uneasy consciousness of the many public differences that might at any time sever us, only made us cling the more tenaciously, although with trembling, to the private ties that united us. For a fortnight after the Irish tidings reached us, Lady Lucy, Aunt Gretel, and even Aunt Dorothy, found a practical bond of union in collecting all the clothes and provisions they could send to the sufferers by the Irish massacre.

Then came the news of divisions in the patriot party in the Parliament, with reference to the framing and printing of the Grand Remonstrance, voted to be printed on the 8th of December. Lady Lucy dwelt much on the conciliatory intentions of the king, on the feastings and welcomes prepared for him in the city of London, and especially on the defection of the gallant Sir Bevil Granvill, Lord Falkland, and Mr. Hyde, from the popular cause. "All moderate men," she said, "felt it was becoming the cause of disorder, and were abandoning it; and my Father, the most moderate and candid of men, would not, she was sure, remain with a little knot of fanatics and levellers."

That Christmas-tide the Grand Remonstrance, with its long list of royal and ecclesiastical oppressions, and its statement of the recent victories of Parliament over evil laws and evil councillors, was read and eagerly debated at every fire-side in the kingdom.

"But what do they want?" Lady Lucy would say. "They seem, from their own statements, to have gained all they sought."

"They want *security* for everything!" my Father would reply, "security for what they have won; a guard of their own appointing to keep them free, to secure them against the guard of his own appointing, with which they believe the king is endeavouring to surround and make them prisoners."

"Will no promises, no assurances of good-will satisfy them?" she said. "They have sent ten more prelates to keep the archbishop company in the

Tower. What further guarantees would they demand?"

"It is hard indeed," he said, sorrowfully, "for all the concessions in the world to restore broken confidence. All the fortresses in England, or a standing army of a million, would not be such a safeguard to the king as his own word might have been. There is no cement in heaven or earth strong enough to restore trust in broken faith."

"It is not always so easy to be sincere," she said, "and God forgives and trusts us again and again."

"God forgives because he sees," he said. "Nations are not omniscient, and therefore cannot forgive, nor trust when they have been betrayed."

"The Parliament is unreasonable," she said, with tears in her eyes; "they judge like private gentlemen. Statesmen and princes cannot speak with the simple candour of private men. Politics are like chess. You would not confide every move beforehand to your enemy."

"The King and the Parliament do not profess to be on opposite sides of the game," he replied. "But if, in fact, it has come to that, can you wonder at any amount of mutual suspicion? Yet our Puritan faith is, that there is but one law of truth and equity in heaven and earth for prince, soldier, peasant, woman, and child. And I believe that, even with hostile nations, not all the diplomatic subtleties in the world would give us the strength there is in a trusted word. Let it once be felt of man or nation, 'They have said it, therefore they mean it;' and they have a strength nothing else can give.

There must be two threads to weave a web of false policy. Withdraw one, and the other falls to pieces of itself. I believe the ruler who could make the word of an Englishman a proverb for truth, would do more for the strength of England than one who won her fortresses on every island and coast in the world."

"But see how the king trusts the people, Mr. Drayton," she said. "His presence in that very tumultuous disorderly city ought to make them believe him."

"I do not see that His Majesty has had reason to distrust the people," my Father replied.

"Ah!" she sighed; "if you had only seen His Majesty amidst his family, his chivalrous tenderness to the queen, his native stateliness all laid aside in playful fondness for his children."

"It might have made it more painful to have to distrust him as a king," my Father replied. "It could scarcely have made it more possible to trust."

"Well," she said, "either the nation will learn, ere long, to trust his gracious intentions as he deserves, or will learn to their cost what a sovereign they have distrusted!"

But scarcely a week afterwards the whole country was set in a flame by the tidings that His Majesty had gone in person—attended by five hundred armed men, many of them young desperadoes, feasted the night before at Whitehall—to arrest the five members (Pym, Hampden, Hazelrig, Denzil

Hollis, and William Strode) in the inviolate sanctuary of the nation, the Parliament House itself.

And after that my Father and Lady Lucy ceased to hold any more political debates.

He simply said, when, on the evening of those tidings, we met in the village,—

"The meaning of His Majesty's promises seems plain at last."

And she replied,—

"But if all good men distrust His Majesty, will he not be driven to trust to evil men?"

"I am afraid the course of falsehood is ever downward," he answered, very sadly, "and the breaches of just distrust ever widening."

"But, for heaven's sake, Mr. Drayton," she said, with an imploring accent, as we returned with her to the Hall, "think before you plunge into these terrible divisions."

"I have thought long, madam," he said, "for I have fought in the Thirty Years' War, and seen how war can devastate."

"But that was easy," she said, "that was church against church, state against state, prince against prince. This will be the church divided against itself, the nation divided against itself, subject against king, one good man against another. Think, if you join Mr. Hampden and Mr. Pym what noble and wise men you will have against you! (for you honour Sir Bevil Grenvill and Lord Falkland as much as we do); what violent and fanatical men with you!"

"If all good men were on one side," he said, sorrowfully, "there need be few battles in church or state."

"It seems to me," she added, "there is no party one would willingly join save that of the peacemakers."

"That indeed is the very party I would seek to join," said my Father. "But that seems to me the very party which, from ancient times, has been stigmatized as those who turn the world upside down. Since the Fall peace can seldom be reached save through conflict."

Meanwhile Roger had joined us, and Lettice, as we were about to separate, whispered to me, clasping my hands in hers,—

"They may turn the world upside down, Olive, but they shall not separate us! How happy it is for us," she said, turning to Roger, who was standing a little apart, "that, as Harry says, women have nothing to do with politics."

"I am afraid," he said, in his abrupt way, "women have often more than any to suffer from politics."

"You take things so gravely, Roger," she said. "Everything would be right if you would not all of you be so hard on people who have done a little wrong; and would only try and believe what we must all wish, and so bring it about."

"Everything will be *wrong*," said Roger, with melancholy emphasis, "if you will believe things and people because we *wish*, and not because they are true."

For Roger, true to every one, was truthful to scrupulousness with Lettice; what she was, or became, being of more moment to him than even what she thought of him.

But Lettice only laughed, and said,—

"I am not sixteen, and I have seen the country at the point of ruin, I cannot tell how many times. Other clouds have blown over, and so will this."

And she sped away to rejoin her mother, only once more turning back to wave her hand and say:

"To-morrow morning, Olive, at the Lady Well! The ice will be strong enough on the Mere for skating. To-morrow!"

But the next morning, when Roger and I went to the Lady Well, no Lettice was there.

Snow had fallen in the night.

The frozen surface of the Mere was strewn with it, except in places where it was sheltered by the overhanging brushwood, where it lay black as steel against the white banks. All the music was frozen in stream and wood. The drops, whose soft trickling into the well beneath, had floated Lettice and me into fairy-land last summer, hung in glittering silent icicles around the stone sides of the well.

And Roger and I went silently home.

"The snow has detained her," I said.

"She is not so easily turned aside from a promise," he said.

And when we reached home we found a messenger and a letter from Lettice, saying Lady Lucy had been summoned to attend the Queen at Windsor, that Lettice had accompanied her, and that Harry

Davenant and Sir Walter, being engaged about the king's person, Sir Launcelot Trevor had come to escort them.

"The Princess Mary is about to be married to the Prince of Orange," Lettice wrote; "and as the queen is to accompany her to the Low Countries, she wishes to see my mother before she leaves the country."

"It would be a good service to us all if the queen would stay away for ever," said Aunt Dorothy—and she expressed the feeling of a large part of the nation—"the king would lose the worst of his evil counsellors."

"That depends," said my Father, sadly, "on whether the king is not his own worst counsellor. If the evil has its origin in others, the queen may indeed injure him more by remaining here. But, on the other hand, she may succour him more on the Continent."

"Well, at all events," said Aunt Dorothy, "her absence may be a blessing to Lady Lucy and Mistress Lettice. For that child is not without gracious dispositions. Last week she called when every one else was out, and wishing to turn the time to account, I set her to read aloud from the sermons of good Mr. Adams; and she read two and part of the third, only twice going to the window to see if any one was coming, and never even looking up, after I once asked her if she was tired."

"Do you think she really enjoyed them, Aunt Dorothy?" I asked; knowing how difficult it was to ascertain Lettice's distastes, on account of her predominant taste of doing what pleased other people.

"I think better of the child than to deem she would seem pleased with aught she did not really like," said Aunt Dorothy; and, although unconvinced, I rejoiced that Aunt Dorothy had fallen under the spell.

"What did she say?" I asked.

"The first sermon was 'The Spiritual Navigator Bound for the Holy Land,' about the glassy sea; and she said it was near as pretty reading as Spenser's 'Faery Queen'—a remark which, though it showed some lack of spiritual discernment, was something, in that it showed she was entertained. The second was 'Heaven's Gate;' and when we came to the place about the gate being in our own heart,—'Great manors have answerable porches. Heaven must needs be spacious, when a little star fixed in a far lower orb exceeds the earth in quantity; yet it hath a low gate, not a lofty coming in.' And she said she had thought the Gate of Heaven was only opened when we die, not here while we live, and it was a strange thing to think on. The third sermon was 'Semper Idem, the Immutable Mercy of Jesus Christ,' and in that we did not read far; for when she read 'the sun of divinity is the Scripture, the sun of Scripture is the gospel, the sun of the gospel is Jesus Christ. Nor is this the centre of his word only, but of our rest. Thou hast made us for thee, O Christ, and the heart is unquiet till it rest in thee; seeking, we may find Him—he is ready; finding, we may still seek Him; he is infinite,'—her voice trembled, and with tears in her eyes, she looked up and said, 'I suppose that is what the other sermon means by *entering the Gate of Heaven now.*' And I deem that a wise thing for a child to say, brought up as she has been under the very walls of Babylon. And the poor young thing's ways pleased me so that I gave her the three sermons to keep. And she promised to set store by them, and treasure them in a cedarn box she hath, together with some books by Dr. Taylor. And although Dr. Taylor is an Arminian, I had not the heart to cross the child. Especially as books are not like us; they are none the worse for being in bad company."

But Roger made no comment. Only the next Sunday, as we were walking home from church together, he said sorrowfully—

"Oh, Olive, so ready to be pleased with everything as she is, so pleased to please every one, so sure to please, so true and generous, so ready to believe good of every one; that she should be launched into that false Court! I shall always dread to hear any one say, 'To-morrow.' If we could only have known, there were so many things one might have said or have left unsaid. The last thing I said to her seems to me now so harsh. She will always think of us as rebuking her. And her last look was a defiant little smile! If we could only know the days, or what words, are to be the last. To-morrow," he added, "she was to have met us at the old well, and now she is at the king's Court; and between us lies a great gulf of civil war; and the whole country in such tumult, it seems a kind of disloyalty to England to think of our own private sorrows."

And Roger spoke but too truly. For it is impossible to say how deeply that act of the king's in invading the Parliament had incensed the whole nation. It showed, as nothing else could have done, my Father said, that what was holy ground to the nation was mere common soil to the king. Men had borne to have soldiers illegally billeted on their homes; fathers torn, against law, from their families, and left to die in prisons. Each such act of tyranny was exceptional or partial, and might be redressed by patient appeals to our ancient laws. Much of personal liberty might be sacrificed rather than violate the order on which all true liberty is based. But the Parliament House during the sitting of the Parliament was the sacred hearth of the nation itself. Every man felt his own hearth violated in its violation. Henceforth nothing was sacred, nothing was safe, throughout the land. And from that day, my Father, dreading civil war as only a soldier can who knows what the terrors of war are, never seemed to have a doubt that it must come. Nor, candid as he was, to the verge of weakness (as Aunt Dorothy thought), in his anxiety to allow what was just to all sides, did he ever seem after that to doubt, if the strife came, on which side he must stand.

There was a strange mixture of rigid adherences to ancient forms, with the boldest spirit of liberty, in that scene in Parliament on the 3rd of January 1642.

Dr. Antony wrote us how all the members rose uncovered before the king, how the speaker on his knee beside his own chair, which the king had usurped, refused to answer His Majesty's questions as to the absence of the five members, whom his eye vainly sought in their vacant places, saying: "Please your Majesty, I have neither eyes to see, nor ears to hear, nor tongue to speak in this place, save as the House directs me." "Words," wrote Dr. Antony, "respectful enough for a courtier of Nebuchadnezzar, with a meaning as kingly as those of any Cæsar. Not a disrespectful word or gesture was directed against the king as he retired baffled from the House, saying, that he saw the birds had flown, and protesting that he had intended no breach of privilege. But before he descended the steps of the Hall to rejoin the armed guard outside, the civil war, my Father said, had begun.

The next day the king had returned baffled from another attempt to arrest the five members in the city. The aldermen, true representatives of the great merchants of England, were as resolute as the Parliament. They made His Majesty a great feast, but no concessions.

Within a week a thousand seamen from the good ships in the broad Thames had offered their services to guard the Parliament from their refuge in the city by water to Westminster, and as many 'prentices had entreated to be permitted to render a similar service by land; four thousand freeholders from

Buckinghamshire (Hampden's county) had entered London on horseback with petitions against wicked councillors, and (on the 10th of January) the king had left Whitehall for Hampden Court.

But no man knew he would not return thither until seven years later, on another January day, never to leave it more.

So few last days come to us clothed in mourning announcing themselves as the last. We step smiling into the ferry-boat which is to carry us for a little while, as we think, across the narrow stream, and wave our hands and say to those who watch us from the familiar shore, "*To-morrow!*" and before we are aware the stream is a sea, the ferry-boat is the boat of Charon, the familiar shore is out of sight; the window of the palace has become the threshold of the scaffold, and to-morrow is eternity.

Chapter VII.

WHEN I think of the months which passed between the king's attempted arrest of the five members and the first battle of the Civil War, I sometimes wonder how any one can ever undertake to write history.

In the little bit of the world known to us, parties were so strangely intertwined, so strangely divided, and so heterogeneously composed. The motives that drew men to one side or the other were so various and so mixed, that I think scarce one of those we knew fought on the same side for the same reason; while the differences which separated many men in the same party were certainly wider in many respects than those which separated them from others against whom they fought.

How world-wide the difference between Harry Davenant and Sir Launcelot Trevor! How nicely balanced the scales that made my Father and John Hampden "rebels," and Harry Davenant or Lord Falkland "malignants!"

Yet the distinctions were real, at least so it seems

to me. Nor do I see how, if all were to be again starting from the same point, either could avoid coming to the same issue.

Harry Davenant believed revolution to be ruin, and chose the most arbitrary rule instead.

My Father, equally dreading revolution, believed the king to be the great revolutionist; by his arbitrary will changing times and laws; by his hopeless untruth subverting the foundations of society. Slowly he stepped down into the cold bitter waters of civil war, having for his watch-word, "Loyalty to England and her laws!" His chief hope lay in Mr. Hampden.

Roger again, and others like him, hoping more from liberty than he feared from revolution, and believing the contest would be fiery, but brief and decisive, plunged gallantly into the flood, with Liberty blazoned on their banners; liberty to do right and to speak the truth. His chosen captain was Mr. Cromwell, in whose troop he served from the first. God only knew the bitter pang it cost him (I knew it not till years afterwards) to take his post on the field which must, he knew, make so great a gulf between him and the Davenants. It was seldom Roger spoke of what he felt; scarce ever of what he suffered.

Dr. Antony wrote, meanwhile, from London:—

"Chirurgeons, like women, have indeed their place on the battle-field, and not out of reach of the danger. But their work is with the wounded, and their weapons are turned against the enemy of all; the 'last enemy,' scarce to be destroyed in this war!

I hope to succour on the battle-field those I sought to comfort in the prisons. God grant I find the air of the fieldas wholesome to the spirits of my patients as that of the dungeon."'

Job Forster never hesitated for a moment as to which was the right side. To him England was in one sense Canaan to be conquered, in another the Chosen Land to be kept sacred. The king was Saul; or, in other aspects, Sihon king of the Amorites, or Og king of Bashan. The Parliament, at first, and then the Lord Protector and the army, were the chosen people, Moses, Joshua, David. His only hesitation was whether he himself ought to fight on the field, or to work at the forge and protect Rachel and the village at home. "The Almighty," he said, "has not given me this big body of mine for nought. God forbid it should be said of Job Forster, Why abodest thou amidst the sheep-folds to hear the bleatings of the flocks?—that is, the ring of the hammer and anvil, which is as the bleating of my flocks to me. Yet there is Rachel! And the old law was merciful; and if it forbid a man to leave his new-married wife, how should I answer for leaving her who has more need of me, and has none but me? and she so ailing, and I, to whom the Lord has said as plain as words can speak, 'Be thou better to her than ten sons.'"

It was perhaps the first perplexity he had never confided to her, and sorely was Job exercised, until one morning in August he came to my Father with a lightened countenance, and said,—

"Mr. Drayton, she has given the word, as plain as

ever Deborah spoke to Barak. I've got my commission, and I'm ready to go this night."

Afterwards, in an intimate talk by a camp-fire, he once told Roger how that morning, between the lights, he woke up and saw her kneeling down with her arms crossed upon the Book, and her eyes raised up to heaven, and running fast with tears. "I lifted myself," he said, "on my elbow, and I looked at her. But I didn't like to speak; I saw there was something going on between her soul and the Lord. And last she rose and came to me with a face as pale as the sheet, but without a tear in her eyes or a tremble in her voice, and she said, 'Job, thou shalt have thy way; the Lord has made me ready to give thee up.' And I said, sheepish-like, 'How canst thee know what I willed? I never said aught to thee!' Then she smiled and said, 'Thee never thinks thee says aught except thee speaks plain enough for the town-crier. Have not I heard thy sighs, and seen thy hankering looks whenever any of the lads listed these weeks past? But I could not speak before; now I can. For I've gotten the word from the Lord for thee and for me, and woe is me if I hold my peace.' The word for me was: 'Now I know that thou fearest God, seeing thou hast not withheld thy son, thy only son, from me.' 'And that,' said she, 'means thee, Job; for thou are more to me than that,' said she, 'more than that, only and all. I have no promise to hold thee by, like Abraham had for Isaac, yet if the Lord calls, what can I do?' And there her voice gave way, but she hurried on—'And I've gotten a word for thee, "*Have not I commanded thee?* Be strong and of a good courage, for the Lord thy God is with thee wheresoever thou goest."' "So," concluded Job," I got my word of command; and there was no more to be said. We knelt down together and gave ourselves up; and as soon as it was fairly day I came to give in my name."

That was Job Forster's motive. He believed he had the word of command direct from the King of kings. And this was the motive, I believe, of hundreds and thousand more or less like him; men who, as the Lord Protector said when the strife was over, were "never beaten." Gloriously distinct the two armies and the two causes seemed to him, perplexed by no subtle perceptions of right on the wrong side, or of wrong on the right.

To Aunt Dorothy also matters were equally clear, although her point of view was not precisely the same, and in the subsequent subdivisions she and Job became seriously opposed. Aunt Dorothy believed that she saw in the New Testament a model of church ritual and government, minutely defined to the last stave or pin or loop of the tabernacle; and rather that abandon the minutest of these sacred details she would willingly have suffered any temporal loss. The whole Presbyterian order of church government she saw clearly unfolded in the Epistles; and that godly men like Mr. Cromwell on the one hand, or learned men like Dr. Jeremy Taylor on the other, should fail to see it also, was a miracle only to be accounted for by the blinding power of Satan, especially predicted in these last days. With regard to the Government of the State also, her belief was equally definite, derived, as she considered, from the same Divine source. The king was "the anointed of the Lord." In this, she said, Lady Lucy had undoubted insight into the truth. His wicked councillors might be put to death, as traitors at once against him and the realm; armies might by his Parliament be raised against him; but it must be in his name, with the purpose of setting him free from those evil councillors by whom he was virtually kept a prisoner; his judgment being by them enthralled, so that he was irresponsible for his acts, and might quite lawfully by his faithful covenanted subjects be placed, respectfully, under bodily restraint, if thereby his mind might be disenthralled from the hard bondage of the wicked. But beyond this no subject might go. The king's person was sacred; no profane hand could be lifted with impunity against him. Any difficulty, disorder, or evil, must be endured, rather than touch a hair of the consecrated head. This also was a conviction for which Aunt Dorothy was fully prepared to encounter any amount of contradiction or disaster. The narrow ridge on which she walked erect, without wavering or misgiving, was, she was persuaded, marked out as manifestly as the path of the Israelites through the Red Sea by the wall of impassable waters on either hand, by the pillar of cloud and fire behind. To this narrow way she would have allured, led, or if needful compelled every human soul, for their good, and the glory of God. No vicissitudes of fortune affected her convictions; the sorrows of all who deviated from this narrow path being, in her belief, from the Sword of the Avenger, while the sorrows of those who kept to it were from the Rod of the Comforter. My Father's adherence to very much the same course of conduct, from a belief of its expediency, and Aunt Gretel's from the tenderness of sympathy which inevitably drew her to the side on which there was the most suffering, seemed to Aunt Dorothy happy accidents, or special and uncovenanted mercies, singularly vouchsafed to persons of their uncertain and indefinite opinions. Not that Aunt Dorothy's nature was in any way vulgar, small, and narrow. Her heart was deep and high, if not always wide. To her convictions she would have sacrificed first herself, then the universe. Her convenience she would have sacrificed to the comfort of the meanest human being in the universe. She would not have swerved from her ridge of orthodoxy for the dearest love on earth. She would have stooped from it to save or help the most degraded wanderer, or her greatest enemy.

But the most dangerous conviction she held was unfortunately one of the deepest. It was that of her own practical infallibility. It was strange that, with the profoundest and most practical convictions of her own sinfulness, she never could learn the impossibility that all error should be removed whilst any sin remains; that there should be no darkness in the mind while there is so much in the heart. Strange, but not uncommon. Her sin she acknowledged as her own. Her creed she identified entirely with the Holy Scriptures. It was not her own, she said, it was God's truth to the minutest point, and, as such, she would have suffered or fought for every clause.

Nevertheless, with advancing years Roger and I grew into a deeper reverence for her character. If in our childhood she represented to us Justice with the sword and scales (often in our belief very effectually blindfolded), whilst Aunt Gretel enacted counteracting Mercy; in after years we grew rather to look on them as Truth and Tenderness, acting not counter to each other, but in combination. And in this imperfect world, where truth and love are never blended in perfect proportions in any one character, it is difficult to say on which we leant the most. It was strange to see how often their opposite attributes led them to the same actions. "Speaking the truth in love," was Aunt Dorothy's maxim; and if the love were sometimes lost in the emphasis on truth, neither truth nor love were ever sacrificed to selfish interest. "First pure *then* peaceable" was her wisdom; and I cannot say she always got as far as the "gentle, and easy to be entreated." But it is something to be able to look back on a life like hers, unprofaned by one stain of untruthfulness, or by one low or petty aim. It is only in looking back that we learn what a rock of strength she was to us all, or how the tenderest memories of home often cling like mosses around such rocks; the more closely, sometimes, for their very ruggedness. Thus our home at Netherby contained various elements ecclesiastical and political as well as moral, all of which, however, at the commencement of the civil wars were gathered together under the watchword, "Loyalty above all to the King of kings. Liberty to obey God."

It was this indeed, that, with all our internal differences as to church government and secular government, united us into one party. Whatever varieties of opinion as to church government our party contained: Presbyterian, Independent, Moderate Episcopal, or Quaker; classical, republican, aristocratic, English constitutional, or, finally, the adherents of the Deliverer, chosen (they deemed) as divinely and to be obeyed as implicitly as any Hebrew judge—all believed in the theocracy.

The liberty our party contended for was no mere unloosing of bonds. It was liberty to obey the highest law. It was no mere levelling to clear an empty space for new experiments. It was sweeping away ruins to clear a platform for the kingdom of God.

And this was another point in which the recollections of my life make me feel how vast and complicated an undertaking it must be to write history.

In our early days we used to be given histories of the Church and histories of the world. Profane histories and sacred histories as neatly and definitely separated as if the Church and the world had been two distinct planets.

But in our own times, at least, it seems to me absolutely impossible thus to separate them. The Battle of Dunbar was to Oliver Cromwell and his army as religious an act as their prayer-meeting at

Windsor. The righting the poor folks who lost their rights on the Soke of Somersham was, I believe, as religious an act to Mr. Cromwell as the appointment of the gospel-lectures. And as with the actions so with the persons. Who can say which persons of our time belong to ecclesiastical and which to secular history?

Does the history of the Convocation, of the Star-Chamber, or of the Westminster Assembly, belong to sacred history; and the history of the Long Parliament, where decisions were made for time and eternity, or of the battle-fields whence thousands went to their last account, to profane? Is the making of confessions of faith a religious act, and the living by them or dying for them secular? Are Archbishop Laud, Bishop Williams, Mr. Baxter, Dr. Owen, Mr. Howe, ecclesiastical persons; and Lord Falkland, Mr. Hampden, Mr. Pym, or Oliver Cromwell, secular?

In our times, as in my own life, it seems to me absolutely impossible to say where sacred history begins and where the profane ends.

My consolation is that it seems to me much the same in the Holy Scriptures. We call Genesis sacred history; and what is it, chiefly, but a story of family life? What is Exodus but a record of national deliverances? What are the Chronicles and Kings but histories of wars and sieges, interspersed with pathetic family stories? What, indeed, are the gospels themselves but the record, not of creeds or ecclesiastical conflicts, but of a life, the Life, coming in contact with every form of sickness, and sin, and sorrow in this our common everyday human life? What would the gospels be with nothing but the Sabbaths and the synagogues, and the Sanhedrim, and the Scribes and Pharisees left in them? With the widow's only son left out of them, and the ruler's little daughter, and the woman who was a sinner, and the five thousand fed on the grassy slopes of Galilee, and the one young man who departed sorrowful 'for he had great possessions?' Would it have been more truly Church history for being the less human history?

The Bible history seems to me to be a history of all human life in relation to God. The sins of the Bible are terribly manifest, secular sins; injustice, impurity, covetousness, cruelty. Its virtues are simple homely, positive virtues; truth, uprightness, kindness, mercy, gratitude, courage, gentleness; such sins and virtues as make the weal or woe of nations and of homes. Ordinary ecclesiastical history seems to me too often a record of secular struggles for consecrated things, and names, and places, and of selfish strivings for which shall be greatest. The sins it blames, too often mere transgressions of rules, mistakes as to religious terms, neglect of the tithe of mint, anise, and cummin. The virtues it commends, alas! too often negative renunciations of certain indulgences, scruples as to certain observances, fasting twice in the week (things which, done or undone, leave the heart the same), intolerance of differences, resulting in persecuting or being persecuted according to the relative balance of power.

But underneath all this a Church history like that of the Bible is being silently lived on earth, is being silently written in heaven. Little glimpses of it we see here from time to time. What will it be when we see it all?

All through that summer the country was astir with the enlistings for the king and the Parliament.

These began about April.

On the 23d of February, Queen Henrietta Maria had embarked at Dover for the Low Countries, with the Princess Mary and the crown jewels.

From the time that she was in safety the king's tone to the Parliament began (it was thought) to change. Always chivalrously regardful of her, and indifferent to danger for himself (for none of his father's timidity could ever be charged to him), he began to give more open answers to the popular demands. He hoped also, it was said, much from the queen's eloquence and exertions in his cause on the Continent. It was his misfortune, my Father said, that any favourable turn in his affairs made him unyielding; and thus it happened that he only came to terms when his cause was at the worst, so that his treaties had the double disadvantage of being made under the most adverse circumstances, and with men who knew from repeated experience that not one of his most sacred promises would be kept if he could help it. Such virtues as he possessed seemed always to come into action at the wrong moment; his courage when it could only kindle irritation; his graciousness when it could only inspire contempt.

The queen being safely out of the country, and the king safely out of the capital, from his refuge at York came the renewal of the old irritating demand for tonnage and poundage, rooting the opposition firmer than ever in the irrevocable distrust of the royal word.

The demand of the king for the old usurpations was met by the assertion of the Parliament of old rights, with the demand for new powers to secure these; by the assertion of the power of the purse, and the demand for power over the militia.

But to us women at Netherby all these negotiations and fencings between the king and the Parliament sounded so much like what had gone on for so long, everything was couched in such orderly and constitutional language, that it was difficult to think anything more than Protestations, Remonstrances, Breach of Privilege, and Protests for Privilege, would ever come of it.

The first thing that roused me to the sense that it might end not in words but in battles, was the news that reached us one April evening that the king had gone in person with three hundred horsemen to the gates of Hull, and had summoned Sir John Hotham to surrender the city; that Sir John had refused to surrender or to admit the king's troops (offering all loyal courtesy at the same time to the king himself); that the king and his three hundred had thereon gone off baffled to Beverly, and there proclaimed Sir John Hotham a traitor.

That night I said to Aunt Gretel,—

"This seems to me altogether to introduce a new set of terms and things. Instead of Protestations and Remonstrances, we hear of Summonses and Surrenders. The king and his cavaliers repulsed from the closed gates of one of his own cities! Aunt Gretel, these are new words to us; does not this look like war?"

And she replied, in a tremulous voice,—

"Alas, sweet heart, these are no new words to me. Your people seem to arrange many things others fight about, by talking about them. And it is difficult for me to say what words mean with you. But these words are indeed terribly familiar to me. And in my country they would certainly mean war."

And that night I well remember the perplexity that crossed my prayers, whether in praying as usual for the king I might not be praying against the Parliament, and against my Father and Roger, and the nation; until after debating the matter in my own mind for some time, I came to the conclusion that on whatever dark mountains scattered, and by whatever deep waters divided, to Him there is still "One flock, one Shepherd," and that however ill I knew how to ask, He knew well what to give.

LETTICE DAVENANT'S DIARY.

(From another source.)

"*York, April*, 1642.—It has actually begun at last. The rebellion has begun. Sir John Hotham (Sir I hesitate to call him, for what knight is worthy the name who turns his disloyal sword against the very Fountain of knighthood and of all honor?) has closed the gates of Hull against the summons—against the very voice and person of His Sacred Majesty. At once the king withdrew to Beverley, and under the shadow of the grand old Minster proclaimed the false knight a traitor.

"The rebellion has begun, but every one says it cannot last long. Next Christmas at latest must see us all at peace again; the nation once more at the feet of the king. My Mother says like a prodigal child; Sir Launcelot says like a beaten hound. Mobs, says he, like dogs, can only learn to obey by being suffered to rebel a little, and then being whipped for it. (I like not well this talk of Sir Launcelot. If the nation is like a hound, at what point in the nation does the dog-nature begin, and the human end?) Speaking so, I told him, we might include ourselves. But he laughed, and said, such discerning of spirits required no miraculous gift. Moreover, he said, the king himself had once compared the Parliaments to 'cats, to be tamed when young but cursed when old;' and had called his sailors in the Thames who offered to guard the Parliament 'water-rats.' If the king said so, I confess I think His Majesty might have chosen more courtly similes. But I do not believe he did. I will never believe any evil of His Majesty, whoever says it, scarcely if I were to see it myself, for my eyes might be deceived.

"Only I should be sorely vexed if they heard

these things at Netherby; because they never said rough things of any one. Especially now I am not there to explain things. For I am not allowed to write to them, nor to see them again, until things are right again in the country; which makes me write this.

"However, it cannot last long. Every one here agrees in that. Every one except Harry, whom we call 'Il Penseroso.' He sees such a long way, and on so many sides, or at least he tries to do so; and he talks of the Wars of the Roses, and the Wars in Germany; as if there were any resemblance! In Germany there were kings and states opposed. In the Wars of the Roses royal persons, with some kind of claim to reign. But this is nothing but flat rebellion. The family against the father; sworn liegemen against their sovereign lord; the body against the head. And how can any one think for a moment there can be any end to it but one, and that soon? Yes; at Christmas, I trust, we Davenants shall be at the Hall again, and the Draytons at Netherby, looking back to the end of this frantic and unnatural outbreak.

"And I mean to be most generous to them all about it. I do not mean even to say, 'I always told you how it would end.' They will see, and that will be enough. The king will forgive every one, I am sure, he is so gracious and gentle—(he spoke to me like a father the other day, and yet with such knightly deference!)—except, perhaps, a very few, who will have to be made examples of, unless they make examples of themselves by running out of the country, which I hope they may. For having once re-asserted his rightful authority, the king will be able to be forgiving without being suspected of weakness. There need not be any more poor mistaken people set in the pillory, which really seems to do no one any good, as far as I can see, and to make every one so exceedingly angry. The Puritans (that is, those among them who have any sense) will see that it really can make no difference whether the clergyman says the prayers in a white dress or a black. Perhaps even the bishops and archbishops might own the same. Because, although it cannot be good management to give a naughty child its way for crying, if it stops crying and is good, it is quite another thing.

"And then everything would go on delightfully. The *very* troublesome and obstinate people (on both sides, I think) might, perhaps, all go to America, some to the north and some to the south. For the American plantations are very wide, they say, and by the time they met—say in one or two hundred years—their great-great grandchildren might have given up caring so much about the colours of the vestments and the titles of the clergymen who do the services in the church. So that by that time everything would go on delightfully in America as well as in England. And by next Christmas, from what the gentlemen and ladies about here say, I should think this might all have begun. Only just now this little unpleasant contest has to be gone through first. And I am very much afraid as to what Mr. Drayton and Roger may do, or even

Olive. They are so terribly conscientious. They will pick up the smallest questions with their consciences instead of with their common sense; which seems to me like watering a daisy with a fire-engine, or weeding a flower-bed with a plough. Mistress Dorothy is the worst of them (dear, kind, old soul, I must now and then look at her sermons, in order to make it quite clear to myself I was not a hypocrite in listening to them all that time). But I do not think any of them are quite safe in this way. And yet I know, in my inmost heart, they are better than any one in the world, except my Mother, and perhaps Harry. (Of His Majesty it is not for me to speak.) And I love them better than any one in the world, which, I am afraid, they will not believe, now I am not allowed to write to them. I love them for their noble perverseness, and their heroic conscientiousness, and their terrible truthfulness, and everything that separates us. And these last months at home have been the happiest of my life. I felt growing quite good. And one thing I have resolved. I will not say one word I should mind their hearing, so that when we meet again I may have nothing to explain or to unsay. For it is only misunderstanding that will ever make any of them take the wrong side; nothing but misunderstanding. And facts will set that all right when they see how things really are. As they will, I trust, before Christmas.

"It is not so easy to be good here as at Netherby. People say so many pretty things to me. My Mother says I must not heed them; they are only

Court ways of speaking, which mean nothing; and that rightly used, I might make them means of mortification, saying every time I hear such pretty phrases, as good Dr. Taylor recommended, 'My beauty is in colour inferior to many flowers; and even a dog hath parts as well proportioned to the designs of his nature as I have; and three fits of an ague can change it into yellowness and leanness, and to hollowness and wrinkles of deformity.' But this I find not so easy. If I were a rose, I should be pleased at being a rose, and at being thought sweet and fair. And even a well-favoured dog, meseems, has some harmless delight in his good looks. And as to the ague, I see no likelihood of it. And as to becoming yellow and lean, the more I think of it, the gladder I am to think I am not. And yet there is some little flutter in my pleasure at these fair speeches which hardly seems to me quite altogether good. And I do not think my Mother quite knows what nonsense these young Cavaliers talk. Perhaps no one did ever talk nonsense to her. Or, if they did, I am sure she never liked it. And I am afraid I do sometimes a little. Else, why should it all come back into my mind at wrong times?—in the Minster or at prayers. Heigh, ho! I wish I was at Netherby. No one ever called me fair enchantress there, or my cheeks Aurora's rose-garden, or my teeth strings of pearls, or my hands lilies, or my hair imprisoned sunbeams, or my voice the music of the spheres. Sir Launcelot talked enough of that kind of poetry to me, between Netherby and Windsor, to make a book of ballads.

(For my Mother was in the sedan-chair, whilst I rode most of the way with Sir Launcelot.) And yet, I think, there is more honour in Roger Drayton's telling me in his straight-forward way he thought me wrong, as he so often did, than in all Sir Launcelot's most honeyed compliments.

"Not that I think Olive just to poor Sir Launcelot. If she could have seen his *debonair* and courteous ways to every clown and poor wench we met, and how he flung his crowns and angels to any beggar, she must have felt there is much kindliness in him, with all his wild ways.

"And when he saw I liked not so many fair speeches, he gave them up in a measure. I must say that for him; and he has been as deferential to me ever since at the Court, as if I were one of the princesses. Only I wish he would not always see when I drop my glove or my posy: at least, I think I do. Yet it is rather pleasant, too, at times to feel there is some one who cares about one among so many strange people, and some one who is always ready to talk about poor old Netherby, and who honours the Draytons, moreover, so generously. I wish Olive knew this.

"And I wish I were like my Mother, and had 'a chapel built in my heart.' Or else that I could live at Netherby.

"Sir Launcelot admires the 'beauty of holiness' in my Mother. He says, in all times, happily, there have been these sweet exalted Saints, especially among women, bright particular stars, celestial beauties, and princesses, that all men must revere.

Quite another kind of thing, he says, from the Puritan notion of calling all men to be 'saints,' or else consigning them to reprobation as among the wicked.

"*Note.*—I am at a loss what to call this writing of mine. It is scarcely a Diary or Journal, for I certainly do not anything as regular as write in it every day. It is not 'Annals;' for I hope to have done with it before Christmas, when I shall have met Olive and all of them again at home. 'Chronicles' are more solemn still. 'Thoughts?' where shall I find them? 'Facts?' how is one to know them, when people give such different accounts of things? 'Meditations?' worse again. 'Religious Journals,' 'Confessions,' etc., always puzzled me. I could never make out for whom they were written. Especially the prayers I have seen written out at length in them. They cannot be meant for other people to read. That would be turning the 'closet' into 'the corners of the street.' They cannot be meant for the people themselves to read. For what good could that do? It would not be praying to see how I prayed some years since. They cannot surely be meant for God to read. He is always near, and can hear, or read our hearts, which is quite another thing from reading our Diaries.

"*May* 30, *York.*—The birds begin to sing in the trees around the Minster. Our lodging is opposite. And the courtiers begin to gather once more around the king. Many lords have come these last days from London, with some faithful members of the

Commons' House, and old Lord Littleton has come, with somewhat limping loyalty, they say, after the Great Seal, now in his right hand. So that this grave old town begins to look gay. Cavaliers caracolling about the streets, doffing their hats to fair faces in the windows. Troops mustering but slowly; somewhat slowly. Nor can I make out if these townspeople altogether like us and our ways. There are so many Puritans among these traders. And Sir Launcelot says they have great sport in the Puritan household where he is quartered, in making the Puritan lads learn the 'Distracted Puritan,' and other roystering Cavalier songs, and drink confusion to the Covenant; and in making the host and hostess bring out their best conserves, linen and plate, for the use of the men. Sir Launcelot told them, he said, that they should only look on it as the payment of an old debt the children of Israel had owed to the Egyptians these three thousand years. I do not think such jokes good manners in any other person's house, and I told him so. But he said their ridiculous gravity makes the temptation too strong to be resisted. If they would jest good-humouredly in return, he said, they would soon understand each other. But would they? I am not quite sure how Sir Launcelot enjoys not having the best of a joke. And I could not bear his calling the Puritans all canting, or ridiculous. He knows better. And I told him so. I felt quite indignant, and the tears were in my eyes (for I thought of them all at Netherby). He seemed penitent. Indeed, I hope it did him good.

"*June.*—The Parliament are growing more insolent every day; they dared to say in one of their ridiculous Remonstrances that 'the king is for the kingdom, not the kingdom for the king, that even the crown jewels are not His Majesty's own, but given him in trust for the regal power.' However, they will soon learn their mistake about that, for the crown-jewels are safe in Holland, and have there purchased for the Crown good store of arms and ammunition. These were all embarked in a Dutch ship called the *Providence.* A great Providence, my Mother says, attended her. For although she was wrecked on the coast of Yorkshire, nevertheless, all her stores have this day been safely brought into York.

"Now we shall see what gentlemen can do against tapsters, and tailors' and haberdashers' 'prentices, such as make up the wretched army they have been mustering in London! The citizens' wives actually brought their thimbles and bodkins, it is said, to pay the men; to such mean and ludicrous straits are they reduced. The Cavaliers call it 'the Thimble and Bodkin Army.'

"*July* 20.—Sir John Hotham is said to be wavering back to loyalty. A day or two since, a gallant little army of four thousand men rode forth hence through the Mickle Bar, to demand the surrender of that presumptuous city, Hull, and if refused, to storm it. Better they had listened to His Majesty's gentle summons with his three hundred. How gallant and brave they looked. Plumed helmets gleaming, swords flashing, pennons flying, horses looking as proud of the cause as the riders. Not a cavalier among them who would not face battle as gayly as the hunting-field.

"*July* 22.—Those treacherous townspeople! Not a troop of them is to be relied on. Our gallant Cavaliers came back in disorder. And all because of the faithless train-bands, and those turbulent citizens of Hull. Lord Lindsay, with three thousand men, was at Beverley, and on the lighting of a fire on Beverley Minster, the gates of Hull were to be opened by some loyal men inside. But five hundred rebels within the town, hearing too soon of the intention of these loyal men, made a sortie under the command of Sir John Hotham. The true Cavaliers would have stood firm, every one says, but the Yorkshire train-bands would not draw sword against their neighbours, but ran away to Beverley, and so the whole ended in disgrace and defeat. If we could only have an army entirely composed of gentlemen, and their sons, and retainers, the Parliament could not stand a day. But the worst news that has reached us lately, is the treachery of the Earl of Warwick and the navy. They have all gone over to the Parliament, in spite of the king's offering them better pay than they ever received before. Five ships stood firm at first, but the rest overpowered them. I hope no one ever told them about their being called 'water-rats,' but there are always some malicious people who delight to make mischief by telling tales. I should think royal persons ought to be very careful about their jests.

"*August.*—We are on the point of leaving York

to spend a few days at Nottingham, where the king's standard is to be set up.

"I am sorry to leave this old town. I miss the pleasant walks at home. For here one dare scarce venture much out of doors. If the Cavaliers are as dangerous to their enemies as they are sometimes to their friends, the Parliament has good cause to tremble. The streets echo dismally at night with the shouts of drunken revelry. But, I suppose, all armies are alike. Only it is rather unfortunate for us that gravity and the show of piety being the badge of the Puritans, levity and a reckless dashing carriage are taken up as their badge by many of the young Cavaliers.

"I would they took example by the king. His Majesty has been riding around the country lately himself, calling his lieges to follow him. And his majestic courtesy and grace, with his loving and winning speeches, such as he made at Newark and Lincoln, showing his good intentions and desires for their liberty and welfare, must, I am sure, be worth him a mint of such money as the London citizens can coin out of their thimbles and bodkins.

"The North country is well disposed, they say; and Lancashire, where the queen hath much hold on the Catholic gentlemen of ancient lineage there; and the West country, where brave Sir Bevil Granvill lives, is full of loyalty. Mr. Hampden has done mischief in Buckinghamshire, and Mr. Cromwell (a brewer, Sir Launcelot says, rather than a country-gentleman, though not of low parentage) calls himself captain, and is disaffecting the eastern counties, already disloyal enough with their French Huguenot weavers, and their 'Anabaptists, Atheists, and Brownists,' as His Majesty calls them.

"The towns are the worst, however. I suppose there is something in buying and selling, and tinkering and tailoring, which makes people think more of mean money considerations, than of loyalty and honour. Then there are so many Puritans in the town. Perhaps the narrow dark high streets make them naturally inclined to be gloomy and strait-laced. I think, however, the less our Cavalier soldiers are quartered in the towns, the better, till they mend their manners. It may make the citizens less pleased than ever with the Book of Sports.

"*Nottingham, August* 23.—This evening the king himself set up his standard on the top of the field behind the castle. There was much sounding of drums and trumpets. Several hundreds gathered around the royal party, and we watched a little way off. But I knew not how the act did not seem as solemn as the occasion. The night was stormy; and the trumpets and drums, and then the voice of the herald reading the royal proclamation, sounded small and poor against the rush and howling of the winds. The troops have not yet answered the king's call as they should, and those present were mostly the train-bands. Then His Majesty, on the spot, made some alterations in the proclamation, which perplexed the herald, so that he blundered and stumbled in reading it. Altogether I wish I had not been there.

"The king's standard ought to be something more than a pole no higher than a May-pole with a few streamers, and a common flag at the top. And the trumpets which are to rouse a nation, ought to have a certain magnificence in them, altogether different from the trumpets they blow at the carols at Netherby at Christmas. I am sure I cannot tell how. But I always pictured it so. The words are grander than the things.

"Perhaps all our pomps and solemnities look poor and mean under the open sky. We had better keep them beneath roofs of our own making. The pomps we are used to under the open sky are the purple and crimson and gold of sunset and sunrise, great banners of storm-clouds flung across the sky. And the solemnities are the thunders, and the mighty winds, and the rushing of rivers, and the dashing of seas.

"The things are grander, infinitely, than any words wherewith we can speak of them.

"But when I said so to my Mother, she said, 'And yet, my child, one soul, and even one human voice, is grander, or more godlike than all the thunders. It is their significance, Lettice, which gives the grandeur to any solemnities of ours. If we heard those trumpets summon our countrymen by thousands to the battle, or saw that flag borne blood-stained from the field, we should not think the voice of the trumpet wanted terrible magnificence, or the flag a common thing ever more.'

"Perhaps, after all, it was only a little inward depression that made me feel this disappointment.

For only three days before, Coventry had shut her gates in the king's face, and the Earl of Essex is at hand, they say, with a great army, and so few flocking loyally to the king.

"But worst of all, I think, is this Prince Rupert. His mother's name, Elizabeth of Bohemia, has been like a sacred name in the country for years; a saint and a heroine in courage and patience. But this prince is so noisy and reckless, and takes so much upon himself, that he angers the older gentlemen and experienced soldiers sorely. My Father says he is little better than a petulant boy. Yet he has great weight with the king, his uncle, and takes the command into his own hands; so that the gallant old Earl of Lindsay deems his own command little better than nominal. And, meanwhile, the younger Cavaliers take their colour from him, and use that new low cant word of his, 'plunder,' quite as a jest, as if it meant some new sport or sword-exercise, instead of meaning, as it does, scouring all over the country, burning lonely farm-houses, robbing the inmates, and sometimes hanging the servants at the doors for refusing to betray their masters, sacking villages, and I know not what other wickednesses. In the fortnight he has been here, he has flown through Worcestershire, Nottinghamshire, Warwickshire, Leicestershire, and Cheshire. And not a night but we have seen the sky aglow with the fires of burning villages and homesteads. I should fear to hear how the people along his line of march, coming back to their ruined homes, speak of the king.

"Moreover, it is said, the rebel troops are strictly forbidden to take anything without paying for it, a contrast worth them much.

"*August* 24.—This morning, before I rose, my Mother's waiting gentlewoman brought dismal news. The royal standard, said she, has been blown down in the night, and lies a wreck along the hill.

"My Mother says it is heathenish to talk of omens and auguries. And my Father says these foreigners are the worst omen, and all would be well enough if they would leave Englishmen to fight out their own quarrels, like neighbours, who exchange blows and are friends again, instead of like wretched hired Lanzknechts or Free Companions.

"But Sir Launcelot laughs, and says it is a good thing to give the whining Puritans something to cry for at last. And Harry sighs, and says he supposes it is necessary to make the rebels see we are in earnest.

"Altogether, we do not seem in very good humour with each other just now. However, a few victories will no doubt set us all right again. There can be no reasonable doubt that the king will bring these rebels to their senses sooner or later; in a few months at latest.

"Only I had not understood at all how very melancholy war is. I thought of it as concerning no one but the soldiers. And men must incur danger one way or another. And there is the glory, and the excitement, and the exercise of noble courrage, making such men as nothing but such trials can make.

"But the battles seem but a small part of the misery; the misery without glory to any one.

"On our way hither from York, my Mother was faint and tired, and we stopped at a little farm-house with an orchard. It was evening, and the woman had just finished milking the cows by the door, and she gave my Mother a cup of new milk while she rested on the settle in the clean little kitchen. There were two little children playing about, and the father was at work in the orchard, and one of the children called him, and he brought my Father a cup of cider. And there was a Bible on the table with wood-cuts; and I found the eldest child knew the meaning of them. He said his father had told him. They were very kind and pleasant to us.

"And a few days since Harry told me they had passed a little farm with an orchard, and the man was surly and a Puritan, and refused to tell the way some fugitives had fled; and Prince Rupert had him hanged on his own threshold, and drove off the cows for plunder.

"And from what Harry says I feel sure it is the same.

"And I have scarcely slept since, thinking of that poor man, and the silent voice that will never any more explain the wood-cuts in the old Bible, and the poor hands that will never show their willing hospitality again.

"But it is only one, Harry says, among hundreds;

and such things must be, and I must not think of it.

"But every one of the hundreds is just that terrible *only one*, which leaves the world all lonely to some poor mourner!

"Those gentlemen in Parliament have dreadful things to answer for.

"Why did not Mr. Hampden pay a thousand times his miserable ship-money rather than lead the country on to such horrors?

"For the king cannot have his commands disobeyed. If he did, how could he be a king?

"I do wish he could be more a king with his own troops; I am sure he hates this ravaging and marauding. But so many of the gentlemen serve, and, indeed, keep their regiments at their own cost, which makes them difficult to control.

"*October.*—Prince Rupert has been driven from Worcester. If it were only a lesson in reverence and modesty for the prince, it would not so much matter, some think, that he left twenty good and true men dead there. The Earl of Essex occupies the city. He has been there a fortnight doing nothing. Some remnants of loyalty, we think, hinder him from coming to open collision. But what the use of collecting an army can be unless it is to fight, it is hard to see. The truth is, perhaps, that he begins to feel the peril of setting his haberdashers and grocers' 'prentices, commanded by a forsworn peer, against gentlemen's sons fighting under their king! Meantime, our army is gathering at last, and only too eager, they say, to give the rebels a lesson. Once for all, God grant it be a lesson once for all. Although the battles do not seem to me half so dreadful as these 'plunderings.' But perhaps that is because I never came near a battle; nor, indeed, can the oldest man in England remember any one that ever did on English soil."

OLIVE DRAYTON'S RECOLLECTIONS.

All through the summer the armies were gathering. In our seven eastern counties—Essex, Norfolk, Suffolk, Cambridgeshire, Lincoln, Huntingdonshire, and Hertfordshire — called the associated counties, because bound by Mr. Hampden and Mr. Cromwell into an association for mutual defence, the King's Commission of Array and the Parliament's Ordinance of Militia clashed less than elsewhere. In August Mr. Cromwell seized a magazine of arms and ammunition at Cambridge. The stronghold of the Puritans was in these eastern regions; and except where a few Royalist gentlemen, like the Davenants, led off their retainers, the Parliament had, amongst us, mostly its own way. All the more reason, my Father said, for our men to risk their persons, since our homes were safer than elsewhere.

My Father, from his old military experience, had much to do with training and drilling the men. Strange sounds of clanging arms and sharp words of command echoed from the old court of the Manor. Old arms, the very stories belonging to which were well-nigh forgotten, were taken down; arms which had hung on the walls of manor-house and farm-house since the Wars of the Roses. The newest weapon we had at Netherby which had seen service in England was a short jewel-hilted sword the Drayton of the day had worn at the Battle of Bosworth Field, fighting, by a rare piece of good luck for us, under Henry VII., on the winning side. Since then the Reformation had revolutionized the Church, and gunpowder had revolutionized the art of war; so that instead of the sturdy bowmen, each provided with his weapon and ready trained to the use of it, whom his ancestors brought to the field, my Father could only muster a few labourers and servants, without weapons and without training, with no further preparation for war than hands used to labour, wits ready to learn, and hearts ready to dare.

My Father did not mean to lead his own men. Having had experience of engineering in the German wars, he was employed here and there as his directions were needed. Roger and those who went from Netherby served from the first with Mr. Cromwell's Ironsides; my Father, as his contribution, providing the armour, which, like that of Haselrigge's Lobsters, was complete and costly. Other bands passed and repassed often, and shared the hospitalities of the Manor, to join Lord Brook's purple-coats, Lord Say and Lord Mandeville's blue-coats. Hollis' red-coats were London men, and Mr. Hampden's green-coats all from his own county, Buckinghamshire; while the badge of all was the orange scarf round the arm—the family colours of Lord Essex, the general. Each regiment had its own motto—Hampden's, "*Vestigia nulla retrorsum*;" Essex's (pointing many a cavalier jest, if seen in plunder or retreat), "*Cave adsum.*" On the reverse of each banner was the common motto of all, "God with us"—the watch-word of so many a battle.

Money was not stinted; the city of London heading the contributions in January with £50,000, and the Merchants' Companies with nigh as large a sum (then intended to avenge the Irish massacre); whilst Mr. Hampden gave £1000, and his cousin, Mr. Cromwell, £500.

Women brought their rings and jewels; cherished old family plate was not held back. We in our sober Puritan household had few jewels to bring, but such as we had were disinterred from their caskets, and the few silver drinking-cups which distinguished our table from any farmers round were packed up by Aunt Dorothy's own hands, and despatched to the London Guildhall, not without sighs, but without hesitation, with all the money that could be spared.

Cousin Placidia also offered what she called her "mite," when she heard that the poor citizens' wives in London had even offered their thimbles and bodkins.

"I am but a poor parson's wife," said she, "but I am thankful they will receive even such poor offerings as I can bring."

And she brought those embroidered Cordova gloves, the search for which had so incensed Aunt Dorothy.

"It is remarkable," she observed, "that I always

said one never knew what use anything might be in a poor parson's household; and now I have found the use."

"What use, my dear," said Aunt Dorothy; "do you think the Parliament soldiers will fight in embroidered gloves?"

"Spanish leather is dear," replied Placidia, "and things will always sell. It is only a poor mite I know, but so is a thimble. The Parliament soldiers cannot, of course, fight in thimbles; and the widow's mite was accepted."

"*A* mite and the 'widow's mite,' are some way apart, my dear," said Aunt Dorothy; "your 'widow's mite,' I suppose, might be the parsonage and the glebe, and those cows in your uncle's park and meadow. Take care what you offer to the Lord. He sometimes takes us at our word. And there are plunderers abroad who take their own estimate of people's mites, widows' and others."

Said Placidia, never taken aback—

"Aunt Dorothy, Mr. Nicholls and I regard the glebe as a sacred trust, of which we feel we must on no account relinquish the smallest fraction. And as to the cows Uncle Drayton gave me, I wonder you can suspect me of such ingratitude as to give them up to any one."

"I did not, my dear," said Aunt Dorothy, quietly. "What shall I label your Cordova gloves? A parson's mite? You know I cannot exactly say 'widow's.'"

"An orphan's perhaps, Aunt Dorothy."

"Very well, my dear," said Aunt Dorothy; "I

should think that would affect the Parliament very much. It may even get into history."

With which this little passage at arms closed.

Happily for the popular cause, the common interpretation of acceptable 'mites' differed from Placidia's, so that in a short time a considerable army was levied.

The navy ever remained true to the Parliament; irritated, some foolish persons said, by a report that the king had called them "water-rats." As well say the whole Parliament stood firm, because the king once compared them to cats. The navy had its own watchwords, better pointed than by the sting of a sorry jest. English seamen were not likely to trust too implicitly to the promises of the Sovereign who had tried to sell them to aid in the destruction of the brave little band of beleaguered Protestants at Rochelle.

All through the summer the armies were being levied, and the breach was silently widening.

In July an incident showed, my Father said, as much as anything could, how entirely the king's mind was unchanged, and how "thorough" would have been the tyranny established in his hands, though Laud, and Strafford, and the Queen, and every violent councillor, had been removed. My old friend, Dr. Bastwick, the physician, was seized by the royal forces at Worcester while engaged in levying men for the Parliament, under Earl Stamford, who retreated. It was with the greatest difficulty that one of the judges restrained the king from having him hanged on the spot, although there could be no reason why he should have been sentenced with this exceptional severity except the fact that he had already been scourged, pilloried, and maimed by the cruelty of the Star-Chamber.

The deep distrust which such indications of the king's true mind produced, cost him more than many lost battles.

They tended to inspire such resistances as that made a few weeks afterwards by the brave commoners of Coventry, when, without garrison, without engineers, with no defence but their feeble ancient walls, they shut their gates in the Sovereign's face, defied the royal forces, and when the breach was made by artillery in the old tottering walls, barricaded the streets with barrows and carts, made a sally, carried the nearest lines, seized the guns, and turned them against the besiegers, compelling them at last to retire baffled.

But it was Prince Rupert, "the Prince Robber," who, perhaps, more than any, turned the hearts of the people against the Sovereign who could use such an instrument. Trained in the cruel school of the Palatinate wars, he had read its terrible lessons the wrong way; having learned from the sufferings of his father's subjects not pity, but a savage recklessness of suffering. He brought home to hundreds of burning villages and plundered lonely farms, which no Parliamentary remonstrances or declarations would have reached, the conviction that the king looked on his people, not as a flock, but as mere live-stock on an estate, to be kept up if profitable and manageable, and if not to be sacrificed to any system of management which gave less trouble and brought in more profit.

"*Whose own the sheep are not,*" was written in the ashes of every home ruined by Prince Rupert in the king's service.

With these deeds the people contrasted the well-kept orders of the Parliament to Lord Essex. "You shall carefully restrain all impieties, profaneness, and disorders, violence, insolence, and plundering in your soldiers, as well by strict and severe punishment of such offences as by all others means which you in your wisdom shall think fit."

And we grew to think that whoever the true shepherd and king of the people might be, it was scarcely one who employed the wolf for a sheep-dog.

It was but slowly and reluctantly that this conviction grew on the nation. Those who look back on the king's life, hallowed by the shadow of his death, little know how slowly and reluctantly. We would fain have trusted him if he would have let us. The nation tried it again and again, and only too much was sacrificed before they would believe it was in vain. Still there had been no battle. The Earl of Essex, after following the Prince from Worcester, lingered there three weeks, doing nothing No battle worth the name for nearly a hundred and seventy years, until Sunday the 23d of October, 1642.

Then came the first great shock. All that Sunday afternoon our countrymen, husbands, brothers, fathers, sons of the women left in the quiet villages at home, were fighting in the desperate struggle for life and death, until at night four thousand Englishmen lay dead on the slopes of Edgehill, or dying in the villages around—the day before as tranquil and peaceful as ours.

I remember there was a peculiar quiet about that Sunday at Netherby. So many of the men of the village had gone to the war. Roger had been away many weeks, and my Father had left some days before to join Lord Essex at Worcester. In all our household there were no men left except Bob the herdsman. The church was strangely deserted. Ths Hall pew empty. Scarcely one deep manly voice in response or psalm. On the benches in the village a few old men had an unwonted monopoly of talk, and the lads on anything like the verge of manhood strode heavily about with a new sense of importance. One asked another for news. But there was none, save rumours of mysterious marchings and counter-marchings of troops, without any aim that we knew, or the echo of some far-off foray of Prince Rupert's. There was a dreamy stillness all around. Tib's voice came up alone from the kitchen as she moved about some Sabbath work of necessity, and sung rather uncertainly snatches of the psalm we had sung at prayers in the morning. From the slope where the house stood (which gave us that wide range over the levels which I miss everywhere else), I saw the cattle feeding far off in the marshy lands, too far for any sound of their voices to reach me. The harvest was over on the nearer slopes, so that there was no music of the wind rustling through the corn. The land lay half slumbering in its autumn rest, like Roger's faithful Lion in his Sunday afternoon sleep on the terrace below. But, I knew not why, there seemed to me a kind of expectancy in this calm. A waiting and listening seemed to palpitate through this stillness of the land such as pervaded Lion's gladness as he couched, quivering at every sound, vainly waiting for Roger's voice to summon him as usual at this hour for a walk in the fields.

The feeling grew on me, till all this quiet seemed not as the rest after a calm, but the calm before a storm; and the silence excited in me as if it were the breathless hush of thousands of beating hearts.

Then I thought of Rachel Forster in her lonely home. And it was a relief to rise at once and go to her. Her door was open. She was sitting before the old Bible. It was open, but she was not reading. Her hands were clasped on her knees. There was a stillness on her face as great as that over the country. But in this calm there was something that calmed me.

It seemed to me conscious and victorious, not dreamlike, and liable at any moment to a terrible waking.

I told her the restlessness I had been feeling.

"Can we wonder, Mistress Olive?" said she. "Do we not know what we might be giving them up for?"

"This quietness of the world seems awful to me to-day, Rachel," said I, "but in you there is something that quiets me. You find peace in prayer, Rachel," said I. "Is it not that?"

"I scarce know whether it is prayer, Mistress Olive. It is nothing but going to the Rock that is higher than I, and taking all that is precious to me there, and staying there. It is just creeping to the foot of the Cross, and keeping there."

"You feel, then, as if something terrible were coming, Rachel," I said.

"I *know* something terrible must come," she said, with a tremulousness in her voice which was more from enthusiasm than from fear. "To-day, or to-morrow, or some day. For the Day of Vengeance is come; and the year of His redeemed is at hand."

"Oh, Rachel," I said, "I cannot silently rest as you do. I want words, entreaties for Roger, for my Father, for Job, and also for the good men who, if the battle comes, must die on the wrong side, and for the king; the king who, if he would but be true, might set all right again."

And she knelt down and prayed in words brief and burning, like the prayers in the Bible.

"You do not feel it too lonely here, Rachel?" I said as I left, "Why not come up to us? Your presence would be like a strong wall and fortress to me."

"I am less lonesome here, Mistress Olive," said she. "Job made so many little plans to spare me trouble before he went. I see his hand everywhere. There is the pile of wood close to the fire, and the little pipe carrying the water to the very door. It would seem like making light of his work not to use it all. And besides," she added, "there's a few poor tried folk who used to look to Job for a good word and a good turn, and now some of them look to me. And I could not fail them for the world."

As I wished her good-bye, and walked home and thought of her, a glorious new sense came on me of the strength there is in waiting on God, of the possibility of the feeblest who lean on him being not only sustained, but becoming themselves strong to sustain others.

When I went to see Rachel, the whole solid world had seemed to me, in my anxiety for the precious lives I could do nothing to preserve, but as some treacherous and quaking ground among our marshes, ready to sink down and overwhelm us, beneath the weight of our passing footsteps.

As I returned, the world, though in itself as transitory and uncertain as ever, was once more a solid pathway to me, because underneath it stood the foundation of an Almighty love, one word from whom was stronger and more enduring than all the worlds.

So we sang our evening psalm, and slept quietly that night at Netherby, knowing nothing of the four thousand pale and rigid corpses that lay stretched on the blood-stained battle-slopes at Edgehill, while Lord Essex encamped on the silent battle-field, and the king's watch-fires were kindled on the hill above, where he began the day, and no ground was gained on either side; only the lives of four thousand men lost.

If we may say "lost" of any life yielded up to duty, and called back to God!

In the tongues of men, we speak of lives lost on battle-fields: perhaps in the tongue of angels they speak of lives lost in easy and luxurious homes.

Chapter VIII.

OLIVE'S RECOLLECTIONS.

T was not till mid-day on Monday the 24th of October 1642, that the first tidings reached us of Keinton Fight, or, as some call it, the Battle of Edgehill. Tidings indeed they scarcely were, only rumours, as of far-off thunder faintly moaning through the heat and stillness of a summer's noon, mysterious, uncertain, scarcely louder than the hum of insects in the sunshine, yet almost more awful than the crash of the thunder-peal overhead. "Wars and rumours of wars." Until that Monday I had no conception of the significance of that word "rumours." I had anticipated the sudden shocks, the ruthless desolations of war; I had not thought of its terrible uncertainties, its heart-sickening suspenses.

At noon, when the few men left in the village were all away in the fields at work, a travelling tinker passed by who that morning about daybreak had done some work at a farm where the swineherd keeping his swine the evening before, on the edge of a beech-forest some miles to the south, had heard the sounds far off in the south-west, in the direction of Oxford, like the thunder of great guns, and the sharp cracking of musketry.

The tinker did what tinkering was needed in the village, in the absence of Job the village smith, and went on his way. Just after he left, Aunt Gretel and I went to take broken meat and broth to two or three sick and aged people, and we found all the women gathered around the black and silent forge, or rather around Rachel, while she sat quietly patching in the porch of the cottage; the latticed, narrow cottage-windows letting in too little light for any work that required to be neatly done.

An eager excited crowd it was, the scanty measure of the text only furnishing wider margin for the commentary. Rachel, meanwhile, sat quietly in the middle, like a mother among a number of eager chattering children.

As we reached the group, poor Margery, Dickon's young wife, with her child in her arms, half-sobbed,—

"I wonder, Rachel, thee can bear to go on stitch, stitch. Since the news came I have been all of a tremble thinking of my goodman, who went off with yourn. I couldn't bring my fingers together to hold a needle, do what I would."

"I don't know that I could well bear it without the stitching, neighbour," said Rachel, softly. "When trouble is come, we may well sit still and weep. The Lord calls us to it. But in the waiting-times I see nought for it but to brace up the heart and work."

When we came, all turned to tell us of the dread rumour. Aunt Gretel brought one or two cheering stories of providence and deliverance out of the eventful histories of her youth; and then we went on our errands, Aunt Gretel thinking we should do more to soothe and quiet these agitated hearts by the example of steadily pursuing our task, than by the wisest talking in the world.

"For," said she, "the true tidings have yet to come; and they are like to be sad enough to some. And how will they bear it, if all the strength is wasted before-hand in vain and mournful guesses?"

The result proved her right, for when our baskets were emptied, and Aunt Gretel returned home, while I went to see Rachel again, the village was stirring as usual with quiet sounds of labour in house after house, and the excited group around the porch had dispersed. Only poor Margery lingered, Rachel having found her occupation in lighting the fire and preparing supper, to save her returning to her lonely cottage; while the baby crowed and kicked on the ground at Rachel's feet.

"But, Rachel," I said, "would it not have quieted the neighbours to pray together, you with them?"

"Maybe, sweetheart," she said. "But I did not feel I could. If the news is true, the fight is over. It's over hours since. The dead are lying cold, out of the reach of our prayers. And the living are saved and are giving thanks; and the wounded are writhing in their anguish, and we know not who is dead, or wounded, or whole. And when we look to the earth to think, it comes over us like a rush of dark waters when the dykes are pierced. So I can but look to heaven and work. It's light and not dark where He sitteth. And beyond the thunders and the lightnings He is caring for us in the great calm of the upper sky. Caring for us, sweetheart, as the poor mother cares for this babe; not sitting on a throne and smiling like the king in the picture, with both hands full of his sceptre and his bauble; but with both hands free, to help and to uphold. So I try to do the bit of work He sets me, and to look up to Him and feel, 'There is no fear but that Thou wilt do the work Thou hast set Thyself; and that is, to care for us all.' And I told the neighbours they had best try the same."

The words were scarcely out of her lips, when a horseman came clattering down the village and stopped at Job's well-known forge.

"What news? asked a score of voices one after another, as the women crowded round him.

"Dismal news enough for some, and glorious for others," he said. "The king's army and Lord Essex's met yesterday. Lord Essex below in the Vale of the Red Horse, and the king on Edgehill above. Prince Rupert charged down on the Parliament horse, under Commissary-General Ramsay, broke them in a trice, and pursued them to Keinton, killing and plundering. I heard it from one of the routed horsemen who escaped. Everything is lost, he said, for Lord Essex, and I hasten to carry the news to one who loves the king."

Hastily draining Rachel's can of home-brewed ale, he was off in a minute, and out of sight.

All through the afternoon confused and contradictory news continued to drop in from one and another. But it was not till the next day (Tuesday) that we could collect anything like a true account of the battle,—how for hours, all through the noontide of that autumn Sunday, the two armies had couched, like two terrible beasts of prey, watching each other; the king on the height, and Essex in the plain—as if loth to break with the murderous roar of cannon our England's two centuries of peace.

Prayers, no doubt, there were, many and deep, breaking that silence, to the ear of God; but few, perhaps, better than that of gallant Sir Jacob Ashley, one of the king's major-generals: "Lord, Thou knowest I must be busy this day; if I forget Thee, do not Thou forget me."

Who began the fight at last, we could not well make out. The most part said Lord Essex, directing a sally up the hill, which Prince Rupert answered by dashing down like a torrent, from the royal vantage-ground to the plain, on the left wing of the Parliament army. The men fell or fled on all sides before his furious charge; and he pursued them to the village of Keinton, where Lord Essex had encamped the day before. Deeming the day won, his men gave themselves up to plundering the baggage, and slaughtering the wagoners and unarmed labourers. But meantime Sir William Balfour, on the right wing, charged the king's left, broke it, seized and spiked many of the king's guns, took the royal standard after a struggle which left sixty brave men dead in sixty yards around it, and drove nearly the whole royal army to their morning's position up the hill. There they rallied. Prince Rupert returned, laden with his blood-stained plunder, to find the king's army in confusion. But darkness was setting in; it is said the Parliament gun-powder began to fail; so no further pursuit was made, and on Sunday night again both armies encamped on the ground where they had begun the battle. The king's camp-fires blazed on the hill, and the Parliament's in the Vale of the Red Horse. But between them lay four thousand dead Englishmen,—that Sabbath morning full of life and courage, now lying stiff and helpless on the quiet slopes where they had fallen in the tumult of the mortal conflict.

It is said, most of those who fell on the king's side fell standing firm, and of ours running away; which means, I suppose, that they lost their bravest, and we our cowards.

I found my Father, and many of the soldiers I know, always loth to speak much of the battle-field after a battle. My Father and Roger would discuss by the hour the handling of troops and the strategy of the commanders, and all which related to war as an art or a science, and regarded the troops as pieces on a board. But of the after-misery, when the terrible excitement and the skillful manœuvres of the day were over, and the troops and regiments had again become only men, wounded, weary, dead, I never heard them to speak save in a few broken words.

The difference of language served a little to veil the common humanity in the German wars, my Father said; but to hear the fallen entreating for quarter, or the dying calling on God and on dear familiar names, or the wounded praying for help which, in the rush of the battle, could not be given, in the old mother-tongue, was enough, he said, to take all the pomp and glory out of war, and to leave it nothing but its agony and its horror.

Both sides claimed the victory,—Lord Essex by right of encamping on the field, and the king by the weight of Prince Rupert's plunder.

However that might be, neither side pursued the advantage they both boasted to have gained.

The king, who was between the Parliament army and London, to the great anxiety of the city, did not advance, but retired on Oxford,—the Parliament garrison of Banbury, however, surrendering to him without a struggle.

Lord Essex made no pursuit, but withdrawing to London, left the country open to Prince Rupert's foragers.

But victory or defeat were scarcely the chief questions to us women that day at Netherby.

Margery's anxieties were the first relieved. Her husband Dickon being in the king's army, sent her an orange scarf taken from a Parliament horseman at Keinton, in token of his safety.

Then, on Wednesday, poor Tim, Gammer Grindle's half-witted grandson, who would, in spite of all that could be said, follow Roger to the war, came limping into the village, emaciated and foot-sore, with his arm bound up in a sling. He stopped at Rachel Forster's door, and began stammering a confused account of Master Roger and Job lying wounded at Keinton, and the prince's men murdering some of the wounded, and carring off Roger and Job, pinioned, in a cart to gaol, and Tim's trying to follow on foot, and having his arm broken by a musket-shot, and his leg wounded, and so, being left behind, having limped home to tell Mistress Olive.

But where the gaol was, or how severe Roger's wound was, or Job's, could in no way be extracted from poor Tim's confused brain and tongue! "Poor Tim!" he said, apologising with broken words, as a faithful dog might with wistful looks, for having escaped without his master, "Poor Tim tried hard to follow Master Roger—tried hard! Master Roger knows Tim did not wish to leave him; Master Rogert knows. Master Roger said, 'Tim, you've done all you could. Go home. And tell them Master Roger's all right.'" When first he saw Rachel, he said, "Poor Job said, 'Take care!'" And then clenching his hand, with a smile, "Poor Tim took care!" But he never repeated or explained it. It was quite useless to question him. That one purpose of obeying Roger possessed the whole of his poor brain. The poor creature was faint from pain and weariness, and loss of blood. Rachel would have made him a bed in the cottage, and not one of us at Netherby but would have counted it an honour to have nursed him for his love to Roger; but he shook his head: "Master Roger said, 'Tim, you've done all you could. Go home." And nothing would satisfy him but to go on to the hovel by the Mere, were his grandmother lived.

Gammer Grindle was a poor, wizened, old woman, soured by much trouble and by the constant fretting of a sharp temper against poverty and wrong, until few in the village liked to venture near her. Indeed, there were dark suspicions afloat about her. Many a labouring-man would have gone a mile round rather than pass her door after dusk, and many a yeoman-farmer and goodwife who had lost an unusual number of sheep or poultry would propitiate her by the present of a lamb or a fat pullet. And, in general, in the neighbourhood she was spoken of with a reverent terror much akin to that of the man who, after hastily using the name of the devil, crossed himself, and said, "May he pardon me for taking his holy name in vain."

But Roger and I happened to have come across her on another and very different side. In our fishing expeditions on the Mere her grandson Tim had often followed us with the fish-basket or tackle; and the rare contrast of Roger's kindly tones and words with the jeerings of the rough boys in the village, had won him in Tim's heart an affection intense, absorbing, disinterested, and entirely free from motives of return or hope of reward; more like that of a faithful dog than a human being with purposes and interests of his own.

This had given us access to his grandmother's

hovel, and many a time she had saved me from the consequences of Aunt Dorothy's just wrath by kindling up her poor embers of fire to dry my soaked shoes, and cleaning the mud from my clothes. Simple easy services, but such as made it altogether impossible for Roger and me to regard the poor, kind, shrivelled hands that had rendered them as having signed a compact with Satan. Besides, did we not see how good she was, with all her scoldings, to Tim, and know from broken words which had dropped now and then how she had loved her only daughter, the mother of Cicely and Tim, and how sore her heart was for the poor, lost girl, and what a power of wronged and disappointed love lay seething and fermenting beneath the sour sharp words she spoke?

Roger and I knew that Gammer Grindle was no outlaw from the pale of humanity by seeing it; and Rachel Forster knew it, I believe, by seeing Him at whose feet so many outcasts from human sympathy found a welcome. And so it happened, that of all the village no one but Rachel, Roger and I sought access, or would have had it, to Gammer Grindle's hovel, so that Rachel that day accompanied Tim home, and was permitted to share his grandmother's watch that night.

For Tim's exhaustion soon changed to delirious fever, as his wound began to be inflamed, and it was as much as both the women could do to keep him from rushing out of the hovel to "follow Master Roger."

All the time, they noticed he kept the hand of

his unwounded arm firmly clenched over something. But no coaxing or commands, even from his grandmother's voice, which he was so used to obey, would induce him to unclasp his hand or let it go.

All that night and the next day the two women watched by the poor lad, bathing his head, and trying vainly to keep him still. But towards evening his strength began to fail, and it was plain that the fever, having done its work, was relinquishing its hold to the cold grasp of Another stronger than it.

The poor lad's delirious entreaties ceased, and he lay so still, that Rachel could hear the cold ripples of the Mere outside plashing softly among the rushes, stirred by the night wind; and they sounded to her like the slow waters of the river of Death.

Only now and then he said, in a low voice, like a child crooning to itself, "Poor Tim, Master Roger knows. Master Roger said, you have done all you could. Go home."

Once also his eye brightened, and he said, "Cicely, sister Cicely! Tell her to come soon—soon. I have watched for her so long!"

Rachel tried to speak to him about Jesus, the loving Master of us all; he did not object, but whether he understood or not, she could not tell. He did not alter the words which had been so engraven on his poor faithful heart. Only they grew fainter and fainter, and fewer and more broken, until, with one sigh, "Master—home," the poor feeble spirit departed, and the poor feeble body was at rest.

But Rachel said it seemed to her as if the blessed Lord would most surely not fail to understand the poor lad who could not understand about Him, yet had served so faithfully the *best he knew.* And she almost thought she heard a voice from heaven saying, "Poor Tim! the Master knows. You have done the best you could. Come home!"

It was not until the poor lad was dead that they found what he had been so tightly clasping in his hand.

It was a fragment of paper containing a few words written by Job Forster, of which Tim had indeed "taken care," as the clasp of the lifeless hand proved too well.

The words were,—

"Rachel, be of good cheer, as I am. I am hurt on the shoulder, but not so bad. They are taking me with Roger to Oxford goal. His wound is in the side, painful at first, but Dr. Antony got the ball out, and says he will do well. Thee must not fret, nor try to come to us. It would hurt thee and do us no good. The Lord careth."

Rachel read this letter, with every word made emphatic, by her certainty that Job would make as light as possible of any trouble, by her knowledge that his pen was not that of a ready writer, and by her sense of what she would have done herself in similar circumstances.

"Rachel!"—the word, she knew, had taken him a minute or two to spell out, and it meant a whole volume of esteem and love; and by the same measure, "hurt" meant "disabled;" and "not so bad," simply not in immediate peril of life; and "thee must not come," to her heart meant "come if thou canst, though I dare not bid thee."

It was not Rachel's way to let trouble make her helpless, or even prevent her being helpful where she was needed. God, she was sure, had not meant it for that. She lived at the door of the House of the Lord, and therefore, at this sudden alarm, she did not need a long pilgrimage by an untrodden path to reach the sanctuary. A moment to lay down the burden and enter the open door, and lift up the heart there within; and then to the duty in hand. She remained, therefore, with Gammer Grindle until they had laid the poor faithful lad in his shroud; then she gave all the needful orders for the burial, so that it was not till dusk she was seated in her own cottage, with leisure to plan how she should carry out what, from the moment she had first glanced at her husband's letter, she had determined to do.

Half an hour sufficed her for thinking, or "taking counsel," as she called it; half an hour more for making preparations and coming across to us at Netherby, with her mind made up and all her arrangements settled.

Arrived in the Hall, she handed Job's letter to Aunt Dorothy.

"What can be done?" said Aunt Dorothy. "How can it be that we have not heard from my brother or Dr. Antony? The king's forces must be between us and Oxford, and the letters must have been seized. But never fear, Rachel," she added, in a consoling tone. "At first they talked of treating all the Parliament prisoners as traitors; but that will never be. A ransom or an exchange is certain. Stay here to-night; it will be less lonely for you. We can take counsel together; and to-morrow we will think what to do."

'I have been thinking, Mistress Dorothy; and I have taken counsel. I am going at day-break to-morrow to Oxford; and I came to ask if I could do aught for you, or take any message to Master Roger."

"How?" said Aunt Dorothy. "And who will go with you? Who will venture within the grasp of those plunderers?"

"I have not asked any one, Mistress Dorothy. I am going alone on our own old farm-horse."

"*You* travel scores of miles alone, and into the midst of the king's army, Rachel!" said Aunt Dorothy.

"I have taken counsel, Mistress Dorothy," said Rachel calmly, and, looking up, Aunt Dorothy met that in Rachel's quiet eyes which she understood, and she made no further remonstrance.

"We will write letters to Roger," she said, after a pause.

In a short time they were ready, with one from me to Lettice Davenant.

Neither my Aunts nor I slept much that night. We were revolving various plans for helping Rachel, each unknown to the other.

I had thought of a letter to a friend of my Father's who lived half-way between us and Oxford, and rising softly in the night, without telling any one, I wrote it. For I had removed to Roger's chamber while he was away; it seemed to bring me nearer to him.

Then, before daybreak, feeling sure Rachel would be watching for the first streaks of light, I crept out of our house to hers.

She was dressed, and was quietly packing up the great Bible which lay always on the table, and laying it in the cupboard.

"Happy Rachel!" I said, kissing her; "to be old enough to dare to go."

"There is always some work, sweetheart," said she, "for every season, not to be done before or after. That is why we need never be afraid of growing old."

I gave her my letter. She took it gratefully; but she said—

"Too fine folks for a plain body like me, Mistress Olive. God bless you for the thought. But in one village I must pass there is a humble godly man who has oft tarried with us for a night, and has expounded the word to us, and no doubt he will give me a token to another. And if not, the seven thousand are always known to the Lord. The prophet Elijah, indeed, did not know; but after *he* was told about it once for all, none of us ought ever to say again, 'I only am left alone.'"

"But how will you manage when you get to Oxford?" I said.

"God forbid I should presume to say, sweetheart," said she. "Oxford is many steps off. And the Lord has only shown me the next step. Job is wounded and in prison and wants me, and will my God, and his, fail to show me how to get to him?"

As she spoke these last words, the force of repressed passion, and of faith contending in them, gave her voice an unwonted depth, which made it sound to me like another voice answering her.

At that moment Aunt Gretel arrived, laden with a small basket containing spiced cordials and preserved meats for Rachel's journey.

And not a quarter of an hour afterwards, Aunt Dorothy, on horseback, bent on protecting Rachel through some portion of her way.

And then Margery and the babe, who had come at Rachel's request.

Before mounting her horse, Rachel said,—

"You will have thought of being at poor Tim's burying, Mistress Olive?"

We promise all to be there.

And Rachel from the mounting-steps climbed up on the patient old horse, and was gone, only turning back once to smile at us as we watched her.

She was not a woman for after-thoughts, or last lingering words. She had always said what she wanted before the last.

She had left us the heavy key of the cottage-door, that we might give away the little stores which she had divided the night before into various portions for her poor neighbours. She had intended committing them to Margery, but as we were there first, we undertook the charge. How simply and how unheralded events come which hallow our common tables and chambers with the tender solemnity as of places of worship or of burial. The sound of Rachel's horse-hoofs was scarcely out of hearing when the empty cottage had become to us as a sacred place. The little packets her neat hands had arranged so thoughtfully were no common loaves, or meat, but sacred relics hallowed by her loving touch. And it was hard to look at the firewood Job had piled by the fire for her, and the little stone channel he had made to bring the water near the door, without tears.

LETTICE DAVENANT'S DIARY.

"*Oxford*, *November* 1, 1642.—Victoria! The first step is gained; the first lesson given, though at some cost of noble lives to us and to the king. Lord Essex is fain to retreat to London to console the affrighted citizens, leaving the whole country open to the king. Yet my Father saith privately to us, this victory of Edgehill might have been far more complete had it not been for Prince Rupert's rashness. Indeed, after the fight there had well-nigh been a duel in the king's presence between the prince and a gentleman who expressed his mind pretty freely on the matter. The prince, after pursuing the rebels to Keinton, lingered there, plundering the baggage, and returned with his horses laden with the spoils to find the royal army not in such order as it might have been had his troops kept with it. 'We can give a good account of the enemy's horse, your Majesty,' he said. 'Yes,' said this gentleman standing by, 'and of their carts too.' For which jest the haughty hot-blooded prince would have had severe revenge, had not the king with much ado brought them to an accommodation.

"*Note.*—The young Princes Charles and James, of but ten or twelve years old, had a narrow escape. Their governor, Dr. Harvey, a learned man, was sitting quietly with them on the grass reading his book, and never perceived anything was amiss until the bullets came whizzing round him. I wonder royal persons should be trusted to the care of people whose wits are always at the ends of the earth, like philosophers. Who knows how different things might have been in the world if Dr. Harvey and the young princes had sat there a few minutes longer!

"However, the best fruits of victory are beginning to appear. Gentlemen, whose loyalty had been somewhat wavering, are riding in from all quarters, well accoutred, abundantly attended, finely mounted, to offer their services to His Majesty.

"This grave and stately old city is gorgeous with warlike array, and echoing with warlike music.

"My Father, Mother, and I are lodged in Lincoln College. A distant cousin of ours, Sir William Davenant, who hath writ many plays and farces, and now fights in the army, being of this college, and also others of our kindred from the north country. I feel quite at home in the rooms with their thick walls, and dull narrow arched windows like those in the turret-chamber at the Hall, more at home than the old quadrangles and walls themselves can be with all this clamour and trumpeting to arms.

"Not that there is much to be seen in the great inner court on which my chamber-window looks. An ancient vine climbs up one side of the walls, encircling the entrance arch, and its leaves, brown and crimson with the autumn, stirred with the breeze, are making a pleasant quiet country music as I write. This vine is held in high honour in the college, having illustrated the text of the sermon, 'Look on this vine,' which inspired good Bishop de Rotheram, more than two hundred years since, to become the second Founder of the College.

"Through this entrance-arch I look beyond its shadow to the sunny street, crossed now and then by the flash of arms, and gay Cavaliers' mantles, or the prancings of a troop of horse. That is all the glimpse I have of the outer world. But I think my Mother were content to live in such a place for ever. Every day she resorts more than once to a quiet corner of the new Chapel to pay her orisons, taking delight in the stillness, and in the brilliant colours of the painted windows Bishop Williams (once the antagonist of Archbishop Laud, and now with him in the Tower) had brought but a few years since from Italy.

"Outside this chapel there is a garden, where we walk, and discourse of the prospects of the kingdom, and of those friends at Netherby from whom we are now so sadly parted.

"For Roger and Mr. Drayton are in the rebel army—alas! there is no longer doubt of it—and any day their hands and those of my seven brothers, all in the king's army, may be against each other.

"*November* 8th.—The king and the army are away at Reading, with my Father and my brothers; and the city is quiet enough without them.

"Sir Launcelot is now on service about the Castle. I would he were on the field, and one of my brothers here. However, I am not like to see much of him at present. He will scarce venture to come after what I had to say to him this morning.

"He came in laughing, saying he had just seen an encounter between an old rebel woman at the gate and four of Prince Rupert's plunderers. 'She was contending with them for the possession of a sober Puritanical-looking old horse,' said he. 'They claimed it for the king's service. She said 'that might be, but in that case she chose to give it up herself unto the care of one of His Majesty's court, to whom she had a letter.'

"'Did you not give her a helping word?' said I.

"'I am scarcely such a knight errant as that, Mistress Lettice,' said he; 'I should have enough to do, in good sooth. Moreover, the godly generally make good fight for their carnal goods, and in this instance the woman seemed as likely as not to have the best of the debate, to say nothing of her being wrinkled and toothless.'

"That made me flash up, as speaking lightly of aged women always does. 'Poor chivalry,' said I, 'which has not recollection enough of a mother to lend a helping hand to the old and wrinkled. *We* shall be wrinkled and toothless in a few years, sir, and our imagination is not so weak but that we can fore-date a little while, and transfer all such heartless jests to ourselves. I have been used to higher chivalry than that among the Puritans,' said I.

"He laughed, and made a pretty pathetic deprecation. His mother had died (quoth he) when he was too young to remember. Some little excuse, perchance. However, Roger Drayton's mother also died when he was in infancy. But be that as it might, I was in no mood to listen. And as we were speaking, a serving-man came to tell me a poor woman from Netherby was in the ante-room craving to see me or my Mother.

"It was Rachel Forster.

"Her neat Puritan hood, so dainty, I think, on her pale worn-looking face, was rather ruffled, and although her eyes had the wonted quiet in them, (only a little loftier than usual,) she was trembling, and willingly took the chair I offered her.

"'You did not find it easy coming through the royal lines,' I said.

"'Nothing but a few rude jests at the gate, Mistress Lettice,' said she; 'but I am not used to them, or to going about the world alone. But I have been taken good care of. And I am *here*,' she added, fervently; 'which is all I asked.'

"'Did they try to take your horse from you?' I said.

"'They took him,' she said. 'But that matters little. He was a faithful beast, and I am feared how they may use him. But the beasts have only *now*, neither fore nor after, which saves them much.' Then without more words she gave me a letter from Olive.

"From this I found that Roger is a prisoner in the Castle here, with Job Forster.

"I went into the other chamber, and asked Sir Launcelot had he known of this.

"'I learned it a day or two since,' he replied, hesitating, 'but I did not tell you or Lady Lucy, because you are so pitiful, I feared to pain you uselessly.'

"'*We* might have judged whether it was uselessly or not, Sir Launcelot!' said I.

"'Can I do anything for you?' he asked, in confusion.

"'Nothing,' said I. 'You might have helped an aged woman, a friend of mine, whom you found in difficulties at the gate this morning. But now, excuse me, I have no time to spare—I must go to my Mother.' And I withdrew to the inner room, to bring my Mother out at once to see what could be done; leaving him to retire through the anteroom, where Rachel Forster sat.

"I trow he will not be in a hurry to visit us again.

"My Mother and Rachel had always been friends. They both live a good deal at the height where the party-colours blend in the one sunlight; and they neither of them ever speak half as much as they feel about religion.

"There was not much to say, therefore, when my Mother understood her errand. My Mother's word had weight, and in a few hours she had procured a permit for Rachel to see her husband, provided the interview was in her presence.

"It was a noisome place, she said—many persons crowded together like cattle in dungeons, with scant light or air, and none to wait on them but each other. Job was on some straw in a corner, looking sorely altered—his strong limbs limp and emaciated, and his eye languid. But it was wonderful how his face lighted up when he saw Rachel.

"'I thought thee would come', said he, 'though I bid thee not. I knew thee had learned how "all things are possible."'

"My Mother's intercessions procured for them the great favour of a cell, which, though narrow, low, damp, and underground, they were to have to themselves. And before she left, Rachel's neat hands had made the straw and matting look like a proper sick-bed, while her presence had lighted the cell into a home.

"Then my Mother went to see Roger Drayton. His wound was not so severe as Job's, and his lodging was better, though wretched enough. Great complaints were made about the prisons. But, I fear, all war-prisons, suddenly and not very tenderly arranged, are hard enough.

"'Have you seen Job Forster?' was his first question after greeting her.

"She told him what had been done.

"'I begged hard to be allowed to share his prison. But they would not let me,' said Roger.

"Roger, though far less suffering, looked less tranquil than Job, my Mother said. He did not ask for me until he had read Olive's letter, and then he said abruptly,—

"'Olive says she has written to Mistress Lettice.' And his face flushed deeply as he added, 'Olive is but a child in such things, Lady Lucy, and cannot know the hard laws of war. You will not be offended if she pleads, fancying you could do anything for us. You must not let anything she says trouble you, you are so kind. For I know nothing can be done.'

"'Only one thing troubles me,' my Mother said, evasively, 'I would give much if *that* could be changed.'

"She did not think it generous to say more, but he understood, and answered,—

"'*That* can *not* be changed, unless *all* could be changed. It makes me restless enough to be shut up here, Lady Lucy, but it does not make me *doubt*.'

"'Those Draytons are like rocks—as firm, and almost as hard. No, not hard. Nothing they ought not to be, if only they were on the right side!

"And Roger called Olive a child. I wonder, then, what he thinks me, who am two years younger!

"However, my Mother thinks something *can* be done for Roger. Exchanges can be made. Little comfort in that. He is less dangerous to himself and every one else where he is, than in the field again. Yet my Mother says the air and food of the prison are none of the most wholesome. And, of course, Olive wants to have him free. These are most perplexing times. One cannot even tell what to wish.

"I would send him a message when my Mother goes again, but that he scarcely even asked for me; only defended himself against joining in Olive's pleadings for himself. So proud! I will send him no message, not a word. Nothing but a few sweet autumn violets from the college garden; because the air of the prison is so bad.

"*February* 10.—Job Forster all but sank. He must have died if my Mother had not pleaded hard and got permission at last for him to be taken home to Netherby in one of our Hall wagons. She thought it would scarce be more than to die. But to-day we have had a letter from Rachel, saying, the very sight of the forge and smell of the fields seemed to work on him like a heavenly cordial, and she doubts not he will rally. Dr. Antony hath been to see him, and Olive, and Mistress Gretel, and Mistress Dorothy, and brought him meats and strong waters, and read him sermons, saith she, and they say he could not be doing better. But, she adds, she hopes Lady Lucy will not think it thankless that he should use his liberty to fight for the Parliament, as no condition was made on his return; and he thinks the Covenant under which he fights must stand good, and dares not break it. So my sweet Mother hath on her conscience the guilt of tenderly nourishing a viper to sting what she loveth best!

"But Roger Drayton is to be exchanged for one of our Cavaliers, and is to leave Oxford to-morrow. All these weeks he hath been here, and never a word between us, except some cold thanks for those violets. So proud is he! And it was not for me to begin.

"*February* 11.—Roger Drayton had the grace to pay us his devoirs before he left, at Lincoln College. But he would scarce sit down. I trow he was afraid of being vanquished if he ventured into debate concerning his bad cause. He did not say anything to me. If he had, I felt tempted to say something angry. But he did not begin; and why should I? Until at last, as he was leaving, he said,—

"'Mistress Lettice, I am going to join Colonel Cromwell at Cambridge. But I may see Olive by the way. May I say a word to her from you? Sometimes a message is better than a letter.'

"I could not think of anything to say. It took me so by surprise after his silence. For it was just like his old tone by the Mere, or in the woods, or on the terraces at Netherby, and at the Hall. And it so brought poor old Netherby back to me, and all the old happy days, that I was afraid my voice would tremble if I spoke. I could only think of Mistress Dorothy's sermons; things come into one's head so strangely. So, after a little while, I said very abruptly, 'I sent Olive dear love—and to tell Mistress Dorothy I had read her sermons.'

"But his voice trembled a little as he wished us good-bye; I certainly think it did. And he was not out of the door when I thought of ten thousand messages to send to Olive. But I could not go after him to say them. I could only go to the window and watch him through the court. I was almost sorry I did. For he looked up and saw me, and seemed half inclined to turn back. But, instead, he made a strange little reverence, as if he did not quite know whether to seem to see me or not. I wonder if he also had thought of a few things he would have liked to have said! He was always rather slow in speech; I mean, his words always meant about ten times as much as any other man's.

"And so he strode across the court and under the shadow of the archway into the sunny street outside. To join Colonel Cromwell. Colonel, indeed! By whose commission? Roger might at least have spared us that. If it had been Mr. Hampden even, or Lord Essex, it would not have been so bad. But this fanatic brewer!

"However, I am glad I said nothing angry. One never knows in these days where or when the next word may be spoken. And then alack, this Mr.

Cromwell, they say, is sure to be just where the fighting is.

"He did not look amiss in that plain Puritan asmour. The cap-a-pie armour of the 'Ironsides,' as some begin to call them. It seems to me more martial and more manly than the gay trappings of our Cavaliers. Gallant decorations are well enough for a dance or a masque; but in real warfare I thik the plainest vesture looks the noblest. At Edgehill His Majesty must have looked most stately in his suit of plain black velvet, with no ornament but the George.

"*March* 1643.—There is a Dr. Thomas Fuller lodging here at present, who is a great solace to my Mother, and also to me, being a kind of cousin of ours through his maternal uncle Dr. Davenant, Bishop of Salisbury.

"He is tall and athletic, with pleasant blue eyes, full of mirth, and withal of kindness, of a ruddy complexion, with fair wavy locks. He hath wit enough for a play-wright, and piety enough,—I had almost said for a Puritan—I should rather say for an archbishop.

"He was in London a few weeks since, and preached a sermon to incline the rebels to peace, which is all his desire. But they did not relish it, and would have him sign one of their unmannerly Covenants; which not being able to do, he has fled hither. Yet am I not sure that he is more at home among our rollicking Cavaliers.

"I would I could remember half the wise and

witty things he saith. I like his wit, because is often cuts both ways—against Puritan and Cavalier; and more especially at present against the younger sort sort of the latter, whose reckless manners suit him ill. The poor Puritans are so hit on all sides with the shafts of ridicule, that in fairness I like to see some of the darts flying the other way, especially against such as assume to themselves the monopoly of wit.

"'Harmless mirth,' said Dr. Fuller the other day, 'is the best cordial against the consumption of the spirits, but jest not with the two-edged sword of God's word. Will nothing please thee to wash thy hands in but the font? Or to drink healths in but the church-chalice?'

"He is very busy, and is abstemious in eating and drinking, and is an early riser. Sir Launcelot, liking not, I ween, to feel the jest so against himself, calls him a Puritan in disguise; but Harry and he are good friends, and to my Mother he behaveth ever with a gentle deference, as all men, indeed, are wont to do. With her his wit seems to change its nature from fire to sunshine. So tenderly doth he seek to brighten her pensive and somewhat self-reproachful spirit into peace and praise. She on her part hath her sweet returns of sympathy for him, drawing him forth to discourse of his young wife lately dead, and his motherless infant boy.

"Religion with my Mother is a life of affections, not merely a code of rules; and, I suppose, like all affections, brings its sorrows as well as its joys.

Otherwise I could scarce account for the heaviness she so often is burdened withal.

"One day, when she was fearing to embrace the cheering words of Scripture, Dr. Fuller encouraged her by reminding her how in the Hebrews the promise, 'I will not leave thee, nor forsake thee,' though at first made only to Joshua, is applied to all good men. 'All who trust the Saviour, and follow him,' said he, 'are heirs-apparent to all the promises.'

"But she, who being a saint (by any laws of canonization) ever bemoaneth herself as though she were a penitent weeping between the porch and the altar, put off his consolation with—

"'True, indeed, for all *good* men.'

"To which he, unlike most ghostly comforters I have heard, replied with no honeyed commendation, false or true, but said,—

"'In the agony of a wounded conscience always look upward to God to keep thy soul steady. For looking downward on thyself, thou shalt find nothing but what will increase thy fear; infinite sins, good deeds few and imperfect. It is not thy faith, but God's faithfulness thou must rely on. Casting thine eyes down to thyself, to behold the great distance between what thou desirest and what thou deservest is enough to make thee giddy, stagger, and reel unto despair. Ever, therefore, lift up thine eyes to the hills whence cometh thine help.'

"'The reason,' quoth he afterwards, 'why so many are at a loss in the agony of a wounded conscience, is, that they look for their life in the wrong place—namely, in their own piety and purity. Let them seek and search, dig and dive never so deep, it is all in vain. For though Adam's life was hid in himself, yet, since Christ's coming all the original evidences of our salvation are kept in a higher office—namely, hidden in God himself. Surely many a despairing soul groaning out his last breath with fear to sink down to hell, hath presently been countermanded by God to eternal happiness.'

"His words brought tears to my Mother's eyes, but comfort, said she, to her heart.

"Yet, though she saw sunshine through the clouds, she feared to find the cloud again beyond the sunshine, whereon he heartened her further by saying, 'Music is sweetest near or over rivers, where the echo thereof is best rebounded by the water. Praise for pensiveness, thanks for tears, and blessing God over the floods of affliction, makes the most melodious music in the ear of heaven.'

"Good and fit works for her who needs and deserves such. To me these other words of his are more to the purpose.

"'How easy,' saith he, 'is pen and paper piety. It is far cheaper to work one's head than one's heart to goodness. I can make a hundred meditations sooner than subdue one sin in my soul.'

"He gave my Mother also a sermon of his 'on the doctrine of assurance,' which she much affects. 'All who seek the grace of assurance,' he writes, 'in a diligent and faithful life, may attain it without miraculous illumination. Yet many there are who have saving faith without it. And those who deny this will prove racks to tender consciences. As the careless mother killed her little child, for she overlaid it, so this heavy doctrine would press many poor but pious souls, many infant faiths, to the pit of despair.'

"*April* 1643.—Dr. Fuller hath left us to be chaplain in the regiment of Lord Hopton, an honorable man, who will honour him, and give him scope to do all the good that may be to the soldiers.

"He took leave of us in the college-garden, and gave my Mother a book of his imprinted last year, when he was preacher at the Savoy in London. It is entitled the Holy State and the Profane State, and seemeth wise and witty like himself. As he parted from us, he begged her to remember that 'all heavenly gifts, as they are got by prayer, are kept and increased by praise.'

"*Note.*—I like well what he writes of anger. 'Anger is one of the sinews of the soul. He that wants it hath a maimed mind.' I would I had known this saying to comfort Roger Drayton withal, when Sir Launcelot provoked him to that blow.

"Yet another saying is perhaps as needful, at least for me, 'Be not mortally angry for a venial fault. He will make a strange combustion in the state of his soul who at the landing of every cockboat sets the beacons on fire.'

"We miss Dr. Fuller sorely; my Mother for his words of ghostly cheer, and I for the just and generous things he dares to say of good men on the other side, and saith with a wit and point which leaves no opening for scornful jest to controvert.

"If Dr. Fuller had been the vicar of Netherby, and if the Draytons had known him, maybe many things had gone otherwise.

"Now, alack! there seems less hope of accommodation by this Christmas than I had felt sure of by the last.

"The Parliament Commissioners were here through March, and have but now left.

"Some Lords and some Commons. But nought could they accomplish. How, indeed, could aught be hoped from subjects who presume to treat with their leige lord as with a rival power?

"My Lord Falkland (now the king's secretary) comes now and then to converse with my Mother. Those who knew him before this sad rebellion began, say he is sorely changed from what he was. Whereas his mind used to be as free and open to entertain all wise and pleasant thoughts of others, as his mansion at Great Tew, near this was free and open to entertain their persons, so that they called it 'a college of smaller volume in a purer air;' now, they say, he is often preoccupied, and when in private will sigh and moan 'Peace! peace!' and say he shall soon die of a broken heart, if this dire war be prolonged. This especially since the royal army was driven back from Brentford on its way to London.

"But to us, who contrast him not with his former self, but with other men, he seems the gentlest and most affable of Cavaliers, ever ready to give ear and due weight to thought and wish of any, the least or the lowest.

"We had not known him much of old, because he leant to the Puritan party (being a close friend of Mr. Hampden), and thought ill of Archbishop Laud, and spoke not too well of bishops or episcopacy.

"But in this conflict I think the noblest on each side are those who are all but on the other; not, I mean, in affection—for lukewarmness is never a virtue—but in conviction and character.

"The queen is amongst us again, as graceful and full of charms as ever. But some think the king were liker to follow moderate counsels without her. He holds her as ever in a perfect adoration, and it is not likely to conciliate him that Parliament have actually dared to 'impeach' her. Blasphemy almost, if it were not more like the folly of naughty children playing at being grandsires and grandames!

"*June* 26.—Mr. Hampden is dead! By a singular mark of the divine judgment (Mr. Hyde says), he was mortally wounded on Chalgrove Field, the very place where he began not many months since to proclaim the rebellious Ordinance Militia. It was in a skirmish with Prince Rupert. The same night the rumour spread among us that something beyond ordinary ailed him, for he was seen to ride off the field in the middle of the fight (a thing never before known in him), with his head low drooping, and his hands on his horse's neck. Less than a fortnight afterwards, he died in sore agonies, they say, but persevering in his delusion to the end, so that his heart was not troubled.

"The king would have sent him a chirurgeon of his own, had it been of any use.

"He was much on my Mother's heart, since she heard of his being wounded, for he was ever held to be a brave and blameless gentleman. She grieved sore that he uttered no one repentant word.

"(Yet the last word we heard he spoke was not so ill a word to die with; 'O God, save my bleeding country!')

"'But,' said she, 'there are Papists who die without ever seeing anything wrong in the mass, or in regarding the blessed Virgin as Queen of Heaven, who yet die calling on the blessed Saviour with such piteous entreaty as he surely faileth not to hear. And it may be trusted Mr. Hampden's heresy is no worse.'

"To most around us it is simply the rebels' loss in him that is accounted of. And that they say is more than an army. For he was the man best beloved in all the land. Some of us, however, speak of the loss to England, and say that his and my Lord Falkland's were the only right hands through which this sundered realm might have met in fellowship again.

"I see nothing glorious in the glories of this war, nothing triumphant in its triumphs, no gain in its spoils.

"It makes my heart ache to see Prince Rupert and his Cavaliers return flushed with success and laden with plunder from raids all over the country. I cannot help seeing in my heart the poor farmers wandering about their despoiled granaries and stalls, and the goodwife bemoaning her empty dairy, and the children missing the cattle and poultry, which are not 'provision' only to them, but friends; and soon, alack poor foolish babes, to miss provision too and cry for it in vain.

"These are our own English homes that are ravaged and wasted. What triumph is there in it for any of us? I would the hearts of these Palatine princes yearned a little more tenderly towards their mother's countrymen.

"The only hope is that all these horrors will bring the end, the end, the 'Peace, peace,' for which my Lord Falkland groans.

"But I know not; I think of Netherby and the Draytons; and I scarce deem English hearts are to be won back by terror and plunder.

"*August* 28, 1643.—Better hopes! Something like a glimpse of the end, at last,

"Two memorable months.

"Everything is going prosperously for the king and the good cause, north, and south, and west.

"In the north, on June the 3rd, the Earl of Newcastle defeated Lord Fairfax and the rebels at Atherton Moor. A few days afterwards York and Gainsborough and Lincoln surrendered, and now not a town remains to the Parliament between Berwich and Hull.

"On the 13th of July, not a fortnight afterwards, Sir William Waller was defeated and his whole army scattered on Lansdowne Heath, near Devizes; the only offset to this advantage being the death of the brave and good Sir Bevill Grenvill, for whose wife, Lady Grace, bound to him in the truest honour and love, my Mother mourned much.

"The West, they say, is loyal; Cornwall fervent for the king.

"And on July 22nd, not a fortnight after this, Prince Rupert took Bristol, thus doing much to secure Wales, otherwise, moreover, well-affected.

"Our hopes are high indeed. In all the horizon there seems but one shadow like a cloud, and that so small I should scarce mention it but that an old friend is there. Mr. Cromwell (or Colonel, as they call him now, forsooth) gained some slight advantage at Grantham and Gainsborough, and stormed Burleigh House. Indeed, wherever he is, they say, he seems just now to bring good fortune. But this, I think, bodes no ill. Little weight indeed can these unsuccessful skirmishes have to counterbalance victories, and captured cities, and reviving loyalty throughout the North and West and South. And if the rebels are to succeed anywhere, I had rather it were where Roger Drayton is, because it is in the nature of the Draytons to be more yielding in prosperity than in ill fortune.

"His Majesty has just set forth with the army, all in high feather, to besiege the obstinate and disloyal city of Gloucester.

"Lord Essex, they say, is collecting an army to meet him. But we could wish for no better. One decisive battle, my Lord Falkland and other wise men think, is the one thing to end the war.

"*September* 22*nd*, 1643.—I cannot make it out. They say there has been a victory at Newbury, yet nothing seems to come of it. The king is here again, and the siege of Gloucester is given up, and our people begin to quarrel among themselves, treading on each other in their eagerness for places and titles and honours. I think they might wait a little, at all events, till the Court is at Whitehall again.

"One good sign is that three rebel Earls—Bedford, Holland, and Clare—have returned to their allegiance. The Earl of Holland raised the militia for the Parliament, so that he hath somewhat to repent of. There is much discussion how they should be received; the elder Cavaliers recommending a politic forgetting of their offence; but we, who are younger, desire they should be received as naughty children, if not with reproaches, at most with a cool and lofty indifference, to show we need them not. It would not look well to be too glad. And, moreover, they are three more claimants for the royal grace, and the faithful like not that the faithless should be better served than they who have borne the burden and heat of the day.

"I thought prosperity would have made us one, but it seems otherwise.

"And Harry says the noblest is gone. The noblest, he says, always fall the first victims in such conflicts as these, so that the strife grows more cruel, and baser from year to year.

"The Lord Falkland was slain at Newbury. He

was missing on the evening of the fight, but all through the night they hoped he might have been taken prisoner. On the morrow, however, they found him among the slain, 'Only too glad to receive his discharge,' Harry said. On the morning of the battle he was of good cheer, as was his wont; his spirits rising at the approach of danger. His friends urged him not to go into the battle, he having no command, but he would not be kept away. He rode gallantly on in the front ranks of Lord Byron's regiment, between two hedges, behind which the Roundheads had planted their musketeers. 'I am weary of the times,' he said to those who urged him to withdraw; 'I foresee much misery to my country, but I believe I shall be out of it before night.'

"And so he was; and needeth now no more dolefully to moan for 'Peace, peace!' as so often in these last months. He is singing it now, we trust, where good men understand all perplexed things, and each other.

"Falkland and Hampden! Alas! how many more before the peace songs are chanted here on earth!

"The two right hands are cold and stiff through which the king and the nation might have been clasped together again in fellowship.

"Who, or what, will reunite us now?"

CHAPTER IX.

HE winter of 1642–43 was one of uneasy uncertainty to us at Netherby. The whole world seemed to lie dim and hazy, as if wrapped in the heavy folds of a November fog. The next villages seemed to become far-off and foreign, in the unsettled state of the country. There was no knowing the faces and voices of friends from those of foes, in the rapid shifting of parties. The comrade of yesterday was the opponent of to-day. Who could say what the comrade of to-day might be to-morrow? Mr. Capel, the Member for Hertfordshire, who had been the first in Parliament to complain of grievances, had become Lord Capel, and was threatening the seven associated counties with his plunderers.

Lord Essex (many thought) seemed as frightened at success as at failure. Victories lulled him into fruitless negotiations; and the only thing that roused him to action was imminent ruin. Some murmured that "professional soldiers love long wars as physicians love long diseases." Some whispered of treachery, and others of Divine displeasure. The explosion of battle had come; but the only consequence seemed to be the loosening of the whole ground around, the crumbling away of the nation in all directions.

Partly, no doubt, this sense of vagueness and dimness was caused by the absence from most homes and communities of the most capable and manly men in each,—in the garrisons, on the field, taking counsel with the King at Oxford, or taking counsel for the nation at Westminster. Thus events were left to be guessed and debated by old men despondent with the decay of many hopes; or women, draining in anxious imaginations the dregs of every peril they could not share in fact; or boys delighting in magnifying the dangers they hoped soon to encounter, therewith to magnify themselves in the eyes of mothers and maids.

Rachel Forster, on whose gentle strength the whole village was wont to lean, was away; and Aunt Dorothy, the manliest heart left among us, had a belief in the general wickedness of men, and the general going wrong of things in this evil world, which was anything but reassuring to those whose fears were quickened with the life-blood of more vivid hopes than hers.

Thus we were ripe for all kinds of credulities that winter at Netherby.

I can remember nothing rising prominently out of the general hum and fog except two convictions, which enlarged before us steadily, becoming more solid instead of more shadowy as they came nearer.

The first was the impossibility of trusting the King. The second was that everything went right where Colonel Cromwell was; for by this time he was Colonel Cromwell, at the head of his regiment, which he was slowly sifting and compressing into the firm invincible kernel of his invincible army.

A dim, dreary time it was for us from the Edge-hill Fight, in October, 1642, to the beginning of February, 1643. Roger in prison at Oxford with Job; my Father at Reading or in London with Lord Essex and the army.

But in the beginning of February a new time dawned on us. My Father came home to us for a few days, to make the old house as tight as he could against any assaults from Lord Capel, or any straggling party of Prince Rupert's plunderers, who were always making dashing forays into the counties favourable to the Parliament, and appearing where they were least expected. The old moat, which in front of the house had long been the peaceful retreat of many generations of ducks, and elsewhere had been partially blocked up with fallen stones and trees, was carefully cleared out and filled with water. The terraces which led to it on the steep side of the house were scarped, all but the uppermost, which was palisadoed, and had two great guns planted on it. The drawbridge was repaired, and ordered to be always drawn up at night. We were provided with a garrison of four of the farm-servants, drilled as best might be for the occasion, and placed under the command of Bob, which virtually placed the whole fortress under the command of Tib, whose orders were the only ones Bob was never known not to disregard. Meantime my aunts and I, with the serving-maids, were instructed how to make cartridges, and prepare matches for the match-locks; and Aunt Gretel gave us the benefit of her experience in pulling lint, preparing bandages, and other hospital work.

If an attack, however, were ever made, the general belief in the household was that Aunt Dorothy would take her place as commandant, her courage being of the active rather than the passive kind. Indeed, I think the sense of danger to ourselves was a kind of relief to most of us. It seemed to make us sharers in the great struggle, which we believed to be for God, and truth, and righteousness. It took us out of the position of uneasy listeners for rumours into that of sentinels on the alert for an attack. And the whole spirit of the household rose from dreamy disquiet into cheery watchfulness and activity.

My Father brought us the story of the king's attempt to surprise London. "It was a treacherous, unkingly deed," my Father said, "enough to quench in the heart of the people every spark of trust left in His Majesty."

He said it happened on this wise. On Thursday, the 11th of November, 1642 (my father told us), the king received messengers from the Commons with proposals of peace, declared his readiness to negotiate, and his intention to remain peaceably in the same neighborhood till all was amicably settled. The Parliament, trusting him, ceased hostilities.

Nevertheless, instantly after despatching this message, he set off in full march for London. On Saturday he sent forces under Prince Rupert to surprise Brentford under cover of a November fog, and of his own too loyally trusted word. But Denzil Hollis, with part of his regiment, made a noble stand, and stopped the Prince's progress.

Hampden came up first, and Lord Brook, to the succour of Hollis' imperilled regiment; they tried to fight through the royal troops, which had surrounded Hollis and his men in the streets of Brentford. This they could not effect. But Hollis' little band themselves fought to their last bullet, and then threw themselves into the river, those who were not drowned swimming past Prince Rupert's troops to Hampden and his Greencoats. Lord Essex, hearing the sound of guns in the Parliament House, where he was at the time, took horse and galloped across the parks and through Knightsbridge to the scene of action. Ater this, all through the Saturday night, soldiers came pouring out from the roused city, until, on Sunday morning, four and twenty thousand men were gathered on Turnham Green.

Then the tables were turned, and Hampden fell on the king's rear.

"And then?" asked Aunt Dorothy.

"And then," replied my Father, drily, "Lord Essex recalled him, and so nothing further came of it; but things have gone on simmering ever since; always getting ready, and discussing how things should be done, and never doing them."

"How do Mr. Hampden and Mr. Pym brook these delays?" said Aunt Dorothy.

"Mr. Hampden would have had my Lord Essex invest Oxford," said my Father, "but he is a subordinate, and Lord Essex a veteran; and Mr. Hampden, I trow, deems military obedience the best example he can give an army scarce six months recruited from the shop or the plough."

"And meantime," said Aunt Dorothy, "I warrant Prince Rupert is active enough. There is no end to the tales of his devastations, seizing whole teams from the plough, setting fire to quiet villages at midnight, with I know not what iniquities besides, and carrying home the spoil from twenty miles around to the king's quarters at Oxford. If Lord Essex does not want to fight the king, why does not he submit to him? Keeping twenty-four thousand men armed and fed at the public expense, and doing nothing, is neither peace nor war to my mind!"

"True, sister Dorothy," said my Father, "I know of no method by which war can be carried on in a friendly way. And when Lord Essex has come to the same conclusion, perhaps things will go a little faster."

"Will they ever, under Lord Essex?" said she.

"Time will show," said he. "We have scarcely found our Great Gustavus yet."

"Colonel Cromwell has been doing something better than dreaming what to do, at Cambridge, since he saved the magazine there and £2,000 of plate for the Parliament last June," said Aunt

Dorothy. "Troops are pouring up to him from Essex and Suffolk, and all around, they say; and Cambridge is being fortified; and they say it is owing to Colonel Cromwell we are so quiet in these seven counties."

"Colonel Cromwell has a rare gift of sifting the chaff from the wheat; finding out who can do the work and setting them to do it," said my Father, thoughtfully.

"So strict with his soldiers too," said Aunt Dorothy. "They say the men are fined twelve pence if they swear a profane oath."

"Then," said my Father, "he is doing what he told his cousin Mr. Hampden must be done, if ever the Parliament army is to match the king's."

"What is that?" said she.

"Getting men of religion," my Father replied, "to fight the men of birth. You will never do it," said Colonel Cromwell, "with tapsters and 'prentice lads. Match the enthusiasm of loyalty with the enthusiasm of piety!"

"It is strange," rejoined Aunt Dorothy, "that Mr. Cromwell never discovered his right profession before. A farmer till forty-three, and then all at once to find out he was made for a soldier!"

"What can make or find out soldiers but wars, sister Dorothy?" said my Father. "Moreover, I warrant Colonel Cromwell has known what it is to wage other kinds of war before this. It is only taking up new weapons. It is only the same conflict for the oppressed against the oppressor, in which he contended for those of the Fen country against Royal assumption, and for the poor men of Somersham against the courtiers who would have ousted them from their ancient common-rights; or for the gospel lecturers whom Archbishop Laud silenced. The same war, only a new field and new weapons. At any rate, I am glad the lad Roger is to serve under him; and so you may tell him when he gets his liberty and comes home, as I trust he will in a fortnight."

This was said as my Father was taking an early breakfast alone with us in the Hall, with his horse saddled at the door, ready to take him back to the Lord General's quarters.

Rachel and Job Forster came home before Roger, in Sir Walter Davenant's wagon, stored with provisions and cordials, and soft pillows, by Lady Lucy.

I believe every one in Netherby slept with a greater feeling of security on the night after their return. Poor Margery, Dickon's young wife, said it was like the Ark coming back from the Philistines, regardless of the slur she thereby cast on the Royalist army, in which Dickon fought. And yet there was nothing very reassuring in Job's appearance. He looked like a gaunt ghost, and stumbled into the cottage like a tottering infant, and rather fell on the bed, which had been made up for him in the kitchen, than lay down on it, so broken was his strength. When the neighbours came in after a while, however, he had a good word to hearten each of them. As to Rachel, she settled in at once, without more ado, to her old ways and plans, doing everything with the purpose-like quietness which so calms the sick.

Cheered by Job's greetings to the neighbours, she told me it was not until the place was still, and she was making up the fire for the night, that she knew how low his strength was. As she took the wood from the pile he had made for her close to the fire, she was startled, she told me, by a sound like a stifled sob from where he lay.

"Art laid uneasy?" said she, at his side in an instant. "Does aught ail thee? Is the bed ill-made?"

"Naught," said he. "It's better than the bed of Solomon to me, with the pillars of silver and the bottom of gold. But I am like to them that dream, laughing and crying all in one. For I used to think before thee come to the gaol, how I should never see thee kindle a fire in the old place again, and how every stick thee had to .takke from where I laid it for thee would go to thy heart like a stab. And it shamed me not to have made a better shot at the Lord's meaning for thee and me."

"How could thee tell His meaning," said Rachel, "before He told thee? He gave thee no promise to bring thee out of prison, nor me."

"Nay," said Job, "but it's making very bold with Him, and making fools of ourselves, to guess at His words when they're half spoken, instead of waiting to hear them out. And it grieves me I should have suspected Him when He was meaning us so well. Read me what the Scripture saith about the forgiveness of sins."

"But, Mistress Olive," concluded Rachel, when

she told me this little history, "when Elijah, worn out with trouble, misunderstod the Lord, the angel comforted him, not with a text, but with a cake baken on the coals; so, when Job took to misunderstanding the Almighty like that, thinking He would be angered with what would not have fretted one of the likes of us poor hasty creatures, instead of the Bible I gave him a good cup of strong broth. I knew it was the body, poor soul, and not the spirit that was to blame, and that all those brave words he spoke to the neighbours had cost more than they were worth; and, of course, I was not going to profane the Holy Word by using it like the spell in a witch's charm."

So for several days she kept every creature out of the cottage, which deprived me of her counsel in a moment of difficulty, which happened the week of their return.

Lord Capel's troops continued to hover round, and to keep the district in a state of suspense and alarm, ripe for any marvellous stories of horror, or for any acts of terrified revenge. For in stormy times there are sure to be some cowardly spirits ready to throw any helpless victim as an expiatory sacrifice to the powers of evil.

One Saturday evening, late in February, I was returning home through the village from Gammer Grindle's cottage, which I had very often visited since poor Tim's death. The old woman had seemed gentler in her way of speaking of her neighbours, and once or twice had betrayed her pleasure in seeing me by speaking sharply to me if I stayed away longer than usual, as if I had been one of her own lost grandchildren.

I had made rather a long circuit in returning, not liking to try the high road again, because, in going, I had encountered a dozen or so of the king's troopers, and as I was hurrying past them, they complimented me in a way I did not like, and came after me. I recognized Sir Launcelot Trevor's voice among them, and then I turned round and spoke to him, and begged him to call his men away. Which, when he recognized me, he did; but not without some more idle Cavalier jesting, which set my heart beating, and made me resolve to come back by a quiet path through the Davenant woods, which led round through the village by Job Forster's.

Poor old Gammer was very friendly. I suppose I was trembling a little, though I did not tell her why, for she declared I was chattering with cold, and would have me drink a hot cup of peppermint water, and kindled up the fire, and took off my shoes, which were wet, and dried them, wrapping up my feet, meanwhile, in her own best woolsey whimple. Indeed, she was so gracious and approachable, that I ventured to say something about the benefit of coming to church, and mingling a little more with her neighbours.

"Too late, too late for that!" said she, firing up. "This twenty year, come Lammas, my Joan, Cicely's mother, was buried, she and her man, Cicely's father, in one grave. And the parson would do nothing without his fee. So I sold the cover from my bed to pay him. And I vowed I'd never darken his church-door again."

"But that parson is dead, Gammer," said I, "and it was not his church after all."

"That may be," said she. "But a vow is a vow. Besides, I could never bear the folks' eyes speiring at me. I'm ugly, and lone, and poor, and they make mouths at me, and call me an old hag and a witch. But it's only natural. All the brood will peck at the lame chick. All the herd will leave the stricken deer. Didn't all the village hoot and jeer at my poor, tender, innocent Tim?"

And then she poured forth the story of her life of sorrow as I had never heard it before. A heart trained to distrust and suspect through a childhood of bondage under the petty tyrannies of a step-mother and her children. One year of happy married life, ending in a sudden widowhood, which widowed her heart also of all its remnant of hope in God, and left her to struggle prayerless and alone with a hard world, for bread for herself and her orphan babe. The growing up of this child to be a stay and comfort, and, for three years, a second home with her when she married. This second home broken up as suddenly as the first, by the death of the daughter and her husband in one month, from a catching sickness, leaving the grandmother once more alone to toil with enfeebled strength for two orphan babes; the boy, poor, faithful Tim, half-witted and sickly; the girl, Cicely, wilful and high-spirited, and the beauty of the village. Then the terrible morning when Cicely was gone, and no account could be got of her beyond Tim's confused and exulting statement, that Cicely had cried, and laughed, and kissed him, and told him to wish grandmother good-bye for her, and she would come back a lady and bring Tim a gun like Master Roger's; to Gammer Grindle tidings worse than bereavement or all the misery she had known, for she came of an honourable Saxon yeoman's house that had never known shame. Tim, however, could never be brought to look on his sister's disappearance in any but the most cheerful light, and would watch for hours at the corner of the path leading to the village for Cicely and the "gun like Master Roger's," until, as time passed on, the expectation seemed to fade away, only to be awakened once again by the mysterious touch of death. And since then not a word of the poor lost girl. Tim in the grave, and the vain longing that Cicely were there too. And all the little world around her, as she believed, leagued against her crushed but unconquered heart. She ended with,—

"But it's but natural. When the lightnings have rent the trunk the winds soon snap the boughs. They say the devil stands by me. If he did no one need wish him for a friend. They say the Almighty is against me. And most times I think belike He is."

Then Aunt Gretel's words came back to me, "*Anywhere but there. Put the darkness anywhere but there;*" and I said,—

"Never, Gammer, never. The devil said that thousands of years ago; but the Lord Christ came to show what a lie it was. He stood by the stricken and wounded always. The lame and the blind came to Him in the temple, and he healed them."

She listened as if she half believed, and then, after a silence, she said,—

"The devil is no easy enemy to deal with, mistress, but if I could be sure it was *only him*, maybe I might look up and try again."

At last she was persuaded so far as to let me say I might call for her the next Sunday on my way to church. "It was as like as not she would not go, but at any rate it would do her no harm to see me."

And as I left I heard something like a blessing follow me, and I saw the poor, bent old figure leaning out of the door and watching me.

But when I came back to Netherby I found the whole village at the doors in a ferment of eager talk.

I thought at once of Sir Launcelot and the troopers, and asked if there had been another battle.

"Nay, nay," said the woman I spoke to, "it's naught but folks going to reap their deserts at last."

Then came a chorus of grievances.

"Three of Farmer White's finest milch kine gone in one night!" "Goodwife Joyce's best black hen killed, and not a feather touched; no mortal fox's work it was too plain to see!" "The dogs yelling as if they were possessed, as belike they were, on Saturday evening, seeing no doubt more than they could tell, poor beasts, of what was going on in the air!" "Lord Essex and his army lying spell-bound, able to do nothing, while the Prince Robber was plundering the land far and wide!" "Job and Master Roger, the best in the village, the first stricken; too clear where the blows came from!" "And to-day the squire's own cattle driven off the meadow, with Mistress Nicholl's, by a troop of plunderers, who came no one knew whence, and had gone no one knew whither!" "And finally, Tony Tomkin had been pursued by a headless hound through the Davenant woods, where he had only gone to take a rabbit or two he had snared, and thought no harm, the family being away and fighting against the country!" "And," but this was muttered under the breath, "there *were* those who said they had seen something that was *not smoke* come out of Gammer Grindle's chimney—something that flew away over the fens faster than any bird. And this was only on last Saturday night, and every one knew that Saturday was the day of the witches' Sabbath ever since the Jews had brought the innocent blood on their heads!"

Then suddenly it flashed on me what it all meant. They were going to execute some dreadful vengeance on Gammer Grindle, believing her to be one of the witches who were causing all the mischief in the land.

It was no use to set myself against the torrent of fear and rage, so I said as quietly as I could,—

"What are they going to do, and when?"

"First," was the reply, "they're going to duck her in the Mere before her own door. If she sinks they will pull her out if they can, as it mayn't be her doings after all. If she swims she's a witch, clear and plain."

"And what then?" I said.

"Nothing too bad, Mistress Olive, for the like of them. But the lads 'll see when it comes to the point. It isn't often their master helps the wretches out at last, they say. And if they don't sink natural, as a Christian ought, belike the lads 'll make her."

"When did they go to do this?" I asked.

"They're but just off," was the answer. "But they'll make short work of it, never fear. It's time a stop could be put to such things, if ever it was."

"If Rachel and Job had been among you this would never have been," I thought. I longed to have consulted Rachel, had it been possible. But there was no time to hesitate.

My first impulse was to rush after the cruel boys; but I felt that in the maddened state of terror in which the village was, they would most probably keep me back. So, without saying a word or visibly quickening my pace, I walked quietly on towards home.

In the porch I found Aunt Gretel. She was watching for me.

I took her arm, not violently, I was so afraid of frightening her from doing what I had determined must be done. And I said quite quietly,—

"Aunt Gretel, we must go together this instant to Gammer Grindle's."

"What is the matter?" she said.

"I will tell you as we go," I said. "There is no time to be lost."

She came with me. I turned into the path by the meadows.

"Not this way, Olive," she said. "The plunderers have been there to-day. Your Father's best cattle are taken, and Placidia's."

"If the cattle are gone, then belike so are the plunderers," I said. "But if the king's whole army were there we must take the shortest way."

And I told her the whole story.

She said nothing but,—

"Then the good God guard us, sweetheart, and don't waste your breath in words."

We went quickly on.

Only once I thought I heard shouts, and I said,—

"Aunt Gretel, what do they do with witches at the worst?"

"They *have* roasted them alive," she said, under her breath. And we said no more.

As we came to the creek of the Mere, on the opposite side of which the cottage was, we heard yells and shouts too plainly borne across the water in the stillness of the evening, unbroken by the lowing of the stolen cattle which had been feeding there that morning. And in another moment we saw the reflection of torches gleaming in the water, as we stumbled along in the dusk among the reeds. I listened eagerly for poor old Gammer's voice. But I heard nothing. Indeed, my own heart began to beat so fast, I could hear little but that. Until, just as we reached the cottage, there was a dull splash, and then a silence. It was followed by a low moan, but by no cry. They were drowning the poor old woman, and the brave broken heart would vouchsafe them the triumph of no entreaty for mercy and no cry of distress! I knew it as if I saw it. And the next moment I had flown along the shore and was in the midst of the crowd on the brink of the water, clinging with one hand round the stem of an alder, and stretching out the other till it grasped the poor shrivelled hands which had caught at the branches which drooped over the water.

"Cling to me, Gammer!—to me, Olive Drayton! I am holding fast—cling to me!"

I was scarcely prepared for the desperate tenacity of the grasp which returned mine. I never felt till that moment what it means to cling to Life. My other arm held firm, but the bank was oozy and slippery, and I felt as if I were losing my power, when at that instant Aunt Gretel came and knelt beside me, and clutching Gammer Grindle's dress, between us we dragged her to land.

Then the second part of the work of rescue began, and the hardest.

The men, or rather lads (for they were few of them more), who formed the crowd, had been startled into inaction by our sudden appearance among them; but now they began to mutter angrily, and would have pushed us rudely away, saying "it was no matter for women to meddle in. They had not come there for nothing, and they would have it out.

The whole country-side should not be laid waste to save one wicked old witch, that no one had a good word to say for."

By this time Gammer Grindle had recovered so far as to rise out of that mere instinct of self-preservation with which she had desperately clung to me. And disengaging herself from me, she said, standing erect and facing her assailants,—

"Let me alone, Mistress Olive. They say right. They are all gone who would have said a good word for me. Let me go to them."

Two of the men seized her again.

"Confess!" said one of them, shaking her rudely; "confess, and we'll leave you to the justices. If not you shall try the water once more to sink or swim."

And they dragged her again to the brink. The touch of the cold oozing water made the horror and weakness come over her again. Her courage forsook her, and she cried like the feeble old woman she was,—

"Have pity on me, neighbours. I'll confess anything, if you'll leave me alone—anything I can. I've been a sinful old woman, and the Lord's against me; the Lord's against me!"

"Hear her, mistress," said the men with a cry of triumph; "she'll confess anything. She says the Almighty's against her. It isn't fit such should live."

They were forcing her on; her poor, patched, thin garments tore in my hands as I clung to them. Aunt Gretel, driven to the end of her English, as usual with her in strong emotion, was pouring forth entreaties and prayers in German, when I caught sight of a Netherby lad well known as the pest of the village, and the ringleader in all mischief. He was carrying a torch. I caught his arm and looked in his face.

"Tony Tomkin," I said, "Squire Drayton shall know of this, and it shall not be unpunished. It is *your* wickedness, and such as your's, that brings the trouble on us all, and not Gammer Grindle's. God is angry with *you*, Tony, for breaking your little brother's head, and idling away your time, while your poor mother toils her life away to get you bread. You will not give up your hearts to be good like brave men, which is the only sacrifice God will have; and instead, like a pack of cowards, you are sacrificing a poor helpless old woman to the devil. Isn't there one man here with the heart of a man in him? What harm can the devil do you, much less a witch, if you please God? And which of you thinks God will be pleased by a troop of you slinking here in the dark to murder a helpless old woman at her own door? Can none of you lads of Netherby remember poor Tim, and how he died for Master Roger, and how good she was to him? Or can't you trust Squire Drayton to do justice, and leave her to him?"

Tony let his torch fall and slunk back. Then two Netherby men came forward and said,—

"She's right; Mistress Olive is right! Squire Drayton 'll see justice done."

Two or three others joined them. The cry arose,

"No one shall touch the old woman to-night, as long as there's any Netherby lads to hinder it."

A scuffle ensued, during which Aunt Gretel and I got hold of Gammer Grindle once more, and led her back into the cottage.

Once there, we barricaded the door with the logs and fagots which formed Gammer's store of fire-wood, and felt safe.

But it was not until the angry voices had quite died away in the distance, and we heard again the quiet plashing of the water among the rushes, that we could quiet the poor old woman so that she would let go her clasp of our hands. Then she let us kindle a fire, and wrap her in warm dry things.

We wanted to lay her in a clean comfortable bed which was made in the corner of the hut. But this she would not suffer. "It is Cicely's," she said. "It's not for me." So we had to pack her up as comfortably as we could upon the heap of straw and rags laid on an old chest, which was her hed.

There she lay quite still for a long time, while Aunt Gretel and I sat silent by the fire, hoping she would sleep.

But in about an hour she said, in a quiet voice—

"Take away those logs from the door."

I went to her bedside.

"In the morning, Gammer," I said, "when it is quite safe."

"This moment!" said she, starting up any trying to walk. But the terrors of the night had made her so faint and feeble, that she fell helplessly back.

"This moment, Mistress Olive!" she repeated, in

a faint querulous voice, very unlike her usual sharp firm tones—"this moment! The poor maid might come and try the door, and go away, and never come again. I've been sharp with her, I know, and she might be afraid, not knowing, poor lamb, how I watch for her."

Aunt Gretel went to the door and began to unpile the logs.

"God will care for us, Olive," said she with a faltering voice. "He will know and care; He who never closes the door against us."

And gently we withdrew the logs which formed our protection.

"Set the light in the window," Gammer said.

By the window she meant a rough crevice in the wall, with a canvas curtain hung before it.

Aunt Gretel ventured a little remonstrance.

"Hardly that to-night," said she. "It might guide any evil-disposed people here."

"It will guide *her*, and what does it matter for anything else?" said Gammer Grindle, almost fiercely. "She knew there was always a light burning, and if she saw none, she might think I was dead, and turn away."

And the lamp was placed in the window.

Then another long silence, broken again by Gammer.

"What'll they think's come to you, my mistresses? What a selfish old woman I've been. Why didn't I let them do for me, and be quiet. I never knew before what fear was. I've wished to die scores of times; but when death came near, I clung to life like a drowning dog or cat, and never cared who I pulled in to save myself. I never thought I should live to be such a pitiful old coward. But the Lord's against me," she cried, going back to her old wail—"the Lord's against me. Everybody says so, and it must be true. He not only leaves me to be drowned; He leaves me also to be as selfish and wicked as I will. The Lord's against me. Why did you try to save me? I must fall into His hands at last!"

This was exactly what Aunt Gretel never could hear with patience.

"You are a little better than those bad men, my dear woman," said she. "You, none of you, can see the difference between the good God and the devil. You talk of falling into His hands, as if His arms were hell. And all the while He is stretching out His arms that you may fall on His heart. You slander, grandmother, you slander God!" she added. "He is not against you; you are against Him."

"Much the same in the end," moaned poor Gammer, "if we're going against each other."

"It is *not* the same," said Aunt Gretel. "You can turn and go with Him, and He will not have to drive you home. You can bow under his yoke, and you will not feel it heavy. You can bow under His rod, and you will find it comfort you as much as His staff."

"Not so easy, mistress," said Gammer, after a pause. "I have turned from Him so long, how can I know if I should have a welcome?"

"That is what Cicely is waiting for, Gammer,"

I whispered, kneeling down beside. "But the door *is* open and the light is burning for *her*. If she could only know! if she could only have a glimpse *inside!*"

"If she could only know!" murmured the poor old woman, her eyes moistening as she turned from the thought of her own sorrows to those of her lost child.

And she said no more. But there was something in the quiet of her face which made me hope that she herself had got a "glimpse inside."

And soon afterwards she fell asleep.

Aunt Gretel and I were left to our watch. Then, for the first time, when we ceased to watch for sleep to come over the poor exhausted aged frame, I began to watch the noises outside, and feel a creeping horror as I listened to the slow cold plashing of the water among the rushes, and the soughing, and wailing, and whistling of the wind among the leafless boughs of the wood behind us. There was one gnarled old oak especially, just outside the house, whose dry boughs creaked in the wind as if they had been dead beams instead of living branches.

Often I thought I heard long sighs and wailings as of human voices, and with difficulty persuaded myself that it was fancy. But at last there came sounds which could not be mistaken—low whistles, and short, peculiar cries, responded to by others, until we became sure that a number of men must be moving about in the darkness around us. At first Aunt Gretel and I thought it must be the witchfinders come again for Gammer Grindle, and very softly we replaced the logs to barricade the door.

But other sounds began to mingle with those of human voices, like the lowings of cattle forcibly driven. Suddenly I remembered my encounter that very morning with the royal troopers, which, with all that happened since, seemed weeks distant.

"It is Sir Launcelot and the plunderers!" I exclaimed.

"That accounts for their not sending after us," said Aunt Gretel. "They have tried to reach us, no doubt, and cannot."

And we listened again.

Then came something like a soft knock and a low cry, which seemed close to the door, and a heavy thud as of something falling. But, though we listened breathlessly, no second sound came; and the old stories of supernatural horrors haunting the place crept back to us, and kept us motionless.

By this time the dawn was slowly creeping in, and making the lamp in the window red and dim.

We sat crouching close together by the embers of the dying fire, and took eack others' hands, and listened.

The voices came nearer, till we could plainly distinguish them, and with them the sound of trampling feet of men and horses, and then of men springing from the saddle and approaching the hut.

"It's the old witch's den," a gruff voice said; "she's burning a candle to the devil. No one ever got good by going near her."

Then a laugh, and Sir Launcelot Trevor's mocking voice,—

"One would think you were a Roundhead, from the respect with which you mention the old enemy's name. At all events, witches don't live, like saints, on air and prayers. We'll get some warmth and comfort this bitter night out of the old hag's stores. Some sack or malmsey, perchance, and a fat capon or two bewitched from good men's cellars and larders. Stay here, if you are afraid. And I will storm this witch's castle for you." And his long heavy stride approached the door. We sat with beating hearts, expecting the rickety door to be shaken or forced in by a strong hand. But instead, the steps suddenly ceased, and the intruder seemed to start back as if struck by an invisible hand on the threshold.

Then there was an exclamation of amazement and horror, ending in a fearful oath in a low deep tone, very different from Sir Launcelot's usual bravado. Afterwards a few hasty retreating steps, and as he rejoined his men, some words in the old light tone, but hurried and wild as of one overacting his part.

"Belike you are right, lads. Black art or white, better keep to beer of mortal brewing than seize anything from a witch's caldron, or touch anything of a witch's brood. Besides, the country will be awake, and it's as well we were in safe quarters with the booty. Steady, and look out for pitfalls in this cursed place."

After which there was a splashing of horses' feet

on the reedy margin of the Mere. Then a heavy trampling as they reached firmer ground, succeeded by a sharp gallop across the meadow, until every sound was lost in the distance, and we were left in the silence to listen once more to the cold plashing of the water among the rushes, and to the breathing of poor old Gammer in her heavy sleep, as we watched the slow breaking of the morning.

We had not sat half an hour after the last tramp of the horsemen had died away, when we heard a faint sound as of something stirring on the threshold.

Aunt Gretel laid her hand on mine.

"*What* made Sir Launcelot turn back, Olive?" she whispered. "He is scarcely a man likely to dream dreams or see visions."

By one impulse we softly removed the logs with which we had barricaded the door, and opened it.

There was a rude porch outside to keep off the beat of the weather, and under it a low seat where Gammer used to sit in summer and carry on any work that needed more light than could be had in the hut.

Across this lay stretched, in a death-like swoon, the form of a woman. She was half kneeling, half prostrate, her head towards the door, resting on the seat, one arm beneath it, the other fallen helpless by her side, half hidden in a heavy mass of long hair. A puny little child lay cuddled up close to her, clasping the unconscious form with both arms, asleep.

The features were sharp as with age, and pallid

as with the touch of death, and the long soft hair was gray, but it was still easy to recognise in the sharp and altered face what memories it had brought back to Sir Launcelot, and why that poor faded form had guarded her threshold from him better than an army of fiends.

It was the flaming sword of conscience which had guarded us that night.

Poor pallid wasted face, so terrible in its mute reproach!

We took her up between us. It was easy. She was light enough to carry. We laid her on the old bed which her grandmother had kept always ready for her. Aunt Gretel loosened her dress and chafed her hands, while I took the poor puny child to the fire to keep it quiet while I made some warm drink to revive the mother.

But the poor sickly little one was not easily to be quieted. In spite of all my soothing it awoke, and began wailing for mammy. Perhaps, after all, the best restorative! The sharp fretful cry aroused the mother from her swoon, and the grandmother from her heavy sleep.

In another instant the old woman was kneeling by the poor girl's bedside, clasping and fondling her, and calling her by tender, endearing, childish names, such as no one at Netherby would have dreamed could have poured forth from Gammer Grindle's lips. The first words Cicely spoke when she fully recovered consciousness and sate up (her beautiful large gray eyes gleaming from her faded hollow cheeks like living souls among a pale troop of ghosts), were,—

"Gammer, I heard him—I heard his voice. Where is he? I thought I saw his face. But it was dusk, and faces change. But voices will be the same, I think, even in heaven or in hell. And I heard his voice, the same as when he called me darling and wife."

"Wife!" said the old woman, starting and standing erect. "Say that again, Cicely."

"All in vain, Gammer!" she said, with a slow hopeless tone. "With the priest and the ring! But it was all false. He told me so when it was too late. He said I must have known. But how was I to know, Gammer? I trusted him; I trusted him. Yet, perhaps, I ought to have known better, Gammer? I suppose it must have been wicked of me. Every one seems to think it was."

"Not me, sweetheart!" the old woman cried; "never me! Thank God, my lamb comes back to me as pure as she went. Thank God, Cicely my darling, thank God, sweetheart, and take courage. If all the cruel world hunted my lamb to death and cried shame on her, there's one in the world who knows she's as pure as the sweetest lady that ever trod the church floor in her bride's white, with her path strewn with roses." Then, taking the child in her arms, and cuddling it to her, she added, "And thy child's as much a crown of joy to thee and me, Cicely, as to any lady in the land. Take courage, sweetheart. What does all the world matter, if grandmother knows; and Him that's above, darling," she added, in a voice faltering again into feebleness. "For He *is* above, Cicely, and He's *not* against us, for He's brought thee home."

All this time the old woman and Cicely had seemed quite unconscious of our presence, as we sat in a shadowed corner of the dark old hut, keeping as quiet as sobs would let us. But when the poor girl was calmed by the long-forgotten relief of a burst of tears on a heart that trusted her, she looked up and around with a quieter glance, and began to ask again how it could be that she had heard the voice.

Then I stepped forward to explain.

She started, and covered her face with her hands, as if she would have hidden herself.

"It's only me, Cicely, Olive Drayton," I said, as plainly as I could for weeping. "You've come back among those that know you and trust you, Cicely."

Then, after giving her such explanation as I could of the events of the night, and after Aunt Gretel had made up the fire, we bade them farewell, and left the three together to go over the mournful history that lay between their meetings; while we hastened away to assure those at home of our safety.

"What a night, Aunt Gretel!" I said, as we went. "It seems like a life-time."

"Things come often thus in life," said she, "as far as I have seen; the fruits ripened through the long silent year, reaped in a day." I scarcely understood her then, but since, I have often thought she was right. Sowing-times and growing-times, long, silent, underground; and then bursts of flowering days, reapings and gatherings; a life-time in a day; a thousand long-prepared events bursting into flower in a moment. A thousand ghosts of forgotten deeds gathered together and confronting us at one point. The probation thousands of years; the Judgment a day.

Aunt Dorothy was a little doubtful as to our having too much commerce with Gammer Grindle or Cicely. "If Gammer was not a witch," said she, "which God forbid—though that there are witches who ill-wish cattle, and ride on broom-sticks, is as certain as there are wandering stars and sea-serpents; at all events it is a solemn warning to every one on the danger of not going to church like your neighbours. And if Cicely was not as bad as had been feared—for which God be praised—she was nevertheless an awful example of the danger of dancing round May-poles, and wearing bits of ribbons and roses on your head."

But when Job heard of it, his anger was greatly kindled.

"One would think," said he, "the Book of Job had been put into the Apocrypha, that men who profess themselves Christians should go worrying the afflicted like Zophar, Bildad, and Eliphaz, heaping coals on the devil's furnace. Witches there were, no doubt, poor wretches, or they could not have been hanged and buried, although for the most part he believed the devil was too good a general to let his soldiers waste their time in cavalcading about on broom-sticks. But, be that as it might, it was ill work piling wood on fires that were hot enough already, especially when you could not be sure who had kindled the flames. The only comfort was, that after all the devil was nothing more than the Almighty's furnace-heater. All his toil only went to heating it to the right point to fuse the silver. The Master would see that none of the true metal was lost."

At the end of February, Roger came to us. He was pale with prison-air and meagre from prison-fare, and the hair had grown on his upper lip. In my eyes he had gained far more than he had lost. His eyes had a look of purpose and command in them, pleasant to yield to; though little enough of command had he exercised during the last four months, except, indeed, that command of himself which is true obedience, and lies at the root of all true command.

He was even less given than of old to long narratives or orations of any kind.

The history of what he had seen and heard dropped from him in broken sentences, as he went about seeing to various little plans for strengthening the defences of the house, or as he repaired or cleaned his arms in the evening. Of what he had suffered he said nothing, except to make light of it in answer to any questioning of mine. More than once he mentioned, in a few brief words, Lady Lucy's kindness. But he did not speak at all of Lettice except once, when we were all sitting together round the Hall fire—Aunt Dorothy, Aunt Gretel, and I—when he said carelessly, as if he had just remembered it by accident,—

"Mistress Lettice told me she had read the sermons you gave her, Aunt Dorothy. And she sent you her love, Olive."

"There are gracious dispositions in the child," said Aunt Dorothy. "I have been sure of it for a long time."

And I ventured after a little while to say,—

"She sent me her love, Roger, and was that all?"

"Her dear love, I think it was," said he dryly, as if the adjective made little difference in the value of the substantive.

"And she said no more, Roger? Not one message?"

"I only saw her for ten minutes, Olive," said he, a little impatiently, "and most of the time she was talking to a little French poodle, a little wretch with wool like a sheep and eyes like glass-beads."

"You are hard on the poor child, Roger," said Aunt Dorothy; "consider her bringing up. I warrant she never spun a web, or learned a chapter in Proverbs through in her life. What can you expect from a mother who is a friend of the Popish queen, and, I am only too sure, wears false hair and paint?"

"Aunt Dorothy," said he, firing up, "the Lady Lucy is as near a ministering angel as any creature I ever wish to see. And if it were not so, it's not for me, who have lived on her bread and on her kind looks for months, to hear a word against her."

And Roger arose, and strode out of the hall and across the court, whistling for Lion; leaving Aunt Dorothy in perplexity as to whether he were more aggrieved with her for defending Lettice or for assailing Lady Lucy, and me in equal perplexity as to how I could ever venture to introduce Lettice's name again, longing as I did to hear more of her.

"You never saw Lettice after she gave you that message?" I ventured at last to say one day when we were walking alone together.

"How could I, Olive?" said he, "I went away instantly; except indeed," he added, "when I happened to look back, as I was leaving the court, I saw her standing at the window with that poodle in her arms. But I did not look again, for at the same moment Sir Launcelot Trevor came out of another door, looking as if he were, as no doubt he is, quite at home in the place with them all."

"O Roger," I said, "some of us ought to write to Lady Lucy at once to say how wicked he is!"

"What is the use, Olive?" said he, sadly. "It is not from us, rebels and traitors, she will believe evil of a good Cavalier. Least of all from me or mine about Sir Launcelot!" he added, in a lower voice.

"But he may be deceiving them all," I said, passionately. "It is a sin to let him. Can nothing be done? Have you never thought of it?"

"You had better ask me could I think of nothing else, Olive?" said he. "For I had to ask myself that many times as I paced up and down in prison, and knew about it all. And the more I thought, the more helpless I saw we were about it."

"And what did you decide on at last?" I asked.

"I decided that *this was what the Civil War cost*," he replied; "not battles and loss of limb or life only, but misunderstandings and loss of friends. To have all we say and do reported to those we love best through those who think the worst of us, and to have no power of saying a word in justification or explanation. To be identified with the worst men and the most violent acts on our side, and, in loyalty to the principles of our party, not to be able to disown them. To see often the people we love best estranged more and more from the principles we hold dearest; and to watch a great gulf widening between us which no voice of man can reach across."

"I feel sure nothing and no one could make Lettice think harshly of us, Roger," I exclaimed; "I feel as sure as if I had been speaking to her yesterday."

"How can it be otherwise, Olive?" said he, "especially when I am under Colonel Cromwell. You should have seen the little start and scornful look she gave when I mentioned his name. 'Colonel!' said she, almost under her breath, as if she were talking only to that poodle. But I heard her. There is no one the Cavaliers hate like him."

"It seems almost a pity you must be with him!" I said, thinking only of Roger and Lettice.

"A pity, Olive!" said he, flashing up. "The

Cavaliers hate Colonel Cromwell, *because* wherever he is there is doing instead of debating. And for what better reason can we hold to him? If we fight at all, it is because we believe there is something worth fighting for to be lost or won; and where Colonel Cromwell is, it is won. The country he defends is defended; the city he holds is held; the men he trains fight; and, thank God, my lot is with him, to defend the old liberties under him, Olive, or, if he fails, to find new liberty in the New England across the seas."

The next day Roger went off to join his regiment at Cambridge, where Colonel Cromwell was.

How silent and languid the old house seemed when he left us, without his firm, soldier-like tread clearing the stairs at a few bounds, and his whistle to the dogs, and his voice singing with a firm precision, like the tramp of a regiment, snatches of the grave, grand old psalm tunes which the Ironsides loved to march to!

A fortnight afterwards, Job Forster followed him. And then came again months of listening and waiting, and of contradictory rumours, ending too often in ill-tidings worse than the worst we had feared.

For that whole year brought little but disaster to the Parliament troops. Day after day in that yellow old Diary of mine is marked with black tidings of defeat and death.

First comes—

"*June* 18.—Mr. Hampden wounded in trying to

keep off Prince Rupert's plunderers, until Lord Essex came. Lord Essex did not come in time, and Mr. Hampden went off the field sorely wounded. They say he felt himself death-stricken, and turned his horse towards the house of his first wife, whom he loved so dearly, that he might die there. But his strength failed. It was as much as he could do to make one last effort, and spurring his horse over a little brook which bounded the field, to find his way to the nearest village, and home.

"*June* 24.—Mr. Hampden died, thinking to the last more of his country than himself. In the midst of terrible pain he wrote (my Father tells us) to entreat Lord Essex to act with more vigour, and to collect his forces round London. He received the sacrament, and spoke with affection of the services of the Church of England, although not altogether so of her bishops. He received the Lord's Supper, and for himself looked humbly and peacefully to God. But for England his heart looked sorrowfully onward. And his last words were, 'Lord, have mercy on my bleeding country;' and then another prayer, the end not heard by mortal ears. My Father writes: 'His love for his country will scarce fail in the better country whither he is gone. But his counsel and all his slowly garnered treasures of wisdom are lost to us for ever.'"

The next death marked is—

"*September* 20.—A battle at Newbury, in Gloucestershire. Lord Falkland killed. Once Hampden's friend, and *now* (must it not be?) his friend again. A good man, and gentle, and wise, they say. I wonder how it all looks and sounds *there* where they are gone."

And the next—

"*November.*—Mr. Pym is dead. They have buried him among the kings in Westminster Abbey. I wonder how many of the people who began the war will be fighting at the end of it, and whether they will be fighting for the same things as when they began."

Then, mixed up with these notices of the dead, are long accounts of skirmishes and fights, which every one thought all-important then, but which no one thinks of now, save those who have their beloved dead lying beneath the fields where they were fought.

And through it all a steady going downward and downward of the Parliament cause, from that fatal June, 1643, when Hampden died, to near the close of the following year.

"*June* 30, 1643.—The Fairfaxes defeated at Atherton Moor.

"*July* 13.—Sir William Waller (once vainly boasted of as William the Conqueror) defeated, and his army scattered, in Lansdowne.

"*July* 22.—Prince Rupert took Bristol."

And so the war surged away to the Royalist West and Royalist North, until in all the West Country not a city was left to the Parliament but Gloucester; and in the North Country, not a city but Hull, which the Hothams had been baffled in an attempt to betray to the king; whilst in the counties between, Prince Rupert and the plunderers were having it much their own way. Very evil times we thought them. And many different reasons were assigned for the failure of the good cause. Aunt Dorothy feared it was a punishment for a licentious spirit of toleration to zealots and sectaries, and the sins of the Independents. The zealous preacher who came from Suffolk occasionally to expound at Job Forster's meeting, was sure it was carnal compromise lording it over God's heritage, and the sins of the Presbyterians. And Rachel believed it was the sins of us all, and of herself in particular, who had, she considered, been too much like Ananias and Sapphira, in that she had professed to give the whole price to God and then would fain have kept back the half, having indulged the deceitful hope that Job was so wounded as never to be able to go to the wars again.

Placidia and Mr. Nicholls were much "exercised." Especially since the loss of the three parsonage cows, which were (by what Aunt Dorothy considered a very solemn warning to Placidia) swept off with my Father's by the plunderers from the meadow by the Mere. "There were two texts," said Placidia, "which had always seemed to her exceedingly hard to reconcile. One was, 'Godliness hath promise of the life which now is as well as of that which is to come.' And the other, 'Whom the Lord loveth He chasteneth.' What could be done with texts so exceedingly difficult to reconcile as these?"

To which Aunt Dorothy replied,—

"Give up trying to reconcile them at all, my

dear. Let them fight, as frost and heat do, fire and water, sunshine and storm; and out of the strife come the flower and the fruit, spring-time and harvest, which shall never cease. Not that I see any difficulty in it. The promise is not meadows or cows, but grace and peace. The perplexity is over when you make up your mind that what you want is not to feel warm for a day or two, but to *have things grow;* not a few sunny hours, but the harvest."

Perhaps among us all, the person least perplexed by these continued disasters was Aunt Gretel; because, leaving the whole field of politics as altogether too complicated for her to comprehend, she continued to see only the links which bind every day to the Eternal Day, and every event to the hand of the merciful Father; and thus her chief wonders ever were the pity which forgave so many sins, and the love which provided so many mercies. Overlooking all the battles and skirmishes around us, she saw but one Battle and one Battle-field, and but two Captains. Overlooking all the subordinate divisions of nations and parties, she saw only a flock and a Shepherd, and the Shepherd calling each one by one, from the Great Gustavus to little Cicely and poor Tim; folded, one, in the heavenly fold of which he knew nothing till he was in it, and the other in the poor earthly house which she and her child and her grateful love had made, once more, a home and a refuge for poor old Gammer. For since Cicely's return, Gammer's broken links with her fellow-creatures began to be knit again; and more than one at Netherby took Job's words to heart. The broad shield of her love and welcome which she threw around the wanderer had shielded herself.

But side by side with the doleful records in my Diary run two series of letters full of victory and hope.

One was to my Father from Dr. Antony, who spent most of that period in London. And there, throughout all these disasters, the courage of the citizens seemed never to fail.

When Lord Essex returned from Edgehill with very doubtful success, which he had entirely failed to convert into lasting gain by his hesitations and delays, London, of as brave and generous a heart as old Rome, voted him £5,000.

When Bristol fell before Prince Rupert, and every city in the west save Gloucester fell into the hands of the king, and Lord Essex timidly recommended accommodation with His Majesty, and the Lords would have petitioned him, the Commons, the Preachers, and the citizens (knowing that no accommodation with the king could be relied on unless secured by victory) rejected all such wavering thoughts. The shops were all shut for some days, not to make holiday, but for solemn fasting. These days were spent in the churches, and the people came forth from them ready for any sacrifice for the eternal truth and the ancient liberty. It was determined to surround London with entrenchments. Knights and dames went forth, spade in hand, to the beat of drum, to share in the digging of the trenches, and to hearten others to the work. And in a few days twelve miles of entrenchment were dug. Whereof we heard His Majesty took notice, and lost heart thereby.

Throughout all those adverse times London never lost heart. Plate and jewels kept pouring into the Parliament's treasury at Guildhall. Time spent by the 'prentices in the Parliament army was ruled to count as time served in their trades. And jests against the courage of men bred in streets and trained behind counters lost their point. Dr. Antony's letters through all that dreary time had the cheer and stir of a triumphal march in them, although he had no triumphs to relate, but only defeats borne with the courage which repairs them, and although he himself went to the battle-field not to wound but to bind up wounds.

The other series of letters was from Roger. And these cheered us, because they always told of victory. They were brief, and mostly written from the battle-field, to assure us at once of victory and safety. They crossed the dark shadows of my Diary like sunbeams. In June, when we were mourning over the death of Hampden, and over the slow debates of the Lord-General what to do first for the bleeding country, wounded in every part by the stabs of plunderers and reckless Cavaliers, came Roger's first letter, delayed on its way, dated, "Grantham, 18th May, 1643." It spoke of a glorious victory won that day against marvellous odds of number, the enemy running away for three miles, four colours taken, and forty-five prisoners, and many prisoners rescued. Again in July, when we were bewailing the Fairfaxes defeated at Atherton Moor in the north, Sir William Waller's army routed at Lansdowne Heath in the west, and Bristol lost, Roger was writing us, on the 31st, news from Gainsborough of a "notable victory with a chase of six miles."

Mingled with these good tidings were sayings which Roger had heard of Colonel Cromwell's. Some of these sayings were like proverbs, so closely did the word fit the thought. Others had in them the ring of a war-song, as when he wrote to the Commissioners at Cambridge. "You see by this enclosed how sadly your affairs stand. It's no longer disputing, but out instantly all you can. Raise all your bands; send them to Huntingdon; get up what volunteers you can; hasten your horses. Send these letters to Norfolk, Suffolk, and Essex without delay. I beseech you, spare not. You must act lively; do it without distraction. Neglect no means." Yet often it seemed, when you listened to Colonel Cromwell, as if it were by some marvellous accident his thoughts did ever tumble into their right clothes, so strangely did they come lumbering out. But every now and then, if you had patience, amidst the rattling of the rough stones and pebbles, flashed a sentence, sharp cut and brilliant as a diamond, although, apparently, as unconscious of its polish and sharpness as the rest of their uncouthness. "Subtilty may deceive you, integrity never will;" "Truly, God follows us with encouragements, who is the God of blessings; and

I beseech you, let him not lose his blessing upon us! They come in season, and with all the advantages of heartening, as if God should say, 'Up and be doing, and I will stand by you and help you!' There is nothing to be feared but our own sin and sloth." "If I could speak words to pierce your hearts with the sense of our and your condition, I would. It may be difficult to raise so many men in so short time; but let me assure you it's necessary, and, therefore, *to be* done." "God hath given reputation to our handful (the Ironsides), let us endeavour to keep it. I had rather have a plain, russet-coated captain that knows what he fights for, and loves what he knows, than that which you call 'a gentleman' and nothing else. I honour a *gentleman* that is so indeed."

"Yet," said Roger in one of his letters, "it gives you little knowledge of what the Colonel is to extract these bits of his sayings, and make them emphatic, as if he meant them for epigrams, when the force is that they are said without force; the thought and purpose in him, which always go to the point in deeds, from time to time flashing straight to the point in words, which are then as strong as other men's deeds. But this I know, when he says of us, 'We never find our men so cheerful as when there is work to do,' or, 'God hath given reputation to our handful,' we all feel as if we were dubbed knights, and were moving about glorious with Royal Orders."

So, slowly as the year passed on, some of us began dimly to feel that a kingly being had arisen among us, such a king as David was before he was crowned, when he ruled in the hearts of the thousands of Israel by right of the slain giant and the secret anointing of the seer; a mighty man, who felt nothing impossible which he believed right, with whom, if a thing was "necessary," it was "*to be* done."

Chapter X.

LETTICE DAVENANT'S DIARY.

OXFORD, *January* 30*th*, 1644.—Another Christmas, and another birthday, shut up within these monkish old stone walls. To my mother the chapel, with the painted windows, and the organ, and the daily services, makes up for much that we lose. But as to me, when I hear the same sounds, and see the same sights, from day to day, I scarcely seem to hear or see them at all. They do not wake my soul up. The sacred music of the woods and fields seems to do me more good, at least on week-days. For it is sacred, and it is never the same. And the choristers there, while they are singing their psalms, are busy all the time building their nests, and finding food for their nestlings, which make their songs all the more tender and sacred to me.

"Not a word from them at Netherby. And not a step nearer to the end.

"Yet it is wrong to complain. It is something to have my Father and my seven brothers still untouched, after being exposed during all this time to the risks of the war. I dread to think what a gulf would yawn between me and Olive, and all of them, if once one very dear to either of us fell in the strife.

"I have nothing to complain of, but that things do not change; and with what a passion of regret I should long for one of these unchanging days, if one of the terrible changes that might come, came.

"A wretched phantom of a Parliament appeared here on the 22nd of January. I would the king had not summoned it. We should leave it to the rebels, I think, to deal with shows and phantoms of real things, with their presumptuous talk of colonels and generals. I would his Majesty had not encountered their pretence of royal authority, with this pretence of Parliamentary debate. Sixty Lords and a hundred Commons, or thereabouts, moving helplessly about these old University streets, with no more power or life in them than the effigies of the saints and crusaders in the churches. Indeed far less, for the effigies are memorials of persons who once were alive, and this Parliament is nothing but a copy of the clothes and trappings of a power now living. The king does not consult them, and the nation does not heed them, and they only show how real the division is amongst us. The king himself calls them the 'mongrel Parliament.' His Majesty is so grand and majestic when he is grave, I feel one could give up anything to bring a happy smile over his sad and kingly countenance. But I would he did not make these jests.

Many grave persons, I have noticed, when they set about jesting, are apt to do it rather cruelly. Their jests want feathers. They fall heavily, weighted with the gravity of their character, and instead of pleasantly pricking and stimulating, they wound. Therefore I wish His Majesty would not jest. Especially about Parliaments and the navy. People are apt not to see the wit of being called 'cats,' or 'water-rats,' or 'mongrel.' They only feel the sting.

"*March.*—The Scottish General Leslie has led an army over the Borders. Traitor! When the king was so gracious as to create him Earl of Leven but a few years since. Oh, faithless Scottish men! Infatuated by a thing they call Presbytery, and treacherous to their compatriot and anointed king!

"*June*, 1644.—Another summer within the walls of this old city. Another summer away from the woods at home. I am tempted sometimes to wish the war would end in any way. Politics perplex me more and more. So many people wishing the same thing, for contrary reasons. So many people wishing contrary things for the same reasons. So many on our side whom one hates; so many against us whom we honour. The best men doing the worst mischief by beginning the strife; and then dying, or doubting, and giving place to the worst men, who finish it—if ever it is to be finished. Hampden gone, and Lord Falkland; and the names one hears most of now, Prince Rupert and this Oliver Cromwell. They call him General now. What next? A country gentleman, none of the most notable or of the greatest condition, eking out his farming, some way, with brewing ale, at Huntingdon, until he was forty-two—and at forty-five, forsooth, General Cromwell, with men of condition capping to receive his orders. A fanatic, moreover, who preaches in the open-air to his men between the battles.

"A cheerful life for Roger Drayton, methinks! For commander, this fanatic brewer; for comrades, preaching tailors and fighting cobblers; for recreation, General Cromwell's sermons; and for martial music, Sir Launcelot says, Puritan Psalms, entoned pathetically through the nose. A change for Roger Drayton from Mr. Milton's organ-playing, or the madrigals we sang at Netherby. And yet I question whether our Harry would not find even that doleful Puritan music more to his taste than many a mocking Cavalier ditty wherewith our men entertain themselves. The times are grave enough, and I doubt sometimes but the Puritan music suits them best.

"*July* 20.—Terrible tidings, if true. Lord Newcastle and Prince Rupert defeated at Marston Moor, on the 2nd of July, by the Earl of Manchester and Cromwell. A hundred colours taken, and all the baggage; the royal army scattered in all directions. And ten days afterwards, York surrendered. Loyal York, in the heart of the loyal North, His Majesty's first retreat from his faithless capital!

"Strange that men speak more of Oliver Cromwell than of the Earl of Manchester in this battle. Strange, if it is true, as some say, that this firebrand was already in a ship bound for flight to America a few years since, when the king forbade him to go. My Father says, however, that the man who really won the victory for the Parliament was Prince Rupert, who, saith he, is no general, but a mere reckless chief of foraging-parties. It was he who hurried the Marquis of Newcastle into battle, against his judgment. And now it is reported that my Lord Newcastle, despairing of himself, with such associates (or of the cause with such leaders), has taken ship for France. I would it were the Palatine princes instead. Their standard was taken at Marston Moor.

"Three of my brothers were there; one wounded, but not severely; the other two have gone northward we know not where.

"Harry is much with us, being about the king's person. He will have nothing to do with the prince's plundering parties. But he chafes at having missed this battle, and is eager for the king to go westward to inspire and reward loyal Devon and Cornwall by his presence, and to pursue my Lord Essex, who has gone thither with the rebel forces.

"*August.*—The queen embarked on the 14th of July for France. I marvel she can bear to put the seas between her and the king at such times as these. But my Mother says she could not help it, and sacrifices herself most, and most to the purpose, by taking off the burden of her safety from His Majesty, and going among her royal kindred, whom she may stir up to fight. And indeed she did essay to rejoin the king. After the birth of the little princess at Exeter, she asked my Lord Essex for a safe-conduct to the Bath to drink the waters; but he offered her instead a safe-conduct to London, 'where,' quoth he, 'she would find the best physicians.' A sorry jest I deem this, inviting her to run into the very den of the disloyal parliament, which lately dared to 'impeach' her.

"Rebel galleys followed her from Torbay, but she escaped safe to Brest, and I trow the king's affection for her is so true he had rather know her safe than have her with him. Yet, methinks, in her case I would not have left it to him to decide. The more one I so loved cared for my welfare and safety, the more I would delight to risk and dare all.

"*August.*—They are off to the West, the faithful West—the king, and my Father, and Harry, with an army enthusiastical in their loyalty, and high in hope and courage. Prince Rupert not with them, and Oliver Cromwell not with the rebels. Surely there must be great things done!

"*September.*—The glorious news has come:—

"Lord Essex's army is ruined, gone, vanished. Not routed in a hard fight, but steadily pursued to Fowey, in a corner of loyal Cornwall, there cooped up ingloriously, closer and closer, until the general was fain to flee by sea, and the whole of the foot had to surrender. The cavalry, indeed, fought their way through, which, being Englishmen, I excuse them. But never was ruin more complete.

"Harry writes from Tavistock, where His Majesty has retired, a small town nestled among wooded hills at the foot of the wild moors. Mr. Pym was member for it; nevertheless the place seems not ill-disposed.

"*November.*—Harry is with us. I have never seen him so in spirits since the war began.

"The royal army received a slight check at Newbury, a place fatal already with the blood of the brave Lord Falkland.

"But Harry seems to think nothing of that in comparison with the state of things this battle hath revealed among the rebels. Rebellion, saith he, is at last obeying its own laws, and crumbling away by its own inherent disorganization.

"After the second battle of Newbury the quiet of our life was effectually broken by a threatened attack on Oxford.

"Artillery booming at our gates, bullets falling in our streets. At last I had a little taste of real war. I did not altogether dislike it. There was something that made my heart beat firmer in the thought of sharing my brothers' and my Father's danger. But then, I must confess, it did not come very near. The walls were still between us and the enemy. After a short cannonading the rebels drew off, from a cause, Harry says, worth us many victories. Lord Essex and Sir William Waller, their two generals, could not agree, and between them the attack on Oxford was abandoned; and what was more, the king, who was encamped outside the city, with a force in numbers quite unequal to cope with their combined forces, was suffered to retreat without a blow to Worcester.

"But better than all. Harry says the rebel generals are assailing each other with all kinds of reproaches in the Parliament, accusing each other as the cause of all the late failures. Lord Essex, Lord Manchester, and Sir William Waller, none of them cordially uniting with each other against us, but all most cordially uniting in assailing Oliver Cromwell, who is the only one among them we have cause to dread. And to complete the mêlée, the Scotch preachers are having their say in the matter, and solemnly accuse Mr. Cromwell of being an 'Incendiary!'

"Which is quite plain to us he is. So that now, when the Incendiaries themselves have set about to fight each other, and to put out the flames, it is probable the arson will be avenged, the flames *will* be put out, and we quiet and loyal subjects shall have nothing left to do but to rebuild the ruins.

"Then we will try to say as little as we can about who began the mischief, and only see who can work best in repairing it.

"The King and the Parliament throughout the land, and the Draytons and the Davenants at dear old Netherby."

OLIVE'S RECOLLECTIONS.

At the end of July, 1644, we had a letter from Roger:—

"*Marston Moor*, *July* 3*d*.—To my dear sister Mistress Olive Drayton.—On the battle-field. A messenger going south will take these.

"Thank God we are here this day. And the

enemy is *not* here, but flying right and left, over moor and mountain. No such victory has been vouchsafed us before.

"Yesterday, the 2nd July, early in the morning, we were moving off the ground—Lord Manchester, General Leslie, and General Cromwell.

"Prince Rupert had gallantly thrown provisions into York, which we were beleaguering; but the generals thought he would not venture an attack on our combined forces.

"But when we were fairly in order of march the prince fell on our rear.

"It took us till three in the day to face round, front them, and secure the position we wanted. There is a rye field here with a ditch in front, where the dead bear witness how we had to fight for it.

"At three, Prince Rupert gave their battle-cry: '*For God and the king;*' and we ours: '*God with us.*' From three till five we pounded each other with the great guns. But little impression was made on either side. And at five there was a pause. Two hours' silence, confronting each other, from five to seven. Such silence as may be where many are wounded, and many are waiting in agonies for the summons to die, while the rest were waiting for the summons to charge. At last, at seven, it came.

"Our foot, under Lord Manchester, ran across the ditch before that rye field for which they had fought so hard. Thus far was clear to all. The rest we know only from comparing what we did, and seeing what we had done afterwards. For immediately on the attack of the foot came the charges of the horse. The left wing of the king's army on our right they all but routed, driving the Lord Manchester, Lord Fairfax, and the old veteran Leslie from the field. Meantime our right—that is, we, the Ironsides with the general—charged their left. We were not beaten. I trust we gave him no reason to be ashamed of us. But everywhere the fighting was hard. Having discharged our pistols, we flung them from us and fell to it with swords. Then came the shock, like two seas meeting, each man encountering the foe before him, but few knowing how the day was speeding elsewhere, till we found ourselves with the whole front of the battle changed, each victorious wing having wheeled round as they fought, and standing where the enemy had stood when the fight began. Then came up General Cromwell's reserves with General Leslie's, and decided the day, sending Prince Rupert and his plunderers flying headlong through the gathering dusk. It was the first time they had encountered the Ironsides. Their broken horse trampled, as they fled, on the broken and flying foot, we spurring after them, till within a mile of York. Arms, ammunition, baggage, colours, all cast away in the mad terror of the flight. To within a mile from York we followed them, and then turned back, and slept on the battle-field.

"Another silence, Olive; not as before, in expectation of another fight, but with our work done, and four thousand dead around us to be buried.

"Job Forster is safe, and would have you tell

Rachel that the Lord has sent Israel a judge at last, and all must go right now.

"He went about with Dr. Antony all night, seeing to the wounded and the dying.

"When I awoke, the summer morning was shining on the field, and I wondered how I could have slept with all those sights and sounds around me. But, thank God, I did, for there is more to be done yet. York has to be taken.

"Tell Rachel, by using my military authority, I got Job to lie down in my place, while I went round with Dr. Antony. At first he wavered. But I said: 'The general is sharp on any of us who neglect our arms or powder. And the body has to be looked to as well as the powder.' Whereon he lay down in my cloak, and in a minute was beyond the reach of any rousing, short of a cannonade.

"*N. B.* —Two young Davenants fought well a few yards from me; scarcely more than lads.

"God grant we gained yesterday a step towards peace."

A fortnight after, another letter, dated:—

"*York, the* 15*th July.*—York has surrendered. The North is ours. This moment returned from a thanksgiving in the minster. The grandest music of the organ scarce, I think, could have echoed more solemnly among the old roofs and arches than that psalm, sung by the thousands of rough soldiers' voices. King David was a soldier, and knew how to make such psalms as soldiers need. Nor do I think the old minster has often seen a congregation more serious and devout. If some on the Cavalier side had heard it, they could scarce have said afterwards, our Puritan religion lacked its solemnities. Our solemnities begin indeed *within*; but when the tide of devotion is high and deep enough, no music like that it makes in overflowing."

To Roger, as to any one borne on the chariot of the sun, the whole world seemed full of light. To us, however, meanwhile in the Fens, things seemed verging more and more from twilight into night.

Not much more than a month after the letter of Roger's concerning the surrender of York, came tidings which, it seemed to us, more than counterbalanced these advantages.

The royal letter post, lately established on the great North Road between London and Edinburgh, and southward between London and Plymouth, had been interrupted during the war. Netherby lay in the line of one of the more recent branch-posts; and we missed at first the pleasant sound of the horn which the postman was commanded to blow four times every hour, besides at the posting-stations.

At first Aunt Dorothy had rather rejoiced. She had been wont to say it was a grievous interference with the liberty of the subject, that we should be compelled to send all our letters by the hands of the king's messengers, instead of by any private carrier we chose. And, moreover, she deemed it highly derogatory to His Majesty to demean himself to take a few pence each letter for such services. But a few months of return to the old private method, with all its uncertainties and suspenses, made her receive the public posts again as a boon, when the Commonwealth government re-established them.

It was from Dr. Antony, therefore, that we first heard the tidings of the Lord Essex's flight from Fowey, and the ruin of his whole army.

This was not until November.

He brought two letters from my Father and Roger. My Father's was sad; Roger's was indignant. Both spoke of divisions among the supporters of the Parliament. They were written at different times, but reached us together by Dr. Antony's hand as the first safe opportunity. The first was from Roger, dated late in September, speaking of the surrender of Lord Essex's foot:—"Marston Moor with the four thousand that lie dead there," he wrote, "was after all, it seems, *not* a step towards the end. Everything gained there is thrown away again by the indecisions of noblemen who are afraid to win too much; and old soldiers who will not move a finger except in the fashion some one else moved it a hundred years ago. As if when war is once begun, there were any way to peace but by the ruin of one party, except, indeed, by the ruin of both; as if a lingering war were a kind of half peace, instead of being as it is, the worst of wars; the opening of the nation's veins at a thousand points, whereby she slowly bleeds to death. Lieutenant-General Cromwell takes sadly to heart the sad conditions of our army in the West. He saith, had we wings we would fly thither. Indeed, wings he hath at command, in the hearts of his men, 'never so cheerful,' he says, 'as when there is work to do.' But there are those whose chief business is to clip these wings, lest affairs fly too fast. The general saith, 'If we could all intend our own ends less, and our ease too, our business in this army would go on wheels for expedition.' If he were at the head of affairs, we should not, in sooth, lack wheels or wings."

The second letter was from my Father written early in November, after the second battle of Newbury (fought on the 27th of October).

He wrote,—

"It is the old story, I fear, of our Protestant lack of unity. People do not seem able to see that the military unity of the Roman Church being broken, the only ecclesiastical unity possible for us is the unity as of an empire, like that of Great Britain, with different races and local constitutions under one sovereign; or the unity as of a family of grown-up children, in free obedience to one father. If Lutherans and Calvinists could have merged their lesser differences in their real agreement, probably that terrible war, which is still crushing the life out of Germany, need never have begun. If Prelatists, Presbyterians, and Independents could agree now to yield each other liberty, this war of ours might end. But while they had power, Prelatists would rather let the nation be torn asunder than tolerate Presbyterians. And now the Presbyterians think they have power, they had rather lose everything we have gained than tolerate Independents. The merit of the Independents and Anabaptists being, perhaps, only this, that they never have had the power to persecute. I cannot see whither it is all tending.

"We have lost an army in Cornwall; but that is little. It seems to me some of us are losing all hold of what we are fighting for. This success at Newbury shows our weakness more than the ruin at Fowey. Lord Manchester will not pursue the king, lest our last army should be lost; in which case, he says, His Majesty might hang us all. As if the block or the gallows had not been the alternative of success from the beginning. In consequence of a disagreement between him and Sir William Waller, the combined attack on Oxford failed; and eleven days after our success at Newbury, His Majesty's troops were suffered quietly to withdraw their artillery from Donington Castle, in face of our victorious army lying inactive.

"The indignation in the army is unbounded. But all minor divisions bid fair to resolve themselves into two great factions of Presbyterians and Independents; Lieutenant-General Cromwell having addressed a remonstrance to the Parliament against Lord Manchester, and Lord Manchester, Lord Essex, and Hollis, with the Scotch Commissioners, being set on crushing General Cromwell.

"The quarrel is of no new origin. The affair of Donington Castle did but set the tinder to the train. It dates back to the first setting of the Westminster Assembly, when the Presbyterians, not content with absorbing the Church revenues, which would have been conceded to them, would have had the magistrate imprison and confiscate the goods of all whom they excommunicated. 'Toleration,' said one of them, 'will make the kingdom a chaos, a Babel, another Amsterdam, a Sodom, an Egypt, a Babylon. Toleration is the grand work of the devil; his masterpiece and chief engine to support his tottering kingdom. It is the most compendious, ready, sure way to destroy all religion, lay all waste, and bring in all evil. As original sin is the fundamental sin, having the seed and spawn of all sin in it, so toleration hath all errors in it and all evils.' They call toleration the 'great Diana of the Independents.' Yet no one contends for toleration to extend beyond the orthodox Protestant sects. These divisions set many of us thinking what we are fighting for. It would be scarcely worth so much blood-shedding to establish one hundred and twenty popes at Westminster, instead of one at Lambeth. They are golden words of General Cromwell's: 'All that believe have the real unity, which is most glorious, because inward and spiritual, in the Body and to the Head. For being united in forms, every Christian will, for peace' sake, study and do, as far as conscience will permit. And for brethren, in things of the mind, we look for no compulsion but that of light and reason.'"

"What does my brother mean, Master Antony?" quoth Aunt Dorothy, when she came to this passage. "And what doth General Cromwell mean?

'No compulsion!' and 'light and reason!' Most dangerous words. An assembly of godly divines at Westminster to settle everything! That is precisely what we have been fighting for. Not for disorder; not for each man to think what is right in his own judgment, and do what is right in his own eyes. But for those who believe right to have the power to instruct, or else to silence, those who believe wrong. Light and reason indeed! The cry of all the heretics from the beginning. Why, reason is the very source of all error. And light is precisely what we lack, and what the Westminster Assembly is providing for us; and when they have just kindled it, and set it up like a city on a hill, does Mr. Cromwell, forsooth, think we are going to let every tinker and tailor kindle his farthing candle instead, and lead people into any wilderness he pleases?"

Said Dr. Antony,—

"There was a great light enkindled and set up on a Sorrowful Hill sixteen hundred years ago. But it has only enlightened the hearts of those who would look at it. And if the Sun does not put out these poor farthing candles, Mistress Dorothy, I am afraid we shall find it a hard matter to do so with our fingers."

"Well," said Aunt Dorothy, "I am sure I cannot see whither things are tending."

And even Aunt Gretel remarked,—

"That Independents and Presbyterians should agree might indeed be easy enough. But Lutherans and Calvinists are quite another question. In the next world—well, it is to be hoped. Death works miracles. But in this, scarcely. The dear brother-in-law is one of the wisest of men. But it cannot be expected that the wisest Englishman should quite fathom the religious differences of Germany."

Of toleration towards Papists, Infidels, or Quakers, no one dreamed. Infidelity, all admitted, comes direct from the devil, and, of course, no Christian should tolerate the devil or his works. The Papists had within the memory of our older men sent fetters to bind us, and fagots to burn us in the Armada, which the winds of God scattered from our coasts. In France they had massacred our brethren in cold-blood to the number of one hundred thousand in the slaughter which began on St. Bartholomew's day. They had assassinated our kindred by tens of thousands in Ireland in our own times. And they were binding, and burning, and torturing, and making galley-slaves of our brethren still on the Continent of Europe. Not as heretics we kept them under, but as assassins. And as to the Quakers, they were reported to be liable to attacks of objections to clothes very perplexing to sober-minded Christians, and were probably many of them lunatics. These should not indeed be burned, but they should at all events be clothed, and, if possible, silenced, until they came to their right mind.

The third letter which Dr. Antony had brought us was from Job Forster. I went with Dr. Antony to take it to Rachel. In it Job spoke much of

Roger's courage and goodness, in a way it made my heart beat quick to hear.

"Master Roger fights like a lion-like man of Judah," wrote Job, "and commands like one of the chief princes. And at other times he can tend a wounded man, friend or foe, or speak good words to the dying, most as tender, Rachel, as thee."

Job's letter was by no means doubtful or desponding. He had the advantage of those in the ranks. He saw only the rank and the step immediately before him, and heard not the discussions of the commanders but only the word of command. "I think," he concluded, "we have come about to 1 Sam. xxii. 14. Some time back we were in 1 Sam. xxii. 1, in cave Adullam: 'Every one that was in debt, and every one that was discontented, gathered themselves unto them,' and a sorry troop they were. But that is over. The General saith himself: 'I have a lovely company; honest, sober Christians; you would respect them did you know them.' And respect us they do; leastways the enemy. And now David (that is, General Cromwell) is in Keilah. And they inquired of the Lord and the Lord said, 'They will deliver thee up.' *But God delivered him not.* The rest has to come in its season."

Job wrote also of "the young gentleman the chirurgeon." "Of as good a courage as the best," quoth Job. "For I hold it harder to stand about among the whizzing bullets, succouring or removing the wounded than to fight. It is always harder to stand fire than to charge. And it is harder to spend days and nights tending poor groaning suffering men than to suffer yourself. That is, if you have got a heart. Which that doctor hath. But every man hath his calling. And Dr. Antony hath his. Straight from headquarters, as I deem."

It was curious that what struck me first in those words of Job's was his calling Dr. Antony "young." It set me wondering what his age might be; and as we walked home together I glanced at him to see. I had always thought of him as my Father's friend, and therefore of another generation. Besides there was the doctor's cap, and a physician is always, *ex officio*, an elder. But when I came to consider his face, it had certainly nothing of old age in it. His carriage was erect and easy; his hair, raven-black, had not a streak of gray; his eyes, dark as they were, had fire enough in them. These researches scarce took me a moment, but his eyes met mine, and it seemed as if he half guessed what I was thinking of, for he said,—

"You wondered at Job's talking of the courage of a chirurgeon."

"Not at all," said I, somewhat confused. "I was only thinking how it was you were always our Father's friend instead of ours."

"Was I not yours?" he said, half smiling.

"Oh, yes, of course," I said, "every one's."

"Every one's, Mistress Olive," he said inquiringly, "only, not yours?"

"Mine, of course," I said, feeling myself becoming hopelessly entangled, "and every one's besides."

"Thank you," he said, gravely, "I should not have liked the exchange."

"Is it easier, do you think, Dr. Antony," I said, breaking hurriedly from the subject, "to fight, than to be a chirurgeon on the battle-field?"

"Easier, probably, to me," he said. "Fighting is in our blood. My grandfather was a soldier, and fought in the French wars of religion. He was assassinated at the St. Bartholomew with Coligny. My father, then a child, was seized, baptized, and educated in a Catholic seminary. But he escaped, at the risk of his life, to England. In France we had enough of wars of religion. I have thought it better work to devote myself as far as I may to succour the oppressed, and heal such as can be healed of the wounds and sorrows of men. There is enough of danger and of warfare in these days in such a calling to satisfy a soldier's passion, and not to let the blood stagnate or grow cold."

There was a subdued fire in his eye and a deep sonorous ring in his voice, which gave force to his words.

"But Antony is not a French name," I said.

"It was my father's Christian name, which he adopted for safety. His name was properly Antoine la Mothe Duplessis, from an estate our family had held for some centuries. But, Mistress Olive," he said, turning the discourse, as if it led to painful subjects, or as if he shrank from continuing on a theme so unusual with him as himself, "I understand you are accused of upholding witches."

Whereby I was led into an earnest defence of Gammer Grindle.

"But even if she had been a witch," I ventured to say, in conclusion, "would it not have been more like the Sermon on the Mount to rescue and then to instruct her, than to drown her? And is not the Sermon on the Mount the highest law we have?"

"It is the last edition of the Divine law yet issued, Mistress Olive," he said. "And one great glory of it is, it seems to me, that it is not only so plain itself as to need no commentary of lawyer or scribe, but if we try to keep it, it has a wonderful power of making other things plain as we go on."

At which point we reached the porch at Netherby.

Said Aunt Dorothy, as Dr. Antony was taking leave the next day,—

"You must not trouble yourself to be our letter-carrier. Less useful men can be spared on such errands. I wonder my brother should have burdened you therewith."

"I thank you, Mistress Dorothy," said he; "but it was my free choice to come. And I promise you I will only come when it is no burden."

Said she, holding his hand,—

"Pardon me; but I am old enough to be your mother. Suffer an aged woman to warn you against new-fangled notions. Beware of 'light' and 'reason,' prithee, and such presumptuous pleas. The light that is in us is darkness, and our reason is corrupt. The spiritual armour your fathers fought in, Master Antony, is proof still."

"I believe it, Mistress Dorothy," he replied; "and if in new times and in new dangers I should need new weapons, believe me, I will only go to my fathers' armoury for them."

I was provoked with myself when he had left, that of all the wise discourse that had been held since he came, the things that kept recurring to my mind were what Job had said of Dr. Antony, and how foolish I had been in the answers I gave him on our way home from Rachel's. He must deem me so unmannerly, I thought. And, besides, so many fitting things now occurred which I might have said. Nothing occupies one like a conversation in which one has failed to say what one ought to have said. It haunts one like a melody of which you cannot find the end.

It was evident, moreover, that Aunt Dorothy took the same view of Dr. Antony's age as Job. It made Dr. Antony seem like some one quite new, to think of this; new, and yet certainly not strange.

The next Christmas, the army being in winter-quarters, my Father spent with us, which made it a holiday indeed.

In February, 1645, he read us a letter which Dr. Antony wrote to him, narrating what was going on in London. At the beginning there was a considerable piece which he did not read to us. He said it related to family matters, which he could speak of hereafter, and contained greetings to us. Thus the letter proceeded—it was dated January 21st, 1645:

"Sir Thomas Fairfax is this day appointed by the Commons' House general-in-chief, in lieu of Lord

Essex; Skipton major-general; while the post of lieutenant-general is *left open.* Most men deem that he who fills it will fill *more than it*, as his name and fame now fill all men's mouths. There have been fierce debates, whisperings, conspirings, mysterious midnight meetings at Essex House; the aim of the whole of these conspirings, the bond of all these gatherings, being to 'remove out of the way General-Lieutenant Cromwell, whom,' said the Scottish Commissioners, 'ye ken very weel is no friend of ours.' This 'obstacle,' this '*remora*,' this 'INCENDIARY,' as they called him (soaring high into Latin in their vain endeavours to find words large enough to express their abhorrence), had hundreds of grave English and Scottish Presbyterian divines, soldiers and lawyers, been labouring for months to remove out of the way; yet, nevertheless, on the 9th of December, there he stood in the Commons' House, as immovable an obstacle and '*remora*' as ever, and about to prove himself an 'Incendiary' indeed by kindling a flame which should consume their eloquent Latin accusations and their authority at once.

"There was a long silence in the House. General Cromwell broke it, speaking abruptly, and not in Latin.

"'It is now a time to speak,' he said, 'or for ever hold the tongue. The important occasion now is no less than to save a nation out of a bleeding, nay, almost dying condition, which the long continuance of this war hath already brought it into; so that without a more speedy, vigorous, effectual prosecution of the war—casting off all lingering proceedings like those of soldiers of fortune beyond sea to spin out a war—we shall make the kingdom weary of us, and hate the name of a Parliament.

"'For what do the enemy say? Nay, what do many that were friends at the beginning of the Parliament? Even this, that the members of both Houses have got great places and commands, and the sword into their hands, and what by interest in Parliament, what by power in the army, will perpetually continue themselves in grandeur, and not permit the war speedily to end, lest their own power should determine with it. This that I speak here to our own faces, is but what others do utter abroad behind our backs. I am far from reflecting on any. I know the worth of those commanders. Members of both Houses who are still in power; but if I may speak my conscience without reflection on any, I do conceive if the army is not put into another method, and the war more vigorously prosecuted, the people can bear the war no longer, and will enforce you to a dishonourable peace.

"'But this I would recommend to your prudence. Not to insist upon any complaint or oversight of any commander-in-chief upon any occasion whatsoever, for as I must acknowledge myself guilty of oversights, so I know they can rarely be avoided in *military* affairs. Therefore, waiving a strict inquiry into the issues of these things, let us apply ourselves to the remedy, which is most necessary. And I hope we have such true English hearts, and zealous affections towards the general weal of our mother-country, as no members of either House will scruple to *deny* themselves and their own private interests for the public good, nor account it to be a dishonour done to them, whatever the Parliament shall resolve upon in this weighty matter.'

"Another member followed and said,—

"'Whatever be the cause, two summers are passed over, but we are not saved. Our victories (the price of blood invaluable) so gallantly gotten, and (which is more pity) so graciously bestowed, seem to have been put into a bag with holes; what we won one time, we lost another; the treasure is exhausted, the country wasted, a summer's victory has proved but a winter's story; the game, however, shut up with autumn, was to be played again the next spring, as if the blood that had been shed were only to manure the field of war for a more plentiful crop of contention. Men's hearts have failed them with the observation of these things.'

"The cause General Cromwell deemed to be the multiplication of commanders. The remedy, that members of both Houses should *deny themselves* the right to appoint *themselves* to posts of military command. The 'Self-Denying Ordinance' and the 'New Model' of the army were proposed, and soon passed the House of Commons. The Lords debated and rejected it; but this day the Commons have appointed Sir Thomas Fairfax commander-in-chief, superseding Lord Essex. And few doubt but they will carry it through.

"Thus may, we trust, a few vigorous strokes bring peace; and peace, order.

"But meanwhile, during these dark January days, another conflict has ended; on Tower Hill.

"The fallen archbishop, whose name was a terror for so many years in every Puritan home in England, there, on this 10th of January, laid down his life heroically and calmly as a martyr, which he surely believed himself to be. He read a prayer he had composed for the occasion. I grieve to say, the scaffold was crowded, not with his friends. He said he would have wished an empty scaffold, but if it could not be so, God's will be done; he was more willing to go out of the world than any could be to send him. A helpless, forsaken old man, heavily laden with bodily infirmities, four years a prisoner, uneasily dragged from trial to trial, I never heard that his courage failed. I would they had let him die in quiet. But Sir John Clotworthy, over zealous, as I think, asked him what text was most comfortable to a man in his departure. 'Cupio dissolvi et esse cum Christo,' said the archbishop. 'That is a good desire,' was the rejoinder; 'but there must be a foundation for that desire, an assurance.' 'No man can express it,' was the calm reply, 'it must be found within.' 'Yet it is founded on a word, and that word should be known.' 'It is the knowledge of Jesus Christ,' said the archbishop, 'and that alone;' and to finish the discussion, he turned to the headsman, gave him some money, and said, 'Here, honest friend, God forgive thee, and do thy office on me in mercy;' and so, after a short prayer, his head was struck off at one blow. The crowd dispersed, and the fatal hill was left once more silent and deserted, with the scaffold and the Tower facing each other, the weary prison of so many, and the blood-stained key, which had for so many unbarred its heavy gates, and also, we may trust, another gate, from inside which our whole earth seems but a prison chamber.

"If we look at the world only as divided into *parties*, truly this death of his were worth to those who think with him, more than many victories in Parliament or in the field. But if we think of the One Kingdom, surely we may rejoice that one who, as it seems to us, erred much in head and heart, and did no little hurt, came right at last, and took refuge with Him who receives us not as Archbishops, or Presbyterians or Independents, but as repentant, weary, and heavy-laden men and women.

"Some few friends reverently buried him in Barking Church to the words of the old burial-service, prohibited by the Parliament a few days before. All honour to them."

Said Aunt Gretel, when my Father had finished reading this letter,—

"It is a great pity the martyrs should not all be on the right side. It would make it so very much easier to know which is the right."

"Martyrs on the wrong side," exclaimed Aunt Dorothy, indignantly; "you might as well talk of orthodox heretics."

But my Father replied,—

"If obedience is better than sacrifice, then obedience is the best part of the sacrifice of martyrdom; and may we not trust that the Master may accept the act of obedience even of some who misread the word of command?"

The next day he left us for London, and we saw him no more for many months.

On the 29th of January, commissioners of the Parliament and of the king met at Uxbridge to negotiate for peace. But they did not get on at all. Dr. Stewart syllogistically defended the divine right of Episcopacy, and Dr. Henderson the divine right of the Presbyterial government. My Lord Hertford and my Lord Pembroke would have passed this by, to proceed to the particular points to be settled; but the divines declined to be hurried, insisting on disputing syllogistically "as became scholars." So, after twenty days, Dr. Stewart and Dr. Henderson, being each confirmed in their conviction of his own orthodoxy, the commissioners separated with no further result.

One evening, indeed, it is said, the king had consented to honourable terms; but in the night a letter came from Montrose announcing Royalist victories, and in the morning His Majesty retracted the concessions of the evening.

Meanwhile the two armies continued fighting; not in two large bodies, but in scattered skirmishes, sieges, surprises, all over the country, making well-nigh every quiet home in England a sharer in the misery and tumult of the war.

The moral difference between the forces of the Parliament and the king became, it was said, more obvious. It could scarce be otherwise. War must make men firmer in virtues or more desperate in sin. Men must get worse with years of plundering, and indulgence in every selfish sinful pleasure. No good woman durst venture near the Royalist army, my Father says, and vice and profaneness are scarcely punished; whereas in the Parliament camp, as in a well-ordered city, passage is safe, and commerce free. It is the armies of the great Gustavus and that of Wallenstein over again.

I think it would be blasphemy to deem such differences can have no weight in a world where God is King.

I wonder if it can be that, after all, it leads to more good to fight out the great battles of right and wrong in this way, than syllogistically, in Dr. Stewart and Dr. Henderson's way. The logical battles making good men fierce, and not hurting the bad at all; the battles for life and death making good men nobler, at all events, if they make the bad men worse. Making good men better seems the end of so many things that God permits or orders in this world. And as to war making bad men worse, it seems as if that could not be helped, because *everything* does that until they change the direction they are going in, which great troubles and dangers sometimes startle them to do. If this be so, the pain and misery and death would cease to be so perplexing. Aunt Dorothy used to say, a Church without a rod in her hand is a Church without sinews. But a Church with a rod seems sometimes as blind and severe in using it as the world. For which reason, I suppose, the best periods of Church history seem often to be those in which the world holds the rod instead of the Church. And a war may sometimes be as effectual an instrument of godly discipline as a synod.

LETTICE'S DIARY.

"*June 14th*, 1645, *Davenant Hall, Three o'clock in the morning.*—We came home yesterday, and I grudge to sleep away any of these first hours in the old house. It is like travelling into some marvellous foreign country, to rise at an unwonted hour in the morning. The sky looks so much higher before the roof of daylight has quite spread over it. For after all, daylight is a roof shutting us in to our own green sunny home of earth. And that is partly what makes the night so awful. We stand roofless at night, open to all the other worlds, with no walls or bounds on any side. And at dawn something of the boundlessness and awfulness are still left. With a majestical slow pomp the morning sweeps the veil of sunlight over star after star, falling in grand solemn folds of purple and crimson as it touches the edge of our world, until the great spaces of the upper worlds are all shut out, and we are shut in with our own kindly sun, and our own many-coloured fleeting clouds, and our own green earth.

"Then the other aspect of the dawn begins. Her first steps and movements are all grand and silent. But when the awful infinity beyond is shut out, and we are left alone, face to face with her, she changes altogether.

"The stars pass away in silence. But the day

awakes with all kinds of joyful sounds. The clouds are transformed from solemn purple banners in some great martial or sacred procession to royal or bridal draperies. They garland the earth with roses, they strew pearls and diamonds; they spread the path of the new sun with cloth of gold. The whole world, earth, and sky, seems to blossom into colour, like a flower from its sheath. Every leaf of the limes outside my window, every spike of the horse-chestnuts seems to awake with a flutter of joy.

"It seems as if infinity came back to us in a new way. For the infinite spaces of night, we have the infinite numbers of day. Instead of the heavy masses of foliage waving an hour or two dimly since against the sky, there is a countless multitude of leaves fluttering in and out of the sunlight, a countless multitude of birds singing, chirping, twittering, among the branches, a countless throng of insects hovering, wheeling, darting in and out among the leaves; there are the infinite varieties of colour on every blade of grass, on every blossom, on every insect's wing.

"It is a wonderful joy to be here again. Every creature seems to welcome me. I seem to long to speak to every one of them, and just add a little drop of happiness to the happiness of them all. I want to take all of them, in some way, like little children, to my heart and kiss them.

"Olive said that feeling was really the longing to be folded to the Heart which is at the heart of all; but nearer us than any other creature.

"'*He fell on his neck and kissed him.*'

"She thought it meant that.

"Leaning out of my window, looking down from the slopes of the Wolds, as we do across the long space of fens which stretches before us like a sea, I see the gables of Netherby.

"Olive is there asleep.

"Olive, and Mistress Dorothy and Mistress Gretel.

"And here, my mother and I.

"Fathers and brothers all at the war. In sight, yet how sadly out of reach! This terrible war that seems as if it would never end. Things have not been going on quite so prosperously with us lately; although many strong places in the North are still loyal; and all the West is ours, and much of Wales. A new vigour seems to have come into the rebel councils. They say the soul of them all is this Oliver Cromwell, that he and his friends have brought in some new regulation, called by some of their unpleasant Parliament names. They call everything a covenant or an ordinance, as if it were all out of the Bible. They call this the Self-Denying Ordinance. The meaning of it seems to be that they are all to deny themselves to give Mr. Cromwell the real command. At least, Harry thinks so. And he looks gloomily on our affairs. He was at home before we came, to make the place ready for us. And he only left yesterday morning to rejoin the king's army, which is in Leicestershire. Not so very far off.

"I wonder, if there were a battle, if we should hear the sound of it!

"A few days since the troops stormed Leicester, and sacked it. Harry would not tell us much about it. He said it was too much after the fashion of those dreadful German wars of religion, which Prince Rupert has taught our men to imitate too well.

"Poor wretched city! We could not hear anything of that. Groans and even helpless cries for pity do not reach far. At least, not on earth. I suppose nothing reaches heaven sooner.

"I wish that thought had not come into my head about hearing the roar of a battle if there were one. Since it came, I cannot help listening, through all the sweet cheerful country-sounds, the twitterings of the swallows under the eaves, the soft cadences of the thrushes, the stirring of the grasses, for *something* in the distance!

"If we did hear anything, it would be very, very far off, fainter than the fluttering of the leaves; like the moan of distant thunder.

"In summer days there are often mysterious, far-off sounds one cannot account for. And now I can do nothing but listen for it.

"For almost the last thing Harry said when he went away was, that there would be a battle, probably, before long, and if a battle, probably a great battle.

"The forces are gathering and approaching each other.

"He took leave of us gayly, my Mother and me. But ten minutes afterwards, he galloped back to the place in the outer field where I was standing looking after him (my Mother having gone to be alone, as she always does when Harry leaves us). His face had lost all the gaiety, and he said,—

"'Lettice, if things were not to prosper with the king, and the rebels were to attack this house, I think it would be better not attempt to stand a siege. The house extends too far to be defended, except with a larger garrison than you could muster. And the country is against us. If it came to the very worst, Mr. Drayton is a generous enemy and a gentleman, and would give you safe harbour for a time. If all on their side or ours had been like the Draytons, there need have been no war. You may tell them that I said so, if you like, if it ever comes to that.'

"'Comes to *what*, Harry?' I said, shuddering.

"He tried to smile. But then, his countenance suddenly changing, he said,—

"'Lettice, we must think of all possibilities. You are young, and my Mother is used to lean on others.'

"'Only on *you*, Harry,' I said.

"'Yes,' he said, hurriedly; 'too much, perhaps. But trust the Draytons, if necessary, Lettice. They will never do anything unjust or ungenerous. If you ask their advice, they will advise you for your good, though it cut their own throats or broke their own hearts.'

"Then, after a moment's pause, he said,—

"'It is never any good to try to say out a farewell, Lettice. If one had years to say it in, there would always be something left unsaid. Partings are always sudden, whether we are snatched from each other as if by pirates in the dead of night, or watch the lessening sail till it becomes a speck in the horizon. The last step is always a plunge into a gulf. But, Lettice,' he added, lowering his voice, 'death itself is not really a gulf, only to those on this edge of it. Do not tell my Mother I came back. If she asks you anything about it, tell her I never went away with a lighter heart. For I see less and less what the end will be, or what to wish for, and I am content more and more to make the day's march, and leave the conduct of the campaign to God.'

"And he rode off, looking like a prince, and I watched him till he disappeared behind the trees. He looked back once again and waved his plumed hat to me, and then galloped out of sight in a moment.

"I crept back by a side-door near the stable, that my Mother might not see me; and Cæsar, Harry's dog, made a dismal whining, and crouched and fawned on me, so that it went to my heart not to be able to grant him what he asked for so plainly in his poor dumb way, and set him free to follow Harry.

"*June* 14, *Ten o'clock at night.*—Some men who came from the North this evening, say there has been fighting towards the North-west, somewhere on the borders of Northamptonshire and Leicestershire. The roar of the guns began early in the day, and then there was sharp interrupted firing, which went on till the afternoon, when it seemed gradually to cease.

"All day it has been going on. All this quiet summer day. My Father there, perhaps, and Harry certainly. And nothing to be heard until to-morrow.

"My Mother will not seek rest to-night. I see the lamp in her oratory-window. And far off across the fields, another light in the gable of old Netherby, where Olive Drayton used to sleep. It is some comfort to think we are watching together. Olive is so good. And she will be sure to remember us.

"*June* 20.—We heard before the morrow. The next morning, when the dawn began to break again, a horseman galloped hastily up to the door. I was in my mother's room; we were both dressed. We had neither of us slept. I looked out. It was Roger Drayton. My Mother sat up on the bed, when I had persuaded her to rest.

"'I will go down and ask,' I said.

"'We will go together, Lettice,' said she.

"Then came a cry from one of the maids.

"'Perhaps it is poor Margery,' I said. For Margery had come to stay with us since we returned. It comforted us to keep together, all of us who had kindred at the field.

"My Mother shook her head.

"She knelt down one moment, and drew me down beside her, by the bedside, heart against heart, and murmured,—

"'Thy will, not mine! Oh, help us to say it. For His sake who said it first.'

"Then she rose, and with a firm step went down into the hall with me.

"She held out her hand to Roger when she saw him.

"His face spoke evil-tidings only too plainly.

"'There has been a battle,' she said.

"'At Naseby, Lady Lucy,' he replied.

"'Was the victory for the king or not?' she asked; unable to utter the question uppermost on her heart and mine.

"'There was hard fighting on both sides,' he replied. 'The king and Prince Rupert have gone westward towards Wales.'

"I could hear that his voice trembled.

"'Then the king has lost,' she said. 'But it was not to tell us this you came. Who is hurt?'

"He hesitated an instant.

"'It is Harry!' she exclaimed. 'You have come to summon us to him. Is the wound severe? Is there hope? Can we go to him at once?'

"There was a pause, and a dreadful irresponsive silence between each of her questions. He answered only the last,—

"'He will be brought to you, Lady Lucy. They are bringing him now.'

"At once the whole depth of her sorrow opened beneath her. Not an instant too soon. For the words had scarcely left Roger's lips when the heavy regular tramp of men bearing a burden echoed through the silence of the morning outside, and paused at the porch.

"My Mother took my hand, and led me forward.

"'He must not come home unwelcomed!' she said.

"For an instant I feared she had not yet grasped Roger's meaning. For this awful burden they were bearing was *not Harry*, I knew. No welcomes would ever greet him more. But I had not fathomed her sorrow nor her strength.

"She met the bearers at the door. They stood with uncovered heads, having laid down what they bore on the stone seat of the porch. They were mostly old servants of the family.

"'My friends, I thank you,' she said. 'You have done all you could. But not there. On the place of honour. He was worthy.'

"And she motioned them to the dais at the head of the Hall, where the heads of our house are wont to receive the homage of their retainers.

"Silently they bore him there, and laid their sacred burden gently down. She thanked them again for their good service. And then as silently they withdrew. I saw many a rough hand lifted to brush away the tears. But she did not weep. She stood motionless, with clasped hands, beside the bier, and murmured to herself again and again, in a low voice,—

"'He was worthy.'

"Then, turning with her own sweet, never-forgotten courtesy to Roger, she held out her hand to him again, and said,—

"'You did kindly to come and tell us. He always honoured you.'

"He held her hand, and said rapidly, as if uncertain of the firmness of his own voice,—

"'I was near him at the last, and he made me

promise to see you, or I could not have dared to come.'

"She looked up with trembling, parted lips, listening for more.

"'He made me promise to tell you he had little pain and no fear,' Roger said, in a low voice. 'And he gave me this for you, and said, "Tell my mother these words of hers have often helped me to believe, through all these evil days, that God is living and commanding still. But, more than all words, tell her my faith in God has been kept unquenched by the thought of *herself*."'

"She took the packet from him. It was a little book, with Scriptures and prayers written in it by her own hand, given to Harry when he was a boy. On the crimson silk cover she had embroidered for it, was one stain of a deeper crimson. As she opened it, a little well-worn leaf dropped out, with a child's prayer on it she had written for him when first he went to school.

"When she saw it, the thought of the hero dying on the battle-field for the good cause vanished, and in its place came the memory of the little hands clasped on her knees in prayer.

"And withdrawing her hand from Roger, a sudden quiver passed through all her frame, and throwing her arms around me, she sobbed,—

"'My boy, my boy! O Lettice, it is Harry we have lost! It is our Harry!'

"When I looked up again Roger was at the door. It seemed to me, from the glance he gave he was waiting to say something more. And I resolved, cost what it might, to hear it. We led my Mother into the nearest chamber, and then leaving her with the maidens, I went back to the Hall.

"Roger was still waiting in the porch.

"He came forward when he saw me.

"'Did he say anything more?' I asked.

"He hesitated an instant.

"He said, 'The Draytons and the Davenants might have to combat one another in these evil times, but that we should never distrust each other, and that he never had distrusted one of us.'

"He said so to me, the last thing before he left us. I said; 'And that was all?'

"'The battle swept on; I had to mount again,' he said, 'and I could not leave my men.'

"'You saw him no more,' I said. 'You could not even stay to watch his last breath!'

"The moment I had uttered them I felt there was something like reproach in my words, and I would have recalled them if I could.

"'I saw him no more until the fighting was over,' he said. 'Then I came back and found him; and we brought him home. It was all we could do,' he added; 'and it was little indeed.'

"'I am sure you did all you could, Roger,' I said; for I feared I had wounded him. 'I should always be sure you would do all you could for any of us.'

"'Should you, indeed!' he said. 'God knows I would.'

"And there was a tremor and a depth of pleased surprise in his tones that startled me, and I could not look up.

"'Would to God I could do anything to comfort Lady Lucy or you,' he said.

"'No one can comfort her, Roger,' I said; and the tears I had been trying to put back choked my voice, 'Harry was everything to her. He was everything to us all. No one will ever comfort her more.'

"'*You* will comfort her, Lettice,' he said, with that quiet commanding way he has sometimes. 'God gives it you to do; and He will give you to do it.'

"And as he ceased speaking, and I went back to my Mother, I felt as if there were indeed a strength through which I could do anything that had to be done.

"*July* 1.—Sir Launcelot Trevor has come with tidings of my Father and my brothers.

"They are in the West, save the two younger, who went across the Borders after the battle of Marston Moor, and have joined Montrose in the Scottish Highlands, deeming that the king's cause will best rally there.

"The good cause is low; lower than ever before. Soon after that fatal day at Naseby the town of Bridgewater surrendered to General Fairfax.

"Prince Rupert (with such courage as one might expect, I think, from a chief of plunderers) thereon counselled the king to make peace. But His Majesty, never so majestic as in adversity, said, 'That although, as a soldier and a statesman, he saw no prospect but of ruin, yet, as a Christian, he knew God would never forsake his cause, and suffer rebels to prosper; that he knew his obligations to be, both in conscience and honour, neither to abandon God's cause, to injure his successors, or forsake his friends. Nevertheless, for himself (he said) he looked for nothing but to die with honour and a good conscience; and to his friends he had little prospect to offer, but to die in a good cause, or, what was worse, to live as miserable in maintaining it as the violence of insulting rebels could make them.'

"What promises, or royal orders, could bind men, with any soul in them, to their sovereign as words like these? Least of all those who, like us, are bound to the cause by having given up our best for it. Nothing, my Mother says, makes a thing so precious to us as what we suffer for it. Indeed, nothing now seems able to kindle her to anything like life, save aught associated with that sacred cause for which Harry died.

"Sir Launcelot saith, moreover, that the rebels have been base enough to lay bare to the eyes of the common people of London the private letters from His Majesty to the queen, found in his cabinet on the field at Naseby. And that these letters contain things which have even lost the king some old loyal friends. Pretty friendship, indeed, or loyalty, to be moved by discoveries, made only through treachery and breach of confidence, which no gentleman would practice to save his life.

"But there is one thing Sir Launcelot hinted to me which I dare not breathe to my Mother. He said there was reason enough why Roger was near Harry when he fell; for it was by the hand of one of the Ironsides, beyond doubt, that he died.

"But never by Roger's hand! Or, if possibly such a curse could have been suffered to fall on one like Roger, it must have been unknown to him. Of this I am as sure as of my life.

"Sir Launcelot said that Roger's hand was wont to be a little too ready to be raised. Ungenerous of him to say it, and yet too true. Slowly roused; but once roused, blind to all results.

"How bitter his vain repentance would be if this terrible thing were possible, and he once came to know it.

"How bitter and how vain!

"But even if it were possible, and he never knew it, but we knew it, what a gulf from henceforth for ever between us and him!

"I cannot breathe this to my Mother. And yet, if Sir Launcelot's fears could have any ground, it would seem a treachery, if ever Roger came to us again to let her touch in welcome the hand that dealt that blow!

"I know not what to do. It is the first perplexity I ever knew in which I could not fly to her for aid and counsel.

"What a child I have been.

"What a child I am!

"Can it be possible that our Lord thought of His disciples being perplexed and bewildered at all, as I am, when, just before He went away, He called them 'little children?' Can it be possible that He meant, Come to me, as little children to their mother; when you want wisdom, come to Me!"

CHAPTER XI.

OLIVE'S STORY.

HE first trustworthy tidings we had of the battle of Naseby were from Dr. Antony. I saw him coming hastily across the fields from the direction of Davenant Hall.

It was very early in the morning. The village had been stirring through the previous afternoon with uneasy rumours, and I had not slept. I was watching the light in the window of Lady Lucy's oratory, and thinking how she and Lettice had watched there together that terrible night so long ago, saying collects for Roger, and how Lettice had hastened to us in the morning, on her white palfrey with the welcome tidings that Sir Launcelot would recover. And now how far we were from each other! What a sea between us! Two moats, (the moonlight was shining on ours just below me,) drawbridges, and fortifications. But deeper and stronger than all the moats and walls in the world lay between us the memories of those bitter years of war, and ever-widening misconception and division. Yet I felt sure Lettice loved us still.

And as I was thus looking and thinking, I saw Dr. Antony coming hastily down the road from the stile which led across the fields to the Hall, where I had parted from Harry Davenant that night when he brought the tidings of Lord Strafford's execution, and would not come in.

My first impulse was to rush down the stairs and unbar the door. But many things held me back. A presentiment that the news he brought might be such as there was no need to fore-date by hurrying to meet it; an uncomfortable recollection of Job Forster's letter, and of that conversation in which I had said nothing right.

I went, therefore, to summon Aunt Dorothy as head of the household. She had so many preparations to make, that Dr. Antony's hand was on the great house-bell long before she was ready. Nothing so slow she said as hurry, besides its being a proof of the impatience of the flesh. She would even fold up scrupulously the clothes she took off, faithful to her maxim, that we should always leave everything as if we might never return to it.

The bell rang again.

I went to see if Aunt Gretel was more capable of being hastened. She, dear soul, was sympathizing, excited, and agitated beyond my utmost desires, for she could lay her hands on nothing she wanted. So that I had to return to Aunt Dorothy, who, by that time, was ready; and feeling how cold and trembling my hand was as she took it to lead me down-stairs, she laid her other on it with an unwonted demonstration of tenderness, and said,—

"Child, we can neither hasten the Lord's steps nor make them linger. But He will do right." There was strength in her words, but almost as much to me in the tones, which were tremulous, and in the cold touch of her hand, which showed that the blood at her heart stood as still as mine.

We went down together in time to meet Dr. Antony just as he entered the Hall.

My Father was wounded, not dangerously, only so as to render him incapable of further service in the field, at least at present. His right arm was broken. Roger was coming home with him.

I wondered that Dr. Antony seemed so heavy at heart, to bring tidings which made my heart leap with thankfulness. What could be better than that Roger was unhurt, and that my Father had received a slight wound just sufficient to keep him at home with us?

Then it flashed on me in what direction I had seen him coming.

"Dr. Antony!" I said, "there is sorrow for the Davenants!" And then he told us how Harry Davenant had fallen.

We had little time for bewailing him, for the household had to be roused, and refreshment and a bed prepared for my Father.

I had scarce ever seen Roger so cast down as he was about Harry Davenant's death. One of the noblest gentlemen the king had on his side, he thought so pure, and true, and brave. If all had been like him there had been no war, and no need for it. "And," said Roger, "I always looked for the day to come when Harry Davenant would understand us. For we were fighting for the same thing, though on opposite sides—for England and her old laws and liberties; for a righteous kingdom. And I always thought one day he would see where it *could* be found, and where it could *not*."

Roger could not stay with us long. But before he went, Harry Davenant was buried very quietly in the old vault of the Davenants in Netherby church.

It was at night, for the liturgy had been abolished six months before, and was unlawful, and the Vicar risked something in suffering it to be read even by Lady Lucy's chaplain, as it was. And we honoured him and Placidia for the venture. Roger had asked to be one of the bearers. Aunt Gretel, Rachel Forster, and I, waited for them in the church-porch. Slowly through the silent summer-night came the heavy tramp of the bearers, until they paused and laid their burden down under the old Lych Gate. Then, while they came up the churchyard, we crept quietly back into the church, dark in all parts except where the funeral torches lit up a little space around the open vault, and threw strange flickering shadows on the recumbent forms of the dead of Harry Davenant's race, knight and dame, priest and crusader. It made them look as if they moved to meet him; for none of the living men of his house were there, although of all his race none had fallen more bravely.

Behind the bier followed four women closely veiled. The first, by the height and movement, I knew was his Mother, and at her side, as the sacred words were read, knelt Lettice. I think in times of overwhelming joy or sorrow, when no words could fathom the depths of the heart, when almost every human voice would fall outside it altogether, or jar rudely if it reached within, there is a wonderful comfort in the calm of those ancient immutable liturgies. They are a channel worn deep by the joys and sorrows of ages. Their changelessness links them to eternity, and seems thus to make room for the sorrow which overflows the narrow measures of thought and time.

"Delivered from the burden of the flesh," "are in joy and liberty," "not to be sorry as men without hope for them that sleep in Him, that when we shall depart this life, we may rest on Him as our hope is, this our brother doth." How tranquilly the simple words sank into the very depths of the heart.

All the more precious and sacred, doubtless, for the tender sanctity which ever invests a proscribed religion.

Not that our Puritan faith is without its liturgies. Older than England, and older than Christendom, fused in the burning heart of the king of old, warrior, patriot, exile, conqueror, and penitent. But it is a perilous thing to make services like those of the Church of England, dear enough already to every faithful heart who has used them from infancy, dearer still by making them dangerous. I never knew how I loved them till we lost them.

And as that night the sacred, simple, time-honoured words fell like heavenly music among the shadows of the dim old church, I felt as if the decree which made them unlawful, and the grave of the brother slain at Naseby, were slowly mining a gulf which could never be crossed between the Draytons and the Davenants.

Alas, alas for truth! or at least for us who fain would ever recognise and be loyal to her, when she changes raiment with error, when the crown of thorns is transferred to the brows of her enemies, and the martyrs are on the wrong side. But such transformations have not hitherto lasted long, and meantime the crown of thorns may imprint its lessons even on those who wear it by mistake.

There was no sound of loud weeping. But when, for the last time, before the coffin was lowered out of sight, Lady Lucy knelt once more to embrace it, she did not rise until Lettice went gently to lift her thence; when it was found that she had fainted, and had to be borne away. But for this, Lettice would probably never have known we were there. I went at Roger's bidding to see if I could render any assistance. And then for a moment Lettice drew aside her veil, and with a suppressed sob clasped my hands in hers, and murmured,—

"Thank God, Olive. I *knew* you would all feel with us. Pray for her and for me, Olive; we have no one like him left."

Then she kissed me once, and hastened on after the rest; as they silently went back through the fields, bearing instead of the corpse of the son the almost lifeless form of the mother.

The day after the funeral Roger left us to go back to the army. I told him what Lettice had said. And he seemed more hopeful than he had been for a long time about her not misunderstanding or forgetting us.

"We must never distrust her again, Olive," he said. "She has trusted us all through."

It was strange that he should thus admonish me, for it was only Roger who ever had distrusted her caring still for us. But such little oblivions are the common lot of sisters situated as I was. I was far too satisfied with his conclusion to dispute as to the way he reached it.

Yet for many weeks after he left we heard nothing from any one of the Davenants.

Sir Launcelot Trevor came and stayed there some days at the beginning of July; and again I was tormented with fears that he had been poisoning their hearts with some evil reports of us. And as I sat watching by my Father's bed-side, many a time I rejoiced that Roger was away, so that he could not share my anxieties.

It so happened that most of the nursing fell on me, to my great thankfulness. Aunt Dorothy's sphere was governing every one outside, and Aunt Gretel's more especially preparing food and cooling drinks. Dr. Antony was pleased to say there was something in my step which fitted a sick-room. Quiet and quick, and not hasty. And in my voice, he fancied, too; cheerful, he said, as a bird singing, yet soft and low.

Be that as it might, my Father naturally liked

best to have me about him; me and Rachel Forster, in whose presence he found that repose she seemed to breathe on every one. As if she had wings invisible, which enfolded a warm, quiet space around her, like a hen brooding over her chickens. Rachel Forster and Lady Lucy, of all the women I ever knew, had most of this. And my Father felt it.

One day Rachel had a letter from Job, written a few days after the battle of Naseby.

"We began marching at three o'clock in the morning of the 14th of June," he wrote. "The day before we, the Ironsides, had come with General Cromwell from the eastern counties to our army. They had gathered after him like Abi-Ezer after Gideon. The horse already there gave a mighty shout for joy of his coming to them. By five we were at Naseby, and saw the heads of the enemy coming over the hill. Such a thing as they call a hill in these parts. A broad up and down moor. We fought it out in a fallow field, a mile broad, near the top, from early morning till afternoon. It began somewhat like the day at Marston Moor. They came on first up the hill. Prince Rupert and the plunderers were on our left, charging swift and steady, crying out: 'For God and Queen Mary.' 'God our strength,' cried we. They broke our left, though this we did not know till afterwards. Our right, that is we, General Cromwell's horse, fell on their left and drove them back, flying down the hill through the furze-bushes and rabbit-warrens. The main body, horse and foot, fought hard, breaking and gathering again, like the sea at Lizard at turn of tide. This raging back and forward lasted till Prince Rupert's horse and ours came back from the chase.

"The difference between keeping the Ten Commandments and breaking them tells in the long run. Plundering, firing villages, and slaughtering innocents, shrinks up the courage of men after a time. Prince Rupert's men could charge to the end like devils, but they could not rally like ours. Neither the prince's nor the king's word can bind their men together again to stand a second shock, as Oliver's word can rally the Ironsides. This difference turned the day. The difference between keeping the Ten Commandments (as far as mortal men can) and breaking them. The king rode about fearless as a lion to the last. 'One charge more and we recover the day,' quoth he. But there was no power in his word to rally them, and the sun was still high when he and they fled headlong into Leicester, and we after them.

"But the Ten Commandments fought against them there too. 'The stars in their courses fought against Sisera." There was no night's rest for the king in the houses he had seen rifled and dishonoured but a few days before, and never lifted up his voice to hinder it. And on and on he had to fly, to Ashby-de-la-Zouch, Wales, and who knows where? The plunder of Leicester lay strewn about the fallow field at Naseby, where we camped that night, with six hundred of the plunderers dead. Yet God forbid I slander the dead. They fought like true men. And brave, young Master Harry Davenant was among them. Belike the true men fell; and the plunderers fled off safe, as such vermin do. Until the Lord and the Ten Commandments take them in hand and bring them to account, whether in the body or out of the body.

"A hundred Irish Papist women were found hanging about the battle-field, armed with long knives, and speaking no Christian tongue. Poor benighted savages! Very strange to think such have husbands, and children, and hearts, and souls. Yet belike so had the Canaanites. These things are dark to me. I have wrestled sore there about, but can get no light on them.

"Two or three days after the battle a young gentleman, a preacher, aged some thirty years, came amongst the army. His name was Richard Baxter, a puny feeble body, marked with small-pox, and bowed and worn at thirty like an old man. Yet had the puny body good quality of courage in it. Courage of the soul, burning out of his dark eyes. Courage, surely, he had of his kind. For he came amongst our men, flushed and strong from the victorious fight, and exhorted us as if we had been a pack of school-boys. Called us—the Ironsides, and Whalley's and Rue's regiments of horse—'hot-headed, self-conceited sectaries,' Anabaptists, Antinomians, and what not—us who had been fighting the Lord's battles for him and the like of him these two years! Took our camp jokes ill, about 'Scotch *dryvines*,' 'Dissembling men at Westminster,' and '*priest* byters.' Called us profane; us who had paid twelve-pence fine for one careless oath ever since we came together.

"Argued with us, dividing his discourse into as many heads as Leviathan, and using words from every heathen tongue under the sun. If we had the best of it, called us levellers and fire-brands. If we were silent under his flood of talk, thought we were beaten, as if to have the best in talk were to win the day. As if an honest Englishman was to change his mind, because he could not, all in a moment, see his way out of Mr. Baxter's Presbyterial puzzles. Scarcely grateful, I think, seeing our men had once asked him to be their chaplain. Some of us reminded him of it, and he said he was sorry he had refused, or we should not have come to what we are. And he rebuked us sore, and called us out of our names in a gentlemanly way, in Latin and Greek, as if we had been plunderers and malignants; us of General Cromwell's own regiment. Of his courage there can after this, I think, be no doubt. Nor forsooth of our patience. And he hath gone back to Coventry and spoken slanders of the 'sad state' of the army!

"Sad state of the army indeed, where every morsel we put in our mouths is paid for, through which every modest wench, if she were as fair as Sarah, can walk, if she had need, as safe as past her father's door. An army which had just won Naseby, by the strength of the Lord and the Ten Commandments—where not an oath is heard—where psalms and prayers rise night and morning as from the old Temple—and where a young gentleman like

Mr. Richard Baxter, could come and go, and call the soldiers what ill names he chose, without hurt. For a godly young gentleman we all hold him to be, and a scholar, and honour him in our souls as such, and for the chastening hand of the Lord on the poor suffering, puny, brave body of him, although in some ways he and the likes of him cost me more wrestlings than even the Irish Papist women with their knives."

Wherever General Cromwell was throughout that summer, there continued to be a series of successes. Job's letters and Roger's were records of castles stormed or surrendered, sieges raised and troops dispersed, in Devonshire from Salisbury to Bovey Tracey.

On the 4th of August, Roger wrote of the dispersing of the poor mistaken Clubmen; a new force of peasants who had gathered to the number of two thousand on Hambledon Hill, in Surrey. Blind, as my Father says peasant armies mostly are. Aunt Gretel turned pale when she heard of them, and talked of dreadful peasant wars in Dr. Luther's time in Saxony; Dr. Luther dearly loving and fighting in his way for the peasants, but not being able to make them understand him, like Oliver Cromwell now.

These poor fellows had gathered like brave men in the West to defend their homes from Lord Goring's band—"the child-eaters" as some called them, the most lawless and merciless among the Cavalier troops, surpassing even Prince Rupert's, whom one of their own called afterwards, "terrible in plunder, and resolute in running away."

"If ye offer to plunder or take our cattle,
Be you assured we'll give you battle,"

was the clubmen's motto. A good one enough. But in time they became hopelessly involved in political plots, of which they understood nothing, demanded to garrison the coast-towns, picked out and killed peaceable Posts, fired on messengers of peace sent by General Cromwell, who had much pity for them, and finally had to be fallen upon and beaten from the field. "I believe," the General wrote to Sir Thomas Fairfax, "not twelve of them were killed, but very many were cut, and three hundred taken—poor silly creatures, whom if you please to let me send home, they promise to be very dutiful for time to come, and will be hanged before they come out again." So men and leaders were taken, and the army dispersed, and came not out again; and the land all around had quiet.

But, as Job Forster said, it was the Ten Commandments that fought best for us.

The king's cabinet at Naseby, with all the false and traitorous letters found therein in his handwriting, did more to undermine his power than a hundred battles. For in it was shown how, while solemnly promising to make no treaties with Papists, and speaking words of peace at Uxbridge, he was negotiating for six thousand Papist soldiers from Ireland, and for more than ten thousand from across the seas; that he had only agreed to call the Parliament Parliament "in the treating with them, in the sense that it was not the same to call them so, and to acknowledge them so to be." He spoke, moreover, of the gentlemen who gathered around him loyally at Oxford, as "the mongrel Parliament." So that many of his old friends were sorely aggrieved, and many neutrals began to see that, call men by what titles you will, there can be no loyalty where there is no truth.

In the North affairs went not so prosperously, though there, too, reckless ravaging wrought its own terrible cure in time. For six weeks Montrose with his Irish, and Highlanders, and some English adventurers, laid Argyleshire waste, killing every man who could bear arms, plundering and burning every cottage. It was not like the war in England, save where Prince Rupert and Lord Goring brought the savage customs of foreign warfare in on us. It was a war of clans, bent on extirpating each other like so many wild beasts, and of mountain-robbers set on carrying away as much spoil as they could from the Lowland cities, and on inflicting as much misery as they could by the way to inspire a profitable terror for the future. Perth was sacked by them, and Aberdeen, and Dundee.

At Kilsyth, near Stirling, Montrose and his men killed ten times as many of a Covenanted army, against which they fought, as fell of the Cavaliers at Naseby. Six hundred lay slain at Naseby; at Kilsyth, six thousand.

And the king, meanwhile, speaking of this robber chief as the great restorer of his kingdom and support of his throne, with never an entreaty to spare his countrymen and subjects.

Can any wonder that the sheep he commissioned so many hirelings to fleece, robbers to plunder, and wolves to slay, would not follow him?

In person, indeed, throughout that summer of 1645, His Majesty was pursuing a kind of warfare too similar to that of Wallenstein or Montrose. It was in the August of this year, scarce two months after the victory of Naseby, that the war surged up nearer us at Netherby, than at any other time.

The king had fled from Naseby to Ragland Castle, the seat of the Marquis of Worcester (an ingenious gentleman who spent his living in seeking out many inventions). There he held his court for many weeks; entertained with princely state in the halls of the grand old castle, and hunting deer gaily through the forests on the banks of the Wye, as if his subjects were not themselves in his quarrel hunting each other to death in every corner of his kingdom.

Whilst there tidings came to him of the successes of Montrose, and he endeavored to go northward to join him in Scotland. From Doncaster, however, he fell back on Newark, turned from his purpose by the Covenanted army of Sir David Leslie, which threatened him from the North. And then he turned his steps to us, to the Fens and the Associated Counties, which General Cromwell's care, and their own fidelity to the Parliament, had kept hitherto high and dry out of reach of the war, save for some few stray foraging parties. During this August 1645 we learned, however, at His Majesty's hands, the meaning of civil war. The eastern counties lay exposed to attack, having sent their tried men westward with Cromwell and Fairfax; so that we had nothing but our own more recent foot-levies to defend us.

The king dashed from Stamford through Huntingdonshire and Cambridgeshire, ravaging the whole country as he passed, and detaching flying squadrons to plunder Bedfordshire and Hertfordshire, as far as St. Albans. Several times he threatened Cambridge.

On the 24th of August, he took Huntingdon by assault, and four days afterwards, by the 28th, was safe again within the lines of Oxford, with large store of booty seized from the very cradle and stronghold of the Parliamentary army.

No doubt the Cavaliers had fine triumphing and merry-making over the spoils at Oxford. But to us, around whom lay the empty granaries and roofless homesteads, and the wrecked and burned villages from which these spoils came, the lesson was not one of submission or of terror, but of resistance more resolute than ever. Prince Rupert had been teaching this lesson for three years in every corner of the realm. His Majesty taught it us in person. A lesson of resistance not desperate but hopeful; for we could not but deem that a king who would indiscriminately ravage whole counties of his kingdom, must look on it as an alien territory already lost to his crown.

Many sins, no doubt, may be laid to the charge of the Parliament and its army. But of two sins terribly common in civil strife they were never guilty;

indiscriminate plunder and secret assassination. The ruins and desecrations the Commonwealth soldiers wrought in churches and cathedrals, will tell their tale against us to many a generation to come. The ruins the Royalist troopers wrought were in poor men's homes long since repaired. The desecrations they wrought were also in homes, ruins and desecrations of temples not made with hands, and never to be repaired, but recorded on sacred inviolable tables, more durable than any stone, though not to be read on earth, at least not yet.

The village of Netherby lay just beyond the edge of the royal devastations. But the cattle all around us were seized, with all the corn that was reaped. And at night the sky was all aglow with the flames of burning cottages, and corn and hay-stacks. Our own barns were untouched, but my Father gave orders at once to begin husbanding our stores by limiting our daily food, looking on what was spared to us as the granary of the whole destitute neighbourhood through the coming winter, and as the seed-store for the following spring. Our sheds and out-houses, meantime, were fitted up for those who had been driven from their homes. Every cottage in Netherby gave shelter to some homeless neighbour. Rachel Forster's became an orphan-house. Yet it was the private lesson which was taught our own family through this foray of His Majesty's that is engraven most deeply in my memory.

Throughout the summer, Cousin Placidia had been more than ever a subject of irritation and distress to Aunt Dorothy. The successes of Montrose in Scotland, followed by the plunderings of the king's troops in our own counties, had once more caused her to feel much "exercised" as to which was the right side. In February, after the execution of Archbishop Laud, Mr. Nicholls had obediently substituted the Directory of Worship for the Common Prayer, sorely trying thereby Aunt Dorothy's predilections for unwritten, or rather unprinted prayers; Mr. Nicholls' supplications not having, in her opinion, either unction or fire, being in fact, she said, nothing but the old Liturgy minced and sent up cold. Her only comfort was in the trust that sifting days were at hand. (The *Triers* had not yet been appointed.) But what vexed Aunt Dorothy's soul even more than any ecclesiastical "trimmings," was what she regarded as the gradual eating up of Placidia's heart by the rust of hoarded wealth. Placidia had at that time an additional reason to justify herself for any amount of straitening and sparing, in the expectation of the birth of her first child. This prospect opened a new field for her economies and for Aunt Dorothy's anxieties. Even the general devastations of the country, which opened every door and every heart wide to the sufferers, only effected the narrowest possible opening in Placidia's stores. Her health, she said, obviously prevented her receiving any strangers into the house; and it was little indeed that a poor parson, with a family to provide for, and nothing but income to depend on, and the certainty of receiving scarcely any tithes the next season, could have to spare. Such as she had, said she, she gave willingly. There was a stack of hay but slightly damaged by getting heated. And there was some preserved meat, a little strong perhaps from keeping, but quite wholesome and palatable with a little extra salt. These she most gladly bestowed. Aunt Dorothy was in despair, and made one last solemn appeal.

"Placidia," she said, "a child will shut up your heart and be a curse to you, if you let it shut your doors against the poor; until at last who knows what door may be shut on you?"

But Placidia was impregnable.

"Aunt Dorothy," she said, with mild imperturbability, "everything may be made either a curse or a blessing. But to those who are in the covenant everything is a blessing."

"Sister Gretel," said Aunt Dorothy, afterwards, "I see no way of escape for her. The mercies of God's providence and the doctrines of His grace *freeze* on that poor woman's heart, until the ice is so thick that the sunshine itself can do nothing but just thaw the surface, and make the next day's ice smoother and harder."

Aunt Gretel looked up.

"Never give up hope, sister," said she. "Our good God has more weapons than we wot of, and more means of grace than are counted in any of our Catechisms and Confessions. Sometimes He can warm the coldest heart with the glow of a new human love until all the ice melts away from within. And the touch of a little child's hand has opened many a door, where the Master has afterwards come in and sat down and supped. When the Saviour wanted to teach the Pharisees, He set in the midst of them a little child."

Aunt Dorothy shook her head.

"Children have dragged many a godly man back again to Egypt," said she. "Many a rope which binds good men tight to the car of Mammon is twisted by very little hands."

And the proposition being unanswerable, the discussion ended.

A few nights afterwards we were roused by a suspicious glare in the direction of the Parsonage. The next morning early we went to see if anything had happened there.

As we passed through the village, we heard the news quickly enough.

Just after dusk, on the evening before, a party of Royalist troopers had appeared at the Parsonage gates. The house stood alone, at some little distance from the village, at the end of the glebe-fields. The captain of the little troop said they were on their way to join His Majesty at Oxford; but seeing a light, they were tempted to seek the hospitality of Mistress Nicholls, of which they had heard in the neighbourhood.

Poor Placidia's protestations of poverty were of little avail with such guests. They politely assured her they were used to rough fare, and would themselves render any assistance she required towards preparing the feast. Whereupon they put up their horses in the stables, supplied them liberally with corn from the granaries, seized the fattest of the poultry, and strung them in a tempting row before the kitchen fire, which they piled into huge dimensions with any wooden articles that came first to hand, chairs and chests included; the contents of these chests being meanwhile skillfully rifled, and all that was most valuable in them of plate, linen, or silk, set apart in a heap "for the king's service."

The supper being prepared, they insisted on their host drinking His Majesty's health in the choicest wines in his cellar. The captain had been informed, he said, that Mr. Nicholls had been induced (reluctantly, of course, as he perceived from the fervent protestations of loyalty) to disuse the Liturgy, and even to contribute of his substance to the rebel cause. He felt glad, therefore, to be able to give him this opportunity of proving his unjustly suspected fidelity, and of contributing, at the same time, of his substance to His Majesty's service, by means of the portion of his goods which they would the next day convey to His Majesty's head-quarters in the loyal city of Oxford, and thus save it from being misapplied in this disaffected country, in a manner which Mr. Nicholls' loyal heart must abhor. This we heard from one of the frightened serving-wenches, who had escaped towards morning, and spread the news through the village.

As the night passed on, they grew riotous, and were with difficulty roused from their carouse by the captain, to see about getting their plunder together before dawn. They poured on the ground what wine they could not drink, set fire (whether by accident or on purpose was not known) to the large corn-stack whilst hunting about the sheds and stables for cattle and horses; till finally the inmates were thankful to get them away early in the morning, although they took with them all the beasts they could drive and all the booty they could carry.

The sympathy in the village was not deep, and Aunt Dorothy and I went on in silence to the Parsonage, to give what help and comfort we could. Neither Aunt Dorothy nor I spoke a word as we hastened up the rising ground towards the house.

The homely ruins of the farm-yard moved me more than many a stately ruin. The remains of the corn-stack, the flames of which had alarmed us in the night, stood there black and charred; the stables were empty and the cattle-sheds; the house-dog was hanged to the door of one of them; the yard was strewn with trampled corn, which the sparrows and starlings, in the absence of the privileged poultry, were making bold to pick up; and the silence of the deserted court was made more dismal by the occasional restless lowing of a calf, which was roaming from one empty shed to another in search of its mother.

We went into the house. The kitchen was full of the serving-wenches, and of some of the more curious and idle in the village, who were condoling with each other, by making the worst of the disaster. The hearth was black with the cinders of the enormous fire of the night before, and the floor was strewn with broken pieces of the chairs and chests which had helped to kindle it, and with fragments of the feast. In a corner of the settle by the cold hearth sat Placidia, as if she were stupified, with her hands clasped and her eyes fixed upon them.

When she saw Aunt Dorothy, she turned away, and said,—

"Don't reproach me, Aunt Dorothy; I can't bear it."

"Didst thou think I came for that?" said Aunt Dorothy. "But belike I deserve it of thee."

And with a voice a little sharpened by the feeling she strove to repress, Aunt Dorothy sent the curious neighbours to the right-about, and disposed of the two serving-wenches, by telling them the very fowls of the air were setting such lazy sluts as they were an example, and despatching them to gather up the scattered corn in the yard.

Then she came again to Placidia, and taking her clasped hands in hers, said,—

"I've learnt many things, child, this last hour. I judged thee a Pharisee, and belike I've been a worse one myself. I've sat on the judgment-seat this many a day on thee. But I'm off it now. And may the Lord grant me grace never to climb up there again. I've wished for some heavy rod to fall and teach thee. And now it's come, it can't smite thee heavier than it does me. Forgive me, child, and let us both begin again."

Placidia looked up, and meeting the honest eyes fixed on her, not in scorn but in entreaty, she sobbed,—

"I shall never have heart to begin again, Aunt Dorothy."

"To begin what again?" said Aunt Dorothy.

"Contriving and saving to make up all the things I have lost," replied Placidia. "I've been years heaping it together, and it's all gone in a night!"

Aunt Dorothy looked sorely puzzled, between her desire to be charitable and her horror of Placidia's misreading of the dispensation.

"Begin *that* again, my dear," she said, at last. "Nay; thou must *never* begin that again. It will never do to fly in the face of Providence like that."

Placidia uncovered her face, but as her eyes rested on the desolation around her, she covered them again, and sobbed,—

"Just when there was to be one to save it all for, and make it worth while to deny oneself."

"Nay," said Aunt Dorothy; "that's the mercy. That's precisely the mercy. The Lord will not let the child be a curse to thee. He will have it a blessing; so He says to thee as plain as can be, I give thee a treasure, not to make thee rage and stint and grudge, but to teach thee to love and serve and give, not to make thee poor, but to make thee rich. And He will go on teaching thee till thou openest thy heart and learnest, and thy burden falls off, and thy heart leaps up, and thou shalt be free. I know it by the way my heart is lightened now. He's smitten me down for my sitting in judgment on thee. Not that I'm safe never to climb that seat again. One is there before one knows, and the black-cap on in a moment. Some one is always near, I trow, to help us up."

And turning from Placidia, she proceeded to a

quiet survey of the ruins, which, under her brisk and discriminating hands, with such help as I could give, soon began to show some signs of order.

The fire was lighted; the calf despatched to Netherby to be fed; sundry fragments of chairs and chests to the village carpenter, to be mended; the broken meat put into two baskets.

"This is for the household," said Aunt Dorothy, "and that for the fatherless children at Rachel Forster's. One of the maids can take it at once, Placidia, when she leads away the calf."

Placidia was at length quite roused from her stupor. She looked at Aunt Dorothy as if she thought she were in league with the plunderers.

"Me send meat to Rachel Forster's orphans!" she said faintly; "a poor plundered woman like me!"

"Better begin at once, my dear," said Aunt Dorothy; "the fatherless are God's little ones. Better give the treasure to them. You see our bags have holes in them."

At that moment Mr. Nicholls returned. Placidia appealed to him for his usual confirmation of her opinions.

"Dear heart," he said ruefully, "Belike Mistress Dorothy is right. It's of no use fighting against God. Who knoweth if He may turn and repent and leave a blessing behind Him."

"Nay, Master Nicholls," said Aunt Dorothy, "*not that way*. It's of no use trying to escape in that way. You must *let go altogether* first, or the Almighty will never take hold of you. It's hoping for *nothing* again. If thou and Placidia will send this to the orphans, ye must send it because it has been given to you, and because they want it more than you do. Because thou wast an orphan, Placidia," she added, tenderly, "and He has not failed to care for thee. Take heed how ye slight His staff or His rod. Both have been used plainly enough for thee. I'll divide the stuff," she concluded, "and you must settle what to do with it yourselves, afterwards."

And insisting on Placidia's resting up-stairs while she subjected the contents of the chests strewn about the chamber-floor to the same process of division, she left the house before dusk restored to something like order, with two significant heaps of clothing on the bed-chamber, and two significant baskets of provisions in the kitchen, to speak what parables they might during the night to the consciences of Placidia and Mr. Nicholls.

But before the morning other teachers had been there. Death and Anguish—those merciful curses sent to keep the world, which had ceased to be Eden, from becoming a sensual Elysium, idle, selfish, and purposeless—visited the house that night. Another life was ushered into the world under the shadow of Death itself. In the morning Placidia lay feebly rejoicing in the infant-life for which her own had been so nearly sacrificed. Rejoicing in a gift which had cost her so much, and which was to cost her so much more of patient sacrifices, toil and watching, sacrifices for which no one would especially admire her, and for which she would not admire herself; rejoicing as she had never rejoiced in any possession before. Not by any supernatural effort of virtue, but by the simple natural fountain of motherly love which had been opened in her heart.

One of the first things she said was to Rachel, who was watching with her through the next night. Very softly, as Rachel sat by her bed-side with the baby on her knee, Placidia said,—

"Strange such a gift should have been given to me and not to thee."

"And," said Rachel (when she told me of it), "I could not answer her all in a moment, for there are seas stronger and deeper than those outside our dykes around our hearts. And it's not safe, even in the quietest weather, opening the cranny to let in those tides. So I said nothing. And in a few moments Mistress Nicholls spoke again, 'For thou art good and worthy, Rachel,' said she, 'and it would be no great wonder if the Lord gave thee the best He has to give.'

"Then I understood what she meant, and my heart was nigh as glad as if the child had been given to me. For I thought there was a soul new born to God as a little child, meek and lowly. The Lord had led her along the hardest step on the way to Himself, the first step down. And she said no more. I smoothed her pillow, laid the babe beside her, and she and it fell asleep. But I sat still and cried quietly for joy. And the next morning, when the light broke in, Mistress Nicholls looked up and saw those two heaps Mistress Dorothy had set apart, and then she looked down on the babe, and murmured as if to herself,—

"'Poor motherless little ones! God has given me thee and spared me to thee. The poor motherless babes, they shall have the things.'

"And then," pursued Rachel, "I turned away and cried again to myself half for gladness, and half for trouble. For I thought sure the Lord's a-going to take her, poor lamb, if she's so changed as that."

But Aunt Dorothy, when Rachel narrated this, although she wiped her eyes sympathetically, at the same time gave her head a consolatory shake and said,—

"Never fear, neighbour, never fear, not yet. Depend on it, the old Enemy will have a fight for it yet. Depend on it, there's a good deal of work to be done for her in this world yet, before she's too good to be left in it."

LETTICE'S DIARY.

"*Davenant Hall, Twelfth Night*, 1645–6.—Only four years since that merry sixteenth birthday of mine, when all the village were gathered in the Hall, and Olive and I gave the garments to the village maidens of my own age, and in the evening Roger stayed to help kindle the twelve bonfires.

"And now we are walled and moated out from the village and from the Manor as we were in the old days of the Norman Conquest, when the Davenants first took possession of these lands, and built the old ruined keep, where the gateway is (whence they afterwards removed to this abbey), to overawe the Saxon village, where the Draytons even then lived in the old Manor. I wonder if there is anything left of the old contentions in Saxon and Norman blood now. The rebel army is so much composed, they say, both of officers and men, of the stout old Saxon yeomanry, and the traders in the towns; whilst ours is officered from the old baronial castles, by gentlemen with the old Norman historical names. How many of the higher gentry and nobility are loyal has been proved these last six months, since fatal Naseby, by the sieges (and, alas! by the stormings and surrenders) of at least a score of old castles and mansions, from Bristol, surrendered on the 11th of September by Prince Rupert to Bovey Tracey in the faithful West. Thank Heaven, they gave Oliver Cromwell and Sir Thomas Fairfax much trouble, Basing Hall especially. In future days, when the king shall enjoy his own again (as he surely will), I hold such a blackened ruin will be a choicer possession to a gentleman's family than a palace furnished regally. The rebels called Basing House *Basting*, for the mischief it did them. And our men called it *Loyalty.*

"Roger Drayton hath shared, no doubt, in many of these sieges. So stern in his delusion of duty, I suppose, if this brewer of Huntingdon commanded him, he would not scruple to plant his reble guns against us. 'Thine eye shall not spare,' they say, in their hateful cant. Sir Launcelot says they have been chasing His Sacred Majesty from place to place like a hunted stag; that Mr. Cromwell, whom Roger loves above king and friend, never sets on any great enterprise without having a '*text*' to lean on! That before storming Basing Hall, he passed the night in *prayer*, and that the text he especially 'rested on' for that achievement was Psalm cxviii. 8: '*They that make them are like unto them, so is every one that trusteth in them!*' as if we Royalists were Canaanites, idolaters, Papists, I know not what. Fancy burning down a corn-stack to a psalm-tune, or setting out on a burglary to a text. Yet what is it better to burn down loyal gentlemen's houses about their ears, from one end of England to another. It is all Conscience; this dreadful Moloch of Conscience! It was the one weak point of the Draytons always.

"Sir Launcelot Trevor came here a week since to see if anything can be done to strengthen the fortifications. My Father was in Bristol when it was stormed, and has followed the king ever since; two of my brothers are in Ireland, seeing what can be done there; two fled beyond the seas after the defeat of the gallant Marquis of Montrose last September at Philipshaugh, near Selkirk; and two lie on that fatal Rowton Heath, where on September the 23rd the king's last army, worth the name, was broken and lost.

"We have made sacrifices enough to endear the royal cause to us. I suppose this old house will be the next. For Harry said it would never stand a siege. But, oh, if I could only be sure Sir Launcelot is mistaken in what he says about Roger giving Harry his death-blow, much of the rest would seem light. I have never yet told my Mother of this dread. Sometimes when I think how Roger looked and spoke that morning, I feel sure it cannot be true. But he always said it was so wrong to believe things because I wished them true. And now the more I long to believe this false, the less I seem able.

"Only four years since that merry sixteenth birthday, when I was a child. And then that happy summer afterwards, when the world seemed to grow so beautiful and great, and it seemed as if we were to do such glorious things in it.

"First the birthdays seem like triumphal columns, trophies of a conquered year. Then like mile-stones, marking rather sadly the way we have come. But now I think they look like grave-stones, so much is buried for ever beneath this terrible year that is gone. Not lives only, but love, and trust, and hope.

"I said so to my Mother to-night, as I wished her good-night. It was selfish. For I ought to comfort her. But she comforted me. She said, 'The birthdays will look like mile-stones again, by-and-by, sweetheart. They will be marked on the other side, "so much nearer home," and perhaps at last like trophies again, marking the conquered years.'

"On which I broke down altogether, and said,—

"'Oh, Mother, don't speak like that, don't say you look on them like that. Think of me at the beginning of the journey, so near the beginning.'

"'I do, Lettice,' said she. 'I pray to live, for thy sake, every day.'

"For my sake; only for my sake. For her own she longs to go. And that is saddest of all to me.

"For, except on days like these, when I think and look back, I am not always so very wretched. It is very strange, after all that has happened. But I am sometimes—rather often—a little bit happy. There is so much that is cheerful and beautiful in the world, I cannot help enjoying it. And pleasant things might happen yet.

"I did love Harry, dearly; nearly better than any one. I do. But to my Mother losing him seems just the one sorrow which puts her on the other side of all earthly joys and sorrows, with a great gulf between, so that she looks on them from afar off, like an angel.

"I suppose there is just *the one thing* which would be the darkening of the whole world to most of us, making it night instead of day. Other people leave that sepulchre behind. It is grown over, and in years it becomes a little sacred grass-grown mound, or a stately memorial to the life ended there.

"But to *one*, it has made *the whole earth* a sepulchre, at which she stands without, weeping and looking on.

"*There is only one* Voice which can quiet the heart there.

"*The day after.*—Sir Launcelot and I have had high words to-day. We were looking from the terrace towards Netherby, and I said something about old times, and that the Draytons would probably resume the lands they had lost in old times at the Conquest.

"I fired up, and said not one of the Draytons would ever touch anything that did not belong to them. '*They* were not of Prince Rupert's plunderers,' said I.

"'No doubt,' said he, 'they hold by a better right than the sword.' And with nasal solemnity, clasping his hands, he added, 'Voted, it is written the saints shall possess the land; *voted*, we are the saints.'

"'Sir Launcelot,' I said, 'you know I hate to hear old friends spoken of like that.'

"(When I had written bitter things myself of them but yesterday! But it always angers me when people are unfair.)

"Here he changed his tone, and spoke seriously enough. Too seriously, indeed, by far. He said something about my opinion being more to him than anything in the world. And when I went back into the garden-parlour, not desiring such discourse, he was on his knees at my feet, before I could raise him, pouring out, I know not what passionate protestations, and saying that I could save him, and reclaim him, and make him all he longed to be, and was not. And that if I rejected him, there was not another power on earth or heaven that could keep him from plunging into perdition, which perplexed and grieved me much. For I do not love him. Of that I am sure. But it is terrible to think of being the only barrier between any human soul and destruction. And I am half afraid to tell my Mother, for fear she should counsel me to take Sir Launcelot's conversion on me. Because she thinks everything of no weight compared with religion. But I cannot think it would be a duty to marry a person for the same reason from which you might become his godmother. Besides, if I did not *love*, what real power should I have to save?

"*At night* (*later*).—I have told my Mother, and she says that last consideration makes it quite clear. I could have no power for good, unless I loved. And I do not love Sir Launcelot; and I never could.

"At the same time, when I opened my heart to her about this, I ventured at last to tell her what Sir Launcelot had thought about Harry and Roger Drayton. I wish I had told her weeks ago.

"For she does not believe it. She says Roger would never have come and told us had it been so. She has not the slightest fear it can be true. It has lightened my heart wonderfully. Roger is not quite just in saying I can believe in anything I wish.

"*March.*—A biting March for the good cause. On the 14th brave Sir Ralph Hopton surrendered in Cornwall. On the 22nd brave old Sir Jacob Astley (he who made the prayer before Edgehill fight, 'Lord, if I forget Thee this day, do not Thou forget me'), was beaten at Stow in Gloucestershire, as he was bringing a small force he had gathered with much pains, to succour the king at Oxford. 'You have now done your work and may go to play,' he said to the rebels who captured him, 'unless you fall out among yourselves.' Gallant sententious old veteran that he is!

"*May.*—His Majesty has taken refuge with the Scottish army at Newark.

"We marvel he should have trusted his sacred person with Covenanted Presbyterians. But in good sooth he may well be weary of wandering, and may look for some pity yet in his own fellow-countrymen. Not that they showed much to the sweet fair lady his father's mother.

"We hear it was but unwillingly he went to them at night, between two and three o'clock in the morning, on the 27th of April. A few days since he left the shelter of Oxford, faithful to him so long; riding disguised as a servant, behind his faithful attendant Mr. Ashburnham. Once he was asked by a stranger on the road if his master were a nobleman. 'No,' quoth the king, 'my master is one of the Lower House,' a sad truth, forsooth, though spoken in parable. It is believed amongst us that he would fain have reached the eastern coast, thence to take ship for Scotland, to join Montrose and the true Scots with him. For his flight was uncertain, and changed direction more than once—to Henley-on-Thames, Slough, Uxbridge; then to the top of Harrow Hill, across the country to St. Albans, where the clattering hoofs of a farmer behind them gave false alarm of pursuit; thence by the houses of many faithful gentlemen who knew and loved him, but respected his disguise and made as though they knew him not; to Downham in Norfolk; to Southwell, and thence, beguiled by promises some say, others declare throwing himself of his own free will like a prince on the ancient Scottish loyalty, he rode to Newark into the midst of the Earl of Leven's army.

"*August*, 1646.—The civil war, they give out, now is over. Every garrison and castle in the kingdom have surrendered. In June, loyal Oxford; and now, last and most loyal of all, on the 19th of August, Ragland Castle, with the noble old Marquis of Worcester, who hath ruined himself past all remedy in the king's service, and in this world will scarce now find his reward.

"In June, Prince Rupert rode through the land, and embarked at Dover. Well for the good cause if he had never come. His marauding ways gave quite another complexion to the war from what it might have had without him. His rashness, Harry thought, lost us many a field. His lawlessness infected our army. The king could not forgive him his surrender of Bristol a few days after he was led to believe it could be held for months. But in this some think perchance he is less to blame than elsewhere. Cromwell and the Ironsides were there and they stormed the city, for it seems as if this Cromwell could never be baffled.

"With Prince Rupert went three hundred loyal gentlemen, some despairing of the cause at home, others, and with them my Father, on missions to seek aid from foreign courts.

"*February*, 1647.—The Scottish army has yielded him up ('Bought and sold,' His Majesty said; others say the two hundred thousand pounds the Scotch received was for the expenses of the war,) into the hands of the English Presbyterians at Newcastle.

"*March.*—We have seen the king once more. My Mother has heard for certain the true cause why the king was given up by the Scotch to his enemies. He would not sign their blood-stained Covenant. He would not sacrifice the Church of these kingdoms, with her bishops and her sacred liturgy, though nobles, loyal men and true, nay the queen herself, by letter, entreated him. My mother saith he is now in most literal truth a martyr, suffering for the spotless bride—our dear Mother, the Church of England—and for the truth. We heard he was to arrive at Holmby House in Northamptonshire, and, weak as my Mother is, nothing would content her but to be borne thither in a litter to pay him her homage. I would not have missed it for the world. Numbers of gentlemen and gentlewomen were there to welcome him with tears and prayers and hearty acclamations. It did our hearts good to hear the hearty cheers and shouts, and I trust cheered his also. The rebel troopers were Englishmen enough to offer no hindrance. And we had the joy of gazing once more on that kingly pathetic countenance. He is serene and cheerful, as a true martyr should be, my mother says, accepting his cross and rejoicing in it, not morose and of a sad countenance as those who feign to be persecuted for conscience sake. He scorns no blameless pleasure which can solace the weary hours of captivity, riding miles sometimes to a good bowling-green to play at bowls, and beguiling the evenings with chess or converse on art with Mr. Harrington or Mr. Herbert.

"He will not suffer a Presbyterian chaplain to say grace at his table, and the hard-hearted jailers will allow no other.

"Thank heaven the common people are true to him still, as they took him from Newcastle to Holmby House the simple peasants flocked round to see him and bless him, and to feel the healing touch of his sacred hand for the king's evil. Sir Harry Marten, a rebel and a republican, made a profane jest thereon, and said, 'The touch of the great seal would do them as much good.' But no one relished the scurrilous jest. And the blessings and prayers of the poor followed the king everywhere. Yes; it is the common people and the nobles that honour true greatness. The Scribes and Pharisees, I am persuaded, sprang from the middle-order yeo men, craftsmen, chapmen. "Tithing mint and devouring widows' houses," are just base, weeping, unpunishable middle-station sins. The troubles of this middle class are wretched, low, carking money-troubles. The sorrows of the high and low are natural ennobling sorrows; bereavement, pain, and death. It is the sordid middle order that envies the great. The common people reverence them when on high places, and generously pity them when brought low. My Mother says, belike the sorrows of their king shall yet move the honest heart of the nation to a reverent pity, and thus back to loyalty, and so, as so often in great conflicts, more be won through suffering than through success.

"*April*, 1647.—We are to pay our last penalty.

Our old hall is declared to be a perilous nest of traitors and cradle of insurrection. A rebel garrison is to be quartered on us.

"Our expedition to Holmby, has led to two results; it offended some of the people in authority among the rebels, and thereby caused them to take possession of the hall; and it so taxed my mother's wasted strength that she is unfit for any journey, so that we must even stay and suffer the presence of these insolent and rebellious men in our home.

"*April, Davenant Hall.*—Mr. Drayton hath been here to-day. He looked pale and thin from the long imprisonment he has had, and he hath lost his right arm—a sore loss to him who ever took such pleasure in his geometrical instruments, and played the viol-di-gambo so masterly.

"He gave a slight start when he saw my mother, and there was a kind of anxious compassionate reverence in his manner towards her which makes me uneasy. I fear he deems her sorely changed, and ofttimes I have feared the same. But then this mourning garb which she will never more lay aside, and her dear gray hair, which I love, put back like an Italian Madonna from her forehead, in itself makes a difference. Although I think her eyes never looked so soft and beautiful as now. The golden hair of youth, and all its brilliant colour, seems to me scarcely so fair as this silver hair of hers, with the soft pale hues on her cheeks.

"Mr. Drayton asked us to take asylum at Netherby Hall till such time as we join my father elsewhere. My mother knows what Harry thought, and seems not averse to accept his hospitality. I certainly had not thought to enter old Netherby again in such guise as this."

OLIVE'S RECOLLECTIONS.

The old house seemed to gain a king of sacredness when it became the refuge of that dear bereaved Lady and sweet Lettice. Lady Lucy was much changed. Her voice always soft, was low as the soft notes in a hymn; her step, always light, was slower and feebler; her hair, though still abundant, had changed from luxuriant auburn to a soft silvery brown; her cheeks were worn into a different curve, though still, I thought, as beautiful, and the colour in them was paler. Everything in her seemed to have changed from sunset to moonlight. Her voice and her very thoughts seem to come from afar; from some region we could not tread, like music borne over still waters. It was as if she had crossed a river which severed her far from us, which she would never more recross, but only wait till the call came to mount the dim heights on the other side. Not that she was in any way sad or uninterested, or abstracted, only she did not seem to belong to us any more.

I wondered if Lettice saw this as I did. And many a time the tears came to my eyes as I looked at those two and thought how strong were the cords of love which bound them, and how feeble the thread of life.

Aunt Dorothy welcomed Lady Lucy with as true

a tenderness as any one. The silvery hair in place of those heart-breakers—the hair silvered so suddenly by sorrow—softened her in more ways than one. One thing, however, tried her sorely. And I much dreaded the explosion it might lead to if Aunt Dorothy's conscience once got the upper hand of her hospitality.

The Lady Lucy always had a little erection closely resembling an altar, in her oratory at home, dressed in white, with sacred books on it; the Holy Scriptures, A Kempis, Herbert, and others, and above them a copy of a picture by Master Albert Durer, figuring our Lord on the Cross, the suffering thorn-crowned form gleaming pale and awful from the terrible noonday darkness. Before this solemn picture stood two golden candlesticks, which at night the waiting gentlewomen were wont to light. I shall never forget Aunt Dorothy's expression of dismay and distress when she first saw this erection, one evening soon after Lady Lucy's arrival. She mastered herself so far as to say nothing to Lady Lucy then, beyond the good wishes for the night, and directions as to some possets which she had come to administer.

But the solemn change that came over her voice and face she could not conceal. And afterwards she solemnly summoned us into my Father's private room to make known her discovery.

"An idol, brother!" she concluded, "an abomination! At this moment, probably, idol-worship going on under this roof, drawing down on us all the lightnings of heaven!"

"I should not use such a thing as a help to devotion myself, Sister Dorothy," said my Father; "but what would you have me do?"

"Help to devotion!" she exclaimed, "'Thou shalt not make any graven image, nor the likeness of any thing.' Sweep them away with the besom of destruction, and cast the idols to the moles and to the bats."

"Sister Dorothy," he said, "you would not have me take a hammer, and axe, and cords, and drag this piece of painted work from the Lady Lucy's chamber before her eyes."

"Thine eye shall not spare," she replied, solemnly.

"But in the first place I must know that it is an idol to Lady Lucy," he said, "and that she does bow down to it."

"Subtle distinctions, brother; traffickings with the enemy. Heaven grant they prove not our ruin, as of Jehoshaphat before us."

For Aunt Dorothy, although she had forsaken the judgment seat for private offences, would still have deemed it an impiety to abandon it in cases of heresy.

"Sister Dorothy," interposed Aunt Gretel, "in my country good men and women do use such things and do not become idolaters thereby in their private devotion and in the churches."

"Belike they do, sister Gretel," rejoined Aunt Dorothy, drily. "The hand that would have pulled down the Epistle of St. James might well leave some idols standing. An owl sees better than a blind man. But it is no guide to those whose eyes are used to day.

This profane comparison of Dr. Luther to an owl dismayed Aunt Gretel, so as to throw her entirely out of the conflict, which finished with an ordinance from my Father that liberty of conscience should be the order of his household; and a protest from Aunt Dorothy that, be the consequences what they may, she would not suffer any immortal soul within her reach to go the broad road to ruin without warning.

Which threat kept us in anxious anticipation. We took the greatest care not to leave the combatants alone; one so determined and one so unconscious of danger.

At last, however, the fatal moment arrived.

It was early in April, a fortnight after Lady Lucy and Lettice took shelter under our roof.

Dr. Anthony had arrived from London with tidings which made us all very uneasy.

The Presbyterian majority in the House of Commons, believing the civil war ended, were very eager to disband the army which had ended it, but which, being mostly composed of Independents, they dreaded even more than the king.

In February, they had voted that no officer under Sir Thomas Fairfax should hold any rank higher than a colonel, intending thereby to displace Oliver Cromwell, Ireton, Ludlow, Blake, Skippon, and Algernon Sydney, and, in short, every commander whom the army most trusted, and under whom their victories had been gained.

They were to be disbanded, morover, without receiving their pay, now due for more than half a year. It was also proposed that such of the soldiers as were still kept together should be sent to Ireland to settle matters there, under new Presbyterian commanders, instead of those whom they knew and trusted.

The indignation in the army was deep. But it was as much under the restraint of law, and was expressed in as orderly a way, as if the army had been a court of justice. The regiments met, deliberated, remonstrated, and drew up a petition, demanded arrears of pay, and refused to go to Ireland save under commanders they knew. "For the desire of our arrears," they said, "necessity, especially of our soldiers, enforced us thereunto. We left our estates, and many of us our trade and callings to others, and forsook the contentments of a quiet life, not fearing nor regarding the difficulties of war for your sakes; after which we hoped that the desires of our hardly earned wages would have been no unwelcome request, nor argued us guilty of the least discontent or intention of mutiny."

No one, my Father said, could deny the truth of this. The Parliament army had not eked out with plunder their arrears of pay.

On the 3d of April three soldiers—Adjutators (or Agitators, as some called them)—had been sent with a respectful but determined message to the House of Commons. General Cromwell (attending in his place in the House in spite of the plots there had been during the past weeks, as he knew, to commit him to the Tower) rose and spoke at length of the danger of driving the army to extremities.

And now Dr. Antony came with the tidings that General Cromwell was at Saffron Walden, bearing to the army the promise of indemnity and arrears. He brought also a brief letter from Roger, saying that now all was sure to go right.

This news drew us all together, and it was not until she had been absent some time that it was discovered that Aunt Dorothy had left us.

Aunt Gretel was the first to perceive her departure, and to suspect its cause. At once she repaired to Lady Lucy's chamber, whence, in a minute or two, she returned, and pressing me lightly on the shoulder, she said, in a solemn whisper,—

"Olive, it must be stopped; the Lady Lucy is looking like a ghost, and Mistress Lettice like a damask rose, and your Aunt Dorothy is talking Latin."

This was Aunt Gretel's formula for controversial language. She said English was composed of two elements; the German she could understand; we used it, she said, when we were speaking of things near our hearts, of matters of business, or of affection, or of religion, in a peaceable and kindly manner. But the Latin was beyond her. There were long words in *ation*, *utical*, or *arian*, which always came on the field when there was to be a battle. And then she always withdrew. In this martial array Aunt Dorothy's thoughts were now being clothed. And Aunt Gretel thought I had better summon my Father to interrupt the debate.

I went at once and indicated to him the danger. He looked half angry, half amused.

"Dr. Antony," he said, "your medical attendance is required up-stairs. My sister has recommenced the Civil War."

I flew up to announce the coming of the gentlemen.

At the moment when I entered the room the controversy had reached a climax. Lady Lucy was sitting very pale and upright, and on a high-backed chair with tears in her eyes, and saying in a faint voice,—

"Mistress Dorothy, I am *not* a Papist, and hope never to be."

Lettice, behind the chair, with her arm round her mother, and her hand on her shoulder, like a champion, stood with quivering lips and burning cheeks, and rejoined that "there were worse heretics than the Papists, worse tyrants than the Inquisition." Whilst Aunt Dorothy, as pale as Lady Lucy, and with lips quivering as much as Lettice's, faced them both with the consciousness of being herself a witness or a martyr for the truth struggling within her against the sense that she was regarded by others in the light of an inquisitor and tormentor of martyrs.

"An't please you, Lady Lucy," I said, "my Father thought Dr. Antony, who is down-stairs, might recommend you some healing draught. He has wonderful recipes for coughs."

And before a reply could be given, my Father and Dr. Antony were at the door, and Aunt Dorothy was arrested in her testimony without the possibility of uttering a last word.

Dr. Antony seemed to comprehend the position at a glance. With a quiet courtesy which introduced him at once, and gave him the command of the field, he went up to Lady Lucy, and, feeling her pulse, observed that it was slightly feverish and uneven, ordered the windows to be open, and recommended that as much air as possible should be obtained, by means of all but Mistress Lettice leaving the room. He had little doubt then that some cooling medicines, which he had at hand, would do the rest. As I was going Lettice entreated me to stay, which I was ready to do.

And ere long we were all three quietly gathered around Lady Lucy's chair, Lettice on a cushion at her feet (where she best loved to be), I on the window-seat near, and Dr. Antony leaning on the back of her chair. She was discoursing to him in French, which she spoke with a marvellously natural accent, and which I had never heard him speak before. I know not why, it seemed as if the language threw a new vivacity and fire into his countenance, and I felt very ignorant, and humbled, not to be able to join. But this feeling did not last long, Lady Lucy had a way of divining what passed in the mind, and she called me near, and made me sit on a little chair beside her, and drew my hand into hers, and encouraged me to say such words as I knew, and praised my accent, and said it had just that pretty English lisp in it that some of the countrymen of poor Queen Henrietta Maria had thought charming.

She made Dr. Antony tell us moving histories still in French of his ancestors, their daring deeds and hair-breadth 'scapes. So an hour passed, and we were all friends, bound together by the easy charm of her sweet gracious manner, and had forgotten the storm and everything else, till we were summoned to supper.

"Ah, Monsieur!" said she, giving him her hand as she took leave of him, with a smile, "re-assure Mistress Dorothy as to my orthodoxy, and make her believe my sympathies are on the right side with the sufferers of St. Bartholomew's Day. And Olive, little champion," said she, drawing my forehead down to her for a kiss, and stroking my cheek, "never think it necessary again to interpose in a battle between your aunt and your Mother's friend. I honour her from my heart for her fidelity to conscience. And if she is more anxious than necessary about my faith—we should surely bear one another no grudge for that. I know it cost her more than it did me for her to exhort me as she did. And I am not sure," she added, smiling, "if after all she does not love me better than any of you."

"Mistress Olive," said Dr. Antony, as we sat that evening in the dusk, by the window of my Father's room, while he wrote, "I would that Christian women understood the beautiful work they might do if they would take their true part in theology."

"What would that be?" I said, thinking, after the experience of to-day, it might probably be the part of the Mute.

"To see that Morals and Theology, Charity and Truth, are never divorced," he replied. "To win us back to the Beatitudes when we are straying into the curses. To lead us back to Persons when we are groping into abstractions. For Books full of dogma, Orthodox, Arminian supra-lapsarian, or otherwise, to give us a home, a living world, full of the Father, the Son, and the Comforter, of angels and brothers. To see that we never petrify the thought of the Living God into a metaphysical formula, still less into a numerical term. Never to let us forget that the great purpose of redemption is to bring us to God; that the great purpose of the Church is to make us good. When we have clipped, and stretched, and stiffened the living Truth into the narrow immutability of our theological or philosophical definitions, to breathe it back again into the unfathomable simplicity of the wisdom that brings heavenly awe over the faces of little children, and heavenly peace into the eyes of dying men. To keep the windows open through our definitions into God's Infinity. To translate our ingenious, definite, unchangeable scholastic terms into the simple, infinite, ever-changing—because ever-living—words of daily and eternal life; so that holiness shall never come to mean a stern or mystic quality quite different from goodness; or righteousness, a mere legal qualification quite different from justice; or, humility, a supernatural attainment quite different from being humble; or charity, something very far from simply being gentle, and generous, and forbearing; and brethren, an ecclesiastical noun of multitude totally unconnected with brother. When women rise to their work in the Church, it seems to me the Church will soon rise to her true work in the world."

"You speak with fervour," said my Father, rising from the table, and smiling as he laid his hand on Dr. Antony's shoulder; "the womanhood you picture is something loftier than that of Eve."

"Mary's Ave has gone far to transfigure the name of Eve," he replied. "'Ecce ancilla Domini' shall echo deeper and further and be remembered longer than 'The serpent tempted me and I did eat.' But," he added, "we have a better type than Mary for woman as well as man, in Him who came not to be ministered unto but to minister. I was chiefly thinking of the gifts most common, it seems to me, to women, and least to controversialists, I mean, imagination and common sense. Imagination which penetrates, from signs to things signified, which pierces, for instance, into the depth and meaning of such words as 'eternity' and 'accursed'—which also penetrates behind the adjective 'Calvinistic or Arminian,' to the substantive men and women whose theology they define. And common sense, which, when a conclusion contradicts our inborn conscience of right and wrong, refuses to receive it although the path to it be smoothed and hedged by logic without a flaw.

"In other words," said my Father, "you would say that, with women the heart corrects the errors of the head oftener than we suffer it to do so with us. We must remember, however, that the heart and the conscience also are not infallible, and that the same qualities which can make women the best saints make them the worst controversialists. Theology and morals being in their hearts thus closely intertwined, they fight against a mistake as if it were a sin. They quicken abstractions, and even rites and ceremonies, into personal life, and are apt to defend them with a blind and passionate vehemence as they would the character of a husband or a son."

"Best gifts abused must ever be worst curses," said Dr. Antony.

And I ventured to say,—

"Is it not just the lowliness of our lot that makes it high? Can we help our voices becoming shrill, if we will have them loud?"

"Tune thine then, sweetheart, where first I learnt how sweet it was," said my Father, stroking my cheek. "By sick-beds, or by children's cradles, or in the house of mourning, or wherever good words are needed only to be heard by the one to whom they are spoken; there women's voices are attuned to their truest tones."

And the next morning I had that walk in the orchard with Dr. Antony, when he told me the secret which my Father would persist in declaring (most unwarrantably, I think) lay at the root of his high expectations as to the future work and destinies of women.

And when, a few hours afterwards, after I had been alone a while, and we had knelt together and received my Father's blessing, and I began to understand my happiness a little, and went and said something about it to Lady Lucy, and especially how strange it was that Dr. Antony said he had thought of it so long, whilst I had not been dreaming of it, she kissed my forehead, and said with a smile,—

"Very strange, my unsuspecting little Puritan. For it crossed my thoughts the first hour I saw you together, and that was yesterday evening. Ah, Olive," she added, very tenderly, in a faltering voice, "I had fond thoughts once that it might have been otherwise. If my Harry had lived, and this poor distracted realm had returned to her allegiance, I had thought perchance some day to have the right to call thee by the tenderest name. But God hath not willed it so. And I try hard that his will may be mine. He hath given thee the great gift of a good man's heart. And I have no fear but that thou wilt keep it."

Chapter XII.

LETTICE'S DIARY.

ETHERBY, *May*, 1647.—They have given us the best upper chambers in the house, one for a withdrawing-chamber, the other for my Mother's and my sleeping-chamber. This last has a broad embayed window commanding the orchard, at the bottom of which is the pond where the water-lilies grow that Roger gathered for me on that night when Dr. Taylor and Mr. Milton discoursed together on the terrace, in speech like rich music, about liberty of thinking and speaking.

"England has been echoing another kind of music all these years since, on the same theme; but it seems as if we had drawn but little nearer a conclusion. The Presbyterians seem as convinced of the sin of allowing any one else to think or speak freely as the poor martyred Archbishop was. The Presbyterians, it seems, are for the Covenant (meaning Presbytery), King, and Parliament; the Covenant first. We for King without Covenant and with

Bishops. But the Presbyterians are against conventicles and all sectaries (except themselves). Herein, so far, we and they agree, and herein, some think, may be a hope for the good cause. If we could make a compromise, order might, it is thought, be speedily restored. This, however, seems very hard. They would have to sacrifice the Covenant, which seems nigh as dear to them as the Bible. We, the Church by law established; the sacred links, my Mother says, which bind us to the Catholic Church of all the past, which the king will die, she thinks, rather than do. The only chance, therefore, of agreement seems to be, if the Presbyterians ever reach the point of hating or fearing the Independents more than they love the Covenant. Then, some think the King and the Presbyterians, Scottish and English, might unite and overpower the Independents; and—what then?

"I cannot at all imagine. Because, when the common enemy is gone, Episcopacy and the Covenant still remain, and in the face of each other. Sir Launcelot said the king thinks he has a very plain 'game' to play. 'He must persuade one of his enemies to extirpate the other, and then come in easily and put the weakened victor under his feet.' This he has in letters declared to be his intention. I trust the royal letters have been misread. For such a 'game' seems to me very far from paternal or kingly; and, except on far better testimony, I will not credit it. But for me there is an especial grief in all these matters. Olive, who takes her politics mostly from Roger, seems to lean to the Independents, who constitute the strength of the army, and to General Cromwell, who is their idol; so that whatever cause triumphs, nothing is likely to bring peace between the Davenants and the Draytons.

"At present, however, our peace in this house is much increased. My Mother and Mistress Dorothy have concluded a treaty on the ground of their common loyalty to His Majesty, and their common abhorrence of 'sectaries.'

"Moreover, Mistress Dorothy is marvellous gentle and kind to us. Having delivered her conscience, she treats my Mother with a tender consideration and deference that go to my heart, although sometimes I think it is only from the pity a benevolent jailer would feel for sentenced criminals. They have been condemned. Justice will be satisfied. And meantime, mercy may safely satisfy herself by keeping them fed and warmed.

"She says little; but she watches my Mother's tastes, and supplies her with unexpected delicacies in a way which binds my whole heart to her.

"I scarce know why; but I always liked her. She is so downright and true; manly, as a man may be womanly. She is most like Roger in some ways of any of them, only he, being really a man and a soldier, is gentler. And when she loves you, it seems to be in spite of herself, which makes it all the sweeter. For she does love me. I am sure of it, by the way she watches and exhorts, and contradicts me. Especially, since I read her those sermons that afternoon when we were waiting. I asked Olive, and she told me Mistress Dorothy said, that afternoon, she thought I had gracious dispositions. That meant, I opine, that she liked me. She wanted to excuse herself for liking so worldly and Babylonish a young damosel as she believed me to be. And, therefore, she has invested me with 'gracious dispositions,' and believes herself commissioned to bring me out of Babylon, and to be a 'means of grace' to me, which, I am sure, I am willing she should be. For my heart is too light and careless, I know well. Except on one or two points. And, meantime, I flatter myself I may be an 'ordinance and means of grace' in some little measure to her, little as she might acknowledge it. It does good people so much good to love (really love I mean, not take in hand merely like patients) people who are not so good as themselves. It sets them planning, praying for others, and takes them away from looking within for signs, and forward for rewards; by filling the heart with love, which is the most gracious sign, and the most glorious reward in itself.

"Sweet Mother, mine! we all have been great means of grace to her in that way.

"Think what she may, she would *not* have been a greater saint at Little Gidding, although she had chanted the Psalter through three hundred and sixty-five times in the year.

"I think she and Mistress Dorothy help each other. They make me think of the two groups of graces in the Bible. St. Paul's,—'Love, joy, peace, long-suffering, gentleness, goodness, faith, meekness, temperance.' I picture these as sweet maidenly or matronly forms white-robed, radiant, with low sweet voices. They represent my Mother and the holy people of Mr. Herbert's school. Then there are St. Peter's,—'Faith, virtue, knowledge, temperance, patience, godliness, brotherly-kindness, charity.' These rise before me like a company of knights in armour, valiant, true, and pure. In the kind of plain, manly armour of the Ironsides, as Roger looked in it that morning at Oxford, when he turned back and waved farewell to me in the court of the College. And these represent Mistress Dorothy and the nobler Puritans. They are the same, no doubt, essentially; love and charity, the mother of one group, the king and crown of the other. Yet they seem to represent to me two diverse orders of piety, the manly and the womanly. Together, side by side, in mutual aid and service, not front to front in battle, what a church and what a world they might make.

"But the great event in the house now is the bethrothal of Olive and Dr. Antony, which took place on the very morning after Mistress Dorothy's grand Remonstrance.

"Dr. Antony left a day or two afterwards. And ever since we have been as busy as possible preparing for the wedding, which is to be in July. Not a long betrothal-time. But they needed not further time to try each other.

"It is very pleasant to be all of us occupied for her, who is so little wont to be occupied with herself. She seems in a little tumult of happiness, as far as any Puritan soul can be in a tumult.

"Many of these Puritan ways seem to me wondrous innocent and sweet.

"They have their solemnities, I see, and their ritual, and ceremonial; and their symbolism and sacred art, moreover, say what Mistress Dorothy may to the contrary.

"Tender sacred family rites and solemnities. They have, indeed, no chapel or chaplain. But the family seems a little church; the father is the priest. Not without sacred beauty this order, nor without sanction either from the fathers of the Church (fathers older than Archbishop Laud's), the fathers Abraham, Isaac, and Jacob.

"For instance, when Olive and Dr. Antony were betrothed, Mr. Drayton led them into his room, and laid his hands on them, and blessed them. And that was the seal of their betrothal. Every Sunday morning, Olive tells me, when she and Roger were children, after family prayers, they used to kneel thus for their father's blessing. Sacred touches, holy as coronation sacring oil, I think, to bear about the memory of through life. But then there is this to be remembered. When the consecrating touch is from hands which work with us in daily life, they need to be very pure. No pomp of place, and no mist of distance glorifies the ministrant. He had need, indeed, to be all glorious within.

"Family solemnities must be very true to be at all fair. I can fancy Puritan hypocrisy, or a mere formal Puritanism, the driest and most hideous thing in the world.

"Then as to symbols and sacred art. What else

are these Scripture texts, carved over door-ways, graven on chimney-stones, emblazoned on walls? 'They are not graven images,' saith Mistress Dorothy. But what are words but images within the soul, or images, rightly used, but children's words? Not that even as to 'holy pictures' and 'images' they are quite destitute. What else are the paintings from Scripture on the Dutch tiles in Mr. Drayton's room, where Olive and Roger learned from Mistress Gretel's lips their earliest Bible lore? It is true, they are chiefly from the Old Testament. But Adam and Eve delving, the serpent darting out his forked tongue from the tree, Noah and the animals walking out of the ark, are as much pictures as St. Peter fishing, or the blessed Virgin and the Babe, on church windows? What difference, then, except that the Puritan pictures are on tiles at home instead of on glass at church? 'They are for instruction, and not for idolatry,' saith Mistress Dorothy. But did not the monks in old times paint their pictures also for instruction, and not for idolatry? 'Centuries of abuse make the most innocent things perilous,' saith Mistress Dorothy. 'When the brazen serpent had become an idol, Jehoshaphat called it a piece of brass, and broke it in pieces.' I can see something in that. The sacrilege, then, is the idolatry, not in the destruction of the idol. But alas, if we set ourselves to destroy all things that have been, or can be made into idols, where are we to stop? Some people made idols of the very stones of their houses, without any scriptures thereon, or of their firesides without the sacred pictures.

There are two things, however, which fill me with especial reverence in these Puritan ways. First, this sweet and sacred family piety. Second, or rather first, for it is at the root of all, the intense conviction that every man, woman, and child, in every word and work, has to do directly with God, and that he, by virtue of being divine, is nearer us than all the creatures; that to Him each one is immediately responsible, and that, therefore, on his word only can it be safe for each one to believe or do anything. Such conviction gives a power which ceases to be wonderful only when you think of its source. But alas, alas! what if this Divine word be misunderstood.

"*July.*—Roger Drayton has come, on a few days' leave, to be present at his sister's wedding.

"He hath brought the strange news that the king is in the keeping of the army. We scarcely know whether to mourn or rejoice. It came about on this wise, as Roger told my Mother and me:—

"It was reported in the army that the Presbyterian party in the Parliament designed to remove the king from Holmby, where he was, to Oatlands, near London, there to make a separate treaty, in which the soldiers were not to be consulted or considered.

"On the fourth of June, therefore, Cornet Joyce, without commission, it seems, from any one, but simply as knowing that it would be agreeable to the army; and to prevent this design of a separate Presbyterian treaty, went, with some seven or eight hundred men, to Holmby House, where His Majesty had remained since we saw him in April.

"The Commissioners of the Parliament, who were His Majesty's jailers, were very indignant at this interference of Cornet Joyce, and commanded the gates to be closed, and preparations to be made to resist an assault. Their own soldiers, on the contrary, were of the same mind with the army and the Cornet, and threw open the gates at once to their comrades. Nor was the king himself, it seems, unwilling. When Cornet Joyce made his way to the royal presence, the king spoke to him with much graciousness. He asked the Cornet if he would promise to do him no hurt, and to force him to nothing against his conscience. Cornet Joyce declared he had no ill intention in any way; the soldiers only wanted to prevent His Majesty being placed at the head of another army, and that he would be most unwilling to force any man against his conscience, much less His Majesty. The king, therefore, agreed to accompany him the next day, this happening at night.

"The next morning, at six o'clock, His Majesty condescended to meet the soldiers.

"He again demanded to know the Cornet's authority, and if he had no writing from the general, Sir Thomas Fairfax.

"'I pray you, Mr. Joyce,' he said, 'deal ingenuously with me, and tell me what commission you have.'

Said Joyce,—

"'Here is my commission.'

"'Where?' asked the king.

"'Behind me,' said the Cornet, pointing to his

troopers; 'and I hope that will satisfy your Majesty.

The King smiled.

"'It is as fair a commission,' he said, 'and as well written as I have ever seen in my life; a company of as handsome and proper gentlemen as I have seen a great while. But what if I should yet refuse to go with you? I hope you would not force me! I am your king. You ought not to lay violent hands on your king. I acknowledge none to be above me but God.'

"Cornet Joyce assured His Majesty he meant him no harm; and at length the king went with the soldiers as they desired, they suffering him to choose between two or three places the one he liked best.

"So, by easy stages, they conducted him to Childerley, near Newmarket. And it is said the king was the merriest of the company. Heaven send it to be a good augury.

"Roger said, moreover, that His Majesty continues to be of good cheer, and the army to be friendly disposed towards him. They have hope yet that Sir Thomas Fairfax, General Cromwell, and Ireton may make some arrangement to which His Majesty may honourably accede.

"And, meantime, they allow him not only the attendance of his faithful servants, but his own chaplains to perform the services of the Church, which the Presbyterians refused him at Holmby. Englishmen, especially the common people, and most of all, I think, English soldiers, have honest hearts after all; safer to trust to than those of men armed *cap-a-pie* in covenants, and catechisms, and confessions. Surely the king will yet win the hearts of the army, and all will yet go right. Roger, meanwhile, is as stately in his courtesy to me as a Spanish hidalgo, listening and assenting to all I say in a way I detest. For it means that he feels our differences too deep to venture on."

"*July 2nd.*—Roger has begun to contradict and controvert me again delightfully. This morning we had our first serious battle.

"Yester eve I said something about abhoring all middle states of things. It was in reference to the poor peasants flocking around the king. I said there was no poetry in mid-way things, or times, or states, in mid-day, mid-summer, middle-life, or the middle-station in the state.

"He took this up earnestly after his manner, and went into a serious argument to prove me wrong. It was but a weakling and half-fledged poesy, quoth he, which must needs go to dew-drops, and rosy clouds, and primroses, and violets, for its smiles and decorations, and could see no glory and beauty in summer or in noon. Summer with its golden ripening harvests, and all its depths of bountiful life in woods and fields; noon-tide with its patient toil or its rapturous hush of rest; manhood and womanhood with their dower of noble work and strength to do it. He could not abide (he said), to hear the spring-tide spoken pulingly of as if it faded instead of ripened into summer, or youth as if it set instead of dawned into manhood. And as to the middle station in a nation, its yeomanry and traders, nations must have their heads to think and their hands to work; but the middle order was the nation's heart. If that was sound, the nation was sound, if that was corrupt and base, the nation's heart was rotten at the core. Which (ended he) he thought these last years, with all their miseries, had proved the heart of England was not.

"Roger Drayton has a strange way of his own in discourse, of putting aside all your light skirmishing forces, and closing with the very kernel and core of the people he has to do with. The way of the Ironsides, I suppose. I have been used to little but skirmishing in discourse among the younger Cavaliers; light jesting talk whether the heart or the subject be grave or gay. Even serious feelings being hidden for the most part under a mask of levity. But Roger seldom, perhaps never, exactly jests. His mirth, like a child's laughter, is from the heart, as much as his gravity. He will know and have you know what you really honour, or love, or want, or dread.

"So it happened that to-day on the terrace we came on the very subject I had intended always to avoid; General Cromwell.

"I chanced to allude in passing to some of the reports I had heard against the General, some careless words about his praying and preaching with his men.

"I had no notion until then how Roger reveres this man, like a son his father, or a loyal subject his sovereign.

"He said, quietly, but with that repressed passion which often makes his words so strong, that no man who had ever knelt at General Cromwell's prayers would jest at his praying, any more than any man who had ever encountered him in battle would jest at his fighting. That his word could inspire his men to charge like a word from heaven, and could rally them like a re-inforcement. That after the battle his strong utterance of Christian hope and faith could hearten men to die, as it had heartened them to fight; that after such a battle as Marston Moor, while directing the siege-works outside York, he could find time to go down into the depths of his own past sorrows to draw thence living waters of comfort for a friend (Mr. Walton) whose son had been slain, writing him a letter of consolation (which Roger had seen) containing words deep enough 'to drink up the father's sorrow.'

"Then Roger spoke of the unflinching justice, which was only the other side of this same sympathy and care; how General Cromwell had two of his men hanged for plundering prisoners at Winchester, and sent others accused of the same offence to be judged by the royal garrison at Oxford, whence the governor sent them back with a generous acknowledgment.

"'It is *loyalty* you feel towards General Cromwell,' I said, 'such a disinterested, ennobling, self-sacrificing passion as our Harry felt for the king.'

"He paused a moment,—

"'If God sends us a judge and a deliverer what

else can we feel for him ?" he said, at length ; 'I believe General Cromwell is the defender of the law, and will be the deliverer of the nation, and if he will suffer it,' he added, in a lower voice, 'of the king.'

"'Is it true,' I asked, 'that, as you once told us, General Cromwell and the army are courteous to His Majesty, and anxious to make good terms with him ? Can it be possible that there may yet be an honourable peace ?' 'I believe,' he replied, 'that all things else are possible, if only it is possible for the king to be true. But if a word, king's or peasant's, is worth nothing, what other bond remains between man and man ? Forgive my rough speech. I know your loyalty is a sacred thing to you. If the king will deal truly, I believe General Cromwell will make him such a king as he never was before. But who can twist ropes of sand ? For one who is untrue seems to me not to be a real substance at all, not even a shadow of a substance, but simply a dream or phantasm, simply nothing.'

"I felt myself flush. We have sacrificed too much for His Majesty, not to believe in him. Yet I fear he has other thoughts as to the double-dealing to be permitted in diplomacy than Harry had, or many gentlemen who serve him.

"I could only answer Roger by saying,—

"Adversity makes a king sacred if nothing else can. If the king's cause were once more to prosper, we might debate such things as these. But not now, Roger. I dare not now.'

"He looked as if words were on his lips, he could

scarcely, with all his reserve and courtesy, hold back. But he turned away, and calling Lion from the pond where he was chasing some wild-fowl, we went into the house.

"*July* 4*th*.—Dr. Antony has come for the wedding. He brought us a moving account of the two days spent by the Royal children. James the Duke of York, the Duke of Gloucester, and the Princess Elizabeth, with His Majesty, at Caversham, near Reading. The Independent officers of the army permitted it. And they say General Cromwell himself, having sons and daughters of his own, shed tears to see the affection of the king and the innocent playfulness of the children, knowing so little of the dangers around them.

"*July* 5*th*.—Olive looked wondrous fair as a bride, in her plain spotless dress, without an ornament, partly from Puritanical plainness, and partly because the family jewels went long since with the thimbles and bodkins of the London dames into the treasury at the Guildhall. So grave and serene, pure and young, with her fair pale face, and her smooth white brow and soft true eyes.

"She was married in the church, with some fragments of the marriage-service, the whole being forbidden.

"It was sweet afterwards to see her kneel while my Mother kissed her forehead, and placed a string of large pearls round her neck, with a jewel.

"They had always a singular love for each other, Olive and my Mother. The bride and bridegroom rode away together after noon-tide towards their London home.

"*July* 6*th.*—This morning I rose early and went down to the pond in the orchard, and being led back by the sight of it to the thought of Olive and old times, strayed on towards the Lady Well where first we met.

"By the way I passed old Gammer Grindle's cottage, and finding the door open, early as it was, went in to tell her about the bride.

"And there I saw Cicely and the child again; and heard her terrible story of wrong and sorrow.

"It made me very sad, and as I went on towards the Well, it set me thinking of many things.

"Why did Olive never tell me? But then I thought how I had more than once wilfully refused to believe evil of Sir Launcelot, choosing to believe what I liked. And a cold shudder came over me as I sat by the Lady Well, to think how near danger I had been, and how terrible it would have been if I had cared for him (not indeed that I ever could). I meditated also whether it was not yet possible to get right done to Cicely. And I resolved as far as I could for the future never to believe anything because I wished, but because it was true; that is, to try not to wish about things being true, but to search out honestly if they are. And I was standing looking into the Well, sunk deep in these thoughts, wondering if any one ever really did quite do this, when I heard a footstep and glancing upwards, I met Roger Drayton's eyes.

"And then he told me of his love. I cannot say I had never thought of it before. I had sometimes even thought it might one day come to something like this, and had even imagined a little, what I should say, or perhaps, not so much what, as how I would say many wise things to him and manage it so ingeniously that in some marvellous way all the difficulties about the Civil wars would vanish, he would see he had made some mistakes, and I would acknowledge candidly that our side had not been blameless, and then I might admit, that, perhaps, one day he might speak to me again on the other subject. At least I know these dreams of mine always ended in my being left in perfect certainty that Roger would one day join in the good cause, and Roger perhaps in a very little uncertainty as to the rest.

"But everything went quite the other way. Roger was so much in earnest about what he had to say, that what I had to say about politics unfortunately went entirely out of my head. Roger has left me with anything but a certainty or probability of his ever being a Cavalier, as things are at present. And I have left him in no uncertainty at all about the rest.

"I am afraid it was a golden opportunity lost. But how could I help it? When he showed all his heart to me, how could I help his seeing mine? And since I am sure there is no one in the world to be compared with Roger, how could I help his seeing that I feel and think so? Besides, after all, there is something base in such conditions. It might have been trifling with his conscience. And that would have been almost a crime.

"Wherefore, I am sure I could not have done otherwise, and I think I have done right.

"Yet we made no promises. We know we love each other. That is all. And I know he has loved me ever since he can remember. And I know, with such a heart as his, once is for ever?

"And I know that now, if it were possible, that the whole world could come between us; a world of oceans and continents, a world of war and politics and calumnies, it would always be outside, it would never come between our hearts.

"My Mother thinks so too. I feel now, for the first time, in some ways what it is to have a Mother's heart to rest on. Although through all her tender silence, I feel she sees more difficulties in the way than I do.

"*July* 10*th*.—A world of oceans and continents no separation! How boldly I wrote! Roger is gone back to the army; gone not half an hour, barely a mile away, scarcely out of sight. If I listen I fancy I can almost hear his horse hoofs in the distance. And it seems as if that mile were a world of oceans and continents, as if these moments since he left were the beginning of an eternity, altogether beyond the poor counted minutes and hours and days of time. But a minute since, his hand in mine, and what may happen before I see him again? How do I know if I shall ever see him again? In love such as ours, *ever* and *never* so terribly intertwine!

"Unbelieving that I am. Now I shall have to learn if I understand really anything of what it is to trust God and to pray.

"Prayer and trust must be as deep as *this love*, or they are nothing.

"They must be *deeper*, or they are no support."

OLIVE'S RECOLLECTIONS.

We began our home in London in troublous times.

As we came near our house which was not far from the river and from Whitehall, we saw something which moved me not a little, a coach being drawn to St. James's Palace, guarded by Parliament soldiers. A few people turned and gazed as it passed; and two children were looking out of the window. These were the Royal children being taken back to St. James's Palace after their two days with the king at Caversham. There was something very mournful in beholding these young creatures, born to be children of the nation as well as of the king, taken to their royal home as to a prison, dwelling in their own land as exiles, their Mother a fugitive in France, their Father a captive among his own people.

There is a terrible strength in the pathetic majesty which enshrines a fallen king; a well-nigh irresistible power in the crown which has become a crown of thorns. A captive monarch is a more perilous foe than a victorious army to the subjects who hold him captive. How often during those sad years, 1647 and 1648, I had to go over all the causes of the civil war again and again; Eliot slowly murdered in his unlawful and unwholesome prison; the silenced Parliaments; the tortured Puritans; the imprisoned patriots. How often I had to recall all its course—Prince Rupert's plundering; the king's repeated duplicity, slowly wearing out the nation's lingering trust in him, and baffling all attempts at negotiation. I had to repeat these things to myself, by an effort of will again and again, in order to keep true to our principles at all.

And the conflict with this rebound of instinctive loyalty, which went on in my heart secretly, was going on in the city openly at the time when we took up our abode there.

So strong and general, indeed, was this rebound of loyalty, that in that August, 1647, which was our honeymoon, it seemed that the whole city of London—at the beginning of the war the Parliament's very strength and stay—was panting to return to its allegiance, led by the Presbyterian majority in the House of Commons. The conflict seemed altogether to have shifted its ground. The enemy now dreaded by the city was not the king, but the army which its own liberal contributions and persevering courage had done so much to create. Like the German magician, Dr. Faustus, of whom Aunt Gretel used to tell us, the city crouched trembling before the untameable spirit it had evoked, as from moment to moment it grew into more terrible stature and strength.

Sunday the 1st August, 1647, my first Sunday in London, was a memorable day to me.

Through all the hush of the Puritan Sabbath there was a deep hum of unrest throughout the city, a ceaseless stir of men walking in silent haste hither and thither, or gathering for eager debate at the corners of streets, in the squares, or in any public place. It was a notable contrast to the cheerful stir of animal life and the deep under-stillness at Netherby.

On the Friday before, the House of Commons had been invaded, not as once in the beginning of the strife by the king trampling on "Privilege" in quest of five "traitors," but by a crowd of 'prentices with hats on, clamouring for the king against the army.

Then the two Speakers of the Lords and Commons had fled to the army, with the mace, and all the Independent members.

The eleven banished Presbyterian members had returned; among them Denzil Hollis (one of the king's fated "five traitors" who had afterwards withstood the royal forces so gallantly at Brentford) and Sir John Clotworthy, whose zeal had pursued Archbishop Laud with theological questions even on the scaffold.

Recruitings, gatherings of men and arms, and drillings and gun-practice had been going on in all quarters of the city on the Saturday.

On Monday these were renewed with the earliest light of the summer morning. Drums beating, trumpets calling, 'prentices hurrahing on all sides, "No peace with Sectaries." The London militia, "one and all," against the factious army, then believed to be couching tranquilly near Bedford.

But on Tuesday the army rose from its lair, and

advanced to Hounslow. Then all Southwark came pouring in terrified throngs across London Bridge, demanding peace with the army, and declaring they would not fight. The Presbyterian General Poyntz was indignant, and there was tumult and bloodshed in the streets.

Closer and closer that defied but dreaded monster of an army came, every step forward and every halt watched with fluctuations of hope and fear in the city. The army, meanwhile, strong in the presence of the king, the speakers, the mace, and Oliver Cromwell, looked on itself as not only representing but *being* all the three powers of the state combined, inspired by an invisible power stronger than all states; and so it advanced majestically free from hurry or disorder. Not a provision-cart or pack-horse was stopped on its way into the city. And on Friday, August the 9th, the army appeared in the city, marching three deep through Hyde Park with boughs of laurel in their hats, through Westminster, along the Strand, through the City, to the Tower. In a day or two they were quietly established in the villages around, the headquarters being at Putney. The king was lodged the while at Hampton Court.

Not an act of vengeance nor of disorder, as far as I know, disgraced their triumph. Not that this was any matter of wonder to us. Our wonder was that sober and godly citizens should wonder at the soberness and godliness of the army, every regiment of which was a worshipping congregation, and the soul of it Oliver Cromwell.

Job Forster was sorely vexed at the evil reports spread concerning the soldiers. We saw him often during that autumn.

"Have they forgotten," he said, "that we have won Marston Moor and Naseby for them? that we have been marching through the land all these years, and not left a godly homestead nor a family the worse for us throughout the length and breadth of the country? A man might think it was *we* who sacked Leicester and plundered and burnt villages and farms far and wide. They should have heard the prayers our poor men poured forth by the camp-fires on the battle-fields where we shed our blood for them. Such prayers as might well-nigh lift the roofs from their great vaults of churches, and belike the great stone also from their hearts. Men creeping easily among streets, praying safely as long as they like behind walls, and sleeping every night on feather-beds, might be the better for a good stretch now and then in one of our Cromwell's marches, and a hard bed on the moors, and a good sight right up into the sky, beyond the roofs, and the clouds, and the stars, and the Covenants and Confessions."

Roger also chafed much at the citizens, but most of all at their misunderstanding of General Cromwell. All that autumn, said Roger, the General, with Ireton, Vane, and Harry Marten, and other faithful men, were labouring hard to establish peace on a lasting foundation, as the proposals of the army proved. They would have provided that His Majesty's person, the queen, and the royal issue should be restored to honour and all personal rights; that the royal authority over the militia should be subject to the advice of Parliament for ten years; that all civil penalties for ecclesiastical offences (for instance, whether for using or disusing the Common Prayer), should be removed; that some old decayed boroughs should be disfranchised, and the representation be made more equal; that parliaments should last two years, not to be dissolved except by their own consent, unless they had sat one hundred and twenty days; that grand jurymen should be chosen in some impartial way, and not at the discretion of the sheriff. But no man would have it so. The Levellers in the army clamoured for justice on the "Chief Delinquent," and declared that General Cromwell had betrayed them to the king. The Presbyterians would not give up the right to enforce the Covenant. The king carried on negotiations at the same time with General Cromwell, with the Presbyterians, and with the Irish Papists; intending, as was showed, alas! too surely, from intercepted letters, to be true to none, except, perchance, the last.

On November the 12th, early in the morning, the news flashed through the city, cried from street to street, that the king had fled from Hampton Court; and Roger, who was with us, that morning, said,—

"Once more General Cromwell would have saved the king and the country. But the king will not be saved. Now he must turn wholly to the country."

"But what," replied my husband, "if the country also refuses to be saved by General Cromwell?"

"Then for a New England across the seas," said Roger. "But we are not come to that yet."

For even after the king's flight Roger clung to the hope of reconciliation, his hopes nourished by secret fountains flowing from the very icebergs of his fears. For with the bond which bound People and King, might be snapped for him the bond, not indeed of love, but of hope between him and Lettice.

Still throughout that dreary winter negotiations went on between the Parliament and His Majesty at the Castle of Carisbrook. More and more hopeless as more and more men became mournfully convinced of the kings untruth. Until, in April, 1648, when, from the upper windows of our house, I could see on one side the trees bursting into leaf in St. James' Park, and on the other the river shining with a thousand tints of green and gold with the reflection of the wooded gardens of the palaces and mansions from Westminster to the Temple; when the fleets of swans began to pass by on their way to build their nests in the reedy islets by Richmond or Kew, the news came from all quarters that, amidst all this sweet stir of natural life, the country was stirring with fatal insurrections from Kent to the Scottish borders.

The first outburst was in London itself.

A few 'prentices were playing at bowls on Sunday, April 9th, in Moorfields, during church time. The train-bands tried to disperse them. They fought, were routed by the train-bands, but rallied quickly to the old cry of "Clubs." All through that night we heard the tumult surging up and down through the city. The watermen, a powerful body of men, joined them. The cry was, "For God and King Charles." And not till the Ironsides charged on them from Westminster was the riot quelled.

Then came tidings that Chepstow and Pembroke were taken by the royalists, and that a Scottish army of forty thousand was coming across the borders to undo all that had been done and to restore the king.

About that time Roger came into the chamber where I was busied with confections, and unlacing and laying aside his helmet, he sat down in silence.

His face was fixed and very pale.

"No ill-tidings?" I said.

"I ought not to think so," he replied.

And then he told me of a solemn prayer-meeting, held throughout the day before at Windsor Castle, by the army leaders. How some of them, being "sore perplexed that what they had judged to do for the good of these poor nations had not been accepted by them, were minded to lay down arms, disband, and return each to his home, there to suffer after the example of Him who, having done what He could to save His people, sealed His life by suffering." But others were differently minded, and striving to trace back the causes of their present divisions and weakness, they came at last to what they believed the root, those cursed carnal conferences which their own conceited wisdom had prompted them to the year before with the king's party.

Then Major Goffe solemnly rehearsed from the Scripture the words, "Turn you at my reproof, and I will pour out my Spirit unto you;" and thereupon their sin and their duty was set unanimously with weight on each heart, so that none was able to speak a word to each other for bitter weeping, at the sense and shame of their sins and their base fear of men." "Cromwell, Ireton, and his Ironsides weeping bitterly! It was a thing not to forget," said Roger, pausing.

"Then, Roger," said I, trembling, "if this was the *sin* they wept for, what is the *duty* they see before them?"

Roger bowed his forehead on his hands as they rested on the table before him, and his reply came muffled and slow.

"'To call Charles Stuart, that man of blood, to an account for that blood he hath shed and mischief he hath done to his utmost against the Lord's cause and people in these poor nations.' This is what they deem their duty," he said.

"Call the king to an account, Roger!" I said, "the king!"

I could scarce speak the word for horror.

"Kings have to be called to account," he said.

"Yes, in heaven," I said. "But on earth, Roger, on earth never."

"Herod was called to account on earth, Olive," said he.

"True, but it was by God, Roger," I said. "Not by man! never by man!"

"By the law, Olive," he said; "by God's law, which is above all men."

"But what men can ever have right to execute the law on a king?" I said; "on their own king?"

"Woe to the men who have to do it," said Roger; "but bitterer woe to the man who does not the work God sets him to do, whatever woe it brings on the doing. Olive, who gave," he added, mournfully, "sanction to Laud and Strafford's oppressions, and to Prince Rupert's plunderings?"

I could only weep.

"Oh, Roger," I said, "let the thunderbolt, or the pestilence, or any of God's terrible angels do this work in His time. They are strong and swift enough. It is not for men."

He made no reply.

"What lies between this terrible resolve and its execution?" I asked at length.

"Chepstow and Pembroke to be besieged and taken; Wales to be reconquered; the Scottish army of forty thousand to be driven back over the borders," he replied.

"Then there is a hope of escape for the king yet."

"There is an interval, Olive," he replied. "These things must take time. But they must be done. In a few days, General Cromwell is to lead us forth to do them. The order is given for the army to march to Wales."

I did not venture to mention Lettice's name to him. We both knew too well what a gulf this terrible resolve, if ever it came to action, must create between us. But before he left he said,—

"Olive, I don't think it is cowardice not to say anything of this to Lettice yet. Her mother, she writes to-day, is failing so sadly. And there are so many chances in battle. If I fall, I need not leave on her memory of me what would so embitter sorrow to her.

"And the king might escape," thought I. "His Majesty had all but succeeded in getting through the bars of his chamber-window not a month since. But I did not say this to Roger."

On the next day, the 3rd of May, the army marched forth, and with it Roger and Job Forster. And my husband went with them on his work of mercy.

So that this summer of 1648 was a very anxious and solitary one for me. I longed much to see my Father, but he was occupied in quelling insurrection in the North. And the city was so unquiet, I thought it selfish to send for either of my aunts.

Not that I was without friends. Now and then it fortified me greatly to have a glimpse of Mr. John Milton in his small house at Holborn; to hear his strong words of determination and hope for the English people; and, perchance, to catch some strains from his organ.

But my chief solaces were, first the morning exercises, between six and eight of the clock, at St. Margaret's Church near the Abby, where there was daily prayer, and praise, and reading of God's word, with comments to press it home to the heart, from divers excellent and godly ministers.

And next, a friendship I had made with good Mr. John Henry, a Welsh gentleman who kept the royal garden and orchard at Whitehall, and lived in a pleasant house close on Whitehall Stairs. His wife had died scarce three years before, of a consumption, and it was edifying to hear him and his daughters speak of her virtue and piety; how she had looked well to the ways of her household, had prayed daily with them, catechized her children, and devoted her only son Philip to the work of the ministry in his infancy, and how a little before she died she had said, "My head is in heaven, my heart is in heaven; it is but one step more and I shall be there too."

This friendship solaced me for many causes; primarily for three: in that Mr. Henry was a godly gentleman; in that he lived in a garden by fair water, which reminded me of Netherby; and in that he was a Royalist. For it did my heart good to hear some good words spoken for the captive king, poor gentleman; and I have been wont ever to gain benefit from good men who differ from us on party points. With such we leave the party differences, and fly to the common harmonies, which are deeper.

Many a delightsome hour have I spent in Mr. Henry's house in the orchard by the river, watching the boats, and gay barges, and the fishers, and the white fleets of swans, and the flow of the broad river sweeping by, always like a poem of human life, set to a stately organ music, plying my needle meanwhile beside the young daughters of the house, with cheerful converse. But most of all I loved to hearken to the father's discourse concerning the king and the court in the days gone by. How the young princes used to play with his Philip, and gave him gifts, and had wondrous courtesy for him; and how Archbishop Laud took a particular kindness for him when he was a child, because he would be very officious to attend to the water-gate (which was part of his father's charge), to let the archbishop through when he came late from council, to cross the water to Lambeth; and how afterwards the lad Philip had been taken to see the fallen archbishop in the Tower, and he had given him some "new money."

It was strange to think how the great River of Time had borne all that stately company away, king, court, archbishop, council, like some fleeting pomp of gay barges beneath the windows, or like the masques and pageants they had delighted in, of which Mr. Henry told me. It was good, too, to have such touches of simple kindness, as remembering a child's taste for bright new money, thrown into the dark picture we Puritans had among us of the persecutor of our brethren. It is good for the persecuted to feel by some human touch that their persecutors are human; good while the persecuted suffer, good beyond price if ever they come to rule and judge.

Sometimes, moreover, Mr. Philip the son came home from Christchurch, Oxford, where he was a student, and his discourse was wondrous sacred and pleasant for so young a gentleman. One thing I remember he said which was a special solace to me. He would blame those who laid so much stress on every one knowing the exact time of their conversion. "Who can so soon be aware of the day-break," quoth he, "or of the springing up of the seed sown? The blind man in the Gospel is our example. This and that concerning the recovering of his sight he knew not: 'But this one thing I know, that whereas I was blind, now I see.'" Which words have often returned to my comfort. In that, instead of sending me back into my past life, and down into my heart to look for tokens of grace, they set me looking up to my Lord, to see his gracious countenance; and in looking I am enlightened, be it for the first time, or the thousand and first.

Meantime the great tide of Time was flowing on, bearing on its breast to the sea royal fleets, and little row-boats such as mine.

In July the sailors of the fleet suddenly declared for the king, landed the Parliament admiral, and crossing the Channel, took on board the Prince of Wales, acknowledging him as their commander.

At this news my heart beat as high with hope as the fiercest royalist's. The Prince of Wales with a fleet in the Downs! the king his father in prison close to the shore at Carisbrook! what could hinder a rescue? But no rescue was attempted. Weeks passed on — the opportunity was lost; the fleet was won back to the Parliament, and the king remained at Carisbrook. I have never heard any attempt to explain why the prince neglected this chance of saving the king. It made my heart ache to think of the captive sovereign watching all those weeks for rescue, (for he sent to entreat it might be attempted) and listening for the sound of friendly guns, and the appearance of a band of loyal seamen, all in vain.

For all this time his doom was coiling closer and closer round him.

Pembroke and Chepstow were retaken. General Cromwell wrote from Nottingham for shoes for his "poor tried soldiers," wearied with a hundred and fifty miles hasty marching across the wild country of Wales towards the north. In August came the tidings of the total defeat of the Scottish army at Preston.

I had just received the news of this in a letter from my husband, and was sitting alone in my chamber, tossed hither and thither in mind, as was my wont during those anxious months, scarce knowing at any news whether to rejoice or to mourn, in that every victory of the army seemed but to bring a step nearer the fulfillment of that dreadful purpose of calling the king to account. By way of quieting these uneasy thoughts, I rose to go to good Mr. Henry's, when a little stir at the door aroused me, and in another minute I was clasped to Aunt Gretel's heart, sobbing out my gladness at seeing her.

"Hush, sweetheart, hush," she said, "that is the worst of surprises. I meant to save thee suspense, and to make as little disturbance as possible."

"I wanted thee so sorely," said I. "It is not thy coming that has so moved me; it was the trying to do without thee."

In half an hour she had unpacked her small bundle, and established herself in the guest-chamber, with everything belonging to her as quietly in its place, as if it had never known another. Her presence brought an unspeakable quiet with it. The solitary house became home again. And in another fortnight we were rejoicing together over my first-born, our little Magdalene; the fountain of delight opened for us in the desert of those dreary times.

And in September my husband returned to me.

Preston was the last battle of that campaign worthy the name. The Scottish royalist army was broken up, and General Cromwell was welcomed in Edinburgh, and by the Covenanters everywhere, as the deliverer of the land.

Throughout September the king was holding conferences at Newport with the Commissioners of the Parliament. All bore witness to the ability and readiness with which he spoke. His hair had turned gray, his face was furrowed with deep lines of care, but all the old majesty was in his port, and even those who had known him before were surprised at his learning and wit.

But, alas, it was mere speech. The king wrote to his friends excusing himself for making concessions, by the assurance that he merely did it in order to facilitate his escape.

And more than that, all the actors in that drama, sincere or not, were rapidly fading into mere performers in a pageant. The decisive conferences were held, the true work was done. The doom was fixed elsewhere.

By the middle of November the army, victorious from Wales and Scotland, and mindful of the prayer-meeting at Windsor, was again at St. Albans, calling for justice on the Chief Delinquent.

On the 29th of November the king was removed from Carisbrook to Hurst Castle, a lonely, bare and melancholy fort opposite to the Isle of Wight, whose walls were washed by the sea.

On December the 2d the quiet of Mr. Henry's house and of the royal orchard was broken, by the arrival of a portion of the Parliament army at Whitehall, trampling down with heavy armed tread the grass which had grown in the deserted palace-court.

On Sunday there was much preaching in many quarters, of a kind little likely to calm the storm. In the churches the Presbyterian preachers declaimed fervently against the atrocity and iniquity of seizing the person of the king. In the parks Independent soldiers preached on the equality of all before the law of God. "Tophet is ordained of old," one of them took for his text. For the king it is prepared. A notable example, my husband said, of that random reading of the Sacred Scriptures which turns them into a lottery of texts to conjure with, like a witch's charms.

In the Parliament my old hero Mr. Prinne, with his cropped ears and his branded forehead, stood up and boldly pleaded for the king, never braver, I thought, than then.

On the 5th of December came another invasion of the Parliament House, Colonel Pride and his soldiers turning all the Presbyterian and Royalist members back from the doors. "Pride's Purge."

It was a sorely perplexed time. Had the very act of despotism which first roused the nation to the point of civil war now to be repeated in the name of liberty for the ruin of the king?

What are we fighting for? I used to ask myself. The battle-cries, as well as the front of the armies, had so strangely changed. For the king and Parliament? The king was in prison. The Parliament was reduced to fifty members. For the nation? The nation was half in insurrection. For liberty? No party seemed to allow it to any other.

Roger and the Ironsides alone seemed clear as to the answer. "We are fighting—not under six hundred members of Parliament, nor under fifty, but under one leader given us by God; under General Cromwell," he said. And he is fighting for the country, to save it and make it free and righteous, and glorious in spite of itself. When he has done it, it will be acknowledged. Till then he must be content to be misjudged, and we must content he should be, as the heroes have been too often, and the saints nearly always, until their work, perhaps until their life, is done."

I lay awake much during those nights of December. My little Magdalene was often restless, and I used to listen to the flow of the river through the silence of the sleeping city and think how the sea was washing the walls of the king's desolate prison, praying for him, and for General Cromwell, and all, and thanking God that my lot was the lowly one of submitting instead of that of deciding, in these terrible times.

But a sorer sorrow was advancing slowly on us all. On the 10th of December came an imploring letter from Lettice, saying that her mother had failed sadly during the last week, that she and her mother longed for Dr. Antony, and her mother even more for me and the babe.

The next day we were on the road to Netherby, Aunt Gretel, my husband, the babe, and I.

It was late in the evening of the second day when we reached the dear old house.

We were met with a hush, which fell on me like a chill. The Lady Lucy had fallen into one of those quiet sleeps which of late had become so rare with her, and the whole household was quieted so as not to disturb her.

The subdued tone into which everything falls, in a house in which there has been long sickness, and where everything has been ordered with reference to one sufferer, fell heavily on us, coming in from the fresh autumn air with voices attuned to the bracing winds, and hearts eager with expectations of welcome. It was like being ushered into a church hushed for some mournful ceremony; and we stepped noiselessly, and spoke under our breath, until an unsubdued wail from the only creature of the company unable to understand the change, the baby waking suddenly from sleep, broke the dreary spell of stillness.

The Lady Lucy heard the little one's cry, and sent to crave a glimpse of us all that night.

In her chamber alone, throughout the house that anxious hush was absent. She spoke in her natural-voice, though now lower than even its usual sweet low tones, from weakness. She had a bright welcoming word for each, and while gratefully heeding my husband's counsel, declared that baby would be her head physician. The very touch of the soft little fingers and the sound of her little cooings and crowings had healing in them, she said.

She looked less changed than I had expected. But my husband shook his head and would give little promise. Lettice seemed to me more altered than her mother. Her eyes had a steady, deep, watchful look in them, very unlike her wonted changeful brilliancy. She said nothing beyond a few words of welcome to me that night. But the next morning the first moment we were alone together she took my hands, and pressing them to her heart, she said,—

"Tell me Olive; I have been afraid to ask any one else, but I must know. What do they mean by Petitions from the army for justice on the King?"

I was so startled by her sudden appeal, I could not meet her eyes nor think what to say. I could only murmur something about there having been so many Petitions, Remonstrances, and Declarations, which had ended in talking.

"True," said she, "but the army are like no other party in the state. They do not end with talking. They know what they want, and mean what they say, and do what they mean. What do they mean by Petitions against the Chief Delinquent?"

"Many do think, Lettice," I said, "that the king himself, and not only his counsellors, began all the evil."

"I know," she replied. "But they have had justice enough on the king, I should think, to satisfy any one. They have deprived him of all power, separated him from the queen and the royal children, and all who love him, and shut him up behind iron bars. And now, they petition for justice on him. What would they do to him worse, Olive? What can he suffer more? What has the king left but life?"

I could not answer her.

"To touch *that*, Olive," she continued, looking steadily into my eyes, and compelling me by the very intensity of her gaze to meet them, "to touch that would be crime, the worst of crimes. It would be regicide, parricide."

"But how could it ever be, Olive?" She went on. "They have assassinated kings I know before now. But a king brought to justice (as they call it) like a common criminal! Since the world was, such a thing was never known. It can never be, Olive, she added in a trembling voice, "I have heard the king dreads assassination. Do you? Could his enemies descend to that depth?"

"Never, Lettice," I replied, "never." And in saying thus I could meet her eyes frankly and fearlessly.

Her face lighted up.

"Never! no, I believe not. Then there can surely be little fear. There is no tribunal which can judge the king. No bar for him to stand arraigned before but the judgment-seat of God. A king was never condemned and put to death deliberately and solemnly in the face of his own people, and of all the nations. Never since the world was. And it never could be. From assassination you are sure he is safe. Be honest with me, Olive. There are base men in all parties. You are *sure?*"

"As sure as of my life," I said, "as sure as of my father's word, or Roger's."

"Then there can be no reason to fear," she said. "I will cast away this awful dread. Oh, Olive," she exclaimed, bursting into tears, "you have brought me new life. Do you know that sometimes during these last few days, since I heard of those Petitions, I have almost prayed that if such a fearful crime and curse could be hanging over England, my Mother might be taken to God first, and learn about it first there, where we shall understand it all. But you have comforted me, Olive. I need make no such prayers. What I have so dreaded can never be."

I felt almost guilty of falsehood in letting her thus take comfort. Yet if my husband's fears about Lady Lucy were well-founded, there was little need for such a prayer. And to Time I might surely leave it to unveil the horrors that after all might be averted.

But no intervention from above or from below came to avert the steady unfolding of the great tragedy on which the nation's eyes were fixed.

The king went on to his doom, as the doomed in some terrible old tragedy of destiny, tremblingly watchful for the storm to break from the side whence there was no danger, but all the time advancing with blind fearlessness to confront the lightnings which were to smite him.

In the solitary sea-washed walls of Hurst Castle he listened for the stealthy tread of the assassin. And when at midnight, on the 17th of December, the creak of the drawbridge was heard between the dash of the waves, and then the tramp of armed horsemen echoing beneath the castle-gate, the king rose and spent an hour alone in prayer. Colonel Harrison, who commanded these men, had been named to him as one likely to be employed to assassinate him. "I trust in God who is my helper," said the king to his faithful servant, Herbert; "but I would not be surprised. This is a fit place for such a purpose," and he was moved to tears; no unmanly tears, and no groundless fears. He was not the first of his unhappy race who had been the victim of treacherous midnight murders. But when on the morrow he recognized in Colonel Harrison's frank countenance and honest converse one incapable of such baseness, his spirits rose, and he rode away almost gayly with his escort of gallant and well-mounted men, courteous enough in their demeanour to him. In the daylight, and in the royal halls of Windsor, where they lodged him, he felt strong again in the sacredness of the king's person, and alas he fancied himself strong in those false schemes of policy which, and which only, had divested his royal person of its sacredness in the hearts of his people. "He had yet three games to play," he said, "the least of which gave him hope of regaining all."

On the 5th of January he gave orders for sowing melon-seed at Wimbledon; and dwelt on Lord Ormond's work for him in Ireland. He made a jest of the threat of bringing him to a public trial. Kings had been killed in battle, treacherously put to agonizing deaths in dungeons whose walls tell no tales, and let no cries of anguish through, secretly stabbed at midnight. But the rebels it seemed plain were not foes of that stamp. Even the example three of his Cavaliers had lately given them in treacherously assassinating Rainsborough, one of Cromwell's bravest officers at Doncaster, kindled in the most fanatical of the Roundheads no emulation, but simply a burning indignation and contempt. Save the sword of battle, or the dagger of the murderer, no weapon was known wherewith to kill a king. The Roundheads did not number assassination among their "instruments of justice." The war was over. What then was there for His Majesty to fear?

Strafford, indeed, had been almost as confident up to the last. And neither gray hairs or consecration had saved the Archbishop's head from the scaffold. But between an anointed king and the loftiest of his subjects, according to the royal and the royalist creed, the distinction was not of degree but of nature.

All the courts of Europe surely would rise and interfere ere a king should be tried before a tribunal of his lieges, of creatures who held honour and life by his breath.

Nor only earthly courts. Would the One Tribunal before which a sovereign alone could be summoned, suffer such an infringement of its rights?

So the king went on jesting at the thought of his subjects bringing him to trial, playing his "three games," and peacefully sowing seeds for more harvests than one.

And meanwhile Cromwell came back slowly advancing from Scotland to London; Petitions for Justice on the Chief Delinquent lay on the table of the House of Commons not unheeded; on the 6th of January, Colonel Pride, with his soldiers, guarded the door of the House of Commons, and sent thence every member who disposed still to prolong treaties with the king; in the afternoon of that same 6th of January, General Cromwell was thanked by the "purged" house, or Rump, of fifty members, for his services, and the High Court of Justice was instituted for the trial of "Charles Stuart, for traitorously and tyrannically seeking to overthrow the rights and liberties of the people." And on the 20th of January, not three days after he had been tranquilly planning at Westminster for his summer garden crops, and sowing seed for other harvests in Ireland, the king was sitting in Westminster Hall arraigned before this Court as a "tyrant, traitor, and murderer."

And still only were the heavens unmoved, but not a word of remonstrance or of generous pleading had come from one crowned head in Europe.

But meantime over our little world at Netherby,

that awful Presence was hovering to which all the outward terrors that may, or may not surround it, the midnight dagger, the headsman's axe, the crowds of eager gazers around the scaffold, are but as the trappings of the warrior to his sword, or the glitter of the axe to its edge. Death was silently wearing away the little remaining strength of Lady Lucy Davenant.

There was one amongst us nearer the beginning of the new life than any of us knew, so near that the roar of the political tempest around us was hushed ere it reached her chamber, and she lay on the threshold of the other world almost as unconscious of the storms of this as our little infant Magdalene, whose cradle she used to delight to have beside her.

I can remember, as if it were yesterday, the dim tender smile with which she used to watch the babe asleep beside her.

Once she said to me,—

"There seems to me something strangely alike, Olive, in the darling's place and mine, though to all outward seeming so different. I lie and look at her and think of the angels in the Percy Shrine at the Minster at Beverly, how they bear in their arms to Jesus a little helpless new-born soul, and He stretches out His hands to take it to His bosom —a soul new-born from death, to the deathless life with Him.

"Sometimes it seems like that, Olive, what is coming to me; so great and perfect the change. Sometimes so easy and simple; more like laying aside garments we have worn through the night bathing in the water of life, and stepping refreshed, strong, and 'clothed in raiment clean and white'—into the next chamber, to meet Him who awaits us there. So *little* the change, for we have in us the treasure we shall bear with us. The new eternal life is in our Lord, and not in any state or time; and since we have him with us, both here and there, it seems only like stepping a little further into the Father's house—from the threshold to the inner chambers—and hearing Him nearer and seeing Him more clearly. Tell Lettice I had these comforting thoughts, Olive," she would say; "I cannot speak to her, she is too much moved; and she wants me to say I long to stay on earth, and I cannot, Olive. I cannot feel at home any more here since Harry is gone. And I am so weak and sinful, I may do harm as well as good by staying longer, even to Lettice, poor tender child. The world—at least the world here in England—is very dark to me. And sometimes I think it will all soon end, not this war only, but all wars, and the kingdom come for which the Church prayed so long, and the glorious Epiphany."

One thing I remarked with Lady Lucy, as with others whom since I have watched passing from this world of shadows into the world of real things. The lesser beliefs which separate Christians seemed forgotten, fallen far back into the distance and the shade, in the light of the great truths which are our life—which are Christianity. The spontaneous utterances of such Christian deathbeds as I have watched, have had little of party-beliefs, and of party-politics nothing. As Lady Lucy herself once said,—

"Oh, if all could only see Him as He is! We are divided because we are fragments; the whole race is fallen and broken into fragments. But in Him, in Christ, all the broken fragments are one again and live. Truth is no fair ideal vision: it is Christ."

And again she would speak of her death with infinite comfort. "He died really—really as I must," she said; "the flesh failed, the heart failed, but he overcame. He offered Himself up without spot to God, and me, sin-stained as I am, in Him—the Son, the Redeemer, the Lord. And the Father was in Him, reconciling the world to Himself. And we are in Him, reconciled, for ever and ever."

Now and then she would ask if we had heard news of the king. And we gave her such general and vague accounts as we dared, deeming it unmeet to distress her with perplexities which would so soon be unperplexed to her. And this was easy, her attention being seldom now fixed long on any subject.

On the 6th of January Roger came on his way to London from the North—on the old Christmas day, which Lady Lucy had continued to keep.

In the morning Lettice had read her the gospel for the day.

In the afternoon when she saw Roger, connecting him with the army and the king, she asked at once for his Majesty.

"The king is at Windsor," Roger said.

"At home!" she said with a smile; "at home again for the Christmas. That is well."

Roger made no reply, and, to the relief of all, her mind passed contentedly from the subject. She took Lettice's hand and Roger's in hers, and pressed them to her lips, and murmured, "My God, I thank Thee." And then, as a faintness came over her, we all withdrew but Lettice.

Roger and I were alone in the ante-room. He was waiting to bid Lettice farewell. When she came out of her mother's chamber she sat down on the window seat, her eyes cast down, her trembling mute lips almost as white as her cheeks.

Roger went towards her, and stood before her; but she made no movement and did not even lift her eyelids, heavy and swollen as they were with much weeping.

"Lettice," he said, "let me say one word before I go. Let me say one word to comfort you in this sorrow, for is not your sorrow mine?"

"Of what avail?" she said. "You are taking the king to London to die. The greatest crime and curse is about to fall on the nation, and you will go and share and sanction it, and make it your own. No word of mine will move you—how can word of yours comfort me? You will, if you are commanded by him you have chosen for your priest and king, keep guard by the scaffold while the king is murdered. Did not you tell me so two hours since? Did not I entreat and implore and tell you you were digging a gulf, not only between me and you, but between you and heaven?"

He stood for a few moments silent and motionless, and then he said: "And did I not tell you, that, as a soldier I could do no otherwise unless I deserted my chief, nor as a patriot unless I betrayed my country? It is the king who has betrayed us, Lettice; who has refused to let us save him and trust him. The hand that could have stopped all the oppression aud injustice at the source—from the beginning—and *did not*, must be the guiltiest hand of all. It is *falsehood* that is leading the king to this end, not the country, nor the Parliament, nor General Cromwell."

At last she looked up,—"Do not try to persuade me, Roger," she said, "God knows I am too willing to be persuaded. I cannot reason about it any more than about loving my Mother or obeying my Father. I dare not listen to you. I am untrue," she added, bursting at length into passionate tears, "I have been a traitor, to let my Mother be deceived—toilet her thank God for what can never be!"

"Lettice," he said in a tone of anguish, "if you reproach yourself, if you call yourself a traitor, what am I?"

"You are as true as the Gospel, Roger," she said, her sobs subsiding into quiet weeping; "as true as heaven itself. You would never have done what I did. You would break your own heart and every one's rather than utter or act one falsehood, or neglect one thing you believe to be duty. That is what makes it so terrible."

His voice trembled as he replied,—"You trust me, and yet you think me capable of a terrible crime."

"I know that to lay sacrilegious hands on the king is an unspeakable crime," said she; "but to trust you is no choice of mine. I cannot tear the trust of my heart from you if I would, Roger, and God knows I would not if I could."

A light of almost triumphant joy passed over his face, as, standing erect before her, with folded arms, he looked on her down-cast face,—

"Then the time must come when a delusion that cannot separate us in heart can no longer separate us in life," he said, in tones scarcely audible. "Your Mother said the truth, Lettice, when she joined our hands. Such words from her lips at such a time are surely prophecy."

Lettice shook her head.

"My Mother saw beyond this world," she said, mournfully; "where there are no delusions, and no divisions, and no partings."

He bent before her for an instant, and pressed her hand to his lips. And so they parted.

That night Lettice and I watched together by Lady Lucy's bedside. And all things that could distract and divide seemed for the time to be dissolved in the peace of her presence.

She revived once or twice and spoke, although it seemed more in rapt soliloquy than to any mortal ear.

"Everything grows clear to me," she said once; "everything I cared most to see. The divisions and perplexities which bewilder us here are only the colours the light puts on when it steps on earth. On earth it is scarlet and purple and bordered work; in heaven it is fine linen, clean and white, clean and white."

Often she murmured in clear rapid tones, very awful in the silence of the sick-chamber at night, the words,—

"The king, the king!"

Lettice and I feared to go to her to ask what she meant, dreading some question we dared not answer. We thought belike her mind was wandering, as she did not seem to be appealing to us or looking for an answer.

But at length the words came more distinctly, though broken and low, and then we knew what they meant,—

"The King! King of kings! Faithful and true. Mine eyes shall see the King in His beauty. He shall deliver the needy when he crieth, King of the poor, King of the nations, King of kings, Faithful and true. I am passing beyond the shadows. I begin to see the lights which cast them. Beyond the storms—I see the angels of the winds. Beyond the thunders—they are music, from above. Beyond the clouds—they are the golden streets, from above. Mine eyes shall see the King—as He is; as thou art; no change in Thee, but a change in me. In Thy beauty as Thou art."

All the following day the things of earth were growing dim to her, but to the last her courtesy seemed to survive her strength. No little service was unacknowledged; even when the voice was inaudible, the parched lips moved in thanks or in prayer.

And on the early morning of the 21st of January she passed away from us, her hand in Lettice's, her eyes deep with the awful joy of some sight we could not see.

On the evening of that very day came the tidings that the king had been brought, on the 19th of January, as a criminal, before the High Court of Justice in Westminster Hall, to be tried for his life as the "principal author of the calamities of the nation."

When Lettice heard it, the first burst of tears came breaking the stupor of her sorrow, as she sobbed on my shoulder, "Thank God she is safe, beyond the storms of this terrible distracted world. She is gone where she will never more be perplexed what to believe or what to do."

"She is gone," said my Father, tenderly taking one of her hands in his, "where loyalty and love of country, and liberty and law are never at variance; where the noblest feelings and the noblest hearts are never ranged against each other. And we hope to follow her thither."

"But oh," sobbed Lettice, "this terrible space between!"

"Look up and press forward, my child," he replied, "and the way will become clear. Step by step, day by day; the space between is the way thither."